Viivan —
May the words
of this book leave
you blessed. Never
forget how of
are to God.
Karen Ayers

MW00510616

Sweet Summer Rain . . .
Noah's Story

The *Seasons of Change*
Series—Book One

by
Karen Ayers

Strategic Book Publishing and Rights Co.

Copyright © 2012 Karen Ayers. All rights reserved.

No part of this book may be reproduced or transmitted in any form or by any means, graphic, electronic, or mechanical, including photocopying, recording, taping, or by any information storage retrieval system, without the permission, in writing, from the publisher.

Strategic Book Publishing and Rights Co.
12620 FM 1960, Suite A4-507
Houston TX 77065

www.sbpra.com

ISBN: 978-1-62212-648-4

Design: Dedicated Book Services, Inc. (www.netdbs.com)

To Ken, for believing in me. I don't have to tell you how much you mean to me. Thanks for everything, including the research I needed to make this book possible.

To my six children. You have been a blessing to my life. Angela, Jennifer, Kristopher, Mary, Heather and Lance, I love you all so much.

To my parents, Jerry and Frances Ayers, who taught me who God truly is; for this I owe much, for without Him, I am nothing.

To my sister Connie, who always liked anything I wrote,I hope you know how truly special you are to me. And her husband Brian, who loves her like she deserves to be loved.

To my adopted sisters and brother, Katie, Thomas and Marcy. It is not blood that makes us family; it is the love we feel in our hearts. I love the way you call me Sissy.

To my friends, Kim, Mandy and Darlene, you are all an inspiration to me. (Thank you, Kim, for naming the book series....Seasons of Change.)

To my friends Craig, Shannon, Josh and Gretchen, thanks for trusting me with your Babies, and to Rebecca, who is as much like a daughter as my own.

*To Casey, for telling me all you know
about horses; I love you, sweet girl.*

*To Judy at New Life Assembly and Linda @
Summersville CVB, for supplying me with the
information I needed to make this book a success.*

*To Lorri, my friend and editor. Thank
you so much for all your hard work.*

*And most of all, I thank Jesus Christ, for
wrapping me in His loving arms, and loving
me unconditionally, even when I don't deserve
it. You saved my soul and forgave me by Your
Grace and Mercy. To YOU, I owe EVERYTHING,
and because of You, I have hope and a future.*

Chapter 1

July felt more like August. The forecast promised temperatures in the high nineties, and the local news stations told stories of the elderly dying in older buildings without air conditioning from heat strokes. Warnings had been to stay inside out of the heat. It didn't seem right for this time of year in New York, but nothing did these days.

Brendy didn't worry about the warnings. It seemed everyone she knew was already on their way to Hell and she was sure Hell was hotter than Spanish Harlem.

Besides, her days of walking the streets had long since past. Those days had been replaced by a not-so-shabby apartment with enough money she didn't have to worry about where her next meal was coming from. She remembered those days all too well.

Brendy crossed the floor of her studio apartment and peered out the window to the street below. The same street that, not so long ago,she walked dirty and afraid and so hungry she sometimes went for days without eating. She sighed, watching the people down below. Even on Sunday they never seemed to rest or care for anyone but themselves. Had she become just like them? Brendy was certain her heart had grown stone cold many years ago.

No one was friendly in Spanish Harlem. Being friendly meant risking your life in this part of town. And after six years of living in the city, her only friends were the girls she worked with, and Brendy knew any of them would do her in if it meant their own safety. But she would do the same to them. Love was an unknown word. It was an emotion unknown to her. For loving meant the risk of being hurt, and that was something she knew all too well.

At the tender, but not so innocent, age of twenty-two, Brendy was tired.

Bone tired.

It wasn't getting any better, only worse. The stress of the last few years had taken its toll on her, emotionally as well as physically, and she was sure she looked more like a woman of thirty. She crossed the room again and stared at the reflection of herself in the mirror. She stood for the longest looking at the image that stared back. Who was she? What had she become?

"Who are you?" she whispered, moving even closer to her image. Brendy knew she was beautiful, or so she had been told at least a hundred times. Her eyes told her the outside was worth looking at, but her heart told her beauty was only skin deep, and she knew all too well that beneath the surface lay a soul so dark no decent man could ever love her.

Brendy placed her hands on her face and wept, feeling the tears in the palms of her hands. So many years of pain and anguish flooding out, and she sobbed uncontrollably, wishing she could start over. Nothing would ever be as she had hoped.

Yes, Brendy knew she was beautiful, for it was beauty that had gotten her this far. But beauty could sometimes be a curse, and, for a moment, she wished she wasn't beautiful. Each time she looked at her light green eyes she saw her mother looking back at her.

The mother she hated with a passion.

She was born with her mother's eyes and knew she was more like her than she cared to admit. How could God ever forgive her for doing the unthinkable? Nevertheless, what did it matter? She wasn't even sure if she believed in God. He certainly never helped her when she needed Him. So many nights she cried out to Him and yet He never stopped her abuse growing up. How could she forgive Him for that?

Depression set in years ago, like a grey cloud of doom. Suicide, she knew, would be the easy way out. But, as low as she felt at this moment, she could not bring herself to that point. Knowing no one would be at her funeral was more than she could bear.

The sound of a gunshot brought her out of her trance. She was so tired of being afraid, not knowing what tomorrow held. Sadness was her constant friend, knowing life as it was held no future or hope. There would be no husband to hold her or kiss away her tears. No children to call her mother and depend on her. No house with a white picket fence. She would never have all the things she dreamed about as a child. How could she dream those things now, when her past would surely haunt all of her tomorrows?

Brendy looked at the clock above her kitchen sink. In less than three hours, the car would arrive as it did every night. She would be dressed to kill, in one of her many gowns. Her makeup would be perfect and her light blonde hair would be pinned up, leaving tiny curls cascading down her face. She would be glamorous, and the gentleman the driver took her to meet would be captivated by her beauty. It would be his choice where they went or what they did. He would pay the high price for her escort, and she would make him feel like a prince. After all, that was her job. And to her disgust, she did it well.

Brendy was sick to her stomach at the very thought of it. Nevertheless, her job was to make him as happy as possible and to smile and act as if she actually enjoyed being in his presence.

So many times over the last few months, Brendy thought of running. Each time the same thought haunted her mind. Where would she run? No matter how far she ran, her past would always be with her, to haunt her around every corner. There would be reminders of the things she'd allowed herself to become. No distance would ever erase the pain.

Another shot rang out on the street below, followed by a woman's loud scream. Brendy could feel her heart racing as she looked around her studio apartment that was home for the last several years. Even the trinkets she bought herself that decorated her home held no sentimental value. They were bought with devil's money, and she needed no reminders of how she earned it.

Quickly she ran to her closet and took out two suitcases. As much as she hated life, deep within, she knew there would be no happiness as long as she remained Sasha, the name given to her by Caroline Reese.

Carrying the name Sasha for so long, she'd forgotten what it felt like to be called Brendy. She longed to start over, where people didn't know her past. Perhaps if she kept quiet, no one would ever know her secrets. A chance Brendy knew she must take.

For years, she role-played and smiled at men who made her sick to her stomach. In fact, she was so good at pretending,she knew she could easily pull it off. There would be time to make up stories later. As for now, she quickly packed what clothing she could stuff into her suitcases, and wrote a letter to her landlord telling him to donate her belongings to charity. She placed the letter in an envelope along with two months rent.

"Goodbye," Brendy whispered, looking around her apartment for the last time. She ran from her mother at the age of sixteen. This time she hoped to make better choices.

Brendy was tired of running.

*****

Brendy hadn't been this nervous since the first night she worked for Caroline Reese, the night she lost her virginity.

JFK Airport was jam-packed with commuters and she prayed no one recognized her. She purchased a one-way ticket on American Eagle Airlines, a smaller jet flying into Pittsburgh,and still carried the sum of three thousand dollars in her purse. It was devil's money, she knew, but she'd earned it fair and square, and considering it was all she had, it would have to do her until she found a job, a decent job.

Pittsburgh was not as far away as she hoped to go, but was the next flight out with a vacant seat. At this point she didn't care where she went; she only wanted to get away from Spanish Harlem and the woman who had such a hold on her.

Caroline told her time and time again that she owed her. She liked appearing to her girls as their salvation since she helped them get off the streets and gave them careers that made the big bucks. Night after night she went wherever Caroline told her to go and gave up fifty percent of her earnings. Caroline thought, since she made the deals and kept her girls safe, they owed her half of everything. She felt certain Caroline had taken more than her fair share and she was leaving owing her nothing. Besides, Brendy had no idea what Caroline would do when she found out she was missing, and it frightened her to think about.

Brendy took a seat beside an elderly woman and smiled the best she could. The last thing she felt like doing was smiling. Brendy knew it was time to start this charade that would soon become her life; playing games was her forte' after all.

Looking at her watch, she realized it was six-thirty. The driver would be at her apartment any moment to pick her up. Would he call Caroline right away and report her missing? Would they send others in search of her?

She looked out the window and watched the ground disappear as they soared into the sky. Brendy knew Caroline would call one of her other girls to take her place, one of her many puppets on a string that would do her bidding.

"Are you okay, dear?" the lady in the seat next to her asked politely.

"Huh," Brendy looked from the window to the woman now smiling at her.

"I asked if you were okay. You seem nervous and a little distracted."

Brendy half chuckled and shook her head. "I guess I am a little. I'm ashamed to say I hate flying," she lied, knowing that didn't come close to the real reason she was nervous. "I have never been comfortable with these smaller jets."

The woman patted her hand. "Well, don't be nervous, my dear, these things are perfectly safe. I fly all the time, so you are sitting with a pro. Besides, the larger jets can't fly into the Pittsburgh Airport; it's not as big as JFK."

"Is that so," Brendy smiled at her. "So why do you fly all the time?" She figured she would try to make conversation; perhaps it would be a way to pass the time.

"I have four sons and two daughters and not one of them live in the same state. I spend my time flying back and forth staying a month or so with each."

"Goodness, six children!" Brendy pretended to be interested. "How many grandchildren?"

"Fifteen grandchildren and four great-grandchildren. By the way, my name is Doris Brubaker. Are you from a big family?" Doris reached into her bag and pulled out a needle and yarn.

"No, just my mother and I. I'm Brendy Blake; it's nice to meet you."

"Brendy Blake," Doris said, starting to crochet on the baby blanket she had started. "That name has a nice ring to it, almost like an author's name. Do you write?"

Brendy laughed, "No ma'am, I am afraid I can't write much of anything."

"I bet you can. Have you ever tried?"

"No, I can't say as I have."

"Well then," Doris still crocheted with record speed. "You should try. I just bet you would make a great writer. With a name like Brendy Blake, I just bet you would."

"I'll keep that in mind, thanks."

"Do you and your mother get along well?"

Brendy knew that Doris was trying to make conversation, but this was not a subject she wanted to discuss. "Okay, I guess," she lied, looking again out the window beside her.

Doris quit crocheting for a minute and looked at Brendy. "That didn't sound too convincing, want to talk about it? I'm really a great listener."

"There is nothing to talk about, really." Brendy tried to smile, but her heart wasn't in it.

"We have at least an hour up here, so why not tell me about your mother?" Doris started again moving the yarn quickly through her fingers.

Brendy looked out the window for a moment in silence. No one ever asked about her mother and she was not sure if she wanted to talk about it now.

Doris rested the blanket in her lap and touched Brendy's hand again. "Sorry child, I guess I hit a sore spot. However, you know that the Lord works in mysterious ways, and perhaps He put you and me together today for a reason. Talking about it might make you feel better."

Brendy looked at Doris. "How do you know that my mother is a sore subject?"

"By the tone of your voice. I can detect something is terribly wrong with your relationship with your mother."

Brendy sighed. "I haven't seen my mother in six years. I honestly don't know if she is dead or alive."

Doris squeezed Brendy's hand, and for a moment said nothing.

"I see. I spent thirty years of my life as a Christian Counselor and I really am good at listening; perhaps you need to talk about it. If you disagree, just tell me and I will not speak of it again."

Maybe Doris was right; maybe some things needed to be let out. "My mother is an alcoholic. She drank all the time I was growing up. She used to hit me to get her point across. She didn't have to have a reason to hit me. I guess it gave her power. I learned early the beatings were not as bad as the verbal abuse. I fought for my life each day when I was a girl, and, on my sixteenth birthday, I decided I'd had enough. I stole money from her purse and took a bus to New York where I've been ever since."

Doris placed her blanket and yarn back into her bag and turned sideways so she could look at Brendy as she spoke. "I won't ask you how that turned out or what life has been like for the last six years. It's obvious, by the pain I sense in your spirit, that you are perhaps running again."

"Perhaps." Brendy could not figure out how this woman seemed to know so much about her. Had God truly put them together on this flight? She had never told anyone that story before.

"Do you believe in God, child?"

"Not really."

"Hmmm, I see. I guess you have a right to wonder, considering what you have been through. Can I tell you something, though?"

"Sure." Brendy was not sure why she liked Doris. She never met anyone that seemed to care, one way or the other.

"There is a God. He is a wonderful, loving Father, who just waits for us to turn to Him. I know that you may not want to hear that now; perhaps you even wonder where He has been all your life, but I can assure you He was there throughout it all. I am going to remember you, dear Brendy, and I am going to start today praying for you. I am going to pray that the Lord blesses you so that you will surely know He is real. I am going to pray that He gives you all of your dreams and sends the right people into your path that can help you along the way. And, if I may say one other thing," Doris paused. "You must forgive your mother, even if she never asks. Forgiveness is the key to healing. Without it, you will never truly be happy."

Brendy took her finger and wiped away a stray tear. "That one will be hard," she whispered.

"Then shall we pray?" Doris looked at her and smiled, as she took both her hands.

"You mean right now?" Brendy looked around to see if anyone was watching.

"Of course, right now. There is no better time than the present." Doris closed her eyes, bowed her head, and started praying. "Oh, Heavenly Father, how great is Thy name. I ask that You wrap your loving arms around this dear sweet child and protect her from evil. Let her feel Your presence around her and show her You are truly real and that You love her. I ask that You send her to the right place with the right people, so that whatever plan You have for her life may be fulfilled. I ask that You bless this dear child and help her find true forgiveness for her mother. I ask that You break all strongholds in her life and help her find her way to You, knowing that You are the only way. I ask these things in Your loving name. Amen."

When Doris finished praying she reached over and hugged Brendy tightly. "You are going to be okay, child. I just feel it way down deep inside. Today is the first day of the rest of your life, so make it a happy one. One day being miserable is just one day wasted."

Brendy had never thought of life like that before, and, as much as she wanted to believe in the words that Doris spoke, she knew Doris had no idea who she was. It saddened Brendy to think that if Doris had known the actual truth, she would not have touched her hand.

Or would she?

Chapter 2

Pittsburgh seemed every bit as loud as New York, and every bit as hot.

After saying her goodbyes to Doris, Brendy managed to find her luggage and found a seat outside the airport on a bench no one was using. The adrenaline raced through her from the fear of leaving her old life behind and the excitement of not knowing what the future held. What did it matter where she went, as long as no one that ever knew her as Sasha crossed her path again?

The summer heat bore down upon her. It was interesting watching people come and go. She wondered about their lives and if any happened to be in her situation, but then laughed at the thought of it. Of course, no one was in her situation. They all had homes to go to with families that loved them. She was quite sure she was the only one in the airport with no idea where she was or where she was going. At least this time she had money in her pocket that would be enough to last a few weeks.

Brendy was about to head to the nearest hotel when she spotted a man walking in her direction having a conversation on his cell phone. Most men Brendy knew could not be trusted, and she decided to write off men altogether, never giving them the time of day. She was sure if she never looked at a man again most of her problems would be over. As much as she wanted to grab her bags and run, she sat frozen in her seat, mesmerized by this handsome stranger. He smiled at Brendy and nodded politely, still continuing his conversation on his cell phone as he sat down beside her.

"I just dropped off David at the airport,so I should be home in about three-and-a-half hours. I can't wait to see everyone," he paused, obviously listening to the voice on the other end. Brendy found herself eavesdropping. He was intriguing, not to mention incredibly handsome. Besides, she was in no hurry; no one was waiting on her at home.

"Tell Mom not to wait up; it will be after midnight before I arrive," he paused again. "Okay, I love you too; I will see you soon." He flipped his cell phone shut and slid it back into his pocket. For a moment he sat, as if deep in thought, then turned to look at her.

"Waiting for someone?" he asked politely.

"Nope, are you?" How could she tell him she had been listening?

"No, just leaving." He stood, and then faced Brendy once more.

"You need a ride somewhere?"

"Momma always told me not to accept rides from strangers," she smiled.

His jaws flexed and he slowly smiled. "Then I would say you have a smart Momma. Have a nice day," he nodded, and started to walk away.

Brendy jumped to her feet. "Wait!" she called after him. He turned around once again.

"You change your mind?"

"You don't look like a dangerous stranger, and I really could use a ride."

"Where are you headed?"

Brendy smiled, trying to think of what to say. "Where are you headed?"

"Summersville, West Virginia."

"Sounds like a nice town."

"Some of the most beautiful country you've ever laid your eyes on. Are you headed that direction?"

"I am if you will let me tag along. You can drop me off before your destination, anywhere will be fine. I am sure there is a hotel in Summersville?"

He chuckled, "Summersville is small, but we do have several, yes." He knew there was quite a story to this beautiful woman. "So, you don't care where you are going? You just want to get out of *here*, right?"

"That's right. I hate the city." *That sounded crazy...could I not have come up with something better than that?*

"Well, okay then." He bent down and picked up her suit-cases. "Follow me, pretty lady," he winked, and started for the parking deck.

******

They rode the first few miles in silence. With so much in Brendy's mind, she was not quite sure what to say. What did it matter? After today, he would never see her again. Brendy looked out the window and sighed, knowing, at least,she was getting away from the noise that would slowly disappear be-hind her.

"Are you going to tell me your name, or are we going to ride all three-and-a-half hours in silence?" he chuckled, pull-ing out onto the interstate.

"Sorry," she giggled. "I'm Brendy Blake, and you are?"

"Noah Garrett. Brendy's a great name, never heard that before. It suits you."

"Thanks. My mother meant for me to be named Brenda after my grandmother, but it was misspelled on my birth cer-tificate, so the name sort of stuck, I guess."

"Hmmm, it's a good thing it was misspelled; I can't see you as a Brenda. Not that Brenda isn't a nice name; it's just an older name that doesn't suit you. You look too young and beautiful to be called an old name."

Brendy looked his way and smiled. It was the first time a man had called her beautiful that she didn't feel he wanted something in return.

"What's wrong, you don't take compliments very well?" He laughed, referring to her quietness.

Brendy shook her head and smiled. "I guess not."

"Come on, you must have been told you're beautiful many times."

"Sure, but not from someone like you." As soon as Brendy said it she felt silly. Nothing was coming out right.

"Someone like me?" he looked down over his sunglasses, looking bewildered.

"That didn't come out right. Never mind. Thank you for the compliment."

Noah smiled again, pushed up his sunglasses and continued driving a few more miles in silence.

"So what is a beautiful lady such as yourself doing at the airport with two suitcases caring less where she is going? Are you running from something?"

"Maybe, but nothing you need to worry about. I'm not in trouble, if that's what you mean."

"That's good. Then perhaps it's someone you're running from. Something that caused you harm, maybe?"

"Maybe." Brendy looked out the window again and watched the city disappear from sight.

"Not very talkative, are you?"

"Not really. I never really had anyone that wanted to talk to me."

"Well, I am trying, in case you haven't noticed."

Brendy managed to smile. "Sorry, I'm just not very talkative."

"Sorry for prying. Are you hungry?"

"As a matter of fact, I'm starved." Brendy was glad he changed the subject.

"Good, then let's stop at the Texas Road House for a steak. Does that sound good to you?"

"Sounds wonderful."

*****

Noah Garrett was a man of honor. To his friends they didn't come any better. And even though Noah was known as a handsome, eligible bachelor, his work kept him too busy to pursue the ladies. Noah wasn't looking for good times. He was looking for that forever kind of love that his parents once shared.

Noah dated his share of women, after Jessie, but no one held his interest until now. After Noah dropped David off at the airport, his only intention was to head to his car and get

out of Pittsburgh as soon as possible. He'd looked forward to
his trip home for months and was eager to get going. He was
on his way back to his car when he spotted her, sitting there
alone on a bench just gazing out into space as if her mind
were a thousand miles away. There was something about her
that pulled at him, as if some unknown force was invisibly
pushing him in her direction. True, she was beautiful, perhaps one of the most beautiful young women he'd ever seen.
Yet, even though he'd seen his share of beautiful women,
there was something about this one that was different.

Noah had never been the type to invite a stranger to ride
with him, and he was certainly no player, yet before he could
stop himself he was doing just that. Maybe it was fate, he
thought, that put them both together at that very moment in
the Pittsburgh Airport, or maybe, just maybe, it had been
God Himself; after all, Noah was a Christian and if anyone
believed in divine intervention it was him. He had witnessed
too often the hand of God working, so why couldn't it be
possible that this time God was actually working on *his* behalf? So many prayers he had prayed for God to send him a
good woman to cherish and to love, yet each time he thought
he found her God reassured his spirit that he had not.

Now, as he sat across the table from Brendy he couldn't
help but notice her beauty. Noah didn't want to stare, but he
found it hard to take his eyes away. He ordered a T-bone and
Brendy a sirloin, complete with baked potatoes and a salad.
He liked the fact that she had a healthy appetite, but still had
a shyness about her that made her even more intriguing.

Dinner went by fairly quickly with small talk, and they
were soon back on the road headed toward West Virginia.

It was hard for Brendy to concentrate on the events that
had taken place that day, when all she could do was think
about Noah and wonder about his life. Was he married? Did
he have children? No matter how hard she tried to focus on
what must be going on back in New York, she found herself wondering about Noah instead. Why was this man different from others she had been with? He seemed kind and

compassionate, and his personality was like none other she'd ever known.

Brendy took a breath and decided to break the silence; her curiosity was killing her. "So, what were you doing three-and-a-half hours from home?"

Noah looked to the side and slowly smiled. "So, you were listening to my conversation."

"Well, you were talking quite loud and sitting right next to me; what did you expect?" She hoped she had not said that rudely.

"I guess you're right. Actually, I am not three-and-a-half hours from home. My home is just a few miles from the air-port where I met you. I was dropping off a friend of mine to fly out to visit his fiancé. However, the home I grew up in *is* three-and-a-half hours away and I am going there to visit."

"I see. So, why didn't you fly, too?"

"Because I'm staying a couple of weeks and I hate rental cars."

"I understand. No rental car could be better than this," Brendy said, referring to his red Lamborghini.

Noah chuckled, "Yeah, you're probably right. Since the only bill I have is the mortgage on my townhouse, I thought I would treat myself."

"Not much room for a wife or children in here," Brendy looked around.

Noah took off his sunglasses and placed them above the visor. The sun had already gone down and he no longer needed them. "There is no wife or children. What about you? Do you have a man and kids in your life?"

"What kind of wife and mother would I be to up and leave my family?"

"Many women have done it, I'm afraid."

"Well, not me. If I had a husband and children, I would cherish them and never leave them." Brendy looked out the window, knowing that it would always be just her. Who would want her now? That dream died the same day she started working for Caroline.

Noah glanced her way, and then focused back on the road. It was easy to tell something heavy weighed on her mind and he wished he could break through the walls she was putting up and get to know the beautiful creature that sat in the seat beside him. He had encountered people like Brendy before. It was clear to see she had a past she intended to keep hidden; he only wished she could trust him enough to let him in.

"So tell me, Brendy, you just woke up this morning and decided you wanted out of the city, packed two bags, and left having no idea where you were going?"

"Yep, you're exactly right."

"That's a story I would be interested in hearing more about, but for now I need to grab some gas or we won't be going much farther." Noah pulled into a Quick Trip and hopped out, leaving Brendy alone. Why was she allowing this man to get to her? Just sitting beside him, smelling his cologne was intoxicating. After all these years of swearing she would never let a man stir her emotions, she knew Noah had managed to do just that. If she could hold on a little longer, he would let her out in some small town and she would never have to see him again; after all, men could never be trusted. She knew that, for sure.

Her eyes followed him inside the store and watched him pay for his gas. *What on earth am I doing here? I'm crazy for taking a ride with this man. What was I thinking?*

*****

"So, where were we?" He asked, pulling out onto the freeway.

"I can't recall." She hoped he would change the subject, for she had no intentions of telling him her story. Not to mention, it was none of his business.

"Oh yes, we were talking about you being single and hating the city, I believe. So tell me, Brendy, what exactly do you hope to find?"

"What do you mean?"

"Away from the city, I mean. What are you searching for? I can't help you find it if you don't fill me in."

Brendy sat up straighter and paused for a moment, not knowing how to answer, since she had not given the idea much thought. "I don't know. A small town where people are kind to one another. Not much kindness where I lived."

"What sort of job will you look for? What did you do before?"

"I was a waitress. Waitress jobs are usually pretty easy to find." She knew the lies would start here. She *had* been a waitress before she started working for Caroline, so it wasn't entirely a lie.

"Yeah, a job like that should not be too hard to find. Do you make good doing that? I mean, enough to furnish you a place to live and all?"

"Depends on where you work. The tips can be good if you're in the right restaurant."

"I guess you're right. So tell me why you hate the city."

"I hated the noise."

"You and me both. That's why I love to go back to my roots at least two weeks out of each year."

"Are you from a small town?" Brendy was glad to throw the questions back at Noah. The more questions she asked, the fewer she had to answer.

"I am. Mostly farm land where I'm from. In the beginning, we were known as a sleepy farming community. Summersville is a place where everyone knows everyone and treats each other with respect. It's a great place to raise children."

"Tell me about it." Brendy turned more to face Noah, absorbed in his voice and eager to know more.

"My family boards and breaks horses for folks, and we also have our own that we use to give riding lessons and trail rides. We have about a thousand acres and some beautiful areas for sightseeing. We get a lot of tourists this time of year just wanting to relax and enjoy the trails."

"Did you come from a big family?"

"There are four of us kids; I'm the oldest. My brother Brad and sister Connie still live in the house I grew up in,with Mom. My brother Greg is married to Rene and has a five-year-old daughter named Bethany. We call her Beth. They live in a two-bedroom cabin there on the ranch. All of them work there."

"Must be a lot to do."

"There is. Beth stays in the house with Mom, who is always busy doing something, usually cleaning, cooking, or whatever. The Garrett house is huge, to say the least, and takes a lot of her time. By the end of the day, Mom always has a home cooked meal for everyone."

"Sort of like Thanksgiving everyday."

Noah laughed, "That's exactly right. Brad and Greg take care of the barn, the stalls, whatever needs to be done with the horses. It's a full time job. Brad is into rodeos and Greg breaks horses."

"And what do Connie and Rene do?" Brendy loved hearing about Noah's family. She knew it would've been wonderful growing up in a family that cared about each other.

"Rene does trail rides. We have about two dozen horses of our own. The tours are usually booked way in advance and Rene is their guide."

"Greg got lucky to have married a woman that loves the ranch as much as he does."

"He and Rene went to school together. Never had another love, it was destined to be, I guess. You don't see that kind of love everyday, that's for sure."

"And your sister?" Brendy didn't wish to talk about love.

"Connie takes care of all the paperwork, the financial part of the ranch. She also gives riding lessons a couple of days per week."

Brendy smiled, loving the conversation. "So, what happened to you? Why didn't you love the ranch enough to stay, like the rest?"

"Oh, I loved it enough, and there are days I sometimes wish I'd stayed."

"Then, why didn't you?"

"I love that life as much as the rest of my family; it's just that, ever since I was a small boy, I dreamed of becoming a doctor. My father made sure I went to medical school; unfortunately, he didn't live long enough to see me finish."

"I'm sorry to hear that. So you're a doctor?"

"I am. I had a good job offer at Magee Women's Hospital in Pittsburgh; that's the only reason I left my hometown."

"You don't look old enough to be a doctor."

"Thanks," he laughed, "I'm thirty-two. How old do I look?"

"Not much older than me."

"And that would be?"

"Twenty-two."

"I thought so. My sister Connie is just a couple of years older than you."

"Mind if I ask you something personal?"

"Just how personal?" he smiled.

"At thirty-two, how come you aren't married? Surely, there is a woman in your life."

"Not even a girlfriend. Maybe I'm too picky, or at least that's what Brad and Greg tell me. The truth is, I am just too busy and don't have time to devote to a relationship."

"So, you aren't gay?"

Noah laughed at her comment." No, I can assure you, I'm not gay."

"I warned you it was personal."

"Yep, you did." Noah was smitten with this woman. Where had she been all his life and what was her story? And why did he feel this overwhelming sense that God was drawing them together?

"So, you do like women then?"

"Of course I do. I just don't have time for one, like I said. I am usually working double shifts, and when I get off, I go home and crash from exhaustion. What about you? Why isn't there a man in your life?"

"I don't trust men."

"But you do like men?"

Brendy giggled, "Of course I do; I just don't trust them."

"You've been hurt before, right?" Noah knew he was finally getting somewhere.

"Maybe."

"There's that maybe again, which means you don't want to talk about it."

Brendy looked at Noah and smiled, letting him know he was right.

"Are your parents still alive?"

"I never met my father and I haven't seen my mother in six years."

"Why?"

"Let's just say we don't gee-haw." These were not questions Brendy wanted to answer.

"You left home at sixteen, right?" Noah was trying to figure this out.

"That's right, smart man."

"Well, I figured if you're twenty-two and you haven't seen your mother in six years, it means either she left or you did. Don't you think she's worried about you?"

"Not in the least. You don't know my mother."

"I can see that. I can't imagine what it must have been like, but it couldn't be too good if it caused you to leave home. You went to the city, became a waitress, and after six years you are once again trying to start over. How in this world did a sixteen-year-old make it by herself?"

"Let's just say I was smarter than most and looked older than my age." Brendy hoped he would stop with all the questions; she felt certain he was about to see through her and figure it out. What would he say if he knew the truth?

Noah drove a few miles in silence, contemplating his next move. What he was about to do was so unlike him, but as he silently prayed and asked God for guidance, he

felt in his spirit that it was the right thing. He'd learned
from his past relationships that trust was something that
was earned, but there was something about Brendy that
told him she was not like anyone he'd ever met. He felt
strongly that God was leading him to take this next step,
and he prayed that it was indeed that spirit voice leading
him and not his own.

"If you could care less where you're going, I'm going
to take you to the ranch with me and introduce you to my
family."

Brendy's head shot around in his direction. "What? I can't
do that!"

"Why not?"

"You just met me. You don't even know me." Brendy knew
she could never enter Noah's home with his family. These
were good people, and she didn't belong there.

"Sure, I do. I am sure I will know you better in the days to
come, but, for now, I am sure not going to set you out at some
hotel and wonder the rest of my life what became of you."

"Why do you care what becomes of me?"

"I just do. You said yourself you don't care as long as it's
a small town and the people are nice. Well, our town is small
compared to Pittsburgh, and my family doesn't get any nicer.
Anyway, we don't have to tell them we just met. I will introduce you as my friend that I met in Pittsburgh, which isn't a
lie."

"And what about when you leave? Are you going to set me
out then? I cannot live with them forever, Noah."

"I'm going to be there for two weeks. Let's just take
one day at a time and see how it goes." Noah hoped that
two weeks would give him enough time to get to know
this woman and understand a little better what God had
in mind. Besides, there was so much more to her that he
wanted to know. Many women had come on to him in the
past, and once he'd even thought he was in love, but never
had he been this attracted to another woman and he was not
about to let her get out of his sight just yet.

"I don't know what to say; I never expected this, really." Brendy could feel her heart beating faster in her chest. She had no idea what she was supposed to do now.

"You want to know what I think?" Noah asked.

"What do you think?"

"I think you're not used to having someone care about you. I think you have been on your own so long you don't know how to act when someone is kind to you."

"Perhaps you're right. I have certainly never had anyone that cared in the least."

"Then it's settled. You will come with me to the Garrett Ranch to experience life. I know you will have a great time, and you are going to love my family."

Chapter 3

Brendy knew there was no talking Noah out of it; he was set on taking her to the home where he grew up. She laid her head back on the headrest and closed her eyes. So tired and so many things going on inside her head at once she thought she might erupt.

Maybe if she pretended to be asleep Noah would stop with the questions. She had no idea how she would get through the next two weeks and the lies she would have to tell in order to hide her past. At the moment, she was grateful she would be able to spend more time with Noah. How amazing it would be to have a man like Noah fall in love with her. Of course, a man like Noah would never fall in love with a woman like her if he knew the truth. Was it wrong to lie to him and make him think she was something other than a prostitute? Caroline told her often she was a highly paid escort, trying to make her profession seem almost glamorous, when Brendy knew no matter how you said it it still meant the same.

Caroline never allowed the word prostitute; she said it sounded dirty. And, as the dark set in all around them, she thought back to the time she first met Caroline.

Jobs were hard to find at sixteen. After living a month on the streets out of garbage cans and sleeping in cardboard boxes in the back alleys, Frank Greene took a chance and gave her a job at the coffee shop on the corner of 5th Street.

The lunch rush was over and Brendy could feel the sweat on her forehead. She longed for a hot shower, but the best she could do was wash off in the coffee shop's bathroom.

Frank noticed her digging out of the garbage can behind the shop and found she was sleeping in the alley. He allowed her to come inside, gave her a job, and allowed her to sleep on a cot in the storage room. Brendy wished a hundred times over the next six years that she had remained with him, but thinking and wishing didn't change reality.

Brendy noticed Caroline the moment she entered the coffee shop. She was decked out in jewelry, wearing excessively too much makeup for Brendy's taste, and her red hair was as bright as carrots.

"Can I take your order?" Brendy asked politely. She'd never seen anyone quite like her in all her life.

Caroline smiled at her and gave her the once-over. "Sure can. Why don't you sit down here and take a load off? Let's chat for awhile."

"I'm sorry, but I'm working. Is there something I can get you, coffee perhaps?"

"No honey, I didn't come in this greasy spoon to eat or for coffee. I came in to talk to you. I have been watching you, and came to offer you a job."

"A job? I already have a job." Brendy didn't like the way this woman was looking at her. She didn't know a lot about people but she could tell this woman did not have good intentions, and something about her reminded her of her mother.

"This is hardly a job, dear, now sit and let's talk," Caroline patted the seat beside her.

Brendy looked around and saw that the crowd had died out and it would be a couple of hours before the evening crowd arrived; besides, she was curious about the job offer.

"Good girl, I knew you were the smart type as soon as I saw you. I'm Caroline Reese, by the way."

"I don't have long, I have things to do." Brendy didn't want to make her boss angry; she would have nowhere to go if he threw her out.

"This won't take long. So what's your name?" Caroline placed her long red nail between her teeth and looked at her with a smug smile.

"Brendy."

"How cute. You look like a Sasha to me."

"About the job." Brendy didn't want to be rude, but she didn't have time for chitchat.

"Ah yes, you are a straight to the point type girl, I like that."

"Like I said, I don't have much time."

"Yes, you wouldn't want dear Frank to fire you, would you? Where would you go? I imagine it gets quite cold in the alley."

"Excuse me?" How did she know so much about her?

"Like I said, I've been watching you, and dear old Frank is quite a sweetheart to have offered you such a fine job, don't you agree?"

"He has been kind, yes."

"I'd say using you like a dog and probably paying you not much of anything, but then, that is dear old Frank."

Brendy got up to leave and Caroline reached over and grabbed her hand. "Okay, I won't talk bad about your boss. Now sit, I'm not finished. What if I could give you a job making way more than you are making now? I'd even get you a nice place to live and you wouldn't have to sleep on that hard cot in the back room. What would you say to that?"

"Doing what?" Brendy looked around to see if Frank was watching, but saw no one.

"Working for me, of course."

"What do you do?"

"I run an escort service."

"What is that?" Brendy had no idea what she was talking about, or what an escort service did.

Caroline laughed. "You are a young thing, aren't you? How old are you, Sasha?"

"The name is Brendy, and I'm sixteen."

"Sixteen is such an innocent age. Are you a virgin?"

"Excuse me, I hardly think that is any of your business."

Caroline laughed again. "Perhaps you are right. It doesn't matter anyway. An escort service is a company in which wealthy gentlemen make appointments to have a fine looking lady such as yourself escort them somewhere for the evening."

"You mean pay to have a date."

"Now you're getting it, yes. And by the way, they pay quite a bit."

"Why don't they just ask someone out and pay nothing. If they are so wealthy, I am sure they wouldn't have a hard time finding a date."

Caroline looked at her again and smiled. "I like the way you think, but, dear Sasha, not everyone's date would be at their beck and call."

"Like I said before, the name's Brendy, and what you are saying is that not every date would allow them to paw all over them, right?"

"Ohh, you make that sound so trashy. These men don't paw, dear, they are perfect gentlemen who just need a little bit of attention, and they pay very well for that attention. I can assure you that you will be perfectly safe. I have a driver that will pick you up, take you to your destination and wait on you to take you back home. If anything gets out of hand, he will be there to protect you."

Brendy got up from the table. "No thanks. I will take my chances here."

Caroline chuckled and handed Brendy a card with her number on it. "If you should change your mind and want to see what living life in luxury is like,you can give me a call." And just like that, she got up from the table and left the coffee shop, leaving Brendy confused. Out of all the women in New York, why did she pick her to offer a job to?

*****

Noah watched her sleep for the longest. She was beautiful and slept peacefully. He knew there was much more to her story than she told him, and hoped he was not making a mistake by taking her home to stay with his family. Even though there was mystery about this woman, there was also a childlike innocence about her, and Noah had always been a good judge of character. Besides, he felt so strongly that God had placed her in his life for a reason, so he was going by faith and would trust that feeling.

"Brendy," Noah touched her lightly on the arm to wake her up.

Brendy opened her eyes and stretched. "I'm so sorry, I never meant to fall asleep. How long have I been out?"

"A while. We will be there in just a moment and I wanted you to have time to get ready for what is about to take place."

"And what would that be?" Brendy looked at the clock on the dash that read twelve-ten a.m.

"My whole family should be up waiting; they always are when I return home."

"At this hour?" Brendy reached into her purse and took out her brush to freshen up.

"It wouldn't matter what time it was, believe me, they will be up. Of course, I doubt Greg and Rene will be there; it is too late for Beth.

"I'm so nervous, maybe this was not a good idea after all, Noah."

Noah chuckled. "It's a great idea; you're going to have to trust me."

"At this very moment you are the only person in the world I could even call a friend, so I guess I will have to trust you."

"Believe me, in about ten minutes, you are going to have several more."

"Ten minutes, are you serious?"

"Yep, we are going through Summersville now."

Brendy looked out the window at what appeared to be the courthouse and glanced at the sign in front. "1820?"

"That's when Summersville was established. Nicholas County, though, came about in 1785." Noah laughed. "Are you really interested in the history of our town at the moment?" Noah reached over and took hold of her shaking hand.

"Just trying to make small talk, I guess; I'm actually terrified," she laughed.

"Hey, it's going to be okay. Don't be nervous." Brendy could feel warmth from his hand, which sent chills through her. How did she get as lucky as this? Perhaps it was Doris and her prayer to God that led her to meet Noah, and now she was on her way to meet his family.

"Does it show? That I am nervous, I mean?" she smiled.

"Very much, but there is no reason for you to be nervous at all; my family is great, and you will soon understand that all this shaking was for nothing."

Brendy took a deep breath and closed her eyes. Now was not a time to mess things up. Noah's family would think they had been friends for a while. He had made that clear to her, and only she could blow it.

"Why have you been so kind to me?" Brendy could feel the sting of tears and was not quite sure where they were coming from; she was never the emotional type.

"Because that's who I am, and you deserve it. I have a feeling you've had many tough breaks in your life and it's about time for a change. Just a few more miles to go."

"So, you didn't live that far from town?"

"Only five miles, but the Garrett Ranch is still the biggest in Nicholas County. Just wait until tomorrow when you can see for yourself how beautiful it is with all the mountains."

"I bet it's breathtaking; I can hardly wait. I don't want to get in the way."

"There you go again. How could you get in the way? My family always insists this is my vacation and hardly lets me lift a finger. You will be able to keep me company while they are busy during the day."

"At least I will be good for something." Brendy could hardly wait to keep this man company for the next two weeks and secretly hoped that time would stand still. After two weeks, he would return to Pittsburgh and she would go on her way, wherever that was.

"Well, here we are." Noah pulled onto a long paved driveway and went under an archway that held the letters GAR-RETT RANCH.

"It's beautiful, and quite large. I can imagine your mother does stay busy."

"This is where I grew up. I never lived anywhere else until I went away to college."

"It must have been something growing up here."

"I have no complaints." Noah stopped the car and looked at her once more. "Are you sure you're going to be all right?"

"I'm okay. So, if they ask, how long have we known each other and where did we meet?"

"I have never been one for lying, Brendy, but in this case, if it would make you more comfortable, we met in Pittsburgh at the place you used to work. What was the name of the diner you worked at?"

"Frank's Coffee Shop, but that is in New York."

"They don't know that."

"Yeah, I guess you're right."

"Now let's see, we have known each other six months, is that okay?"

"Okay, I will remember that, but I hate for you to lie on my account."

Noah winked at her, "It's okay; I think God will forgive me for this one."

*****

As soon as they entered the door, Noah's family circled around him, each giving him a hug and telling him how much he was missed. For a moment Brendy was lost in the commotion.

"My, my, people, where are our manners? We are completely ignoring this beautiful girl. Hey there, my name is Edith; I'm Noah's mother."

"Hi Edith, I'm Brendy." Brendy shook her hand and hoped she wasn't still trembling.

"Everyone, I want you to meet a very good friend of mine, Brendy." Brendy could feel everyone's eyes on her and see their smiles. They all looked at Noah as if perhaps he had failed to tell them he had a girlfriend.

"Wait a minute," Noah threw up his hands. "Brendy and I are just friends, so don't go thinking all those things that I know you are all thinking," he laughed.

"Well, big brother, we should have known you don't stand a chance with someone this gorgeous," Connie teased, holding out her hand toward Brendy. "Hi there, I'm Connie, Noah's sister. I'm glad you came to visit us; it's nice to have another female around the house my age."

"Thanks, I couldn't wait to meet you all. Noah has told me so much about you."

"All good, I hope." Brad shook her hand next. "I'm Brad; it's nice to meet you."

"Likewise." Brendy could see the resemblance between Noah and Brad, and guessed they must look like their father. Connie, on the other hand, was the spitting image of her mother, short and pretty.

Edith playfully slapped Noah on the arm to scold him. "Why did you not bother to tell us you were bringing company?"

"I wanted it to be a surprise." Noah smiled at Brendy, who still looked as if she was lost.

"Well, it is certainly a surprise, that's for sure. It's a good thing I have just changed the sheets in the guest room and cleaned it a bit."

"I'm sorry for intruding like this. I feel bad coming uninvited." Brendy could not feel more out of place.

"Don't you dare feel like you are intruding," Edith looked at her and shook her head. "Any friend of Noah's is a friend of ours, and it's nice to know he actually has time to make friends. That surely makes me feel a lot better."

"And such a beautiful friend at that," Brad winked at her. Brendy could tell he was not the shy type. Not as handsome as Noah, but handsome just the same.

"Okay, little brother, I'm sure Brendy would like to have a nice peaceful vacation, and not have you barking at her," Noah teased. Even though he wanted his family to think they were just friends, he wanted to be the one to do the pursuing if there was any to be done. He certainly was not ready to give her up just yet to his handsome brother.

"Hey, you did say you two were just friends, right?" Brad smiled, and Brendy could tell he was teasing her, trying to make light of the situation.

"It's okay." Brendy smiled back at him. "And thanks for the compliment."

"Would you two like something to eat?" Edith asked.

"I wouldn't; how about you, Brendy?" Noah could still sense Brendy's nervousness and wished there was someway he could calm her.

"No thanks, I'm really quite tired from the drive."

"Here, let me take your bags to your room," Brad said, starting to pick up Brendy's suitcases.

"No, big brother, I think we can manage this." Connie picked up Brendy's bags. "Come along, Brendy; I'll show you to your room." Brendy followed Connie, looking back at Noah to see him smiling at her. She couldn't help but wonder what he was thinking and if he already regretted his decision about bringing her here.

Brendy followed Connie down a long hallway and into a room at the back of the house. "Don't let Brad get to you. He thinks he is a lady's man." Connie closed the door behind her and placed the suitcases on the bed.

Brendy giggled. "I think he was just being nice, that's all."

"Yeah, right," Connie rolled her eyes. "You are quite a looker, and believe me, he noticed. So now that we are alone, are you and Noah really just friends?"

"Yep, just friends."

"Darn, I was hoping there was more to it. You know, he hasn't had a girlfriend that he has spoken of since Jessie."

"Jessie?" Brendy wanted to know more. Noah had failed to mention Jessie, but then his life was none of her business.

"Surely he has told you about Jessie?" Connie put her hands to her mouth as if she had perhaps told something she shouldn't have.

"Not yet. Who was Jessie?"

"Oh my, I am sure this is not something Noah wants me to talk about. He always told me I had a big mouth."

Brendy knew better than to push the issue. "I'm sure he just never thought it was important; after all, I'm not his girl-friend in that way, and so his personal life is none of my business. This is a nice room. Thanks for helping me with my bags."

Connie looked at her, wishing she had never opened her mouth about Jessie "Hey, I'm sorry, Jessie was a long time ago. It doesn't matter, really." Brendy could see the regret in Connie's eyes.

"Don't worry about it. Would you mind telling the others goodnight?" She didn't feel up to going back to the living room to answer more questions.

"Sure thing, and I really am glad you're here. If you should need anything, my room is right across the hall. Just knock, okay?"

"Thank you, and goodnight." Brendy smiled as Connie shut the door and left her alone.

Even though she had napped on the road, she felt tired. It was hard to believe this morning she awoke in New York, dreading the day ahead, and tonight she was going to sleep on a ranch in the middle of nowhere, in a town called Summersville, West Virginia.

Chapter 4

Brendy awoke to the smell of bacon and freshly brewed coffee. For the first time in her life, she felt safe. She stretched and climbed out of bed, knowing today was the first day of the rest of her life, and no matter what tomorrow might bring, she vowed to spend the next two weeks as close to Noah as humanly possible, savoring every moment she was lucky enough to have. It would be nice to feel as if she had a family.

Noah was sitting at the table eating breakfast with a small girl that Brendy guessed was Beth. Edith was humming *Amazing Grace* and busy putting dishes away.

"Well, good morning," Noah smiled at her, eating the last of his toast.

"Am I the last one up?"

"Don't worry if you are." Edith wiped her hands on her apron and poured Brendy a cup of coffee. "You sit right down there and eat. I have kept your breakfast warm for you."

"You should have woke me up and I would have helped you with breakfast."

"Nonsense, cooking is my job. That's what I'm here for. How do you like your coffee?"

"Cream and sugar, please." Brendy sat down at the table and smiled at Noah, who winked at her. He'd warned her that his mother did all the cooking.

"So, I guess you're Bethany?" Brendy asked the small girl who sat staring at her.

"Yes, they call me Beth, though."

"Then I will call you Beth. My name is Brendy." Brendy stuck out her hand and Beth took it, smiling a toothless smile.

"Are you Uncle Noah's girlfriend?"

Brendy could feel her face grow warm and looked at Noah, who was waiting to see what her answer was.

"I am his friend, yes."

"And since you are a girl, then that would make you his girlfriend."

Brendy could see Edith smiling from the sink, but neither Noah nor Edith said a word to correct the girl.

"Would you like to ride into town with me, Brendy?" Noah asked. "I know no one is going to let us turn our hand around here, and this will give you a chance to see Summersville in the daytime."

"Sure, I would like that."

"Can I come, too, Uncle Noah?" Beth asked with excitement.

"You are going to help me make gingerbread cookies, re-member?" Edith said.

Noah knew his mother wanted to allow him time alone with Brendy, for it wasn't every day he showed up with a female friend.

"Maybe next time, okay? If you're a good girl, I will try to bring you back something from town."

"Okay, I like Barbies." Beth got down from her seat and put her arm around Noah.

"Oh you do, do you?" Noah laughed, picking her up and hugging her closely. Brendy loved the way Noah interacted with his family. She wished she had been as close to hers. Sometimes she thought it wasn't fair at all that she had been handed the mother of her birth. Beth was lucky to have been born to the Garretts. Fate had certainly been on her side.

*****

"So, how are you doing so far?" Noah chuckled as he cranked the car and backed out of the driveway.

"Your family is extremely nice. You were right. I had no reason to be nervous. I do hate, though, that you only got to see them briefly and now you are out with me."

"We talked about an hour last night after you went to bed. Besides, they are so busy now with daily chores, and since they refuse to let me help them, it's better for me to get out of the way."

"So, where are we headed?" Brendy was excited to be spending time with Noah, yet still nervous to be around him. She hoped he didn't ask too many questions so she wouldn't have to lie more than necessary. There was no way she would ever tell him the truth about her past, or anyone, for that matter.

"It's a surprise, something I thought of this morning, and I am glad to see you are dressed for it." Brendy was wearing black shorts and a white tank top. It had been the fifth outfit she'd tried on, not knowing what to wear.

"A surprise?"

"That's right. I think I have thought of a way to make you fall in love with my town."

"Is that so?" she smiled.

The mountains around Summersville were beautiful, and the town square looked friendly. Quite a few people were out and about, and it made Brendy wonder why Noah would have ever wanted to leave it in the first place.

Noah pulled the car into a parking space at the marina, and cut off the engine. Turning sideways to look at her, he smiled. "Are you ready to go on an adventure?"

"An adventure? You mean, here at the lake?"

"That's right. I am renting us a boat for the day."

"Wow, that sounds like fun. What made you think of this?"

"Mom helped me think of it, actually," he laughed. "She even packed a picnic lunch in the trunk for us."

"Gosh, why all the trouble?"

"Because I wanted to show you how beautiful Summersville is, and there is no better place for that than Summersville Lake. Mom, on the other hand, has wanted me to find a woman for quite sometime, so I am sure she is hoping this will lead to more than just friendship. But don't worry; we will just go with the flow, and in two weeks when I leave you won't have to have my family trying to put us together any longer."

Brendy laughed at his comment, and wondered if he thought she was someone he would want to be with. There was a ten-year age difference and she was certain he probably went for women with an education, someone with the intention of making something of herself. Besides, what did it matter anyway?

Noah handed Brendy the picnic basket and grabbed the cooler out of the trunk. She felt like a child in a candy store. She knew Noah had no idea today would be the first time she'd ever been on a boat in her entire life. There was so much in life she'd never done, going from being raised by a poor alcoholic mother, living in the slums, to working for Caroline doing things most could never imagine. She'd never once taken a day to do anything fun.

*****

Summersville Lake was breathtaking with the high cliffs along the shore. The day was hot and beautiful, without a cloud in the sky. Noah rented a pontoon boat that was perfect for cruising, and Brendy knew this was, by far, the best day of her life.

"That's Long Point Overlook over there," Noah pointed. "It's the highest cliff on the lake, almost 100 feet out of the water." Brendy could tell that Noah was in his familiar atmosphere and felt right at home. She could see the pride in his face as he told her about Summersville. Not many people loved their hometown as much as Noah seemed to love his.

"It's beautiful, but then the entire lake is. Thanks for bringing me out here. It's hard to imagine that we only met yesterday, and today you are entertaining me," she laughed.

Noah cut the engine and dropped in the anchor close to Long Point Overlook. "This looks like a perfect place for a picnic; what do you think?"

"You can't get more perfect than this."

Edith had thought of everything and placed it neatly inside the picnic basket. There was a table on the boat and Noah took a moment to arrange the food just so. He smiled as he extended his hand towards Brendy. "Are you ready to eat, my lady?" he bowed. Brendy laughed at him.

"I am, kind sir." She got up and took his hand and he led her to the table to sit down.

"Mom is a miracle worker, isn't she?" he chuckled.

"She is something else, that's for sure, going through all this trouble for us."

"Do you like fried chicken and potato salad?" Noah handed her a plastic container of chicken.

"I love it. When in this world did she make this?"

"Before sunlight."

"Seriously? Goodness, the poor woman didn't go to bed until one a.m."

"She's normally in the bed by nine, but last night was special. She will be okay, trust me, my mother is a tough bird. And she truly enjoys doing for others."

"She is just too kind."

"She's the best." Noah took a bite out of a chicken leg and Brendy smiled at him. She wondered if he really knew how lucky he was to have a mother like Edith.

*****

Half an hour after they'd eaten, they were still sitting at Long Point Overlook, talking. The sun was at its hottest and Noah made her put sunblock on generously, giving her all the reasons why the suns rays were bad for you. Spoken as a doctor would, Brendy thought he was cute. No one had ever cared whatsoever, especially about something as simple as sunburn.

"I have enjoyed myself. Thank you so much for inviting me to your home and for doing all this for me today. I will never forget your kindness." Brendy had never been treated with such respect from someone who didn't expect anything in return.

"You are very welcome. In case you didn't know, I have had a great time myself. I stay so busy at the hospital all the time; I never have time to relax." Noah looked around the lake and smiled. "I do love Summersville Lake. I have lots of memories here."

"Do tell," Brendy smiled. She loved hearing stories of Noah's long ago.

"When I was a small boy, my mom and dad brought us kids down here often. There are many walking trails and footpaths here, and places to swim. Mom was big on picnics and spending time with the family. As we got older, my dad bought a ski boat, and in the summer months we would come down once or twice a week after the chores were done and go skiing. Of course, we fished a lot, too. Dad always said fishing with live bait was cheating, so he taught us at an early age how to use spinner bait or rattle traps, plastic worms and lizards." Noah laughed, looking at Brendy's expression.

"You don't have a clue as to what I am talking about when it comes to bait, do you?"

"Not in the least," she laughed, "but I must admit, it does sound interesting."

"Oh, it is, if you like to fish."

"Sounds like you've had an exciting life."

"I did, blessed beyond measure. I have no complaints or regrets; God has truly been good to me."

"Wonder why He is better to some than others?" Noah could sense bitterness in her tone.

"I don't know the answer to that, Brendy. I sense bitterness there. Tell me about your life growing up."

Brendy leaned back in her seat and crossed her legs at the ankles. It was bound to happen sooner or later, she knew. She'd thought she would have more time to prepare herself for answers, but everything had happened so quickly.

"It doesn't matter," she shook her head. "It's over, no use dwelling on it."

Noah stared at her for a moment. How would he ever break through the walls she put up so thick in front of her? It was none of his business, he knew, and yet in his heart, he also knew that if she talked about it, maybe she would be able to let it go. It was easy to see it was something that caused her great pain.

"You're not going to let me in there, are you?" he smiled.

"You mean inside my head?" Brendy laughed. "Are you sure you're not a shrink?"

"No, but I want to help you heal. Plus, I want to understand you, see what makes you tick."

"There is nothing to heal; I'm over it. There's nothing to understand."

"If you were over it, you wouldn't mind talking about it. I won't pressure you to talk about something you're not ready to talk about, but know you can if you ever want to."

"I appreciate that. Never really had anyone to talk to, so it isn't something I am used to, you know?"

"I understand. So what do you say we set this boat to motion and see some more of this lake?" Noah decided to let it go for now. After all, it was just their first day together and he knew it would take time for her to feel more comfortable with him. He could tell she had been hurt tremendously and trusted no one.

"That sounds good." Brendy got up from the chair and headed to the front of the boat. "And Noah?"

"Yeah?" He was pulling up the anchor.

"Don't take it personal, okay? My past is not something I like to remember."

"It's okay. Because no matter what's back there, it doesn't change who you are today, and from what I see, that's pretty amazing."

Chapter 5

The house smelled of pot roast and potatoes when they entered, around seven. Brendy could hear laughter coming from the kitchen.

"Sounds like Rene is here. Come and let me introduce you." Noah led the way to the kitchen, with Brendy following close behind.

"Hello there, sweet sister," Noah teased, giving Rene a huge hug.

"Hello there, handsome brother, sorry I missed you last night." Rene pulled away and smiled at Brendy. "Mom tells me Noah brought a new friend." Rene didn't give Noah time for introductions. She walked over and gave Brendy the same hug she had given Noah.

"That's right; this is Brendy Blake, Rene. Brendy, this is my sister-in-law, Rene Garrett."

"It's a pleasure to meet you," Brendy smiled. Rene was pretty with her long black hair pulled back in a ponytail, jeans, and cowboy boots. She certainly looked the part of a trail ride tour guide.

"Greg's around here somewhere. He should be back in a minute. He is looking forward to meeting you, too. By the way, did you two have fun today? Mom told us you were renting a boat."

"I had a great time, thanks for asking. And thank you, Edith, for the wonderful lunch you packed us." Brendy smiled in Edith's direction. Brendy could feel her heart pounding and prayed Noah's family would not be able to see through her disguise.

"I'm glad you liked it; I enjoyed making it."

Noah kissed Edith on the cheek. "That's what I have tried to tell Brendy, that you really do enjoy cooking."

"Thank God for that, or we would all be in trouble," Greg said, coming in the back door of the kitchen. "Hey there, brother, I hear you've been off gallivanting around with this pretty lady here." Greg hugged Noah, and then turned to hug Brendy as well.

"That's right, you don't think I wanted to stay around here and watch you work, did you?" Noah laughed. "Greg, this is a good friend of mine, Brendy Blake."

"Prettiest friend you have had in a while, I bet," Greg laughed.

"Thank you," Brendy could feel herself blushing, and wished they would quit taking on about her looks; it brought back too many memories of the men who paid big money just to spend time with her.

"So, where's Connie and Brad? Dinner is done and going to get cold if them two don't hurry it up." Edith started carrying bowls heaping full of food to the dining room table.

"I hear myself being paged," Connie said, coming into the kitchen from the hallway. "I was working on the summer camp program we are having in a few weeks and lost track of time. Need some help, Mom?"

"Sure, everyone grab a dish and come to the table. I know you young'uns are hungry by now.

"Can I bring the cookies now, too, Grandma?" Beth asked, who had been sitting at the bar coloring in her Disney coloring book.

"You sure can, sweet girl," Edith answered. "We made them for dinner, remember?"

"So, are we not going to wait on Brad?" Noah asked, pulling out a chair for Brendy and then taking one himself beside her.

"No need to wait; I'm finally here." Brad entered the dining room and winked at Brendy as he took a seat at the end of the table.

"It's a good thing," Edith piped up. "We were going to eat without you."

"Sorry,Mom, we had a couple of new horses arrive and I was showing the owners around. So how did you both like Summersville Lake?"

"Wonderful, I forgot how great it was to just take a day off and do nothing," Noah said.

"Okay, you kids can talk about your day in just a second. Noah, would you care to say grace?" Edith grabbed onto Brendy's hand and Noah took the other. Saying grace was not a ritual she'd ever followed, but she'd learned from watching movies she was supposed to bow her head.

"Dear Heavenly Father, we thank You for this wonderful meal that is before us. Thank You for family and for great friends. Thank You for this beautiful day You have given us and for bringing us all together once again. We ask in Jesus' mighty name, we pray, Amen." A round of Amens was heard around the table and everyone started passing food and talking at once.

Brendy looked around in wonder at this incredible family. Everyone got along so well and seemed to genuinely love each other. The feeling certainly wasn't something she was used to, or thought she would ever fit into. What would it have been like to grow up in a family as Noah had? Where would she have been today? Certainly she would not be worried about anyone finding out about her past because her past would have only been filled with wonderful memories. Sometimes, life just wasn't fair.

"So what do you think, Brendy?" Connie asked from across the table.

"Excuse me?" Brendy had been so caught up in her own thoughts she'd lost track of the conversation.

"I was asking Noah why he had not taken you to the Gauley River to go whitewater rafting."

"I told her you were a city girl, and I wanted to break you in slowly," Noah added.

"Well, he is right about being a city girl. I have never been rafting before." She wasn't going to tell them she had never been on a boat either, until today.

"I want to go rafting, Uncle Noah," Beth pleaded.

"You're going to have to grow a bit, kiddo," Greg said, patting his daughter's head.

"That's for sure," Rene added. "Brendy, don't you allow them to get you on that river until you're ready for the adventure of your life. If it isn't something you are used to, it might frighten you."

"Just the thought of getting on a horse frightens me enough," Brendy said.

Connie looked at her with eyes opened wide, not believing what she'd just said.

"You mean to tell me you have never been on a horse before?"

"No, I haven't," Brendy laughed. "I haven't even been around a horse before."

"See, I told you Brendy was a city girl," Noah laughed.

"Would you like to learn how to ride a horse?" Connie asked.

"Yes, I would. That is, if you don't laugh at my ignorance."

"What are your plans for tomorrow, big brother?" Connie looked across at Noah with that look he knew all too well.

"Looks like I am going to do some riding."

*****

After dinner, Noah went out back with Brad and Greg to check on the new foal. Excitement was always in the air when there was a new addition to the family.

Connie and Edith insisted they would do the dishes, and Rene carried Beth home to put her to bed. Brendy went to the front porch swing to enjoy the evening breeze, as Edith suggested, telling her it was her favorite spot on the ranch. After fifteen minutes, Brendy would have to agree with her.

Brendy thought the Garretts were the nicest people she'd ever met. Perhaps they were the first people who were actually kind to her. Of course, there was Frank Greene at the coffee shop six years before. Taking her in off the streets and allowing her to sleep in the stockroom was better than the cardboard box under the alley stairs out back.

If only she could've been satisfied working at the coffee shop, and not had her head filled with dreams of wanting more.

Six months after pouring coffee and waiting tables for Frank, Brendy found herself at the address on the card looking straight into the eyes of Caroline Reese.

"I knew you were a smart girl, Sasha. What size do you wear?"

"I told you, my name is Brendy."

"Not anymore, it isn't. Rule number one in the business, no one knows your real name, you got that?"

"Why?" Brendy knew right off she no more liked Caroline than she did her own mother, but if she could get a better place to live it wouldn't hurt to give it a try. Besides, if she didn't like it, she could always go back to the coffee shop, couldn't she?

"Rule number two, don't ask questions. Now I will ask you again, what size do you wear?"

"Size three, why?"

Caroline laughed, "Why do you think? You have to dress the part, dear, and I know you don't have any nice clothes to speak of. Think of this as a loan, which you will pay back with interest. I'm giving you an advance, knowing you will be well worth it. Now, go in there," Caroline pointed to a room behind a closed door, "and put this on." She handed her a short red dress off a rack behind her. "You will start work tonight."

"I never said I was going to work for you. I just wanted to come and talk to you more about it. I haven't made up my mind yet."

Caroline laughed out loud. "But, of course you have made up your mind, sweet Sasha, or you wouldn't be here, now would you? Now hurry on; we don't have much time."

And just like that, Brendy started working for Caroline Reese. Many times she told Caroline she wasn't happy and wanted out, but Caroline would find some excuse and never let the words Brendy spoke actually sink in. Caroline had her claws in Brendy for the past six years and Brendy knew there was no way she would ever loosen the grip. After three years, Brendy quit fighting it and went with the flow. Feeling like a lightning bug in a mason jar, she knew there was no getting away from what she had become. She felt trapped, with no way out.

Apparently, Caroline told the gentleman the driver took her to the first night that she was young and had not yet been touched. She remembered it as if it were yesterday. Brendy wasn't sure how old he was, but he reminded her of her grandfather and knew they must be around the same age. He was a balding man, who smelled of sweet cigars and Brut cologne that almost made her sick to her stomach. From the time she entered his limousine, he couldn't keep his hands off her. She closed her eyes, remembering the feel of his chubby hands caressing her thighs underneath her short dress. Tears streamed down her face as she remembered him pulling off her panties as he kissed her neck. Caroline told her, no matter what happened, not to speak unless she was spoken to and to allow this man his pleasure. She would be taught what to say and what to do, but as far as tonight, she was to remain quiet.

Brendy knew that no matter how long she lived and breathed on this earth she would never forget that first night and the pain she endured and the awful stench of him. As a bonus to his chauffeur, he allowed him to take a turn, also. As she lay there and went numb, the older man bragged to his driver, who was now on top of her, that this was his reward for being faithful. But what was her reward? Who would love her now?

The pain only lasted a couple of days. After that, Brendy became more of a robot than human. She withdrew even further into her shell and wasn't sure how to find her way out. Caroline did as she promised and found Brendy a small apartment and helped her furnish it with nice things. It was easy to see Caroline wanted to keep her happy, but there was no happiness to be found, only hopelessness.

The more weeks and months that went by, the easier it became for Brendy to work for Caroline. It became routine each night for her to dress up and meet different men to entertain. It seemed she was one of Caroline's most requested girls and many men came back several times until she learned them by name. Brendy always wondered which ones had wives and possibly children. Which ones left their homes for a business trip and never told their wives everything they had done.

Brendy hated men. At least, she had hated them until now. Until Noah.

What made him so different from the rest? Maybe it was the fact that he looked at her like she was a person, and not just an object. She had never felt so respected and been treated so well by any man before.

Brendy had no idea what the future held, but she knew one thing for certain. For the next thirteen days, she didn't care.

Chapter 6

"It's a nice evening, isn't it?" Edith asked, sitting down beside Brendy on the front porch swing.

"It is, and you were right; this is a great spot." Brendy reached up and wiped the tears from her eyes, hoping Edith couldn't tell she'd been crying. If Edith knew, she never brought it up. Instead, she reached over and took Brendy's hand in hers.

"Do you realize how special you are to God?" Edith asked.

Brendy never said a word. Instead, they kept swinging back and forth slowly.

"I am no psychiatrist, and no mind reader, but from having four kids, I have learned to read them like a book. I'm pretty good at telling when something is bothering one of them."

"I'm okay, just thinking about a few things I wish I could forget."

"Must be awful to have things at your age you would like to forget."

Brendy smiled and squeezed her hand tighter. "Well, it is pretty awful and I have quite a few things, actually."

"Does Noah know about these things?"

"No one does." *What am I doing? Shut up, Brendy, just shut up.*

"I didn't think so, nor does it matter. Do you have someone to talk to?" Edith felt an overwhelming sense of love for Brendy that she couldn't explain. Ever since Brendy had walked into her front door the night before, God had been pushing her to speak to her. She prayed for God to guide her and give her the words that would fulfill His purpose.

"Never had anyone to talk to."

"Your parents?"

"No, haven't seen my mother in years and I never knew my dad."

"Grandparents?"

"They both died before I was seven."

"Poor child." Edith reached over and put her arm around her and pulled her close. Brendy felt warmth, not just from being held, but the warmth of a mother's love that she had never known before.

"It's okay; I got used to it. No use feeling sorry for me, I'm grown now and have learned what's important in life."

"And what is that to you, Brendy? What is important in life?" Edith asked.

"Surviving." What else was there, Brendy thought?

"Please, don't be angry with Noah. I guess because I am his mother, I am nosy, and because he doesn't lie he tells me the truth, but I know that you don't intend to go back to Pittsburgh when he returns."

"Oh, did he tell you that?" Brendy wondered just how much he told his mother.

"Frankly, I'm glad he did. Now I don't have to worry about you leaving and breaking my heart, you know? At least you can stay right here where I will grow to know you better and love you deeper."

"Here? You mean here in town?"

"No, right here at the ranch. This house is plenty big enough for you to live here with us, that is, if you want to," Edith chuckled. "If you want to feel more independent, you can stay in the small apartment over the garage. It's not very big, but it has its own kitchen and does have a nice bathroom."

"You are asking me to live here with you and your family?" Brendy sat up straighter and turned toward Edith, looking her in the eyes.

"That's right. Any friend of Noah's is a friend of ours."

"Edith, what all did Noah tell you?"

"That you were sick of the city, and he suggested you come here to visit to see how you liked Summersville, and that you weren't planning on returning with him."

"Is that all he told you?" Brendy knew she needed to tell this woman the truth about just having met Noah the day before. Now was not the time to make her think otherwise."

"Pretty much. What more is there?"

"Edith, I never laid eyes on your son until yesterday at the Pittsburgh Airport. He was so kind to give me a ride. I never intended for him to bring me here. He was only supposed to set me out somewhere in town."

"So you were coming to Summersville? Do you know someone that lives here?"

"No, ma'am. Before last night I'd never been in the state of West Virginia. I was leaving Pittsburgh; I really didn't care where I went."

"I see." Edith didn't say anything for the longest time, and Brendy was afraid that she would be asked to leave at any moment. She felt guilty for misleading this wonderful woman who had opened up her home to her and invited her to stay. Sure, she could have kept up the charade of being Noah's friend, but there were already too many things in her life she would have to lie about,and this was not going to be one of them.

"Do you like it here, Brendy?" Edith asked, moments later.

"Yes ma'am, Summersville is very beautiful."

"No, I mean here on the ranch?"

"Of course I do. Your home is beautiful and your family is like none I've ever encountered."

"Good, then I want you to stay. God sent you here, Brendy. I do believe that with all my heart. He's looking out for your best interest, even if you don't realize it. I have this feeling, if you allow yourself to truly open up to the world around you, that you will realize that there is so much more to life than just surviving."

*****

"So, how do you feel?" Noah looked up at Brendy who now sat on top of a gorgeous buckskin quarter horse.

"Do you want me to lie to you or tell you the truth?" She laughed.

"Beauty is gentle and she knows this trail by heart; you don't have to guide her and she will lead you around and come right back to this spot." Noah had already spent the past hour teaching Brendy all he knew about riding, yet it still didn't make sitting atop this massive horse any less scary.

"Okay, I think I have it. Now what?" Noah thought she was beautiful looking down at him, so afraid, yet trying her best to appear confident.

"Now, we go for a ride." Noah threw his leg over his horse as if he had done this a million times, and Brendy thought perhaps he had.

"Beauty will follow right behind Ginger; all you have to do is hang on to the reins, okay?"

"Okay, sounds good." Brendy gripped the reins tightly, praying she didn't make a fool of herself.

Brendy had never imagined riding could be so easy. She was sure there was much more involved than her one hour lesson, but for now she was enjoying the warm summer day following behind Noah. He'd promised to take her high in the mountains and show her a surprise. Edith had packed them another picnic lunch to enjoy when they were at the top.

Noah rode slower than he would have knowing Brendy was close behind, since it was the first time she'd ever ridden. He was glad for another day with her, and thankful that Connie had suggested it in front of the family. This way, it gave him an outing without their knowing it was what he wanted all along.

Noah planned to go to the top where the old hunting cabin still stood even after weathering years of wind and rain. He remembered helping his dad build the cabin as a young boy. His brothers and sister did what they could, being smaller, and he had felt proud of himself, as if it was a project that he and his dad accomplished alone. Year after year they would gather in the fall and hunt for deer to stock the freezer for winter. It wasn't that they *had* to hunt; it was being together that made it special. With his dad gone, he understood that more now than ever.

"God, I miss you, Dad," Noah said, talking to himself.

"What did you say?" Brendy asked.

"Talking to myself. We're about here. It's just around these bushes."

"Thank God, my butt has never been this sore in all my life."

Noah laughed. "You think it's sore now, just wait until tomorrow."

"Now you tell me," she giggled.

"We're here. So what do you think?" Noah asked, rounding the corner as the cabin came into view.

"Oh my god, it's beautiful! You didn't tell me there was a cabin here. Who lives here?"

"No one, it's an old hunting cabin we built when I was a small boy. We used to come up here all the time with my dad. I'm amazed it's still in the condition it's in. Want to go exploring?"

"Sure, anything to get me off this horse."

Noah dismounted and tied his horse to a post in front of the cabin and helped Brendy down from Beauty. She stretched and rubbed at the small of her back where she felt the most pain. Noah laughed again, realizing how out of shape she was for such a tiny person.

"Do you have a key?" Brendy asked, going up the steps to the small covered porch.

"You bet." Noah lifted a huge rock and retrieved a key. "My dad didn't seem to think anyone would think of looking here. We own this side of the mountain, so no one but family ever comes here anyway."

"Do Rene's trail rides come this way?"

"No, too high up and takes too long. She leads them around the base of the mountain and up through the pasture, but that is still an hour's ride."

"I envy you, Noah."

"Oh, why is that?"

"Just look at this place. It's so beautiful, every last acre of it. I've never seen anything like it, and your family is just amazing, every one of them have treated me with such kindness and made me feel welcome."

"I guess I am lucky to have been born a Garrett. Can't complain any there." Noah unlocked the cabin door and pushed it open. "It's been closed up for sometime; let me open the shutters." Noah went through the one-room cabin and opened the inside shutters to let the light in.

"It's so pretty," Brendy carried on.

Noah chuckled. "I don't think pretty was the look that Dad tried to achieve here."

"Well, you know what I mean. It's lovely."

"Thank you. Still looks like it did the day we finished. My dad never had it wired for power. He said when we came to the cabin it would be like we were going back in time to the good old days. We always used that fireplace over there to warm us in the winter and we used black iron pots to cook soup and beans in. Mom has oil lamps sitting everywhere, and if you look in the old closet there, you will find all sorts of old games we used to play as kids."

Brendy saw two bunk beds that sat along the wall and a double bed on the other side. A couch sat in the middle of the room and faced the fireplace and an old wooden table sat off to the side. Brendy could see that in its time there must have been so much life there, when the kids were little and Noah's father still alive.

"Does it bother you?" Brendy knew it was risky asking personal questions, for that meant having to answer a few herself.

"You mean coming here?"

"Yeah."

"It brings back many wonderful memories, but I wouldn't say it bothered me. I do miss my dad, though. I know I am a grown man, but still miss my dad something fierce sometimes."

"You have a wonderful mom, too."

"That I do; she's great. I know she talked to you last night. Are you mad at me, for telling her you weren't going back to Pittsburgh?"

"No, I guess she had to find out sooner or later, seeing as your leaving is just around the corner."

"I didn't tell her anything else, though."

"But I did." Brendy sat down on the sofa in front of the fireplace and Noah sat down beside her.

"You did? You mean you told her we just met?" Noah chuckled.

"That's right, Noah, my gosh, she was asking me to stay here after you left. I had to tell her the truth; I mean, what if she found out later on?"

"Brendy, she wouldn't have found out, unless one of us told her. I told you I wasn't going to do that."

"She's just too kind, Noah, wanting me to stay and all. I just had to tell her the truth."

"And did that change her mind?" Noah knew the answer even before he asked it.

"Not at all. She got quiet; I thought she was thinking what a fool she had been or something. I thought she might throw me out. Here I am, a stranger, living in her house, you know?"

Noah laughed. "Then you obviously don't know Mom. I have learned when my mom is quiet she is usually praying, asking God for guidance. So she still wanted you to stay, anyway?"

"Yeah, strangely enough she did, isn't that something?"

"Not really, Mom is a good judge of people. She believes, like I do, that people are put together for a reason to fulfill God's purpose."

"Do you *really* believe that?"

"Of course I do, don't you?"

Brendy laughed. "Noah, I'm not sure I believe in God. There's been too many times in my life I really could have used Him, and He was never there for me."

Noah reached over and took her hand in his. It reminded her so much of Doris Brubaker on the plane, and the same thing Edith did last night. It was as if God had all these soldiers here on earth working for Him. Did they really believe He existed?

"It's hard for me to comprehend it," he shook his head. "I mean how a person can not believe in God."

"I've never seen Him, have you?"

"I have, many times," he smiled.

"When? 'Cause I sure haven't."

"Sure you have; you were just too busy thinking about whatever it is that haunts your past that you couldn't see what's in front of you."

"I'm not following here." She tried not to sound rude. The last thing she wanted to do was upset Noah, but it was clear that he'd been brainwashed like so many other so-called Christians.

"Look around, Brendy. All my life I have seen Him. He is the sunrise in the morning when the sky leaves streaks of orange and white that take your breath away. He's in the waterfall that leaves us standing in awe of its beauty. He's in the full moon and the stars that light up the Heavens. He's that tiny baby that is born to this world all covered in the very stuff that kept him alive for the nine months he lay growing in his mother's womb. He's that first cry that same baby takes as he takes his very first breath. He's in the tides being pulled in to the shore from the enormous ocean that is home to so much living and growing beneath its surface. He's inside of me, Brendy, and He will come inside of you, too, if you just invite Him in."

Brendy could feel tears about to pool over from the corners of her eyes and knew if they ever started, they may never stop. "I just don't know, Noah. I mean it all sounds so good, you know. So believable, and yet when I think back throughout my life all I see is darkness and doom."

"Do you blame God for whatever went on between you and your mother?"

"Maybe. That is, if He is real. Because if He is *really* real, then why didn't He stop it, Noah? Why didn't He stop the abuse? I was just a child, for god's sake. I used to beg Him to, you know? I lay in my bed knowing she was coming back for me to hit me some more. I asked Him to please make her stop, yet He never did." Brendy couldn't hold back the tears any longer. They fell freely down the cheeks of her face.

Noah slid closer and reached for her. Pulling her close to him, he let her cry for the longest on his shoulder.

"I'm sorry, Brendy. I'm so sorry, Baby." Noah rocked her slowly back and forth.

"It was so awful, Noah, so awful," she sobbed. Noah finally understood what it was that tormented her and why she had not seen her mother in years, and yet it was as if she was still running, never finding peace within herself.

"Brendy, there is no use in me trying to convince you that God exists." He still held her close as she cried. "All that matters is that He still believes in you. I have never understood why so many terrible things happen to innocent people, especially children. It's something I can't answer. All I know is that when bad things happen to us, it either causes us to flee from God, or run toward Him. I'm sorry that you endured that, Brendy; no one should have to go through that."

Brendy rubbed at her eyes and sat for the longest leaning against Noah's shoulder. As much as she wanted to believe in his God there was just too much of life that told her He wasn't real at all, just some fictional character that man made up to bring them peace,when peace was something she never experienced.

Chapter 7

"Mommy, can I stay up later tonight?" Beth asked, not wanting to go home after dinner that evening.

"No, I'm afraid you can't. You know, every pretty girl has to get at least eight hours of sleep, or she will turn into an ugly old hag," Rene teased.

"Oh, Mommy, you are so funny. You know that's not true," Beth laughed.

"But, of course it is, just look at me. It's from all those late nights and early mornings, and not getting enough sleep."

Greg laughed, "Then we know it's not true because you are the most beautiful woman in Summersville."

"Hey, what about me? You seem to forget I exist, big brother," Connie said playfully.

"Well, there can only be one true beauty in Summersville, and as cute as you might be, dear sweet sister, I will have to say that title belongs to this lady here." Greg pulled Rene close as he sat beside her on the couch and kissed her on the lips in front of everyone.

"Ewww, Daddy, that is disgusting," Beth made a face and everyone laughed.

Brendy loved the way Noah's family seemed so close, every one of them had a love for the other, and she knew that when push came to shove, they would each take up for the other, no matter what.

"But your Mom is right, baby girl," Greg said, getting up from the couch and lifting his daughter in his arms. "You need to get to bed because we all get up with the sun, remember?"

"That's cause we live on a ranch, right Daddy?"

"That's right, sweetheart. Goodnight, everybody," Greg called out and pulled Rene up with his remaining hand. Within minutes, they were out the door, leaving the rest of the family still sitting in the den.

"What's wrong, pretty lady? I noticed you walking a little slow," Brad asked Brendy, smiling at her.

"I'm just a tad bit sore," Brendy answered, knowing that come morning she would be lucky to be able to get out of bed.

"Sore?" Brad laughed. "Guess you're not cut out for riding, huh?"

"Sure I am. Just give me a little time to get used to it. I did enjoy it. And the cabin is so lovely up there, all by itself."

"So, you did go to the cabin?" Edith asked.

"Yeah, I hadn't been up there in so long. I was amazed the shape it's still in."

"Your brothers have done a little work on it when it needs it, they just can't bear for it to fall apart, I guess." Edith looked over at Brad, waiting for him to respond.

"Is that so, little brother?" Noah looked Brad's way.

"Greg and I have gone up several times and replaced this and that. Just can't stand to let something you and Dad built go to waste."

"You helped, too. We all did." Noah could remember Brad handing his dad nails when he asked for them.

"Yeah, right," Brad laughed. "If you say so."

"Well, thanks for keeping it up. I guess if I'd looked around a little better, I would have noticed the changes. I know it would make Dad proud that it's still there and still enjoyable, if we want to use it."

Brendy was glad that by the time she and Noah rode back into the yard her eyes had dried and there was no trace she'd ever cried at all. Brendy hoped Noah didn't tell Edith what transpired up on that mountain. She'd never intended to break down in front of Noah, and the way he reacted to her made her realize that maybe falling in love was possible, after all.

But no matter what her heart felt, she would never be able to let it be known.

*****

Brendy awoke to the pouring rain. She had no idea what Noah had planned for the day or if he'd planned anything, for that matter. She threw on a pair of khaki shorts and a yellow tank top that showed off the tan she was getting from being on the lake one day and going horseback riding the next. Noah had been right about the sunscreen; she'd accomplished not getting burnt, but instead was turning a nice golden color.

Before she could get her hair brushed or her makeup on, she heard a knock on the other side of her door.

"Come in," she called out.

Connie stuck her head in. "Are you decent?"

"I am enough for you, come on in. What's up?"

"I know you probably want to hang out with Noah today, but I was going into town for groceries. Mom gave me this huge list, and I wondered if you wanted to tag along. You know, like have some sister time," she grinned.

"Sure, that sounds good; give me just a sec to finish my face."

Connie laughed, "Your face is pretty enough! You don't have to cover it up and you still look good. I'm afraid some of us aren't that lucky."

"You have never seen me without my makeup; you might change your mind on that thought," Brendy giggled. "Trust me; I look a lot better with it on than with it off. I'll be right there."

*****

"You headed out?" Noah asked, reading the newspaper.

"Yes, I'm stealing her for a bit." Connie stuck out her tongue at her brother and smiled, remembering how she used to tease him as a child.

"Not until she eats first," Edith called out from the kitchen. "I have hot buttermilk pancakes waiting for you. Come on and eat."

Brendy laughed to herself. This was better than any vacation she could have ever dreamed of taking, with the best food imaginable. How could she possibly complain?

*****

"So, what goes on at the ranch on rainy days?" Brendy asked Connie, who was pushing the buggy and putting in several loaves of bread.

"There are no riding lessons or trail rides. They prefer to be in the barn, so Greg and Brad will spend most of the day brushing and checking their shoes to see if they need reshoeing."

"Horses wear shoes?" Brendy looked at Connie with an odd expression that made Connie laugh.

"Don't tell me you never saw a horseshoe? You know, the funny-shaped thing that looks like this." Connie made the shape in the air.

"Nope,I haven't. Guess I'm more of a city girl than you thought, huh?" Brendy shrugged her shoulders, still looking lost.

"I know because I was raised with horses, all my life. I suppose I thought everyone was born with horse knowledge, but that just isn't true, is it?"

Brendy shook her head. "No, it isn't true at all. For some of us, we have no horse sense at all." Connie couldn't help but laugh at Brendy. She was funny, even when she didn't try to be.

"So, what do you think about my brother?" Connie leaned down and picked up two bags of self-rising flour, not looking directly at Brendy as she asked the question.

"You mean Noah?"

"Of course I mean Noah. Who did you think I meant, Brad?"

Brendy giggled. "I wasn't sure. I think he's sweet, why?"

"Sweet?" Connie stuck her finger in her mouth as if she was gagging and laughed. "Come on, you can do better than that. Do you think he's hot, sexy, attractive? Come on, it's fess up time here."

"Fess up time? Is that why you brought me grocery shopping?"

"That's part of the reason, but not the whole reason. So are you going to answer me or not?"

"Yes, he is all of the above."

Connie screamed out. "I knew it. I just knew it!"

"You knew what?" Brendy was great at acting clueless.

"That you and Noah were attracted to one another. It's clear to see he is attracted to you, but you are a hard one to read."

"It doesn't really matter what I think. I am not going back to Pittsburgh. I'm staying here in Summersville."

"What? What on earth for?"

"I hate Pittsburgh. When I left there, I never intended to go back."

"But what about Noah? He lives in Pittsburgh."

"Noah and I are just friends, Connie, nothing more."

"Well, you are both attracted to one another and I want to know just how you intend for it to be anything more, if you are here and he is there?"

"I don't intend for it to be anything more." Brendy knew there was no hope for it to be anything more. That was something she could never allow.

Connie stood and stared at her for a moment, then pursed her lips. "I don't think I will ever figure you two out. My brother is like the best catch ever. He is young enough, he is very attractive, he is a doctor who lives in a nice townhome, drives a killer car and has money to boot, yet he seems to care less if he has a girlfriend or not. And then there's you, very young, very attractive, and you obviously have this thing for my brother and I can see he has this amazing attraction for you, yet you are just going to let him get away from you and he is just going to go, and not try to take you back with him. Did I get that right? You are both just giving up?"

"How can we give up something that never started?" Brendy asked.

"Well, it would start if you would allow it to."

Brendy put some peanut butter into the shopping cart and sighed. "It's complicated; trust me when I tell you it's better to keep things the way they are."

*****

"What can I help you with?" Brendy asked Edith that evening, finding her in the kitchen cooking.

"I usually don't allow any help only because I enjoy doing it, but if you would grab the potato peeler in the top drawer over there, you can peel this bag of potatoes while we talk."

"Sure thing," Brendy was glad to have been given something to do. Up until now she had felt more in the way than anything.

Brendy got out the peeler, took a seat on the barstool, and started peeling as she watched Edith making a peach cobbler.

"So, did you and Connie have fun in town this morning?"

"Yes, she is fun to be around."

"I can imagine she must have played twenty questions with you," Edith laughed.

"Twenty? Good grief, I am sure it was much more than that."

"Yep, that's Connie for you. But, you know what? I think she took that after me." Edith smiled and placed the top on the cobbler and then topped it with sugar before placing it into the oven.

"So, how do you like Summersville? Not so bad, huh?"

"No, it's actually very nice and seems quiet enough. I like that."

"Did you know that in the winter of 1864 and 1865 both Union and Confederate armies encamped here and all the buildings were burned to the ground?"

"Is that so? There is just so much to learn about this town."

"There is. We Summersville citizens are quite proud to call it home. So, have you given it anymore thought to where you want to stay after Noah leaves? You are more than welcome to stay here in the house with us; there is plenty of room. Or would you prefer to be more private and stay in the apartment over the garage?"

Brendy shook her head and smiled. "You are serious, aren't you? You really do want me to stay."

"Of course I do. I would never ask something like that if I didn't want you to stay."

"You are very generous, but you live five miles from town and that is quite a walk to work without a car. I was hoping to get a waitress job. It might be better for me to look for an apartment in town."

"That's something else I want to talk to you about. I need a housekeeper. This big old house is all I can do to keep up with, and I am afraid at my age it isn't easy. Would you consider taking the job? If you do, you won't have to leave the ranch; you can work right here. As far as going into town, one of us takes a trip or two there daily so it wouldn't be a problem for you to get a ride."

Brendy couldn't believe what she was hearing; this was all so surreal. She kept thinking back to the prayer Doris had prayed about her being led to the right people, and sure enough, she could not have asked for a better place to be.

"How much were you going to rent the apartment for?"

Edith smiled, "I wasn't going to rent it. I am going to let you stay there at no charge, and I will pay you to keep the house clean."

"Sounds like the deal of a lifetime. How could I refuse that?"

"So that means you're staying, and I no longer have to slave in this house?"

"I guess so. Gosh, thank you so much, I am very excited about this. I thought it might take me a while to get a job, and I've been here three days and already have an apartment *and* a job."

"The good Lord does look out for us." Edith patted Brendy's hand and started making the tea. "I know you were sent here for a reason, and I know that God has His hands upon you. But don't think of starting the job until Noah leaves; until then, you are on vacation."

Brendy wasn't so sure God ever had His hand anywhere near her, but she knew for certain it was a strange coincidence that the exact thing that Doris had prayed for was happening right before her eyes.

*****

"Want some company, or had you rather look alone?" Noah came around the side of the garage after dinner and found Brendy unlocking the door to the apartment above. Edith had given her the key earlier.

"Sure, come on up with me. I wanted to take a look at it." Brendy unlocked the door and found a set of stairs that led the way to the top.

"I haven't been up there in years," Noah said, following behind her up the stairs.

"Why did they put an apartment here in the first place?"

"There was room, and my dad never left anything unfinished; that was just unheard of. No one has actually ever lived up here. Mom has only used it as a guest room for company from time to time. I know Mom was thrilled you wanted to stay here. Finally, someone is going to get some use out of it."

Brendy opened the door at the top of the stairs to a cute kitchen decorated in apple paraphernalia. The curtains were pulled back, and the evening sunlight still shone through. Everything smelled fresh and clean, and it was hard for Brendy to believe no one had ever lived here.

"It's so gorgeous! I love it, and it's furnished,too. Wow."

Noah laughed. "I want to let you in on a secret. Mom was up late last night going over everything up here. She wanted to rid it of dust and make it presentable."

"Are you serious? How did she know I would want to stay here?"

"She figured you would want your privacy. I'm glad you decided to stay, Brendy. My family really likes you, and they will take care of you. You will be very safe here."

Brendy leaned against the bar that divided the kitchen and the living room and stared at Noah for a moment. "Do you know, I've never felt safe a day in my life?"

"That's what I thought," he shook his head and smiled at her. "Those days are over, Brendy. I knew the day I saw you in that airport God wanted me to give you a ride, and I also knew God wanted you here. Even though you do not believe in Him, as I have said He still believes in you, and He cares about you, and my prayer is that one day you will understand that."

Brendy nodded her head. There was no use telling Noah why God was fiction to her; she somehow felt he understood. It was clear that no matter what she believed or how she felt, Noah did believe in a higher power. Maybe that's what it was that made him different from all the other men she encountered in her life. Not only did he call himself a Christian, he actually lived it everyday of his life.

Chapter 8

Usually after working double shifts at the hospital, by the time Noah was able to lie down and get still, it never took more than five minutes before sleep overcame him, but not tonight. Even though he had spent the day with Greg and Brad, helping them against their wishes, he was still wide-awake.

Brendy spent the morning and afternoon with Connie and helped Edith cook dinner, so Noah occupied his time elsewhere.

He could visualize her lying one floor beneath him, and wondered if she was finding it hard to sleep as well. With so many things of her past tormenting her mind, he guessed she was wide-awake as well.

He always enjoyed coming home to Summersville and visiting his family, but this time would be different. This time, Noah knew that when his two weeks had passed, he would find it more difficult to leave. He could picture himself driving back to Pittsburgh alone, sitting beside the empty seat that was once occupied by the woman he knew for certain would take months, if not years, to erase from his mind. If he closed his eyes and thought about it, he could see every feature her face held. Her emerald green eyes absorbed him every time he caught himself looking into them.

Even though Noah had dated his share of women, only one woman before now had ever captured his heart. He met Jessie Goldman in college. She too, was studying to be an obstetrician. He had been captured by her beauty, and it was as if she'd placed a spell upon him that kept him coming back for more.

When Noah thought back to those early years in college, he was not proud of the man he was then. He accepted Christ at an early age, but even after knowing right from wrong, when it came to Jessie it didn't seem to matter. She captivated him with her long red hair and slim physique. She seemed flawless, like an addiction that left him hungry, and never quite satisfied until the next fix.

After dating Jessie a year, Noah knew for certain there would never be another woman for him but her. After taking her out to dinner and to a movie one evening, he proposed to her and gave her a beautiful diamond engagement ring. Jessie cried as he placed the ring on her finger and told him yes. She wanted more than anything to become his wife and have a family with him. Noah had never been happier.

For six months they planned a big wedding that was to be on the ranch surrounded by family and friends. They talked about opening a practice together someday, treating women and delivering babies.

Noah's best man, Jasper, was the same friend he grew up with, went to school with and was also going to medical school with. He had become friends with Jessie as well, and the three of them often hung out together when they found off times.

Jasper was the same man Noah found in bed with Jessie two weeks before the day of the wedding. Noah wasn't sure if he was more hurt with Jessie who had stolen his heart, or Jasper who had been his friend for as long as he could remember.

It was on that day that Noah decided he would never love again. Not only did he lose the love of his life but also his best friend. Since that time, he had not allowed himself to get close to anyone. Sure, he forgave them because that was what God required, but he wiped his feet of them that day and never looked back.

Edith tried to console him, to listen to him and be there for him to cry on, but Noah found that nothing helped. He felt lost and betrayed. Most would have turned against God after that, but Noah chose to run toward Him, embracing Him and allowing God to comfort him like never before.

That season in his life was the lowest he'd ever felt, even more so than when his father died. At least when his dad died they were expecting it. The cancer had eaten away at his body till there was nothing left of him. In fact it had given Noah peace knowing in his heart that his dad no longer suffered, and he was with Jesus. But this.....this was unexpected, a slap in the face, and something that had taken him by such surprise that he had thoughts he never wanted to have again, as long as he lived.

Two days after Noah found Jessie and Jasper in bed together, he loaded up some gear and rode to the top of the mountain, and closed himself in the old hunting cabin to be left alone. Edith and Connie had taken care of cancelling the plans that were made and calling off the wedding.

His family left him alone, as he requested, for three days. Even though he knew God before that time, on that mountain was when he actually found God and formed the relationship he still had today. He fell to his knees and begged God to forgive him for the sins he and Jessie had committed even though they weren't married, and he promised to be a different man.

Five years had passed since that time, and Noah had lived up to his promise. He had stayed true to God and been faithful. Now, when Noah looked back to the darkest time in his life, he also saw it as the brightest, for that was when God met him there, just like Moses and the burning bush. Now, as he lay awake in the dark of the night thinking back to that time and realizing what God had done for him, he also thought of Brendy and what she must be going through, so tormented with her past and the things her own mother had done to her.

He prayed God would find a way to show her that He was real and help her to see what Noah already knew, that only through God could anyone ever truly be happy.

*****

Brendy heard footsteps above her and knew that Noah must still be awake. What was causing him to not sleep? There were hundreds of reasons she could think of that would keep her awake, but Noah? Noah's life was perfect and always had been. Born to two wonderful parents, with a family that adored him and was proud of him.

She, on the other hand, was a mess. Born to an alcoholic mother who never looked at her as a daughter, but as a punching bag; just someone to take life's anger out on. Never had Brendy heard her mother tell her she loved her or felt the embrace of a hug.

Night after night, for years, all Brendy knew was fear. For as long as she lived, she would never forget the one spot under her bed that she would hide. On nights when her mother was drinking, if she came into Brendy's room and she was under the bed, her mother wouldn't bother to look for her, and on those nights she was left alone. For that reason, Brendy slept on a cold linoleum floor, crying and praying that her mother would go to sleep and leave her alone.

Now that she thought back to it, she had spent many nights praying, but to whom? God was supposed to love you and make things right for you. He was supposed to protect you from evil and keep you safe, but Brendy was never safe. Day after day, she endured her mother's wrath and sometimes wondered why her mother decided to have her at all. Why had she not had an abortion, if she hated her so much? That way she could have just died and not had to be born. But then that would have defeated her mother's purpose in having her. Surely she had her to punch around; if not for her, who would her mother have taken her anger out on?

After she got the courage to run away at sixteen, life on the streets was worse than anyone could have imagined. Hiding out under bridges and in alleyways, eating out of dumpsters behind Frank's Coffee Shop the food people wasted. Never had she dreamed she would have stooped so low as to eat other people's trash, but never had she thought she would grow so hungry there would be no other choice.

When Frank finally caught her, one day, going through his trash, he asked her to come inside and eat a real meal. She was embarrassed at first, after having been caught, but having a real meal sounded so great she jumped at the chance. Of course, he let her eat in the back room away from everyone in the diner; she hadn't been able to take a bath in weeks and even smelled bad to herself.

Frank Greene had taken a chance on her, given her soap and shampoo to use, and even bought her a few outfits to wear. She owed a lot to Frank, and sometimes wondered if he ever thought about her and what had happened to her. She never went back after she left that night to go in search of Caroline; she was too ashamed.

Now, as Brendy lay in the dark of the night, she couldn't help but think of Noah. How good it felt to cry on his shoulder as he held her. The smell of a man who actually acted as though he genuinely cared about her for something other than sex. The feeling was something she had never experienced or expected.

And here this man so strongly believed in a God that did not exist. A God that a whole book was written about, said to be the best selling book ever, and for that reason alone people believed, because they wanted to. They needed to know that there was something there they could count on and have faith in, but Brendy knew it was all just a myth and she hoped someday Noah realized what she already knew, that God was just a made-up fairy tale in a book that was as fiction as most books are.

*****

Greg rolled over and put his arm around Rene and pulled her close. She moaned sleepily and turned to face him. "Can't you sleep?"

"Not really. I was thinking about something Noah said today."

"Oh, what's that?" Rene loved to cuddle with her husband after midnight. It seemed it was the only time they were ever able to find alone, since they stayed so busy during the daylight hours.

"Nothing really that was significant. He just made a statement that he really hated going back to Pittsburgh this time, right after he told us that Brendy was staying in Summersville and wouldn't be going back with him."

"Brendy's staying here? I wonder why?"

"It appears that she was leaving Pittsburgh to escape the city life, and Noah wanted to show her where he grew up."

"How long has Noah known her?" Rene asked.

"I don't know, I didn't ask, but I do know one thing. Noah has it bad for her."

"You mean he is in love with her?"

"Yeah, I think he is, and I honestly never thought he would allow his heart to feel that again after Jessie."

"Well, that's a good thing, don't you think? Jessie was years ago, it's about time he got over that and moved on with his life."

"I agree, but then why is Brendy staying here?" Greg got out of bed and headed to the bathroom.

"Maybe Noah has never told Brendy how he feels, or maybe Noah hasn't even admitted it to himself yet," she yelled out.

Moments later Greg crawled back into bed and pulled her close again. "There is more to the story than anyone knows. I have this feeling that Noah and Brendy haven't known each other that long, and Noah is just now realizing he can feel things for someone other than Jessie."

"Maybe I should do a little snooping, huh?" Rene giggled.

"Do you think Brendy will talk to you?"

"It's worth a shot. At least I will find out when they met and if she has any feelings for him."

"Do you think she will tell you that?"

"She might, couldn't hurt to try. In the meantime, it wouldn't hurt for you to do a little snooping with your brother."

"What are we going to do if we both find out that each one of them has feelings for the other? What then?"

"Well, my wonderful husband, we will try to play a little match-making. It never hurts to have a little help; look at what Noah did for us."

Greg laughed, remembering. "He just realized we were more than just friends and came right out and told us we were blind if we didn't see it, too. I remember."

"I did like you," she laughed. "Your mom let me work that whole summer just to be close to you. But I thought you weren't paying me any attention."

"Oh, I noticed all right, just didn't want to be too obvious."

"Obvious? Good gosh, Greg, you never acted like I existed."

"I most certainly did. We had been friends forever."

"True, but that's just it. You acted like my friend, but you didn't seem interested in being my boyfriend."

Greg kissed her passionately on the lips, and nuzzled his face in her long black hair. "But just look at us now."

Rene chuckled, "Yeah, just look at us. I think Brendy and Noah might need a little pushing. Give me a day or so to perform a little magic, and you try to do the same on the other end."

"Maybe I'm not as magical as you are."

"I have a feeling that with Noah you won't have to perform too much magic. It has been way too long since he allowed himself to love. I think if he thought Brendy was interested, it wouldn't take much magic at all."

*****

"Hey there, big brother, where's your little lady at this morning?" Greg asked Noah, coming into the barn to find him picking a stall. "And what on earth are you doing? This is supposed to be your vacation, remember?"

"I do remember, but I will go nuts just sitting around the house. I have to do something, and it looked like this needed to be done. For your information, if you are referring to Brendy, she is not my little lady, and your wife took her into town to buy Beth a new Barbie since I forgot to get one three days ago, like I promised. I'm paying for it, of course, and Brendy is picking it out."

Greg laughed. "Beth never forgets anything, does she?"

"You aren't kidding. I hate myself for forgetting. My forgetfulness cost me time away from Brendy again this morning. Connie had to have her turn yesterday."

Greg watched as Noah threw the old shavings into a wheelbarrow, and wiped the sweat off his face with his forearm. It was easy to see his big brother was very much missing his little lady, and Greg knew for certain that Noah wished she were, even if he cared not to admit it.

"So, I guess this morning Rene gets a turn, huh?" Greg smiled.

"Yeah, it appears that way. I guess Brad will want to be next?"

"Next what?" Brad asked, coming into the barn.

"The next one to have a turn with Brendy," Greg laughed.

"Oh, are we getting turns? Oh boy," Brad winked at Greg behind Noah's back. Noah turned around quickly and gave Brad the evil eye, causing Brad to chuckle.

"Look here, little brother, you may be handsome and all, but I want to ask that you leave Brendy alone, is that okay?"

"Well, well, I do detect that you would like it if you two were more than just friends, am I right?" Brad loved to tease Noah.

Noah leaned the pitchfork against the side of the stall and rested up against it, as well. "She's a little young for me, don't you think?" This was something that Noah had been wondering himself and now was his opportunity to get his brothers' opinion.

"Just how old is she?" Greg asked.

"Twenty-two."

Brad whistled. "Man, I thought she was at least twenty-eight."

"Are you serious? She doesn't look any twenty-eight, and you know it!" Noah commented.

"So, that's just ten years. There are many great marriages that have a ten-year age difference, look at the Smiths on the next farm. They have been together forever." Greg wasn't positive if there actually was a ten-year age difference there, but he felt certain Noah would never know, since he'd never actually met the Smiths.

"Come on guys, Brendy is beautiful. I think she is a little above my league."

Now Brad laughed hard. "Man, oh man, you *really* do have it bad, don't you, big brother?"

Noah chuckled and shook his head. "It shows, huh?"

Greg put his arm around Noah's neck. "It sure does, so what are you going to do about it?"

"Nothing." Noah shrugged his shoulders and felt like an elementary school kid again.

"Nothing?" Brad shook his head at Greg and rolled his eyes. "Do Greg and I need to give you some pointers on how to hook a woman and reel her in?"

"Oh yeah? What makes you the expert?" Noah looked at Brad and smiled. "I mean, I don't see too many women lined up around here waiting on you. I haven't even seen one in the past four days."

"That's just because it isn't the weekend yet. Don't think I will be dateless. As a matter of fact, I dated Linda last Friday and Barbara on Saturday."

Noah looked in Greg's direction and Greg shook his head and laughed to confirm that what Brad said was true. "Yep, big brother, it seems that Brad doesn't have a problem at all. So, when is the last date you actually had?"

"Come on, when do you think I have time to date? The hospital doesn't give me anytime at all. And that is the reason I'm not going to pursue Brendy. I am going back in a little over a week and she is staying here; there is no use wasting either of our time."

"Do you really believe that?" Greg asked. "You are the one that is most like Dad, and Dad never gave up on anything. I know you believe in divine destiny. Don't you think

God has someone for you? He wouldn't just leave you alone for the rest of your life."

"I used to believe that, remember? Now, I am not so sure anymore." Noah picked up the pitchfork and started to grab more shavings, when Brad took it out of his hands.

"You mean Jessie? You are going to throw away your chance of happiness and leave her and never know what could have been, because of Jessie?"

"Don't you think if Brendy and I were meant to be anymore than friends we would have been by now?" Noah knew that neither of his brothers knew they had just recently met.

"Not if you never tried. Dang it, Noah," Greg said. "Don't let that woman you were in love with so long ago ruin your chance for happiness. I see you look at Brendy, and I see her look at you. So what if there's a few years between you, who cares? I don't care, do you?"

"No, but she might. Besides, she hates the city. And why would she waste her time on someone who can't give her anytime?"

"Do you think Rene and I have a lot of time together?" Greg asked. "This ranch keeps us both so busy the only time we get alone is just a few hours at night, but that's all we need. We love each other and we make time. We adjust and you will, too."

"Greg's right," Brad agreed. "I think you're afraid of rejection. You are afraid you are going to get hurt again, so you are afraid to love again."

Noah didn't say anything for a moment, and then he looked at Brad. "Perhaps you're right. I honestly don't think I could stand losing her if I allowed myself to love her."

"Big brother, it was you that told me to recognize what I wanted for my life. You were the very one that made me realize Rene had my heart all those years. I was too stubborn and prideful to realize it. You told me never to be afraid to love because, without love, what else was there? Sometimes, we have to take risks, and even if we get hurt, at least we tried. How else will we ever know?"

"Look, I have a meeting with the vet in a few, so I have to leave you two alone," Brad added, "but listen to him, Noah, what he says is true." Brad gave Noah a brotherly hug and left the barn, leaving Noah and Greg alone.

"Well?" Greg was still waiting on Noah to comment.

"I know you're right. And even though Brendy and I are friends, I really don't know that much about her yet. I'm only here ten more days, which isn't enough time to pursue her at all."

"Good grief, so you have ten days. Much can happen in ten days. Besides, you both have a phone, right? This isn't the Stone Age. There is a thing called the Internet. You two can talk daily no matter where you are, and who says she wouldn't like the city if she was with you? Have you ever thought of that? Besides you are *only* three-and-a-half hours away."

"I just don't know," Noah shook his head.

"All I am saying is, if you leave here in ten days and Brendy Blake doesn't know you care about her, then it's your own fault if some other country boy takes her away. I mean, after all, she will be fair game to anyone, even Brad. And maybe, since she doesn't think you give a hoot about her anyway, she just might look in his direction." Greg knew what to say to push Noah's buttons. He knew the last thing Noah wanted was for Brendy to be attracted to his handsome brother.

"Okay, you win. I will try to move a little bit closer. I do feel that God pushed us together as friends; I'm just not sure if He wanted it to be anything more than that."

"You're a Christian man, Noah, pray about this and ask God for guidance. I feel that you and Brendy belong together, but it isn't up to me. I have always thought that God helps those that help themselves. Who's to say God didn't place her right under your nose for the very purpose of you two being together? Follow your heart, big brother, just follow your heart."

Chapter 9

"That's a nice one," Brendy said, picking up the Wedding Barbie. "Do you think she will like this one?"

Rene took the Barbie in her hand and looked it over. It was wearing a long white wedding dress. "She should; every little girl likes to pretend they are getting married. I know I sure did when I was small, how about you?"

"I never thought that much about it."

"Really? Maybe I was just strange, then," Rene laughed. "Come on, this one should do."

Brendy followed Rene to the checkout at Wal-Mart and headed for the car. She was glad Rene hadn't kept on at her about Noah the way Connie had the day before. In fact, Rene had not mentioned Noah's name all morning.

"So, would you mind to stop at Family Dollar with me? I need to pick up some new sheets and the ones at Wal-Mart are a little pricey."

"Sure, that sounds good. I would like to look around myself, actually. I'm very excited about moving into the garage apartment and I wanted to look for a few knickknacks."

"Knickknacks are all you will need unless you need personal stuff," Rene laughed. "Edith has that place furnished with dishes, pots and pans, and everything."

"Really? I never thought to look in the cabinets."

"So, where were you living before Summersville? Did you leave all your stuff behind?" Rene was trying to be careful how she approached Brendy. She hoped her plan worked.

"I did. I donated my things to Good Will. I decided to start over."

"Amazing, I have heard of people doing that but never knew anyone to actually do it."

"Well, now you know someone," Brendy smiled. "I didn't have anything sentimental, so it was no big deal. I brought what clothes I liked and the rest I got rid of."

"So, I have been dying to ask you a question. Dying of curiosity, to be exact." Rene parked the car in front of the Family Dollar and turned toward Brendy.

Brendy had known this was coming; she'd expected as much. It seemed everyone wondered about her and Noah.

"So, tell me what you think about Brad," Rene grinned. Brendy's mouth dropped open for a moment, and she didn't quite know what to say. That wasn't at all what she thought Rene was going to ask her.

"Brad?"

"Yeah, Brad. I mean that *is* why Noah brought you to Summersville, right? It was Noah that put me and Greg together, and if I know Noah he is trying to do the same for Brad."

Brendy sat speechless for a moment. "Do you really think that is what he is doing?" Maybe Rene was right. Maybe Noah wasn't interested in her at all.

"I am almost certain of it. So, what do you think? He's handsome, isn't he?" Rene was enjoying seeing Brendy squirm, and she thought that perhaps her plan would work, after all.

"Sure, but I'm really not interested in Brad."

"Well, of course not yet, but soon. I mean, after all, you are going to be living right here in Summersville, sharing the same acreage as him, and he isn't taken yet, you know?"

"That may be true, but I'm really not interested. I don't mean to sound rude or anything."

Rene laughed. "Just wait until Brad puts the moves on you; you won't be able to resist. I mean, you are fair game, right? You and Noah are just friends?"

"That's right, but still…."

"But still, what? I bet you in six months time, you will be smitten with him."

"So, you really think Noah is in on this, getting me set up with his brother?" Maybe Rene was right; they were closer in age than she and Noah. Perhaps Noah thought ten years was too much. But what did it matter, and why did she care?

"That's what Greg and I think."

"Greg thinks that, too?" Brendy wasn't sure she liked this. She had to admit that Brad was handsome but it wasn't him she was interested in. It was Noah that kept her mesmerized and left her breathless.

"I know that Brad has left you alone because Noah is here, but just wait until he leaves; he will be on you like white on rice."

"Noah hasn't come on to me at all; why should Brad?"

"Noah is saving you for Brad. He wants Brad to think you two are only friends. Why else would he not like you for himself? I mean, you are very attractive and he is very single."

"Maybe I am just not Noah's type." Brendy didn't like being put off on Brad, and she hoped Rene was wrong.

"Doesn't really matter, Noah will be gone in a few days," Rene shrugged her shoulders. She loved this. It was easy to tell Brendy was attracted to Noah.

"How long has it been since Noah had a girlfriend?"

"Noah? Five years, I think. I mean, that is, since he had anyone serious."

"Five years? Why? He is gorgeous."

"Because the only woman he really loved so far didn't love him."

"Oh, what happened?" Brendy wasn't interested in hearing about Brad. She wanted to talk about Noah.

"That's probably not for me to tell. Why don't you ask Noah to tell you about her? I mean, you two are friends and all, so I am sure he won't mind." Rene had wanted to talk about Noah all along and Brendy had taken the bait...hook, line, and sinker.

"What did this woman look like?"

"Jessie? She was pretty. She went to college with Noah; they were the same age."

"Oh. I see." Brendy knew her age would be a factor for him.

"So anyway," Rene smiled, still turned sideways in the seat outside the Family Dollar parking lot. "We got off the subject.

Don't you think if you gave Brad half a chance he could be a real catch? I would love having you for a sister-in-law."

"Rene, I'm really not interested in Brad, but I don't want to hurt his feelings. You don't think he's interested in me, do you?"

"It appears that he is. I was just sure you were staying because you found him attractive."

Brendy's eyes grew wide. "Oh my, you don't think he thinks that, do you?"

"He might." Rene put her hand to her face as if she was thinking something over. "Unless, of course, he thinks you are interested in Noah. Yes, that's it. If he thought you were interested in Noah, then he would lay off. He would never mess with you if he thought Noah had a chance."

"But Noah is not interested in me."

"Yes, I see what you mean. Let me think a second." Rene was having fun playing match- maker and Brendy was falling for all of it. It was too easy.

"Maybe if you made Noah think you were interested in him he might see you differently, you know? That might be the only chance you have."

"I have no idea how to do that."

"Maybe you could flirt with him. I don't know; I haven't been available for quite some time now, so I am not used to this."

"But what if Noah bought it and actually liked me back, then what?" Brendy was not sure if she was ready for this. After all, she knew she could never be anymore than friends with Noah, but she sure didn't want Brad coming on to her.

"Would it matter? He is leaving for Pittsburgh soon, and you won't have to worry with him anymore, and Brad will leave you alone. That way you will have them both off your back. I know you aren't interested in Noah, but you can make him think you are."

"Isn't that mean?" Brendy wasn't sure this was going to work, but she was sure she didn't want to be fixed up with Brad and pretty certain Rene was right. Noah had this planned all along to set his brother up with her. Why else would he want to bring her to his home?

"Mean? No meaner than him trying to set you up."

"That's true." Brendy thought a moment. "I will try my best to make him think I am interested, but I'm not sure he will buy it."

Rene reached over and took Brendy's hand and squeezed it. "Oh, I think he will buy it." Rene knew for certain if Noah thought she was interested, then maybe he would let her know of his feelings, too. It was clear they both needed a tiny little push in the right direction.

*****

The rain let up by three in the afternoon and Brendy was busy decorating her new apartment with the things she'd bought at the Family Dollar. Excitement filled her as she looked at the small quarters she would call her home. It was a great feeling to feel safe. To feel that her mother and Caroline were behind her, and for the first time in her life, she was headed in the right direction.

Brendy laughed to herself as she hung the Serenity Prayer in her small hallway. Even though God was a myth, she always looked at the prayer and memorized it because it was something that was true in her life. A prayer she could read and ask herself if the situation she was in was something she could change or something she had to learn to live with.

Lord, grant me the serenity to accept the things I can not change, the courage to change the things I can, and the wisdom to know the difference.

She read the prayer out loud and straightened it on the wall. Leaving her mother at sixteen and Caroline Reese were both things Brendy could change, and she changed them by moving and starting over. Her past and the things she had done were things she knew she would never be able to change. No matter how many years came and went, her past would follow her everywhere.

Her past would keep her from being able to fall in love with a man like Noah, a man who put God above everything. A man who believed in praying for guidance and hoped, one day, to find the love of his life who believed in the same God as he. Brendy knew in her heart that woman was not her. As much as she wanted a fairy tale kind of love, she knew it wasn't in the cards for her.

Brendy moved to the bathroom to put out the new soap dish and bath mats she had bought.

Edith had the apartment clean and smelling fresh. Curtains hung from the windows and everything was dust free, but Brendy wanted to add her special touch and give it that homey look that made a place her own.

She decided to go ahead and move into the apartment to give Noah time alone with his family. She'd felt like she was intruding ever since she'd been there. Now all she needed to do was make Noah think she was interested in him, so he would stop trying to set her up with Brad. It just didn't make any sense that he wanted to take her on a boat ride and horseback riding in the mountains if he wanted to fix her up with his brother. Maybe that was only to see what sort of person she was first. After all, he wouldn't want just anyone with his brother.

Brendy hoped Rene's plan worked; this was not something she wanted to backfire on her. The last thing she wanted to do was hurt Noah or lead him on, but she felt certain she was not someone he would be interested in to begin with, and because of that he would go back to Pittsburgh and forget all about the young girl he felt had a crush on him. He would laugh it off and realize she wasn't right for Brad, either. Or, at least, that was what she hoped.

"So how's it coming in here?" Noah asked, coming in the door. "I would have knocked, but the door was open."

"Oh, that's okay," she smiled. "Come on in. It's coming quite nicely. Doesn't everything look great?"

"It sure does, smells great, too. You baking apple pies in here?" he sniffed.

"Unfortunately no, that's the new Apple Cinnamon candle I have lit on the table."

"Well, it smells great, good enough to eat."

"I'm sorry to say I am not the best cook in the world. In fact, I don't even come close."

"I thought you worked as a waitress."

"I did. Waitresses don't cook, Noah, they serve." Brendy laughed.

"Oh, I guess you're right. Well, if you want to learn, hang around with Mom when she is cooking; she would love to teach you everything she knows."

"Sounds like a plan. I would like to learn to cook, even if it's just for me."

"Why do you say that? You are only twenty-two years old. One day you'll get married and have a house full of children. Then you will have a gang to cook for."

Brendy looked at Noah and smiled. "I don't see that in my future."

"What, a husband or a house full of children?"

"Both. I don't think I'm cut out for that, too much baggage."

Noah laughed. "Come on, Brendy, too much baggage? I know you were abused as a child, but that doesn't mean you won't still make a great wife and mother some day. Give it some time. I can see you need time to heal, but you will, eventually. You know what they say; time heals all wounds."

"It's not just that, Noah," Brendy shook her head and pulled out a barstool to sit down. "Some people aren't cut out to have a family life; I always knew I was one of those people. You, on the other hand, are. You were raised with a great family and you are family oriented. I am not; I was born to be a loner."

Noah pulled out the other stool and sat down beside her. She was so beautiful sitting beside him, even with her hair pulled pack in a ponytail and wearing shorts and a tee shirt. Why had God placed this woman in his path? Did He actually have a plan, or was this temptation from the devil? Brendy didn't believe in God, and yet he still felt her goodness. It was easy to visualize her getting up in the mornings, wearing her pajamas, with no make up and her hair in a mess, going to the kitchen to make pancakes for her family before she got the kids up for school. Why was God allowing him to see these visions in his head? Why would God want him with a woman who clearly did not want a family?

Noah reached over and placed a strand of loose hair behind Brendy's ear and smiled. "That's not what I see." He wanted to pull her close and kiss her lips, but only four days had passed since they'd first met. What kind of Christian would he be if he took advantage of the situation?

"And what do you see?" Chills went up Brendy's arms just from his touch. The brush of his hand against her face, the look in his eyes, told her he was the one who was interested in her. Maybe Rene was wrong after all.

Noah shook his head from side to side and grinned. "I see much more than you do, apparently." Noah knew he had to change the subject before it got too deep. As much as he wanted Brendy to know he was interested in her, now did not seem the time.

"Well, I am glad someone does," she returned the smile. "So what's for dinner? It smelled wonderful when I was in the house getting my clothes a while ago. Your mother insists that I keep eating with her until you go back to Pittsburgh. I hope you don't mind."

"It's fried chicken and mashed potatoes, and why would I mind? I'm the one that brought you here, remember?"

"Yes, and I still wonder why you did that."

"Because God spoke to me and told me to, if you want to know the truth."

"God speaks to you personally?"

"He does. But I guess you don't believe that, either."

"Not really. If you want to believe that, that's great; we all need to believe in something."

"And just what is it that you believe in?" Noah asked.

"I believe you are a very good man that believes you talk to God and He talks to you. I believe I have never met anyone

quite like you in all my life, and I am amazed at your goodness and the way you treat people."

"Thank you, but that is not exactly what I meant."

"I know what you meant. You wanted to know if I believe
in a higher power, and the answer is no. I hope you don't hold
that against me."

"Not at all. I understand why you believe that way. And I
hope you won't hold it against me if I continue to pray for
you daily."

Brendy smiled. "I guess I can't stop you for that. I don't
see what it would hurt."

Edith caught them both by surprise when she stuck her
head inside the door. "Hey you two, mind if I come in?"

"Not at all," Brendy got off the stool and slid it under the
bar. "Come on in."

"Man, oh man, you have this looking like a home. I love
the décor, good job. Rene told me you done a little shopping
today."

"I did. Now all that's left to buy is groceries."

"Not until Noah leaves, okay? Then you can cook here all
you want, but remember you don't have to; I cook enough
each night for an army."

"Yes, I see that. And thanks again for letting me move up
here. It's beautiful."

"You know you could have stayed in the house, though,"
Noah said.

"I know, but this is so cute, don't you think? I just love it."
Brendy looked around the room as she spoke. Edith came to
her and wrapped her arms around her, squeezing her tightly.

"I'm so glad you are happy. Just wanted to come take a
look for myself. It does my heart good to know someone
is getting use of this place. Anyway, I need to go check my
cake; it's probably done by now." Edith turned to leave, then
stopped at the door and looked back.

"By the way, we attend New Life Assembly on Sundays. I
can't wait to introduce you to our pastor."

"Your pastor?" Brendy looked confused, and Noah smiled.

"Yes, our pastor. I just know you will love him."

"Ah, I don't have a dress to wear." Brendy knew she must find some way to get out of going to church. She had never stepped foot in a church a day in her life.

"Well, that's perfectly okay; you are welcome to wear your pants. God doesn't look on the outside. He only sees our hearts. Anyway, we'll eat at seven, so I'll see you two then." Edith left just as quickly as she came, leaving Brendy standing with her mouth agape.

Noah chuckled and shook his head. "So, why didn't you tell her you didn't believe in God?"

"Are you serious? She would hate me if she knew."

"My mother doesn't know the meaning of the word hate. I guess that means you will be going to church with us on Sunday."

Brendy sighed. "I guess so. Just what is it one does in church?"

Noah looked amazed. "Are you telling me you have never been in church before?"

"That's right."

"Well, dear lady, I guess you will find out on Sunday."

"Do you think your pastor will be able to tell?"

"Tell what?"

"That I don't believe in God." Brendy was starting to feel nervous already.

"I have a feeling that when he is done with you, you will at least question the possibility."

"You think so?"

"No, I don't think so. I know so." Noah smiled and knew God's plan had already started to work; it was just a matter of time now before He found His lost sheep.

Chapter 10

Connie convinced Edith to lie down after dinner; she told the family she had a headache and was not acting like herself. It wasn't in Edith's nature to lie down before dark, but she did as she was told and left Brendy and Connie in the kitchen, doing dishes.

"I'm sorry. I've been so busy I've completely ignored you," Connie said, handing a plate to Brendy to dry.

"You haven't ignored me. Besides, I've been busy with the apartment. I can't tell you how excited I am about this move."

"We are all excited, especially Brad," Connie smiled. Rene had told her of the conversation that morning, and now Connie was eager to play along.

"Oh no, not you, too?" Brendy sighed.

"I want to apologize for yesterday; I shouldn't have gone on about Noah, and it was foolish of me. I mean, now that I have had time to think, I realize that you and Noah together would never work anyway."

"Why is that?"

"Because he is older and set in his ways, and because I have seen the way Brad has been looking at you. I guess I just put you and Noah together because you are friends. So anyway, please forgive me."

"Connie, I am not interested in Brad. I already told this to Rene. I hope Brad doesn't think that I am. Rene seems to think Noah brought me here just for Brad and says I should make Noah think I'm interested in him so he won't pursue this craziness."

"That's a good idea, but how do you intend to do that?"

"Beats me. I'm no good at this sort of thing, and it really makes me sick to my stomach to think about."

Connie laughed. "Well, I am sure you will figure it out, and if worst comes to worst, Brad is really good looking, don't you think? I don't care which one you like as long as I snag you for a sister-in-law."

"Good grief," Brendy giggled. "You and Rene are terrible."

*****

It felt strange sleeping in her new apartment. So much had happened in just four days. Brendy knew that when the sun rose, Friday would be upon them, the end of the week,with the weekend and one more week left. So much had happened already, yet so much more could happen depending on how she played the next few days.

Was it right to make Noah think she was interested in him? Brendy knew that wouldn't be too hard, considering she was. Maybe Rene was right, though; what could it hurt? He would go back to Pittsburgh for another year and Brad would leave her alone because he would think she was interested in his older brother.

Brendy sighed and rolled over. It was all so complicated. And yet Brendy knew if her past wasn't her past, she would have no problem grabbing on to this man and never letting him go.

*****

Noah was going insane wondering what he should do. Here he was, a grown man who had a high education, graduated at the top of his class, and yet when it came to love he was clueless, especially with a woman of Brendy's caliber. She was young, yet she was classy and appeared to have a good head on her shoulders. It was easy to see that she had grown up fast and knew how to take responsibility for herself.

Dear Father, this time around I will need all the help I can get. I want to do things Your way. I feel in my heart it was You that put us together, so it will have to be You that guides me to do and say the right things.

Dear Father, please help her to understand who You are and that You love her. Help her to feel Your Holy presence so there won't be any doubts. Help to erase the painful memories of her past and cover them with nothing but love and forgiveness.

You are everything to me, Father, and I know her entire life would change if she could actually see that You are everything to her also. In Jesus' name I pray, Amen.

*****

Brendy smiled when she sat up in bed to the sunlight shining in her apartment window. It was such an incredible feeling to know that Caroline no longer had control over her life. No longer did she have to walk on pins and needles, and wonder about the night ahead. Never had she felt so free and so alive, yet still there was something that weighed on her. Pressed on her like a heavy weight. Brendy knew it was her past, the past of a thousand pounds or more.

Edith made it clear that she was to eat breakfast with them until Noah had gone back to Pittsburgh, so she dressed in black capris and a pink short sleeve top. Instead of pulling back her blonde hair, she left it down.

Looking into the mirror, she saw something she had not seen five days prior—the face of a woman who was slowly starting to be happy with life. Excitement filled her each morning, not knowing what the day would bring with Noah's family. Everyday on the ranch brought new adventures and laughter. And even though she did not believe in God, she knew how strange the coincidence was that she had been led to just the right people who actually cared about her. The very prayer that Doris Brubaker prayed for her on the plane, which had to be proof there was no God. Because if God were real, she would be the last person He would be blessing.

*****

Brendy found a letter on the table telling her breakfast was in the microwave. The rest of the family had already eaten, and Edith had cleaned up. If there was one thing she knew she would never get used to, it was rising with the sun. It was only nine a.m. yet everyone had been up for several hours by now and was busy outdoors.

Brendy ate her waffles and drank a cup of coffee. The house seemed quiet, and she wondered where Edith and Beth had gone. She guessed they had gone into town shopping, since it was Friday. Perhaps Noah had gone with them. She longed for more time with Noah, but it seemed that since the first two days after they arrived, he'd stayed busy doing other things. Maybe he found her unattractive or much too young. He was probably looking for a more educated woman like Jessie. No wonder he'd been in love with her.

Brendy headed out back towards the stables in hopes of finding Noah somewhere close around. He told her he had been helping Brad and Greg, even though they refused his help. It seemed Noah wasn't good at resting, but then, he came by it honestly.

"Hello, beautiful lady, what brings you out here?" Brad asked, as Brendy entered the barn.

"Just wandering around. I thought I might find Noah out here." Now was as good a time as any to make Brad think she was interested in his brother for more than just friendship.

"Is that right?" Brad laughed. "He was here earlier. Was he not in the house?"

"Nope, I just came from there."

"Then, I don't know. Give him a call on his cell." Brad was busy brushing a beautiful black mare. He was handsome, Brendy thought, more rugged and cowboyish, with a smile that would make any woman turn her head. And, although she could tell he was attracted to her, it was not Brad who had stolen her heart in five days. Noah was the first man in Brendy's life she would consider falling in love with. It was too bad she had to keep her guard up and have in-depth conversations with her heart.

"That's okay; I don't want to bother him. I'll take a walk around the ranch. I wanted to get a better look anyway." Brendy didn't want to tell Brad she didn't have a clue what Noah's number was. After all, they were supposed to be old friends, and because of the fact that she didn't have a cell phone of her own.

"Would you like me to go with you?"

"Oh no, you go ahead and work. I'm going to walk down the path toward the creek, if anyone should wonder where I am. I'll be back shortly. Just want to enjoy this beautiful summer day."

"Well, be careful and keep a look out for copperheads; they are pretty bad in the summer."

"Copperheads?" Brendy sounded confused.

Brad laughed. "Snakes, keep a look out for snakes."

"Oh, okay," Brendy giggled. "Guess there's a lot I need to learn, huh?"

"You will in time." Brad nodded and tapped his cowboy hat and winked as she started out the door. "You be careful, now."

*****

Brendy would love to have ridden a horse down to the creek, but knew that would have taken Brad's help and she didn't dare ask. Maybe after living on the ranch for a while, she would be able to learn more and be a little more independent when it came to horses. She so longed to ride back up the mountain, and back to the cabin that Noah had shown her. She knew for certain she could spend countless hours at that cabin, and be lost to everything else going on in the world. The quietness was priceless.

The Garrett Ranch was beautiful with its green meadows and mountain ranges. The back view of the house and barns from far away was stunning, as if she were observing a view from a movie, and not something that actually existed, a place that people actually lived.

After the view of the house was gone, Brendy made sure she followed the trail and kept her eyes open for snakes as Brad suggested. She'd never seen a snake in New York and had no idea how she would react if she walked up on one.

Not much farther down the path, the creek came into view. The entire area was so peaceful, just as Noah told her it would be. The sound of the water cascading over the rocks and the birds above gave Brendy the sense that everything was right in the world. It was hard to go back in her mind to the noise of Spanish Harlem, the gunshots and the screams that were forever being heard, the kind that left chills going up your arms and made you glad it wasn't you. Being in a place where you could trust no one and knew that no one trusted you, either.

Brendy smiled at the footbridge someone had built across the creek, and the hammock that hung beside the creek bank. It was easy to see this must be the place chosen to relieve stress, or to come so one could kick back and relax after a hard day. Someone took care of this place, making sure all the weeds were kept away. Flowers and ferns grew along the creek bed, and Brendy could tell they had not grown there wild, but had been placed there by someone who loved gardening. Brendy placed her bet on Edith. She could picture the fifty-something-year-old woman down on her knees, wearing her sunbonnet and loving every minute of making the home where she raised her children beautiful. The same home where she'd loved and lost the love of her life. If Noah's dad was anything like Noah, Brendy imagined it must be hard living without him.

Brendy lifted her body into the blue hammock that moved slightly in the July breeze. How comfy it felt to lie back and stare up at the cloudless sky, and feel the warmth of the sun on your face. All her life of struggles and problems had led her to this moment. The only thing now that clouded her future was knowing she would always be alone. Sure, she would have the friendship of the Garretts, but would never truly know the kind of love that Edith had shared with her husband. The same love that was easy to see that Greg and Rene shared.

Brendy sighed and closed her eyes. The breeze felt wonderful, with the large oaks up above that gave her just the right shade from the sun. Maybe next time, she thought, she would bring a good book and enjoy the afternoon reading.

*****

"I should have some sort of say in who you set me up with!" Brendy was upset at Caroline for not telling her she would have to be with more than one man the first night.

"I had no idea that was going to go down, Sasha, and you will learn not to raise your voice at me! I am the boss here, do you understand me, little girl? You will go and do as I tell you and not complain, ever!"

Brendy trembled as Caroline yelled at her. How could she have gotten herself into this mess? This was not what she wanted, and yet Caroline made it clear that there was no way out.

"I don't know why you look at me like that." Caroline's voice softened. "I am really not a bad person to work for. Just look at all I have already given you: a home, nice things, and gorgeous clothes. Look at all the people out there that don't have half the things you do. I will talk to Mr. Carter, and you better believe he will get a piece of my mind for what he did to you. He knew you were a virgin; he had no right to allow his chauffeur to have his way, too. I am truly sorry about that, Sasha. That will never happen again."

Brendy hung her head in shame. Caroline spoke the truth, for Brendy knew she would never be a virgin again. They had taken from her what was not theirs to take, yet she had given it freely, all for the price of money.

"Can I have a night off, please?" Brendy asked the second night. "I am still sore from last night."

"Sorry, Sasha, I already have you booked. Besides, it will never get better until you get used to it. How do you think that soreness goes away, huh?" she laughed a wicked laugh.

Brendy could feel tears in her eyes. "I don't want to do this anymore."

"Heavens, girl, you can't stop now; you have just started. Just wait and see, in no time at all, you won't think anything of it. Tonight you will be seeing a very handsome gentleman, probably not but about ten years older than you. All the girls love their turn with him, and I made sure you were his for tonight." Caroline smiled as if she were doing Brendy a great favor. "Yes, I do believe when Mr. Logan gets a look at you, it will be you he requests each month when he is in town. All the other girls will just hate you." Caroline laughed again and sent chills down Brendy's spine.

Brendy had already been sick to her stomach, and lost her lunch twice before the car arrived. Caroline helped her get ready, in a short black dress that left nothing to the imagination.

She was driven to the docks and told to enter a very nice yacht that was docked there. All Caroline told her about Mr. Logan was that he was very wealthy. Once a month, he would splurge and hire a date for the night. Caroline was flattered that he chose her escort service, and tried to keep him happy.

"Well, look what the dog's drug in," a very handsome man said, smiling at her as she entered the door of the yacht. "You're every bit as young as Caroline said, aren't you?"

"I'll soon be seventeen." Brendy's voice trembled when she spoke.

Mr. Logan chuckled. "Seventeen? What is a beautiful girl like you doing working for Caroline Reese? It must be my lucky night." He walked over to Brendy and pulled her close to him. His lips pressed into hers and she felt his tongue slip inside her mouth. He was not forceful, as the men the night before, and the smell of him was intoxicatingly pleasant. It was true he was handsome, and Brendy closed her eyes as he unzipped her black dress and let it fall to the floor.

*****

"I wondered where you had gotten to." Noah's voice jolted Brendy awake. She had fallen asleep on the hammock and was dreaming about her past. She reached up and wiped the tears from her face, realizing she must have been crying as well.

"I'm sorry. I must have fallen asleep." Brendy sat up and swung her legs out of the hammock.

"Well, this is certainly a nice place to take a nap. I see you found my mother's secret garden."

"It's beautiful. I've never saw anything like it. It's almost like a fairy tale."

"It is. I used to play here as a boy. It was always one of my favorite spots, this and the cabin, that is." Noah took a seat beside the hammock on a cement bench.

"I can see why it would be. I'm sorry I just wandered off. I didn't know where everyone had gone and I wanted to take a look around. I hope that is okay."

Noah laughed, "Of course it's okay. This is your home now; you *should* take a look around."

Brendy shook her head. "It just seems so surreal, that this is my home. It still amazes me. I don't think it has actually sunk in yet, you know?"

"I hate the fact that I will be leaving to go back to Pittsburgh in nine days."

"Why is that? You hate the city, too?"

"I do, but that's not why. I will be leaving and never really have the chance to find out who you are." Noah looked into Brendy's eyes and hoped she could see everything that he didn't know how to say.

"There really isn't much to know. I've never been much of anyone special."

"I have a feeling you are much more special than you give yourself credit for."

"Trust me, Noah, I am not that special." Brendy knew she would love to tell Noah the truth, but fear of him asking her to leave kept her from it. Surely it wouldn't hurt keeping her past hidden for her happiness; after all, she wasn't working for Caroline any longer.

"So, what do you think of Brad?" Noah asked.

Brendy stared at him for a moment, realizing what Rene said was true. He had been trying to set them up all along. "He is nice, favors you, why?"

"I think he might think you are attractive. If I know my brother, after I am gone he will make his move. I guess I just wanted to warn you." The last thing Noah wanted was for Brad to go after Brendy, but he knew there would be no way to stop the inevitable. She was young and attractive, and Brad was much closer to her age. Perhaps that was what God wanted.

"I'm not interested in Brad. I hope you know that." Brendy could feel her heart pounding in her chest.

"Can I ask you why?"

"I'm not looking for a relationship at this point in my life. If I was looking for a relationship, it wouldn't be Brad I would be interested in."

"Oh?" Noah looked at her in wonder. "Why is that?"

"Because it would be you I'd be interested in." There, Brendy had said it. She hoped Rene was happy.

A smile slowly came over Noah's face as he cocked his head to the side. "Me? You would be interested in me?"

"Sure, why not?"

"Because?" Noah needed to hear more, longed to hear more.

"Because you are the kindest man I've ever met."

"Brad is kind." *What am I doing?*

"Brad was not the man that was kind to me; you were."

"I guess it's too bad I will be leaving in nine days, isn't it?"

"Yeah, it's too bad." Even though Brendy wanted Noah to think she was interested in him, he had no idea how much truth was in the words she spoke.

"You are a very beautiful woman, Brendy, but not just that. You are also beautiful inside, where it counts the most."

Brendy looked at him with a crooked smile. "That's because you chose to see me as a good person. You have no idea the person I really am. Besides, I have confessed to you that I don't even believe in your God, so how can you think me to be a good person?"

"Because I see you as God does."

"And how does your God see me?"

"He is everyone's God, Brendy. He sent his Son to die for us, so that if we only just believe we will have everlasting life. He sees you as he has since the beginning of time, a time when you still believed in Him. A time way back before you suffered from your mother's abuse. He sees you as the wonderful, caring woman He designed you to be."

Brendy held back the tears that she felt would surely come if she allowed them. "And you see me as wonderful and caring?"

"Yes. The only problem you have is that you don't see that yourself. I honestly don't think you like yourself at all. It's a shame you allowed your mother to ruin you for life. To cause you to value yourself less than you are."

"Noah, what if I told you it isn't just my mother's abuse that made me this way?"

"Then I would say its more baggage you need to release and give to God."

"Give to a God I don't believe in?"

Noah smiled at her sweetly and reached over and took her hand and squeezed it. "I think you do believe. I think you are angry and bitter at God, but you believe."

"Maybe you're right." Brendy shrugged her shoulders.

"So, now that we got that out of the way, let me say that just like God, I don't care what your baggage is. And I feel that if you didn't dwell on it so much, and worry about what everyone else thinks, you would be able to find peace within yourself. Of course, true peace comes from knowing God and Him knowing you."

"That may never be possible."

"He won't give up on you any more than I intend to." Noah still held tightly to Brendy's hand. She had never been touched by a man such as Noah, a man who had no ill intentions at all. A man like none other that she had ever met. A man with such integrity and honor that it almost made her want to fall into his arms and believe every single word he told her.

Chapter 11

Brendy enjoyed spending the afternoon with Noah, walking around the ranch and talking about his family and the way he grew up. Noah never made it clear to her that he was interested. He only said he didn't intend to give up. Brendy wasn't sure if he meant give up on their relationship, or give up trying to convince her there was a God, or both.

Noah took her to Bob Evans Restaurant to have lunch and to The Kirkwood Winery for a tour. It felt good to be able to go on a real date with someone who wanted nothing in return but friendship.

By the time they entered the house, everyone had already eaten dinner. Edith called them to the kitchen to get their plates she'd been keeping warm.

"Sorry we're late, Mom," Noah apologized.

"Goodness son, don't apologize for that. Just tell me you had a great day."

"Oh, we did," Brendy answered. "One of the best days I've had in my life. Almost felt like a real date." She laughed and winked at Noah.

"Oh, so what would a real date feel like?" he teased.

Edith smiled at them from a distance and realized they had no idea she was even in the room; their eyes were only for each other. It did her heart good to see Noah caring about someone again.

"Well, a real date would be more than just a friend. But hey, you did a very good job, I might say."

"If you think today was good, just wait until tomorrow."

"Tomorrow? What's tomorrow?"

"Tomorrow is the Nicholas County Fair. It's held each year at the Nicholas County Veterans Memorial Park. If you like to eat, ride rides, hear music, and look at crafts, you are going to have a ball."

"I've never been to a fair before, but I always wanted to."

"Goodness, child, you never been to a fair?" Edith was amazed.

"No, there is a lot I'd never done until I came here."

"I don't think we have ever missed The Nicholas County Fair, have we, Noah?"

"Nope, I don't think so. I can't wait to take you. Make sure you wear plenty of sunscreen; it's going to be a long hot day."

*****

Saturday morning was bright and sunny, the perfect day for The Nicholas County Fair.

Noah loved seeing the fair through Brendy's eyes. It was almost as if he were seeing it for the first time himself.

Brendy was amazed with all the country crafts and even bought a plaque with her name printed on it that read Brendy's Apartment…Come in and take a load off.

Brendy's eyes lit up like a child's on Christmas morning when they rode the double Ferris wheel. Noah realized that because of her past with her mother she'd never had the opportunity to be a child, and she loved every minute of this.

"Look Noah, I can see everything from way up here!" she exclaimed.

"I love your excitement," he smiled.

"Sorry, this is the first ride I ever rode, you must think I'm crazy the way I carry on," she laughed.

"Just the opposite, I think it's great that you carry on. I knew you would have fun today."

"I've had a great time, thanks for bringing me. I really do hate to see you leave." Brendy knew the Ferris wheel may not be the appropriate time to talk about Noah leaving, but at least this way she didn't have to get so serious.

"Do you? Not as bad as I hate to leave. Only eight more days, and there is still so much to see. How do you like Summersville?"

"It's amazing, really. The people are so nice, too. After living in the city for so long it's hard to imagine places like this exist in America."

"There are plenty of places like Summersville. You've just got to know where to look."

The Ferris wheel stopped at ground level, and a scruffy looking man with his hair in a ponytail helped them off. Noah had been to the fair each year throughout his life, but he knew this had to be the best time yet.

"Well, if it isn't Noah Garrett," a beautiful red haired lady said in a sultry voice, coming up beside them.

Brendy knew immediately it was Jessie, and she could see by Noah's reaction that he was caught off-guard. He reached down and took her hand in his, pulling her closer to his side.

"Hello, Jessie, how've you been doing?" Noah tried to sound as polite as possible, but it was easy to hear his discomfort in his tone.

"Just fine. I have no complaints, if that's what you mean." As Jessie spoke, she gave Brendy the once-over.

"Well, that's something then, isn't it? This is Brendy Blake. Brendy, this is Jessie, an old college friend."

Jessie laughed. "Noah, we were a little more than college friends, but I'm sure you know that, right dear?"

"That's right," Brendy answered.

"So, how is Jasper these days?" Noah was growing angrier by the moment. Leave it to Jessie to ruin a perfectly good day.

"He's good, stays busy with the hospital, and with the nurses, if you know what I mean," she laughed, as if she could care less that he might be running around on her.

"Well, you know what they say; a leopard doesn't change his spots." Noah turned to walk away, still holding onto Brendy's hand. "Take care of yourself, glad to see you are doing so well." And just like that, they walked away and left Jessie standing there watching them leave.

Noah didn't say anything for awhile. He kept walking, holding on to Brendy's hand. Brendy could tell he was set on a destination by the way he led her through the crowd. She wasn't sure what had just transpired between Jessie and Noah, but it was easy to see it made him uncomfortable and had changed his mood.

Noah led her to a picnic table surrounded by beautiful flowers. "I hope this spot is okay for lunch," he asked." Are Caesar salads okay?"

"It's perfect."

"Okay, I'll be right back." Noah took off into the crowd and left Brendy sitting alone. It looked as though Noah had a past as well, just not nearly as bad as hers.

Within ten minutes he was back with two ice waters and two salads. People walked all around them enjoying the festival, yet Brendy felt alone with Noah sitting in front of her sipping his water and looking out at the crowd as if Jessie may come back at any moment. He was shaken, and Brendy felt terrible for him.

"We can go home after lunch, if you like," she tried to sound polite.

"No, we haven't finished. Besides, I want you to see the parade." Noah grew quiet again thinking about the past.

"Noah, what happened back there?"

Noah took a deep breath and let it out slowly. "I guess I have a few things I'm not very proud of either. Jessie is one of them."

"Was she your girlfriend?" Brendy thought it best she didn't tell Noah she already knew a little about Jessie. She wanted to hear the story straight from him, if he wanted to share it with her.

"She was, back years ago. We were engaged to be married." Noah took another sip of water.

"So that's why she said you were a little more than friends. I get it now."

"I'm really sorry about that."

"Nothing to be sorry about. Why didn't you two get married?"

"Because she chose my friend Jasper right before the wedding. The three of us were going to medical school together. We were all close; I had no idea how close the two of them really were until days before we were to get married."

"Did she come to you and break it off, tell you the truth?"

"I wish. I honestly don't think she would have told me, who knows? I found them together in bed. Talk about a shock." He half laughed, as if remembering now he found it humorous.

"Oh Noah, I am so sorry. That must have been so hard for you. What did you do?"

"What could I do? I felt hurt and betrayed. I turned and walked out. I drove home in shock and walked in to find Mom and Connie working on some final plans for the wedding and told them the wedding was off. I think they could see by the look on my face that something terrible had happened, yet they never asked. Not then, anyway."

"Is that why you chose to move away, because she still lives in town?"

"No, I really did leave because of the opportunity in Pittsburgh. Jessie moved away, too. Last I heard they live somewhere in New York. They are both doctors there." Noah shook his head. "I guess she came back to visit family the way I did. That's probably what brought her here today."

"So, she married your friend?"

"Yes, she did. Six months after we broke it off, they got married. I guess I not only lost her that day, but him as well."

"So, you never talk to either one anymore?"

"I talk to Jasper from time to time. We grew up together. Even though he is a couple of years older than me, we were very close. He came to me afterwards and apologized. As a Christian I forgave him, but I could never get back that trust. After that, we went our separate ways."

"I can tell it still bothers you deeply." Brendy reached across the table and laid her hand on top of Noah's.

He smiled at her. "It does. So I will be the first to admit that when something traumatic happens in your life, it's not easy to push aside and forget. I don't dwell on it any longer, but if I run into one of them it brings it all back to reality."

"Nothing that happened was your fault, Noah."

"Yes, it was. I went against God from the very beginning with my relationship with Jessie. We were having premarital

sex, and even though that was not the way I was raised, it
didn't seem to matter then."

Brendy swallowed, realizing how Noah felt about sex before marriage. What in the world would he say if he knew
she'd had sex with hundreds of men? She became light-
headed and she braced herself by grabbing the sides of the
table.

"Are you okay? You look a little pale," he commented.

"Yes, just got a bit dizzy. It must be the sun and the lack
of food."

"Then eat," he pointed at her salad. "And if that isn't
enough, I'll go get you something else." Brendy started eating slowly, still not feeling much better.

"Are you sure you're okay?"

"Yes, I will be fine." Brendy chewed her food and looked
at him again. "So you think because you had premarital sex
that it was your fault?"

"When I chose to sin, knowing better, I went against God's
will for my life. God no longer blessed my relationship with
Jessie. So yes, I feel that if I had stayed true to God it might
not have happened."

Brendy shook her head. "I don't believe that."

"You don't?"

"Absolutely not. You are a good man, Noah. I know your
Bible may say that you should not have sex before marriage,
but I don't think you are the one that caused your two friends
to do what they did. I believe that even if you and Jessie
had never been together, that still would have happened. You
can't create their destiny, only your own."

Noah smiled. "Thank you. I still feel bad for going against
God. I know God forgave me; that part was easy. It was forgiving myself that was hard."

"Is that why you don't have a girlfriend now? Is it trust issues?" Brendy knew she was getting personal, but it pained
her to see the hurt in his eyes.

"I'm too busy with my career to devote time to women.
And yes, I do have trust issues, but God is helping me deal

with that. I am learning more everyday to lean on Him and let Him guide me."

"So how did you handle it all? I mean, right when it all went down?"

"Mom and Connie cancelled the wedding. It must have taken them days to call everyone and tell them we decided now was not the best time for us without giving too much detail. What they did for me was something money can't buy."

"I guess what I am asking is, how did you handle the rejection? How did you handle it emotionally?"

"I threw some clothes in a backpack, and headed up the mountain to the cabin. I closed myself in for three days. When I rode back down that mountain, I had been reborn. I still hurt. It was still hard, but I made my peace with God and was ready for whatever He wanted of me for the rest of my life."

"Three days did all that?"

"There is no way to explain to you the peace you will find when you truly let go and let God own you. When you tell Him that you are a sinner, and you cannot do this alone. When you finally are able to forgive all the people that hurt you and also give them to God, then, and only then, do you find peace within yourself."

"But Jessie still gets to you; that's easy to see."

"She does. But it's not because I am not over her or I didn't forgive her. I am human, and I still get uncomfortable when I run head-on into my past. Besides, I know she and Jasper are not living for God, and I still pray for them daily."

"You pray for them?" Brendy seemed amazed.

"Of course I do."

"Aren't they your enemies?"

"In Luke 6:27–28, it reads….*Love your enemies. Do good to those who hate you. Pray for the happiness of those who curse you. Pray for those who hurt you.*"

Brendy looked at Noah for a long moment. She had never encountered anyone like him. It was hard to comprehend the goodness in him. "Your Bible may say that Jesus said that, but very few are ever able to do it."

"True, and this is why so many will never be able to find inner peace."

"I'm happy that you found that, and happy that many do. But, as you said, so many don't. There is no way I will ever be able to forgive my mother. Besides, she never asked."

"The Bible tells us to forgive, even when it isn't asked of us."

"How can you be so sure that the Bible you have based all your principles on is *really* God's word?"

Noah smiled and took another bite of his salad. He loved this conversation. He had been so agitated being confronted with his past, yet God had turned it around and into something good.

"The Bible is the best selling book of all time. It is a true account of events that took place thousands of years ago. The men who wrote the Bible were men of God. It is more or less the greatest history book that was ever written."

"Then how come there are so many different kinds?"

"You mean Bibles?"

"Yes, it's been translated several times, right?"

"It has. But the translations don't change the meaning, just make it easier to understand. There are many different types of religions; each has their own Bible. Some, I am afraid, have been very misled."

"Why do you say that?"

"Because they leave so much out and add so much, too. Some religions leave Jesus out altogether."

"And why is Jesus so important?"

"Because He is the only way to the Father. God, Jesus, and the Holy Spirit are all in one. It's like an egg. You have one egg, yet you have the shell, the yolk, and the white. Do you understand that? We can't believe in one without believing in all three."

"It sounds complicated."

"It's not. Once you understand that God sent his only be-gotten Son to be born of a virgin, to live a perfect life on this earth, and to be persecuted, ridiculed, beaten, and left to die on a cross for you and for me, you will understand what Jesus did for us was the greatest love of all."

"But how do you know He was the Son of God?"

"Because it is all written in God's Holy Word, Brendy. All the miracles he performed. He made the lame walk and the blind see. He even made the dead get up and walk again. After Jesus died, He rose again after three days. Thousands saw Him. He told his disciples, before He left them again, that they would be better off without Him, for now they would be left with His Holy Spirit, and not only them, Brendy, but all of us. We are all greater now that He walked the earth and died for us; all we have to do is believe."

"It does sound like such a fairy tale, doesn't it?"

Noah chuckled. "What sort of books do you like to read?"

"That's getting off the subject, don't you think?" she laughed.

"Not really, what kind?"

"Suspense."

The Bible is loaded full of suspense."

"I like romance as well."

"And it's also full of romance. The Bible has everything you can imagine rolled into one. It is our guideline from God to live a life pleasing to Him."

"What if we have already done things that are not pleasing to Him?"

"That's the beauty of it, Brendy. We have all done things that are not pleasing to God. No one is perfect. Jesus was the only man that ever lived a perfect life. That is the very reason Jesus died for us, so that we would all be forgiven; all we have to do is ask."

"And what if we sin again?"

"Then we ask forgiveness again."

"You make it all sound so simple." Brendy finished her salad and wiped her mouth. If only life could be as simple as Noah made it sound.

"It is, Brendy. There's an amazing life just waiting for you, if you trust in God."

"I can see that the God you believe in means everything to you. I guess I am just not ready to trust in anyone other than myself right now."

"That's fair, but can you do me a favor?"

"I guess. I mean, after all, if it weren't for you I wouldn't be so happy right now."

"You don't owe me this favor. In fact you don't owe me anything. It's just something I would like for you to do."

"What's that?"

"I want to take you to the Daystar Bible Bookstore and buy you a Bible you can understand. A New Revised Version, means the same as King James, just easier to comprehend. I will even get your name engraved on the cover. Something you can keep as a gift from me."

"You want to buy me a Bible as a gift?" Brendy smiled.

"That's right, but I also want you to read it. Read it with an open mind and let it touch you in places that need to be touched."

"You think I will believe if I read it, do you?"

"I am praying that you believe, in time, yes."

"How can I refuse that? I will accept your gift and I will read it, but I can make you no promises."

"Fair enough."

Everyone was friendly and helpful in Daystar. Noah bought Brendy a beautiful pink Bible and had her name engraved on the front cover. Other than the clothes and trinkets that Caroline got for her, the pink Bible was the very first gift Brendy had ever received. She felt certain one book would never change her mind about the way she believed, but for one incredible moment she held tight to her new gift and had never been so proud of anything in all her life.

Chapter 12

Brendy was restless and knew sleep would not come easy. Tomorrow morning the family would go to church together, and she felt almost as nervous as the first night at Caroline's.

What on earth was she doing going to church? At dinner, Edith had been so excited about Noah being home and the family once again going to church together. It was easy to see that, to Edith, having the whole row filled with Garretts was important and made her proud. Brendy wondered how proud she would be if she knew a prostitute sat on their row tomorrow, a woman who was not fit to wipe her boots.

Brendy looked around the room and towards the pink Bible that now sat on her bedside table. Noah had given her a choice of colors, and pink was her favorite. He told her it suited her.

Brendy reached over and brought the Bible back to bed with her. Slowly she ran her fingers over the gold letters. *Brendy Louise Blake.* It was the first time she had seen that name written out in years. She had been called Sasha for so long. It felt nice to see it there in print.

Her name.

Her Bible.

Even though this Bible she held in her hands was just made-up stories from someone's imagination, it still meant the world to Brendy because it was a gift from Noah. A gift she would treasure all the days of her life.

Brendy opened the back of the book and rested her finger on Revelations 3:20.

Here I am! I stand at the door and knock. If anyone hears my voice and opens the door, I will come in.

Brendy closed the Bible and laid her head back on the pillow. Even the words of this book were begging her to believe. How would she ever get through it? And yet she'd promised Noah that she would.

Noah explained to her about the Old and New Testaments. He explained about the words in red being the words that

Jesus spoke to the multitudes of people. He told her to start
with John, which gave an overview of the days Jesus spent
on earth.

Brendy laid her Bible back on her bedside table and turned
off the lamp. Morning would come early, and the last thing
Brendy wanted was to fall asleep in church.

*****

"Can't you sleep, son?" Edith asked, sitting down on the
porch swing beside Noah.

"There's too much on my mind. I know it's almost midnight, but my mind doesn't seem to care."

Edith patted Noah on the leg and remained quiet for a few
moments. She loved it when her oldest son was home; having all her children on the ranch meant the world to her. She
missed Noah when he was away, but that was life. Every tiny
bird has to leave the nest; Noah had chosen to fly farther than
the rest.

"Do you know how much I love you?" Edith spoke quietly.

Noah smiled and took her hand in his. "About as much
as I love you, I would say. I miss you too, Mom, very much.
There are times I wish I could come home and start a practice right here in Summersville."

"Why can't you?"

"I guess I could. I've really been contemplating it the last
few days."

"Because of Brendy?" Edith knew her son well.

"Yes. I hate to leave when I feel I don't really know her at
all."

"Can you take another week off?"

"No, I have obligations. Patients who hope I am back before their babies are born."

"I see. So what are you thinking? You were in deep thought
when I sat down beside you."

"Mom, I am actually confused. I feel in my heart that God
pushed me toward Brendy. I felt in my spirit He wanted me

to bring her here. I am not sure if it was to draw her closer to Him, or if He was showing me that this is the woman I have been praying for all of my life."

Edith smiled. "Son, I am pretty sure it just might be both."

"It doesn't make any sense, though."

"What doesn't?"

Noah turned more toward his mom on the swing and looked at her. "Mom, Brendy doesn't believe in God. I am not sure she wanted me to tell you that, but I wanted you to know, so you could pray for God to open her eyes. That's what doesn't make any sense. Would God send me the woman of my dreams if she didn't believe in Him? You know how I feel about Him. He is everything to me and all my life I have prayed for a Christian woman to stand beside me."

"Son, just because she doesn't believe now doesn't mean she won't forever. God can see your future and you know as well as I do that He works in mysterious ways. We are not to question God, but to have faith that all things happen for His good."

"She's young, Mom, very young." Noah was trying to think of all the reasons possible he should not pursue Brendy. Even though his heart told him she was all he ever wanted.

"Yes, and she will get older, as you will. What does age have to do with anything?"

"Nothing, I guess. Just trying to think of reasons it wouldn't work. I guess I am wondering why a woman like that would be interested in me."

"Are you serious? You are handsome and have a promising career, not to mention you are a godly man."

"I don't think Brendy cares that I am godly."

"She will Noah, she will. If it was God that put you two together, then He has it already planned out. Just be patient and see what He does next."

"I'm running out of time, Mom. I leave in eight days."

"Noah, with the technology we have today, you two can stay in touch as often as you like. Besides, you only live three-and-a-half hours away."

Noah laughed. "That's what Greg said. I don't know, Mom. I guess I was just praying, asking God for guidance. I'm trying to decide if I should make Brendy know, without a shadow of a doubt, that I want more than friendship, or if I should leave well enough alone. I mean living the distance I do, is that fair to her?"

"Is it fair to leave her, and not tell her how you feel? Especially if she is the woman you have been praying for. Are you going to leave and never find out what could have been?"

"You're right. I would be crazy not to go after her. But Mom, you alone know that Brendy and I have just met. I have only known her six days. Don't you think this is a little premature on my part, to think that this is the woman of my dreams? Can love really happen that fast?"

"Son, thirty-eight years ago I met your father. I was working at the pharmacy in town. I will never forget the day he wandered in to buy a camera. He might have been in there all of half an hour, but I knew beyond a shadow of a doubt that this was the man I wanted to grow old with."

"Just like that? Love at first sight?"

"That's right. It's a good thing he felt the same way, because he came in the next night and asked me out. We were married within the next two years, and had you four years later, after we purchased the ranch."

"It's too bad you never got to grow old with Dad."

Edith looked off, as if thinking about a day long ago and smiled. "Yeah, it would have been nice, but that wasn't in God's plan. For some reason, God wanted him to go on to Heaven and me to be left here for awhile."

"You know, Mom, you are still young enough to find someone else. I think Dad would want you to be happy."

"Do you not think I am happy?" she grinned.

"You might be happier if you found love again."

"Noah, when you have the kind of love your father and I shared, you realize a love like that only comes once. If I met another man, it would just be for companionship, and he would always feel like he was second best, because in my heart he would be. No one would ever take your father's place and that is why I don't want another man."

"What if God saw differently and sent someone to you?"

"Then it would have to be God. If that time ever comes, I will know it. As for now, I truly am happy with the way life is. I am healthy and have my family surrounding me. I have no complaints."

"God really did bless us all, didn't He, Mom?"

"He sure did, Noah. And I think that He sent Brendy your way for a reason. I know you are busy with your work and don't have time to pursue women, as you say, but I really feel that you need her as much as she needs you."

"It does get lonely. Maybe that's why I stay so busy working double shifts; that way, I don't have to face the loneliness as long. By the time I get home, I fall asleep and leave the moment I wake up. It's quite convenient, if I think about it. I really don't have time for loneliness."

"Edith patted Noah's leg again. "You know what, son? I have this feeling all your lonely days are about to end. You have been a good man of God. You have made Him proud, and I think you are about to be blessed more than you can imagine. And Brendy may not realize it now, but the same God she doesn't believe in is about to bless her as well."

*****

Brendy was aggravated, messing with her hair. She put it up and back down several times and couldn't make up her mind. Finally, she decided to leave it up since it looked more sophisticated and church-like.

She looked in the full-length mirror at the black skirt and white blouse she'd bought in town the day before. She felt sick to her stomach at the very thought of entering a church. It would be almost as if Satan had walked in the doors himself. If they only knew, she thought.

Noah decided to drive Brendy to church. He wanted to talk to her before they got there. He knew that only he and his mother knew how hard Brendy was having it this morning and wanted to make sure she was okay.

He smiled when she entered the house for breakfast all smiles and confidence, not letting on she was terrified inside. He liked that about her, the ability to smile and laugh despite how she really felt. He hoped that by driving her to church she would open up a little and tell him what was on her mind.

"You can breathe now," he laughed, when she buckled her seatbelt.

"Does it show?" she giggled. "I am a nervous wreck. I don't think I slept a wink last night."

"I was afraid of that. By the way, you look amazing this morning, but then you always do, no matter what you wear."

"Well thank you, but if you are trying to butter me up so I will get my mind off what's coming the next couple of hours, it won't work."

"Well, you can't stop a man from trying. There's really nothing to be nervous about. No one will be paying attention to you directly, once the service starts. I will make sure you sit at the end of the row, in case you want to go to the bathroom, or get so overwhelmed you need air."

"Overwhelmed?" Brendy said, confused.

"Our pastor doesn't hold anything back. He tells it like it is. People who aren't Pentecostal, or people who have never been to church, for that matter, might get a little overwhelmed."

"I understand. I might need to run for my life."

Noah laughed. "Nothing like that. Everything he says today will be Bible facts. I'd like to ask you to listen closely and absorb what you hear."

"I'll be okay, if you promise to sit beside me and hold me up." Noah could hear the nervousness in her voice and almost felt sorry for her. On the other hand, he knew God was working miracles today, and he prayed that the message would be something that would be absorbed in every corner in Brendy's mind; something she could take back and ponder over for days and weeks to come.

"I won't let you out of my sight, I promise. Oh, and there's one other thing." Noah looked at her as if he was a little nervous himself, and Brendy wondered what could have caused that look.

"Oh no, I'm afraid to ask."

"I know quite a few people that attend New Life Assembly, and they haven't seen me in a year now, so there will be lots of introductions."

"How will you introduce me?"

"As my friend, of course."

"They will think I'm your girlfriend, won't they?"

"Probably. Will that be so bad?"

"No, I guess not. I don't mind being your girlfriend for today." Brendy smiled, thinking how wonderful that would be if it were true.

"Also, the family is going to Carnifex Ferry State Park after the services for a picnic; that's why I asked you to bring a change of clothes. Mom reserved one of the shelters; she's planning on grilling burgers."

"Sounds like fun. Summersville is just filled with things to do, isn't it?"

"It is, makes me wonder why I ever left to begin with." Noah had been thinking about that more and more over the last seven days. Why he was in Pittsburgh, when the people he loved were in West Virginia?

Chapter 13

The parking lot was packed by the time they arrived for the 10:45 service. Noah parked his car and turned towards her. "I do thank you for coming with us this morning. It means so much to Mom to have the whole family together."

"It's the least I can do. No one has to know how nervous I am except you, right?"

"That's right. Just stay close." Noah got out of the car, and opened Brendy's door for her. She smiled, knowing that he could be sure she would be staying close.

Noah greeted several people on their way in,including Judy, the church secretary, who was an old family friend. He introduced Brendy as his friend, as he'd said he would. Brendy could tell from Judy's smile that she hoped it was more. Perhaps at thirty-two, people were starting to get worried that he may remain single the rest of his life.

The sanctuary at New Life Assembly was beautiful. It seated about two hundred and fifty people and had the most amazing stained glass window of the events in Jesus' life that made up most of the back wall behind the pastor.

Brendy took a seat at the end of the aisle, just as Noah had promised, not too far from the back of the church. All seven of the Garretts sat beside her in the same row, and Brendy could see the happiness that radiated from Edith's face. She was so proud to have them all there with her. The Garretts were a family that loved like none other she had ever known.

After they took their seats, people still crowded into the sanctuary and took the empty seats. So far, so good, Brendy thought. Maybe this wouldn't be as bad as she'd anticipated. Just a little over an hour, and she would be having a great time with the family at the park. For now, she would tough it out and get through this.

Brendy stood, with everyone else, as the music started. She was amazed at the fast-paced music the congregation sang, instead of the old hymns found in hymnals. She'd seen the inside of churches from movies she'd watched, but never did the words of the songs touch her heart the way this one did.

She is running.......a hundred miles an hour.......in the wrong direction...... She is trying...But the canyon's ever widening........ in the depths of her cold heart.

Brendy knew she'd been running all her life, first from her mother's abuse, as a little girl when she'd hidden under her bed. She ran as a teenager, when she'd left home for good, having no idea where she would end up. Finally, she'd run from the woman who had controlled her life.

So she sets out on another...... misadventure just to find.... She's another two years older and she's three more steps behind....

What was happening? Was this song written just for her? It was as if someone had written her story.

Does anybody hear her?.......Can anybody see?......Or does anybody even know she's going down today. ...Under the shadow of our steeple.....With all the lost and lonely people.....Searching for the hope that's tucked away in you and me.

Brendy felt the sting of tears in her eyes. What was happening to her? She had not been inside more than fifteen minutes, and already she felt as if she couldn't breathe.

She is yearning....For shelter and affection...That she never found at home.....She is searching for a hero to ride in...To ride in and save the day....and in walks her Prince Charming....and he knows just what to say.....momentary lapse of reason and she gives herself away.

Brendy felt the first tear slide down her face. Noah had forgotten to warn her about the music. She'd had no idea it would hurt this much.

If judgment looms under every steeple...... If lofty glances from lofty people....can't see past the scarlet letter.....And we never even met her.......

Brendy whispered to Noah that she would be right back; she had to go to the restroom. She slipped out of the aisle, and quickly went to the restroom. Noah pointed her in the right direction.

Brendy stared at herself in the mirror. She was grateful everyone was in the sanctuary, and she was there alone. She wet a paper towel and wiped her face of the stray tears that mysteriously made their way down her cheeks.

She hoped Noah couldn't tell she was crying when she left. What would he think of her if he knew the very first song had gotten to her like that? And how on earth was she going to go back into that sanctuary, and listen to the pastor preach for an hour?

After spending about ten minutes in the bathroom, Brendy knew she had to return, or they would send someone to come looking for her, and what would she say? I'm hiding out in the bathroom?

Noah smiled at her as she walked back beside him. The choir was finishing up their last song, and everyone was once again finding their seat.

"Are you all right?" he whispered.

"Yep, just fine," she smiled. How could she tell him the truth, which was that she wanted to go to the car and sit because she couldn't breathe? It felt like an elephant was sitting on her chest, and all she could see, staring at her, was the stained glass picture of Jesus, behind the pulpit. The stained glass covered so much of the wall, and was beautiful, yet it screamed out to her.

Look at what I did for you! How could you not believe in me?

Brendy rubbed at her temples. She felt a migraine coming, and hoped it would be gone before the service was over.

"It's wonderful to see everyone with us on this beautiful July Sunday." the pastor spoke. He was a middle-aged man, and he smiled at everyone. Brendy heard hellos around the sanctuary. It was easy to see that he was liked by the congregation.

"Today I want to read from John 8:12..... *I am the light of the world. Whoever follows me will never walk in darkness, but will have the light of life."*

Brendy saw Noah open up his Bible and follow along. She wished she had brought her Bible; she'd had no idea she was supposed to.

"I also want to talk to you about going left before you go right. Follow along now, as some of you I have already lost." Brendy heard a light laughter coming from the congregation.

"When we follow Jesus, He is the light. When we don't follow Jesus, or don't have that relationship with Him, then we live our lives in darkness. When we are in darkness, we allow Satan to come in and control us. We may not realize it, or we might even think that we are controlling our own life, but we aren't."

"Each of us lives our life serving either Satan or God. If you are not serving God and trying to live by the commandments and lead a godly life,then you are serving Satan. Satan comes to steal, kill and destroy us. He takes away our joy,and leaves us feeling worthless, defeated, unloved, unworthy, depressed, angry, and bitter. We wonder why our life is such a mess. We start to blame our failures on God, and some even stop believing in Him altogether."

Brendy slid down a little in the seat. Even though two hundred and fifty people or more now sat in the sanctuary, Brendy was sure he was speaking directly to her. She watched him for the longest time pace back and forth across the stage, and speak words that seemed to be meant only for her. Surely she was the only one in the church who did not believe.

"I ask you today, who do you serve? Think about it. If your answer didn't come to you quickly enough, then perhaps that is something you need to consider."

"You may be asking yourself why bad things just keep happening to you. Maybe you do serve God. Maybe you are trying harder than you ever have to live by the commandments. You read your Bible, you come to church, you pay your tithes, you help out in your community, and yet you still struggle each day. Your finances are terrible, your husband or wife left you, your children are living out in darkness, your health is bad, and your car won't start. You ask yourself, why? Why do these things happen, when you are doing everything humanly possible to live in God's will?"

"Good things happen to bad people as much as bad things happen to good people. Many of the things that happen to us are of our own doing. But many of them are things out of our control. Sometimes God allows us to go left before we go right. Okay, now you are looking at me confused."

The sound of quiet laughter rumbled through the sanctuary again. "Let me explain. Just because you may have gone left doesn't mean you aren't headed for the right. Sometimes God sends us on a detour to build us up, and make us stronger. Look at Paul, Job and Abraham. God sent Paul left for three years. Look how many times throughout the Bible God led his people on detours, in order to make them stronger. Job lost everything he had, yet he never once gave up and cussed God. Because he overcame the evils that were thrown his way, God blessed him with more than he had to begin with."

"I need you to remember this. Post it on a sticky note if you have to, and read it everyday. The longer your left, the greater your right. It's okay if you are in a left season of your life. As long as you are serving God, I can assure you, He will bring you out of it with more strength and faith than you ever had before. God will pour out His blessing on you, if you keep the faith and don't stray from His will."

"If you are living for Satan, then don't be sitting there thinking….man, I have been in left for so long, it's terrible. My friend, you are not left; you are in darkness, which is much worse. You, my friend, are lost to a dying world with nowhere to go. Not only can you not take a detour, but you are totally lost with only one way to go, and that's down."

Brendy was shocked when Noah reached over and took her hand in his and gave her a gentle squeeze, as if saying, it's okay; no matter what happened in your past, it's okay. Brendy could feel the tears starting to pool in her eyes again.

Oh, don't let me cry now. Please, not now.

"Which brings us back to John 8:12.... *I am the light of the world. Whoever follows me will never walk in darkness, but will have the light of life.*"

"Living in the darkness is not fun, my friends. For those of you that are living in the darkness, you know I speak the truth. To make this simple for you to understand, if you are still trying to figure out if you are at a left or just living in the darkness, ask yourself if you have ever asked Jesus Christ into your life. Have you made him your Lord and personal Savior? If you answered those questions no, then, my friend, you are living in the darkness. And this is not something that you want to hear. You might even be offended by what I am about to tell you, but not only are you living in the darkness, you are serving Satan. And since you cannot serve but one God, which one do you choose? It's your choice."

Brendy watched the choir walk back up onto the stage and start singing softy, as the pastor continued to preach.

"If you think that you will have time to make up your mind later, let me ask you this. What if you leave this church today, and never make it home? What if this is your last day on this earth? What if you don't have time to make it right with Jesus later? Where will you be when your soul leaves your body? Your soul will never die. And when you take the risk of not accepting Jesus as your savior, you take the risk that you will spend eternity in Hell. Many churches today don't like to talk about Hell. But Hell is mentioned over five hundred times throughout the Bible. In fact, it is mentioned more times than Heaven is. Don't let people tell you there is no Hell. If I offend you, I am sorry, you are in the wrong church."

"Everyone, please stand. I want every head bowed and every eye closed. Jesus said in John 11:25 *I am the resurrection and the life. Those who believe in me, even though they die like everyone else, will live again.* You must believe in Jesus Christ, and accept Him as your personal Savior in order to have everlasting life.....He didn't say we all make it, no matter what. No, he plainly says all throughout the Bible that we MUST accept Him, there is no other option."

"If you are here today and say, Pastor, I have lived in darkness all my life. I want what you speak of. I want Jesus to come into my life and save me. I'm tired of the darkness. I'm tired of the loneliness, the anger, and the bitterness. I don't care if I have to go left before I go right; at least I will know I am on the right road, and headed in the right direction, even if I have to take a few detours. If that is you, please raise your hands as high as you can. Raise them high and unashamed. Jesus will not go where He is not invited."

"I see many hands here; that is good. If you are one of the ones who raised your hand, I want to ask you to get out of your seat and come to the front."

Brendy remained still. She was sure Noah was disappointed that she had not raised her hand, and as much as she longed to have what Noah and his family had, she still felt that if God really did exist, salvation did not apply to her. There would be no way that a loving God would forgive her of her past sins; she had gone too far, too long ago.

Chapter 14

Noah and Brendy rode most of the way to Carnifex Ferry State Park in silence. Brendy felt certain he was disappointed in her, yet he never spoke a word about the church service, or even asked her what she thought about it.

The day was beautiful and warm, and perfect for grilling burgers and playing horseshoes. Beth rode her small bike around the shelter, and begged everyone to take turns pushing her.

After everyone ate, they teamed up and played volleyball. Brendy, Noah, and Connie were on one team, while Brad, Rene, and Greg were on the other. Brad's team won, and blamed it on the fact that he had two guys and one girl instead of the other way around. Connie, of course, refused to believe that.She said it was just luck.

Only seven days had passed since Brendy left New York, and she had already fallen in love with the Garretts. Brendy had never understood until now what that four-letter word meant, but with each new day she understood it more and more.

*****

Monday morning came early. Noah found it hard to believe that a week had already passed since the day God put Brendy in front of him, and yet, in just one week, Noah was falling more in love everyday.

Noah wanted so badly to ask Brendy what she thought of the church services the day before, but he knew better than to push her. He could feel God working on her, and in his heart, he knew it was just a matter of time before she came to Him of her own free will, and not his. If there was one thing he had learned, it was that a man convinced against his will was of the same opinion still.

Only seven more days until he left for Pittsburgh. He always enjoyed his time with his family, but had always been eager to get back to work with his patients who counted on him. But not this time. There were other doctors who could deliver babies in Pittsburgh. For the past week, he'd felt his heart calling him home. Perhaps it was calling him because he had already been away so long, or because the woman he wanted to spend the rest of his life with was there. How strange it was that one single week could turn your whole life around.

Noah thought about his next move. As much as he loved his family and loved being around them, he knew he was going to have to get Brendy alone in order to talk about his feelings, his life, and open up to her about his dreams. He hoped that a trip to the cabin to stay overnight alone would be enough.

He ran his plan by his Mom, and she thought it was a great idea. She even packed the things he would need, as far as food, in the large backpacks that would hang over his horse. Now he had to run the idea by Brendy, and hoped she would be as excited about the time alone as he was.

*****

"Good morning, are you decent?" Noah called from the other side of Brendy's door.

Brendy laughed, and opened the door to find him standing there in a pair of jeans and button down shirt with boots, and wearing a cowboy hat. He could have passed as Brad's twin, only better looking. He had gone the past two days without shaving, and the scruff on his face was rather sexy, she thought.

"What are your plans for the day?" he asked.

"I don't have any. I was hoping you did."

"Oh, really?" he smiled. "Well, I do have some, if you want to hear about them."

"Come in, then." Brendy moved aside and let Noah enter. "So what's on the agenda for the day?" She loved this, and was going to hate it when Noah left her. There would be no more surprise visits, or trips to the lake, or horseback riding, just days of cleaning, and longing for the year to pass so she could see him once again.

"I was wondering if perhaps you wanted to ride with me back up the mountain to stay overnight in the cabin."

Brendy looked at him for a moment without saying anything. "Just the two of us?"

Noah laughed. "Yes, but let me tell you this—I have no ill intentions, I promise. You will be perfectly safe with me up on that mountain, I can assure you."

"Well, of course I would be, I didn't think otherwise. I guess it just caught me by surprise. I mean, why would you want to waste a day of being with your family to spend it with me?"

"Brendy, I actually talk to my family each day of my life, either by phone, Facebook, or email. It isn't like I never get to talk to them. It's you I would like to get to know better, and always being surrounded by family doesn't really give us anytime to talk. So what do you say? Do you want to go?"

Brendy smiled. "I would like that very much."

"Great, I'm glad to hear that, especially since Mom and I have already packed the kitchen stuff," he laughed. "I would sure hate to have to put all that back."

Brendy laughed. "Let me pack an overnight bag, and I will be right there. Is there anything I need to remember to bring?"

"Nope, just you, and very good ears. I not only plan to talk to you. I plan to listen as well. When we come off that mountain tomorrow afternoon, I want us to know each other and understand each other. I want to be one person you feel that you can talk to, and I would love it if you were that person for me as well."

Brendy watched Noah leave, and packed a few things in a bag. She was sure she would be able to listen to Noah as long as he desired to talk, but he would be awfully disappointed if he expected her to tell him anything he didn't already know. There were just some things she had to keep to herself.

*****

Following Noah back up the mountain was even more exciting than the last time because Brendy knew where they were headed. She was anxious for her time alone with Noah yet afraid that he would ask too much of her. Here she was, a stranger to him, and she knew Noah was expecting to get to know her better by isolating themselves from the others.

"Looks like we might get a storm," Noah called out, a few feet ahead of her. "Guess I should have paid more attention to the weather."

"A little rain never hurt anyone," she teased.

"That may be true, but no one likes to get drenched, and quite honestly, it doesn't look like we are going to make it." The wind had started to pick up, and the sky grew dark overhead.

"How much farther?" Brendy called out, to be heard.

"Not that much, just enough to get wet. Beauty will stay close; just keep your head ducked and hold on."

The rain started slowly at first, and then came down in huge drops, splashing Brendy on the head. Thunder rolled in the distance, and a strike of lightning flashed not too far from them. Beauty stopped and whinnied out.

"Nudge her with your heels, and talk to her gently," Noah yelled out. "Just hold tight."

"Come on girl, let's go." Brendy nudged. Beauty did as she was told, and stayed right behind Noah's horse. Within minutes, they were at the cabin.

"Follow me over here," Noah yelled, heading for a lean to beside the cabin. "We'll leave the horses under here for tonight. I'll come back as soon as the rain lets up, and take care of them." Noah helped Brendy off her horse, and tied them to the post of the lean to. Now they stood under the shelter in the downpour, not far from the entrance to the cabin.

Brendy laughed as she felt the water dripping off her face. Her hair was soaked and her clothes plastered to her body; she was sure she looked frightful, in this condition.

Noah looked at her and laughed, as she stood before him, drenched. She was so beautiful. Oh, how he hated to leave her in six days. With his thumb, he slowly wiped a drop of water off her face.

"How sweet," he smiled.

"Sweet? So you think I look sweet, do you?" Brendy couldn't help but giggle.

"Oh yes,that sweet summer rain. And this just proves that you are as beautiful wet as you are dry." Noah came to her in slow motion, caught up in this incredible moment, the two of them high on the mountain, with the storm raging all around them and placed his lips on hers. Slowly, he let the kiss linger. He could feel that her response to him was not one of shock or refusal. Instead, she responded with sweet innocence that told him beyond a shadow of a doubt that she, too, felt the same way. There was a longing between the two of them that told a love story Noah thought he would never find, this side of Heaven. A sweet, beautiful love story that was as real as his parents had shared. Noah had no idea how he would make their love story work, but was determined, now more than ever, that he was going to do everything possible to hold on to this feeling as long as he lived.

Brendy was the first to slowly pull away, and smile at him through teary eyes. "Wow," was all she could manage at the time. Never had she felt love behind a kiss. Never had she wanted to be kissed, the way she wanted it from Noah.

"Sorry, guess I just got caught up in the moment. Is this more rain, or tears I see?" Noah looked confused for a moment, looking into her teary eyes.

"I'm sorry, Noah." Brendy started to turn away, but Noah stopped her.

"What's wrong, baby? Talk to me."

And there, as the thunder rolled in the distance and the rain still poured, Brendy could do nothing but look at this handsome rugged man before her in amazement, amazed with all the emotions running through her all at the same time. How could she tell him she loved him, in just eight days? But the strangest thing to her of all was how she knew what love was.

"I'm no good at this, Noah...relationships. I don't know how to love someone like you. For that matter, I don't know how to love at all."

Noah took her face in both his hands and kissed her on her forehead. "What do you mean, someone like me?"

"I'm not a good person, Noah. I've never been a good person. I've never loved a good person."

Noah smiled at Brendy with love in his eyes. "Don't cut yourself short. You are a good person, Brendy. You just don't realize it. I'm like Mom when it comes to being a good judge of character."

"Can we go inside and get dried off? I think I would feel better talking to you if I weren't freezing." Brendy crossed her arms in front of her chest as she shivered. The pouring rain and wind caused goose bumps, not to mention the conversation at hand.

"Sure we can. Goodness, look at me just standing here letting you shiver. Give me just a second to get the key and unlock the door before you make a run for it."

Noah took off for the house, and quickly unlocked the door. Within minutes, Brendy was behind him and inside the safety of the cabin. Noah grabbed a couple of towels and handed Brendy one. "I'll be right back. I need to go get our bags off the horses, so you can change clothes. While I am out there, I will tend them. Give me a few minutes."

Noah took off again and left Brendy in the cabin alone. She walked to the window that faced the lean to and watched him, as he took care of the horses for the night and unhooked their bags from them.

Slowly, she ran her fingertips over her moist lips. She'd only been kissed by men who paid for her time in advance. Men she catered to, who didn't love her or care about her feelings.

What was happening? She knew how Noah felt about sex before marriage, and because of that, she knew he had not brought her up on this mountain alone to lure her into bed. What were his intentions? Did he expect to sweep her off her feet and leave her in six days to go back to Pittsburgh, as if nothing ever happened?

And how could she allow him to fall in love with her, a woman who sold her body for trinkets and material things, a woman who was angry and bitter with the world, while he was vibrant and full of life?

Noah pushed the door open with his foot and carried in an armload of wood to place into the fireplace. "I know it's July, but we will need the fire to heat our soup Mom made us for lunch. The bags are on the porch under cover. I will get them in just a second."

"Oh no, I will get them." Brendy took off to the front door and carried in their bags. "Might as well make myself useful for something. I would have lit the lamps, but I didn't know where the matches were."

Noah started the fire and lit the oil lamps around the cabin, while Brendy changed her clothes. Noah had already put the soup in the kettle that hung over the fire, and the room magically came to life.

"Smells good." Brendy sniffed the air.

"Mom makes the best homemade vegetable soup there is."

"I bet. Your mom makes good everything. I don't think I have eaten anything yet I didn't like."

Noah ladled out a bowl of steaming hot soup and handed it to Brendy before getting his own. "Let's sit at the table; it's been years since I sat at that old table."

"Bet it holds many memories."

"That's for sure. Had some really good meals here, too."

Noah and Brendy ate their soup slowly and sat in silence for a bit, each thinking about what had transpired between them under the lean to and exactly what it meant.

To Noah, it meant the start of a relationship that would only grow stronger as years passed, yet to Brendy it meant she would have to find a way to let him down gently. She was not what Noah needed, not now, not ever.

"That was great." Brendy ate the last of her soup. "Thank you for bringing me back to the cabin. Out of all the places we have been so far, this has to be my favorite."

"Mine, too." Noah looked around the room. "I see my dad everywhere when I am here. I can close my eyes and still remember the days we nailed the boards, the things he said to me."

"Oh, and what was that?"

Noah chuckled. "I remember the day we placed the last window. He looked at me and said,' Son, one day you will bring the woman you love here to this place, and you will remember me telling you this. For as high on the mountain that we are, you're just that much closer to God and Heaven. But one day, when you truly find the kind of love that will last your lifetime, you will already feel you're in Heaven.'"

"So he was a man of words. A kind man, like yourself?"

"He was kind, yes. And he was right." Noah reached over and took Brendy's hand. "It does feel like Heaven."

"Noah," Brendy lowered her head to keep from looking directly into his eyes. Noah took his hand gently under her chin and raised her head back up to face him once again.

"Brendy, it is clear you have a very low self-esteem. I have no idea what your life was like as of eight days ago, but I know who you are in your spirit. You carry a broken heart. I'm not sure if it is still there from your mother's abuse or from something else, but a heart can be mended. I had a broken heart once, too."

Brendy got up from the table and walked to the fireplace. The fire still blazed, and the crackling sound it made reminded Brendy of days long ago when she was a little girl, before her grandparents died. She would sit upon her grandfather's knee and he would tell her stories. Brendy was only five back then. Her mother didn't become violent until after they passed, leaving her a single mother, alone, with no one to turn to.

Noah came up behind her and placed his hands upon her shoulders, turning her to face him. He wrapped his arms around her and held her like that. Never had she felt so surrounded by love.

"My heart can never be mended, Noah. It is broken in places that no glue will hold."

Noah stood holding her, rocking her slowly from side to side. How could he make this woman realize how special she was to God? How could he make her realize that this was in God's plan for her life, that they were destined to be together from the beginning of time?

"Brendy, I know that it has only been eight days since God put us together, and don't dare say this wasn't God's doing, just hear me out. All my life, I have prayed for Him to send me the woman He had chosen for me to spend my life with. I didn't want to do as so many do, and run from one to the other, in search of something that just wasn't there. I wanted to find her and know she was the one. I thought I'd found that with Jessie, but I realize now it was more lust than love, and because it wasn't real love from the beginning, it didn't last; unfortunately, it never does."

Noah pulled away and took her hand and led her to the couch to sit down. There, he faced her and continued to talk.

"I have dated quite a few women since Jessie, but it never lasted because they wanted something I was never able to give them. I promised God five years ago, up here on this very mountain, that I would never again go against His will for my life. Most thirty-two- year-old men can not say this, but I have never been with a woman sexually besides Jessie, and I won't again until my wedding night, so please don't think I brought you up here to lure you to bed; that was not my intention."

Brendy smiled at him as he looked at her with such love in his eyes. She'd already figured that part out. She just wasn't sure what his intentions were.

"Which brings me back to the beginning; I know it has only been eight days, but there is no doubt in my mind that you are the woman I have been praying for all of my life. You being on that bench outside the airport at just the moment

I walked by was no coincidence. I know you say you don't believe in God, and I am not trying to sound conceited like you will never have a better choice, but God blessed both of us that day, Brendy, don't you see that?"

"I see that you believe that. You believe in divine destiny. You believe in a God that you feel controls our life and moves us around like chess pieces on a chessboard. I also believe that you truly think I am a good person, but as your pastor said, I am living in darkness, darkness you don't need in your life."

"Brendy, the only reason you are living in darkness is because you choose to live there. You are afraid to let go and give it to God, not because you don't believe in Him but because you think He has never been there for you, so it's easier to turn against Him than to acknowledge Him, am I right?"

Brendy breathed in deeply and let it out slowly. "Maybe you're right. I do understand that there is *probably* a higher power. I understand that Jesus came here and died on a cross and people saw Him walk again after three days, but I also understand that the same God that you say blesses you has *never* been there for me, not ever." Brendy put her hand to Noah's lips to stop him from protesting. "And I know, surely, you didn't drag me up on this mountain to show me the light. I promise you I will read my Bible. I will even read it with an open mind, but please don't push me. You have no idea where I came from, or what has happened to me during the course of my life."

"You are right." Noah took her hand and lightly kissed her fingertips. "I have no idea about any of that, but I can assure you, that no matter what it is, God can heal your broken heart if you allow Him. And you're also right about something else. I did not drag you up here to show you the light about God. I feel you will see that for yourself when the time is right. I can't convince you against your will, and I'll not try."

"Thank you for that," Brendy said, pulling her feet up on the couch and underneath her to get more comfortable.

"What I did drag you up here for was to be able to spend one-on-one time with you. I've never met a woman I felt God had actually placed in my path for a certain purpose. I feel that there are many reasons, but I also feel that you are the woman I've been praying for. Yes, I do believe in divine destiny. I believe our stories are written out since the day we are born. I believe God has someone for everyone to love, to grow old with."

"You really think that woman is me?"

"I do."

"What if you found out I was not the woman you thought I was?"

"Are you telling me you left a husband or boyfriend behind?" This was something Noah had been considering.

Brendy laughed. "Goodness no, I have no ties; I can assure you of that."

"Then, what is so bad you think I would run from it?"

"Noah, I am not a virgin. I know how you feel about that."

"Neither am I. Does that bother you?"

"Of course not."

"Then, why would you think it would bother me?" Noah asked.

"When you slept with Jessie, you thought you loved her, right?"

"That's right. I'm not sure what you are getting at."

"Noah, I have never in my life loved anyone. I have never even *thought* I loved anyone."

"So, you're saying you had sex with someone you didn't love?"

"That's right. Doesn't that bother you?"

Noah smiled and shook his head. "Brendy, our past is our past. We all do things we are not proud of, but we can't allow our past to control our future."

"Noah...." Brendy sighed, not knowing how to tell him the truth. Oh, how she wanted to scream out the truth to him but couldn't find the right words.

Noah moved a bit closer to her on the couch and took her hand again. "Brendy, I know that *our* God will never give up on you as long as you still have breath, just like me. I have fallen in love with you. I can't explain how it happened so quickly, but it did. I have not worked out the details in my mind yet of how this could work with the distance between us, but I will. Until the day you look me in my eyes and tell me you do not feel the same, and that I am not someone you would even consider living your life with, then how can I back off? When you kissed me, I felt it. I wasn't sure until then, but now I am convinced that there is love there. You may not be head over heels at this moment, but you are certainly on your way. I won't rush you. If there is one thing I've learned, it's patience. Take all the time you need, but please don't push me away and not try to find out how good we could be together just because you think I would be upset from something you did in your past. That's why they call it a past, Brendy; it's over, so let it go."

Chapter 15

"Full house, I win." Noah laughed, laying his cards on the table. It was almost ten, and yet Brendy felt wide-awake. They'd had a great time so far, playing board games and now cards. Noah was so much fun to be around. Brendy could only imagine what life would be like if she actually belonged to this man.

Of course, she knew her life would never be all laughs and board games; he was a doctor, after all, and a very busy one at that. Besides, what did it matter? She couldn't allow him to ever be anymore than a friend anyway.

"I have to say, Brendy, I will never forget this day. I have had a great time beating you in about every game we have played."

Brendy laughed. "That's only because of your experience. I've never played any of these games before, so you had an advantage."

"It amazes me when I think of all the things you've never done. I mean, who hasn't played a board game?"

"I never had a childhood. I was always running and hiding out. I never had any brothers or sisters, so there was no one to play with."

"I know talking about your mom is a sore subject, but have you ever thought of finding her, just to see if she is alive?"

"No, not ever. This will make me sound very cruel, I am sure, but I don't really care."

Noah knew there was no use giving her the lecture on making peace with your enemies and about forgiveness; that would all come later. It was clear she wasn't ready for that.

"What did you dream about when you were little?" Noah hoped she would open up a little, just enough for him to get a tiny glimpse inside.

"I honestly didn't know what a dream was."

"Come on, Brendy, every little girl has dreams." Noah wanted to be patient with her, but he knew healing would come only when she could let go. Maybe talking about it would somehow speed up the process.

Brendy's eyes filled with tears as she thought about days long ago. "I dreamed that she would die. That she would go to work and never come back. I used to lie there under my bed and pray to God, a God that never heard me. I would ask Him to kill my mom, so she wouldn't hit me anymore."

"Do you understand why God didn't kill your mom?"

"Because He didn't care if she hit me?" Brendy wiped at a tear and smiled, realizing she was crying again.

"No, because it wasn't her time to die. God saw what was happening and wanted her to draw near to Him. It's hard for you to believe, but He loved her as much as he loved you and me."

"But I was so little. I couldn't defend myself, and He is all-powerful. He could have stopped it if He wanted to."

"True, but you have to understand something. He does not control our lives as if we were chess pieces on a board. He allows us to make our own choices, no matter what they are. I'm not giving your mother excuses, because there is no excuse for hurting a child, but perhaps your mother drank because she had inner issues of her own. What was her life like? It's apparent she didn't live for God, so, as you said, she lived in darkness. Everyone's darkness is different. She had her own battles raging inside her that she didn't know how to deal with, and, unfortunately, she took them out on you. Everyone in darkness takes it out on someone, even if it is themselves."

Brendy looked at Noah and let what he'd said sink in. "Are you suggesting that I am taking my battles out on myself?"

"I am. You choose to believe you are not worthy, not good enough. Your past is too bad, in your mind, so you close yourself off to love."

"Maybe it's easier than being hurt again."

"If you never take risks, how can you be sure of the outcome?"

"And what risks would that be?" Brendy knew where Noah was going with this conversation.

"You never risk to believe that God loves you, and to have faith. You never risk loving someone and allowing someone to love you. You find it easier to close yourself off from the world, from God, and from me."

"Is that what you think?" Brendy knew Noah was right.

"It's what I know. Do you have any idea how much happier your life would be if you just stopped trying to do everything for yourself and let someone else help you?"

"I have. I am here, aren't I?"

"I mean, to just give your life to God, and allow Him to help you. I know you think He wasn't there before, but He was. I know you suffered, Brendy, but you are still here. You are still breathing, which means you made it. And if you allow it not to ruin you, you will become stronger for it."

"How is that?"

"Do you know the blessing you can be to victims of abuse? Just your story alone and how you overcame it."

"Did I overcome it, Noah? I hardly think so."

"Not emotionally. But with God's help, you will. You might even need counseling; it couldn't hurt."

"It probably wouldn't help much, either. Look, Noah, I understand what you are trying to do. You have been trying to help me ever since last Monday. You are a truly great person, and I appreciate that, but you have no idea what you are dealing with."

"Maybe not. Maybe I just don't care," he smiled.

"You're just like a doctor, always wanting what's best for everyone. So tell me, do you like being an obstetrician?" Brendy wanted so badly to get off the subject they were on.

"I love it. There is nothing like bringing a baby into the world. Hearing it cry out for the first time."

"I've never seen a baby being born. I bet it's amazing."

"It is. Of course it can be sad, too, when things go wrong."

"Does that happen often?" Brendy asked.

"No, but it does occasionally. It's hard to see a parent lose a child when you know you did everything humanly possible to save it."

"I can imagine. So what do you want out of life, Noah? What are *your* dreams?"

"Why don't you answer me first? You must have dreamed about something as a child, besides wishing your mother dead."

Brendy looked away for a moment and smiled. "I used to dream I would grow up and a handsome man would fall in love with me and take me far away from my mother. He would love me and protect me from her, and we would live in a little white house with a picket fence, and I would have two children that I would love and protect and treat them like a mother should treat a child."

Noah smiled. "Do you still want that?"

"No, not anymore."

"Why is that? Why did your dream change?"

"Because I changed. That is a fairy tale dream, and reality just isn't like that."

"Then I guess I am hoping for a fairy tale, too."

"Maybe we all are. Maybe there are certain people who can live that, like Rene and Greg and your mother and father, but for most people that just doesn't happen."

Noah looked at her for a moment, thinking about what he wanted to say next. "If that is the case, then for those that it doesn't happen for, it's either that they were with the wrong one to begin with, or they just didn't care enough to try. Marriage is give and take. It's not a matter of trying to change the other to suit you; it's a matter of trying to change yourself to be the best partner possible."

"That may be true. But as I said, some things just can't be fixed. Anyway, enough said." Brendy laughed. "We can talk all night and there are just some things that may never change with me. But I have had a terrific day with you in this pouring rain, high on this mountain. I shall never forget it, as long as I live."

Noah got up from the table, walked over to Brendy, and pulled her to her feet. He stood there before her, holding both hands in his, and smiled. "You have that right. This is, by far, the best day of my life." Noah's lips touched hers once again. This time there was no shivering from the rain, no thunder or lightning piercing the sky. There were only two people, high on a mountaintop, with the warmth of the fire behind them. One knew he would treasure this moment forever, and planned to do whatever necessary to have her in his future for the rest of his life. The other knew this as one of the last times she would feel his lips upon hers. A future as he dreamed would never be possible, as long as he included her in it.

*****

Brendy awoke to the smell of fresh coffee drifting through the cabin. Noah had the shutters open and the curtains pulled back. The sunlight streamed in, and gave Brendy a sense of peace she'd never felt before. Even though she knew in her heart it would never work out for the two of them, as she knew Noah hoped, at least the safeness she'd never felt before was something she welcomed and would always be grateful for.

"I could get used to this place." Brendy sat up in bed and stretched.

Noah looked her way and smiled. "I was wondering when you were going to grace me with your presence."

Brendy giggled. "Come on now, it can't be that late."

"It's nine a.m., but I guess that isn't late for you."

"Not when you keep me up until two a.m., it isn't. How do you do it, get up at the crack of dawn each day?"

"Habit, I guess. I usually have to be at the hospital by six. Of course, many nights are spent there anyway; babies tend to come after midnight."

"I think I was born at three in the morning myself." Brendy got out of bed and took the cup of coffee Noah handed her.

"Oh, really? So you and your mom talked about when you were born?"

"No, my grandmother and I did. My grandmother used to tell me all sorts of stories. My life wasn't so terrible before they died. Of course, that was before I was seven. After that, my whole world changed."

"I'm sorry. I guess I need to stop dragging it up."

"It's okay. I'm actually getting better talking about it. Maybe it's what I needed all along."

"Could be. I enjoy being that person you can talk to. In fact, I want to know why you don't have a cell phone."

Brendy chuckled. "Never had the use for one. People have phones so they can stay in touch with people. I never had anyone I wanted to stay in touch with."

"Well, I hope you don't still feel that way. I would love to be able to stay in touch with you after I go back to Pittsburgh. We could talk at least once a day, and text throughout the day. Would that be okay with you?"

Brendy crossed her legs under her on the couch and stared at him. "Won't you be too busy to chat throughout the day?"

"There are times I am too busy, yes, but that is how I stay in touch with my family. Just because I only come down once a year doesn't mean I don't talk to them daily. Besides, how am I going to get to know you if we don't stay in touch? I would suggest the Internet, but I rarely have time to sit at a computer unless it's work-related. On the other hand, I always have my phone with me, wherever I go."

"You're not going to give up, are you?"

"Not until you tell me you want me to. Do you want me to?"

Brendy took a sip of her steaming hot coffee and looked him in the eyes. How could she push him away without hurting his feelings? Why did she want to?

"I don't mind getting to know you better. I would like that, but let me warn you now; I only want to be friends. Is that okay with you? I am not looking for a relationship with you, or anyone, at this point in my life."

"That's fair enough. I will stop pushing, but you have to promise me you will stay away from my brother."

Brendy laughed at that. Now she knew her plan to make him think she was interested had worked. "Oh really? Isn't that why you brought me here, so you could pawn me off on your brother?"

"Is that what you thought?" Noah smiled. "Honestly, I brought you here on a whim. It's something God placed in my heart, and now I know why. So, I guess with that said, we will get up in the morning and go cell phone shopping for you. How does that sound?"

"In the morning, huh? What about today?"

"Today, Miss Brendy, is going to be spent right here on this mountain. We will leave in time to make it down before sundown; in the meantime, I think I want to spank your butt in cards some more."

Brendy laughed. Who was this incredible man before her? If there really was a God, and He loved Noah as much as Noah thought, then why did He place her before him? Poor Noah, he would soon realize that she was not a blessing at all, but a curse he had to endure to pay for the sins in his life, and it made her sad to think about. Yes, she knew in her heart that she would be Noah's punishment for it all.

*****

The day remained sunny and beautiful. After they'd spent the afternoon laughing and playing cards, walking around outside, and eating ham sandwiches and iced tea, they started back down the mountain.

Following Noah back down was not as exciting as following him up. Brendy had a heavy heart thinking about leaving this beautiful place of solitude, a place of utter peace with nature, knowing that not one soul, besides Noah's family, knew where she was.

Brendy could not keep her eyes off him as he rode in front of her down the narrow trail. At last, she knew a man that cared about her well being. A man she'd spent an entire night with, and not once had he wanted anything more than her friendship and conversation. In fact, he spent the entire night on the couch and gave her the bed. Nothing more than a kiss was all that he asked for, a kiss that left her breathless and wishing beyond wishes that she could return the love he desired to give her. If only she could forget everything she'd done, but she knew in her heart that not telling him about her past would not be fair to him, and that it was something she could never look him in the eyes and say.

*****

"Did you have fun, Uncle Noah?" Beth asked, as they entered the house.

"We sure did, sweet girl." Noah picked Beth up in his arms and swung her around. Brendy looked over at Rene, who was sitting on the couch beside Beth, and smiled at her. Rene winked and smiled back as if to say, I'm glad you both had a great time. Brendy knew that Rene was wondering if their plan had worked.

"So when do I get to go to the cabin?" Beth asked.

"That is something you will have to work out with your mom and dad." Noah looked in Rene's direction.

"Greg and I were talking about taking her up there before the end of summer for a couple of nights. It's just been too busy to take off, at the moment."

"Well, it's a great place to spend time, that's for sure," Brendy smiled at her.

"So, it looks like the city girl might like the country just a bit," Greg said, coming into the living room from the kitchen.

"It does," Brendy giggled. "In fact, I think I wouldn't mind to move up on that mountain and never come back down."

"Oh, really?" Greg seemed amazed. "If we ever get to missing you, we will know where to look first."

"That's right." Brendy loved the way she could interact with Noah's family. What luck she had to be given the opportunity to live among them.

"Come on and eat; dinner is served." Edith stuck her head out of the dining room door and smiled when she spotted Brendy and Noah. "So, you two are back already? How did it go?"

"It went great, Mom, and your soup was awesome," Noah said, taking Brendy's hand and leading her to the dining room.

Brendy didn't think she would ever get used to it. It felt strange with him holding her hand that way in front of everyone else, but he didn't seem to care. It was as if he wanted everyone to know that she was becoming more than just a friend and he was proud of that fact. Brendy could tell by the look on everyone's face that they were also thrilled with the idea, even Brad, who didn't seem to mind that she was now off-limits to him. What would it hurt, she thought. After all, Noah would leave in five days, and besides a few text messages that would pass between them, nothing more would ever become of their relationship. Surely, within the next year, Noah would meet the woman his God had planned for him all along, and he would realize Brendy was just a stray girl who had stolen his heart for a brief period in his life.

*****

Noah turned over and hugged his other pillow closely, imagining it was Brendy he held. Strange, here he was a grown man, and yet, he hugged a pillow. He laughed to himself. How did he fall so hard so fast, and with a woman younger than his sister? Perhaps, to God, age was not important.

Noah thought of all the beautiful nurses that worked at Magee Women's Hospital who had pursued him over the past couple of years. They might be a bit disappointed there would be no more occasional dinners or plays to attend. Not that he had time to do much, but he had occasionally taken turns taking them out when he found the time. Of course, it was never more than a friendship type of thing. Noah could always tell from the first date if this was the woman he'd prayed for, and when she wasn't, he never allowed himself to become serious.

Now, of course, he knew there would be no more occasional anything. He would devote his time to taking care of his patients, and in his free time he would call and text the woman he'd fallen in love with. No, he did not intend to give up easily.

So much now weighed on his mind. There would be no way he would be able to wait an entire year to hold her in his arms again and kiss her sweet lips. How could he stand the distance between them? Even though Brendy made it quite clear she wanted no more from him than friendship, her kiss told another story. Noah knew he would have to take this slowly. Perhaps the distance would make her miss him and long for him to be back; at least, that's what he silently prayed. If, for one second, he thought she felt the same about him he would have no problem putting in his notice at Magee's. Of course, Noah knew that was not going to happen soon, if ever.

Noah drifted off to sleep dreaming of the two of them high up on a mountain in front of a raging fire, with the sound of thunder and pouring rain. He imagined his lips upon hers and saw her face there in the firelight. She smiled at him and cried, and as he wiped the tears from her face, she told him she loved him and she could not imagine her life without him.

Chapter 16

Brendy was excited about shopping for her new cell phone. She'd had money in the past to get one, but, as she told Noah, there had been no reason for her to. Now, she actually had someone to stay in touch with. It was exciting to her that after he left she would still know his whereabouts, and she would be a person he would talk to as she'd heard him that day at the airport talking to his family.

"This one is nice," Noah handed her a pink phone that looked extremely complicated.

Brendy smiled and took the phone. "Noah, you have to remember, I have lived my entire life without a cell phone or a computer and I am a bit technically challenged. This looks a little complicated."

"It might look that way, but it's a great phone. You can even get on the Internet with it. I'll teach you how to use it; it won't be hard, I promise."

"It is cute. I like it." Brendy felt like a kid in a candy store getting a new toy, and could hardly wait to learn how to use her new phone.

"Great, let's go to the counter and I will fill out the paperwork. I'm adding you to my plan, so you won't ever have to worry about a bill; I will take care of it for you."

"That doesn't seem quite fair."

"It was my idea, remember? It's my way of keeping track of you, pretty lady. Come on now, I don't want to hear you complain about this." Noah headed for the counter and started talking with the salesperson at the front about adding her to his plan.

Brendy strolled around the front of the store and tried to look interested in the other phones. It was hard for her to accept a gift such as this, and she wasn't quite sure how to act.

The bell rang on the door and another customer entered. Brendy's heart sank, and fear overcame her. Quickly, she turned her back to the customer so he would not be able to see her face. Mr. Logan, the man who had paid for her escort each month for the past several years, had entered. What on earth was he doing in Summersville?

Oh my god, don't let him see me...... he will go back and tell Caroline...everything will be ruined!!

Brendy knew if Mr. Logan saw her, she would have to run again. Caroline would know of her whereabouts, and she was sure someone would come after her. She headed back to the counter to tell Noah she was feeling ill, and she would wait for him in the car. So far, Mr. Logan had been too busy looking at phones himself to realize it was her.

She took a deep breath when she climbed into the car and shut the door behind her. Maybe Summersville was his hometown. How would she ever be free to take a trip into town for fear of running into him? Of course, this was and had always been her life....God had never been on her side, not even once.

Within half an hour later, Noah got into the car and took her hand in his. "Are you okay? You looked a little pale back there. You were fine all morning, right?"

"That's right. It just hit me all of a sudden. I'm actually feeling a bit better now."

"Perhaps you just need some lunch; you ate earlier than usual and you didn't eat that much. How does Shoney's sound? It's not far from here."

"If you don't mind, I think I will just grab something back at the house. I'm really not that hungry."

"It might make you feel better."

"That's okay. If you don't mind, I would like to go lie down for a bit." Brendy still felt sick to her stomach, but didn't want to let on. The last thing she wanted to do was run into Mr. Logan at Shoney's. She knew the best thing for her to do was to go back home, and never come into town again.

Noah looked concerned. "That isn't like you. Are you sure you're okay?"

"Yes, thank you for your concern, but I am fine, really."

"If you don't mind, when I get you back to the house I would like to check you over, perhaps check your sugar level."

Brendy tried to laugh. "Are you serious? You want to play doctor with me?"

"That's right; you are too young to suddenly feel ill enough to look as though you might pass out, so I would like to check your vitals and sugar level, won't take but a second, I promise you."

"If you insist. I do feel a little better, just not very hungry at the moment." Brendy was aggravated that Mr. Logan had ruined the day she and Noah had planned to spend in town. He'd planned to take her to a few of his favorite shopping places, but now she would have to pretend she wasn't up to it, and it made her sad, considering they only had four more days together.

"By the way," Noah chuckled as if he'd thought of something funny. "Remember when we ran into Jessie a few days ago?"

"Yes, how could I forget that?"

"Well, you will never guess who I ran into in the cell phone store."

"Don't tell me you saw Jessie again." This day was turning into more and more coincidences, she thought.

"No, just the opposite. I ran into her husband, my old friend, Jasper Logan."

Brendy sat speechless as Noah talked on about how they were only in town for a few days to visit family. He said something about how he'd tried to be nice, considering, and that he wished she had still been there so he could have introduced her, and how he was certain Jasper would have seen the happiness on his face.

Oh my god...Jasper is Mr. Logan? Mr. Logan was Noah's best friend as he was growing up.....how could this be happening to me?.....What are the chances in all the world that this could possibly happen?

Noah had already driven into the driveway and parked the car, and was looking at Brendy who now appeared to be zoned out.

"Sit right there; something is not right." Noah jumped out and ran around to her side of the car and opened her door. "Come on, let me help you inside."

Brendy remembered Noah helping her out and going to the top of the stairs to enter her door when her world went black.

*****

When Brendy awoke almost an hour later, Noah was sitting beside her on the bed holding her hand. "Well hello, pretty lady, glad to see you back in the land of the living. You had me worried there for a minute."

Brendy started to sit up, and Noah very gently pushed her back down. "Just lie there a while longer, and when you do get up, you need to get up very slowly. What happened back there? Did something happen to upset you from the time we picked out your phone until you went to the car?"

"No, why do you ask?"

"Because I checked your vitals, your heart rate and your sugar level, and I didn't find anything wrong. Brendy, could you possibly be pregnant?"

Brendy's eyes grew wide. "Heavens no, is that what you think?"

Noah shrugged. "I wasn't sure. You had the signs. I thought that you might have run from a man you were trying to get away from in Pittsburgh; perhaps you just found out you were pregnant."

"No Noah, I wasn't running from a man in Pittsburgh, and I'm not pregnant."

"Are you positive of that?"

Brendy smiled. "Would you like me to take a pregnancy test?"

Noah shook his head. "No, that won't be necessary. I was just trying to figure this out. Has this ever happened to you before, passing out like that?"

"Not that I recall."

"I would like for you to go for an exam."

Brendy sat up slowly and smiled at him. "Noah, you are a doctor and you said you just checked me. I am fine, really."

"I want to know if there is something going on you need to know about. Do you ever have headaches?"

"No, I never have headaches."

"Are you sure?"

"Noah, come on now, I wouldn't lie to you."

"Brendy, people don't just pass out, for no apparent reason. It would make me feel better if you let me take you to the ER and get an MRI."

"Noah, please, let's wait and see how I feel later, okay? I promise, if this continues I will go."

"But I am leaving in four days. Will you get Connie or someone to take you?"

"Yes, I promise. Right now all I want to do is concentrate on that pretty pink phone you bought me, and let you show me how to use it."

For the next hour, Noah taught Brendy all she needed to know about using her new phone and how to text. It was clear to him that either she wasn't telling him the truth about her health, or there was much more to Brendy's past than he would probably ever know, something so bad that it caused her to lose consciousness. How would he ever help her if she didn't open up, and what had happened today to bring it all back?

*****

Noah made sure Brendy lay still the rest of the day. He stayed with her until that evening and left her to rest alone. Edith brought her some of her homemade chicken noodle soup for dinner and checked on her. Everyone had been so nice, sticking their heads in just long enough to see how she was feeling. How wonderful it would be if she actually belonged in a family like the Garretts'. It was too bad she would have to leave again soon; it was just a matter of time until her past would catch up to her. It had already started in town today, and Brendy felt certain that no matter where she ran from here, it would find its way to her, just as it always had.

She could remember Noah telling her that Jasper Logan was only in town a few days to visit family. Perhaps, as long as she kept herself out of town for a few days, she would be able to venture back. How else would she get to the grocery store and places she needed to go?

Brendy got out of bed and made it to the mirror. Her long blonde hair hung around her shoulders as it had for years. Perhaps if she cut it short and colored it dark brown? Brendy pulled her hair up on top of her head and visualized her new look.

She dropped her hair back around her shoulders and headed for the kitchen for a cup of hot chocolate; it always seemed to smooth out the rough edges. What did it matter what her hair looked like? Jasper Logan was bound to know it was her, just as soon as he got one look into her light green eyes. That was something she couldn't disguise.

After Brendy crawled back into bed, her cell phone let her know she had a text message. She smiled picking it up, knowing the only person it could be.

Goodnight, pretty lady. If you need me let me know, I will always be there for you.

Brendy started to send him one back but decided against it. Maybe it was better to let him think she was already sleeping.

*****

Brendy's heart pounded as she pressed her body to the cold floor. As much as she was growing, it was becoming impossible to hide in the place she had hidden since she was seven. She could see her mother's worn tennis shoes walking slowly around her full-size bed.

"I know you're under there!" her mother screamed. "Go ahead and hide from me! You will have to come out sooner or later, and when I catch you, it will just be that much worse! Do you hear me, Brendy Lousie?" It had always been the same thing, night after night. Her mother came home from work, drinking, and used Brendy as a punching bag. For the past few weeks Brendy had started sleeping under the bed instead of in her bed. That way, her mother had time to let some of the alcohol wear off before she found her. The beatings weren't so bad when her mother wasn't drinking. At those times, she got slapped around instead of punched.

Brendy lay crying as quietly as possible, praying her mother was too drunk to drag her out and throw her against the wall.

Oh please Jesus, make Mommy stop. I know You love me; Grammy said You did. If You love me, You will make her go away. It hurts.

Brendy cried, knowing that the Jesus Grammy spoke of was as fictional as Santa and the Easter Bunny. No one was ever there for her except Grammy and Papa, and now that they were gone, there was no one left to save her, no one at all.

Brendy was awakened by a flashing red light coming from outside. She pulled the blanket over her face, knowing she'd had another bad dream. It was bad enough to have lived the nightmare once, but to have to live it over and over was something else.

Brendy quickly sat up in bed, realizing she was no longer in Spanish Harlem. Where were the flashing red lights coming from? In New York, she was used to lights shining into her windows in the dark of the night, but not here on the Garretts' ranch.

Brendy got out of bed and looked out the window to the driveway below. An ambulance was parked there with the doors opened in the back. What on earth had happened? Who needed an ambulance?

Brendy grabbed her housecoat and tied it around her and took off down the stairs.

Outside, she saw two men coming out of the house rolling a stretcher down the sidewalk and toward the back of the ambulance. It was hard for her to tell who was lying on the stretcher. Connie and Noah were following behind, and Connie was crying hysterically.

"What on earth happened?" Brendy asked.

Noah came to her and wrapped his arms around her. She could feel him shaking all over. "Noah, what's wrong?"

"Brendy, I found Mom unconscious on the kitchen floor. She didn't have a heartbeat. I did CPR until the paramedics arrived. Thank God we finally got a heartbeat, but she is in critical condition. I'm going to ride with them in the ambulance. Would you mind trying to get Connie to calm down, and go and tell Greg and Rene what's happened? I have already called Brad. He was at a friend's house, and he is going to meet us there."

"Can't we call Rene and Greg?"

"Tried that. They aren't answering."

"Look, you go on and do what you need to do. I will take care of this and we will be there shortly." Brendy hugged him tightly, and as she pulled away she could see tears in his eyes.

"Thank you. I don't know what I will do without her, Brendy. I don't think I can take losing her right now."

"You're not going to lose her, do you hear me? You are not going to lose her, now go on. I'll see you soon." Brendy watched as Noah climbed into the ambulance and they sped away down the driveway.

Brendy and Connie stood there watching them until there were no more flashing lights and no more sounds screaming in the darkness. Connie was still sobbing uncontrollably. Brendy went to her and put her arms around her.

"Shhh Shhh....it's going to be okay. Come on now, let's calm down so we can go to the hospital. Noah is a good doctor; she is in good hands." Connie still cried hard on Brendy's shoulder.

"I lost my daddy; I can't lose my momma, too. I just can't."

"You're not going to. Come on now, you have to get a hold of yourself for Edith. Take a deep breath." Brendy pulled away and looked at Connie. Connie tried to stop crying and took a deep breath in and out.

"That's good. Now listen, I want you to go in and put on some clothes, so we can go to the hospital. I'm going to run next door and wake up Rene and Greg, and then come back and change clothes as well. I will meet you back down here in about fifteen minutes, okay?"

"Okay," Connie sobbed. She had calmed down a little, but it was clear to see she was shaken badly. Brendy didn't see how she was going to keep from passing out, herself.

Brendy took off through the yard to the small cabin on the other side of the house. There were no lights on, but since it was four a.m. Brendy knew everyone was sleeping. She ran around to the back side of the cabin to where she guessed the bedroom window was, and started banging on the window, hoping she'd gotten the right room and was not going to scare poor Beth half out of her wits.

Within seconds, Greg pulled back the curtains and saw her standing there. He motioned for her to come back around to the front of the house.

"What on earth has happened?" he asked, standing there in his shorts. Rene was behind him looking sleepy-eyed.

"It's your mother, Greg. An ambulance just left with her for the hospital. Noah is with them. He sent me to tell you."

"Oh my god, what happened? Is she okay?"

"Apparently, he found her unconscious and revived her; that's all I know."

"Where are Connie and Brad?" Rene asked.

Brad was with a friend. He's meeting the ambulance there, and Connie is hysterical. Do you mind if we ride with you? I don't think she is up to driving."

"That's not a problem," Greg said. "Give us just a minute and we'll all ride together."

Chapter 17

Beth lay sleeping on one of the couches in the waiting room. Daylight was breaking, and still no one had heard from Noah. He'd been with Edith since they arrived. One of the nurses had been out to tell the family that she was still in critical condition, yet still hanging on, which was a good sign.

Connie sat off to herself and cried, looking out the large window that was now becoming brighter by the minute. Brad and Greg talked amongst themselves and Rene sat beside Brendy, nervously thumbing through a Better Homes and Gardens magazine.

"What do you think is going on in there?" Rene asked Brendy, throwing the magazine to the table.

"I have no idea, but I know she is in good hands."

"Yeah, she is a strong believer. I know God is with her now. He will take care of her."

Brendy was referring to Noah, not God. It was clear that all the Garretts believed as Noah did.

"Let's all join hands and pray. I think that is all we really can do at this point," Greg suggested. Everyone came together in the middle of the room, including Brendy. No one knew about her unbelief except Noah. It would be strange if she weren't willing to pray now, so instead of saying anything, she took Connie and Rene's hands.

Greg bowed his head, as well as the rest of the family, and started to pray out loud.

Dear Heavenly Father, we come to You this morning asking that You spare our mother's life. As much as I know she would like to be with our dad at this moment, I ask You to please keep her on this earth a while longer. Selfishly Lord, we aren't ready to give her up just yet. She is a wonderful, vibrant, strong-believing woman of God and I know she still has a mighty work to do down here on this earth. Please send Your spirit into her room and heal her body, Lord. Lord, You promised where two or three are gathered, there You are in the midst…we know You are with us, Lord, and we know You love our mother more than we do. Thank You, Jesus, for hearing our prayer, and for placing her into the palms of Your hands. Amen

Everyone said Amen around the room, and Brendy looked up, teary-eyed. Why could she not have the faith this family had? Faith in a God who loved her and took care of her. Silently she said her own prayer to herself as she made her way back to sit down.

God, if You hear me, prove to me this day that You are real. Don't allow that sweet woman to die. I don't care what You do with me, but help her, God, help her to go back home with her family just as it was.

Several hours passed before Noah walked into the waiting room. He looked exhausted, and Brendy could tell he'd been crying. Everyone stood and walked towards him. A smile spread across his face as he looked at them.

"Give us some good news, big brother," Brad said.

"Mom is, at the moment, undergoing heart surgery. I called in Jasper to take over. I know we've had our differences, but he's the best, and I wanted her to have the best. So far everything is going good, and I trust it will continue to go well. I have been in the chapel praying, and I feel at peace about this. I don't think God is going to let Mom go just yet. I think she still has a purpose on this earth." He looked at Brendy and smiled and she could see the love in his eyes. How would she ever get through this night knowing Jasper Logan was now performing surgery on Edith? Surely he would be out to talk to the family when it was over.

Everyone hugged Noah before he left again, including Brendy. She was glad she could be here for the family; it was the least she could do, but where could she hide when Edith's doctor walked out? What would he do if he realized his friend's new girl was the same girl he'd slept with more times than he could count? And how would Noah feel when he found out that Jasper didn't only sleep with the woman he was engaged to, but the woman he was sure he had been praying for all of his life?

*****

Everyone was anxiously waiting on the results of the operation by mid-afternoon. Everyone except Brendy, of course. It wasn't that she didn't want to hear the results; it's that she wasn't sure how she could get out of being here when Dr. Logan arrived. Funny, she'd never called him doctor before now. He seemed too sneaky to be a doctor, and now she knew why.

Movement caught her attention. She was sitting in a daze of what ifs, when she realized that Jasper and Noah had entered the room. Everyone got to their feet and walked towards them, everyone except for Brendy, who stayed back on the couch hoping she wouldn't be seen.

Noah spotted her and motioned for her to come over, letting her know it was okay; she was as much a part of their family now as anyone. He had no idea why she stayed behind except to give his family privacy.

Brendy got up and walked slowly in their direction. Jasper was talking to the family, telling them about the operation and how everything went. Almost as if in slow motion, she saw Jasper look in her direction and do a double-take. His words froze as he looked at her face-to-face. Brendy immediately felt sick again. She had no idea what was going to take place in the next few minutes. Either she would act like she didn't know him, or he would explain how she did, in which case she would be leaving the ranch for good.

"Sasha?" Jasper looked utterly confused.

Brendy took a deep breath and walked straight towards him. "I'm afraid you must have me mistaken for someone else. Hi there, I'm Brendy Blake." Brendy held out her hand, shaking, praying that he would take it and realize she did not want to be known as Sasha, and leave it at that. This was the time she would find out just what kind of man Jasper Logan really was.

Jasper took her shaking hand, with a bewildered look across his face.

"Jasper, this is a friend of mine from Pittsburgh," Noah said.

"Pittsburgh?"

"That's right. She's going to be staying here with my family."

"Is that so?" Jasper shook her hand and smiled. Brendy could see wheels turning in his head, wondering how in the world did Sasha become Brendy and wind up in Summersville with his best friend's family?

As much as Brendy wanted to run and hide she knew everyone was looking at them, and no one knew the truth except for her and Jasper. She hoped the pleading look in her eyes told him to please not say anything that would give her away.

"It's nice to meet you, Brendy. You'll have to forgive me; you looked so much like someone I used to know."

Brendy managed to smile despite the turmoil raging through her body. "I've been told that before. I guess I just have a familiar face."

"Yes, that must be it." Jasper took a breath and started again. "As I was saying, your mother has undergone a triple bypass. She will be in intensive care until she is out of the woods; that might take a few days. Then she will be moved to a private room. When she gets home, she needs to take it easy for six to eight weeks. Don't allow her to do any heavy lifting or anything, just lie around and rest and take it easy. I know that won't be easy for her."

"You got that right. Mom does not know the meaning of the word rest," Connie commented.

"As you all know, I don't work in this hospital. Noah just called me in to do the surgery. Your mother's care will be transferred to Dr. Eric Banks who is known as one of the best heart doctors in this hospital. I have confidence that he will take very good care of Edith. He assisted me in the surgery, so he is already aware of what's going on up until this time." Jasper looked at Noah as he spoke. "I'm glad you happened to go into the kitchen last night;

otherwise,this would have been an unpleasant day for everyone."

Brad and Greg patted Noah on the back as they realized what the outcome would have been if Noah had not been there and found their mom in time.

"It wasn't me," Noah rubbed his head. "It was God." Noah looked at Brendy and back at his family. I was dreaming that Mom was calling my name over and over. I asked her where she was. I could hear her but couldn't find her. She told me she was in the kitchen and to please hurry. The dream was so real it woke me up. I lay there for a moment and got the strangest feeling that I must go to the kitchen, so I got up and went. I am telling you, if it weren't for that dream, I would never have gotten up. So it was God who woke me up. I truly believe that, with all my heart."

Connie grabbed Noah and cried. "Oh Noah, you saved Mom's life. God is so good to us, Noah." Noah hugged his sister gently and agreed with her.

The family seemed to lose focus on their surroundings for a moment and didn't notice the strange look Jasper gave Brendy. Brendy was sure that just because he chose not to say anything for now, it was hardly over; she could sense that in his eyes. She had no idea what he was up to, but she hoped it didn't have anything to do with Caroline Reese.

*****

Noah was tired when he finally got the chance to lie down that evening. He made sure his mother was stable before he rode home with Brad. Brendy had ridden home with Greg and Rene, and Connie stayed. They decided they would take turns around the clock staying with Edith, in case she needed anything.

Each of them made sandwiches in the kitchen and acted more like robots than family; all seemed to be tired and in a world of their own. It wasn't the same without Edith running around the kitchen waiting on everyone. Edith was clearly the backbone of the Garrett family.

Noah noticed Brendy acting strangely all evening. There was definitely something weighing heavily on her mind. Noah thought it was strange the way she had not gotten up with the rest of the family. He figured it was to give them a chance to have a private conversation with his mom's doctor, but when she got up, the looks that passed between Jasper and her were so quick Noah thought for sure no one had caught it, no one except him, of course. It was apparent that Brendy and Jasper knew each other and were hiding something.

What was it he'd called her? Sasha? Noah had noticed her shaking as she took Jasper's hand. Was he the only one who'd noticed? Everyone else was so caught up in their mother that they had not paid attention to what transpired between Brendy and Jasper.

Maybe that was why she'd become ill the day before. Maybe she had seen Jasper in the cell phone store and took off before he could realize it was her. That would certainly explain a lot.

Noah knew that if Jasper and Brendy knew each other, she'd done a great job hiding that fact today in the hospital. Of course, the look on Jasper's face told otherwise. He was not as good an actor as Brendy was an actress.

Exactly who was this woman he'd fallen in love with, and what was God's plan next?

*****

Brendy was awakened by a light knock on her front door. It was totally dark when she sat up and looked at the bedside clock. It registered one-fifteen a.m.

Quickly she got out of bed and tied on her housecoat. She headed for the door, thinking something had happened to Edith and she dreaded hearing the news.

She opened the door expecting to see Noah and was shocked to find Jasper Logan standing there. Brendy took several steps backwards until she rested up against the bar and could go no farther.

"Don't look so worried. It isn't like I'm a stranger, is it?" Jasper walked towards her and placed his hands on her hips and pulled her into him.

Brendy placed her hands on his chest and pushed herself back. "Please, Mr. Logan, I can't do this anymore."

"Why not? Is it because I haven't paid yet? Is that what you want Sasha, money?

"No, I don't want your money. I just want you to leave me alone."

Jasper laughed and released his grip on her. He pulled out a barstool and sat down.

"So tell me, how did you end up here at the Garretts'?"

"I met Noah and he asked me to come back here to meet his family."

Jasper put his hand under his chin, thinking over what she had said. "I know Noah, and I know he did not pay to be with you. How did you meet him?"

"We met at the airport. He gave me a ride."

"Does Caroline know you are here?"

Brendy looked down at the floor as she spoke. It was so hard to look Jasper in the eyes. "No, she doesn't, and I would appreciate it if you didn't tell her."

Jasper took his finger and ran it up Brendy's arm slowly as he spoke. "That might be arranged. I mean, I can keep your secret safe, for a price, of course."

Tears fell down Brendy's cheeks. How could she have ever thought she would be safe, even here? "Mr. Logan, please, sir."

"I bet Noah doesn't know you are a high-paid prostitute, does he?" Jasper chuckled. "And I could see how smitten he was with you. But then, you are more beautiful than his first love by far."

"Noah is a good man," Brendy said. "He doesn't care that I am beautiful. He treats me better than I have ever been treated."

"Is that so? That's only because he doesn't know the truth. You know how Noah is, a man of God. He would never love a woman who had slept with so many, especially his best friend. Been there, done that, remember?" Jasper smiled.

Brendy could do nothing but cry. For the first time in her life she'd found happiness. Why did this have to happen now? She wanted so badly to argue and yell, but what good would it do? He would only call Caroline. "Please, Mr. Logan, I beg of you. Please just walk away, and leave me in peace."

Jasper laughed again. "First of all, the name is Dr. Logan, and second, whether you realize this or not, I do care about Noah, and I can not just sit back and allow him to fall deeply in love with a woman like you. Of course, he will be going back to Pittsburgh, so you really won't be that much of a threat. No, no, I think I will just keep you to myself. I mean, you do want to continue to live here, right? It's got to be better than working for that dreadful woman in New York."

"What do you mean, keep me to yourself?" Brendy couldn't imagine what he meant.

"I asked questions about you and found out that you were living here in the apartment over the garage. I knew Noah would never be here with you after bedtime, oh no, not Noah; his God would never allow that. I knew I would be able to find you here alone. So I parked my car at the end of the road and walked in. Everyone is sound asleep in the house and not one soul knows I'm here. That is quite convenient, don't you think?"

"Are you blackmailing me?"

"Blackmailing you? That word seems rather harsh, don't you think? After all, you were the one I paid for all those years. I thought we had something special." Jasper's grin gave Brendy chills.

"You meant nothing to me. I was just doing my job, a job I no longer do."

"Well, you certainly meant something to me, or I would not have wasted all that money. And since I wasted all that money, it's time I started making up for what I lost."

"What do you mean?" Brendy knew what Jasper meant, and it made her sick to her stomach.

"I mean I don't see why anything has to change between you and me. I know where to find you. I'll pop in every now and again and continue as before, only this time there will be no money passing between us. Look at it this way; you won't be considered a prostitute if you don't charge, and no one will ever have to know about our little agreement."

"And what agreement would that be?" Brendy had stopped crying and was becoming angry.

Jasper laughed. "That as long as you continue to give me what I want, no one on the ranch will ever know you were a prostitute, and Caroline will never know your whereabouts. Your secret will be safe with me."

"I can't do that to Noah. Don't you understand that?" Brendy pleaded. "He loves me; it will kill him!"

Jasper reached for her and pulled her close again. "Noah will never have to know. On the other hand, if you refuse, not only will the Garretts know your dirty secrets, but I will also call Caroline and she will send one of her men to get you. Now, come here to me and kiss me like you used to."

Brendy stood unmoving and now looked Jasper in the eyes. "Please, don't you have a heart? How could you make me do this?"

Jasper smiled. "I think you have me mistaken for Noah. I haven't had a heart in years; I just doctor others'."

Jasper got off the bar stool and wrapped his arms around Brendy, kissing her with such force she wanted to push him away, to scream out for Noah to come and help her, but she knew that could never be. Noah could never know the sins of her past, and for that reason she did nothing to stop Jasper from having it his way.

Chapter 18

Brendy knew that if Edith had not been in the hospital, she would have left the ranch before daybreak and never looked back.

As much as she would have hated leaving, that would have been the only way Jasper would never know her whereabouts. As it was, she knew that with Noah going back to Pittsburgh and Edith having to be laid up for a few weeks, she would need her help now more than ever. How could she run from the only woman who was ever good to her when she needed her the most?

Maybe, with Jasper living in New York, he wouldn't show up often. That would buy her some time until Edith was up and able to take care of the house again.

It pained her to know what she had to do as soon as that day came. She would pack a few things, leave a note, and be gone again. She was getting so good at running, and even though she knew there was no other way around it, she had no idea where she would go.

Brendy stepped out of the shower and dried off. She felt disgusted with herself for what she'd done. Never had she felt so dirty and tainted. She hated the fact that Jasper had the upper hand, and at the moment there wasn't anything she could do about it. If she didn't care so much about Noah and his family, she would just laugh and tell them the truth so Jasper wouldn't have a hold on her, but she did care, maybe too much, and she knew it would be better for them to think she'd left because she wanted to move on than to know the awful truth.

*****

"Would you like to ride to the hospital with me this morning?" Noah asked Brendy, as she entered the house for breakfast.

"If you don't mind, I think I will wait until tomorrow and hopefully she will be out of intensive care. I thought I would go ahead and start with the house; that way it will be clean when she gets home from the hospital. You know, change her sheets and stuff like that."

"That's nice of you, but it isn't necessary."

"Sure it is, that's my job, remember? Besides, I am only starting a couple of days early. You go to the hospital and visit with your mom. Are you still leaving for Pittsburgh tomorrow?"

"It was my plan until this happened with Mom. I called Magee's and made arrangements for another week's vacation; I just can't leave Mom like this. In a week she will be out of the woods, and soon to be coming home. I would take more time if I could, but I have so many obligations."

Brendy poured herself a bowl of cereal and sat down at the table beside Noah.

"I can understand that. Don't worry about your mother; we will all take good care of her when she gets home."

Noah smiled at her and drank the rest of his orange juice. "Thank you, I appreciate that. I had no idea Mom had a heart condition. We were just sitting on the swing the other night and she was telling me how healthy she was, so obviously she didn't know, either. It's times like this I wish I'd never moved away."

"So, are you and Jasper friends again?" Brendy wasn't trying to change the subject. She was just curious to know.

"Jasper and I will never be close again, ever. The only reason I called him in for Mom was because he is a great cardiologist. He asked me a few questions about you." Noah smiled.

"Oh, did he?"

"Yes, he said you were beautiful and wanted to know if I was in love with you. He asked how we'd met and why you were staying here when I went back to the city."

"And what did you tell him?"

"I told him you were living in the apartment above the garage, and yes, I was in love with you."

Brendy blushed. "Noah, don't you think that is a little premature?"

"Not at all. I know how I feel."

"And as I have said before, you might feel differently if you *really* knew me."

"I know this...I know Jasper Logan won't ever get his hands on you."

Brendy felt sick at his comment. What would he do if he knew Jasper already had his hands on her and had for years? How would she ever explain that she'd never loved Jasper; it was just a job. That would be even worse.

No, Brendy knew Noah could never know the truth. As soon as Edith was able, she knew she would leave before she hurt Noah any more than necessary. The last thing she wanted to do was lead him on to believe that there might be a future for the two of them.

"You got awfully quiet. What's on your mind?" Noah asked.

"I'm sorry; I was just thinking about how hard that must have been for you to have come home and found Jasper and Jessie, and now have to socialize with him again."

"I forgave him a long time ago, but that doesn't mean I have to buddy with him. In a way, I guess Jasper did me a favor. If he had not gone after Jessie, I would be married to her now, and when I look at what kind of person she really is, and what she has become today I thank God my eyes were opened before it was too late."

"Has Jasper left for home yet, or is he going to wait until your mom is out of the woods?"

"He is leaving this morning. Mom has already been turned over Dr. Banks. Can I ask you something, Brendy?"

"Sure, what's up?" Brendy smiled.

"When you and Jasper met, I noticed a strange exchange between the two of you. I know he said you looked like someone he knew. Do you perhaps know him from some-where else? You know you can tell me, right?"

No Noah, I really can't tell you, not now or ever. "No, I guess I just had a familiar face. I looked at him weird be-cause I was trying to figure out why Jessie ever went to him when she had you."

"Thanks, but Jasper has a wilder side than I do, guess that is what attracted her to him."

"Perhaps." Brendy knew about the wilder side more than anyone.

*****

Brendy spent the day giving the house a good cleaning. She spent extra time on Edith's room, and was sure that the older woman she had grown to love would be pleased with the results.

It was hard to smile at the family and go about life as she had a couple of days before. Since the day she'd seen Jasper in the cell phone store, she had once again sunk into a de-pression that she hoped the Garretts had not noticed.

Nothing at the Garrett house seemed normal anyway, with Edith gone. Everyone seemed a little off or not quite right. It was as if the part of the family that kept everything running smoothly had disappeared, and with it taken everyone's will and energy.

"The room looks terrific," Connie smiled, coming into Edith's room as Brendy was putting the sheets back on the bed.

"Thanks, I hope she likes it."

"She will. She stays so busy with the rest of the house she tends to neglect hers; this will surely cheer her up. I want to thank you for starting work a couple of days early. I stay so busy with paperwork and riding lessons that I don't get a lot of time to help Mom in the house. Now that Mom is in the hospital……" Connie let her words die off and tears came to her eyes.

"Are you okay? Would you like to talk?" Brendy offered.

Connie sat down in a rocking chair, and Brendy sat on the edge of the bed. The least she could do was listen.

"I'm so worried about Mom. Brendy, I have no idea what this family will do when something happens to her."

Brendy reached over and took Connie's hand in hers and smiled. "She's going to be all right. You heard what Dr. Logan said."

Connie shook her head. "For now maybe, but sooner or later she is going to leave us just like Dad did."

"That may be true, but sooner or later we are all going to leave; we all just live on borrowed time." Brendy wasn't sure where that came from, but it sounded good.

"I guess I just realized that nothing is the same without her. She is the backbone that keeps this family together. I mean, look at us. We are all moping around like we don't know what to do next." Connie tried to laugh.

"How was she last night?"

"She was good; everything seems to be going as Dr. Banks wants it to. They kept her too sedated to even realize I was there. She opened her eyes several times, but I don't think she realized where she was or what was going on. They say that she will come around more today. I just came home to get a few hours sleep and I will go back again this evening."

"Then go lie down. Is there anything I can do for you?" Brendy offered.

Connie smiled. "You are already doing it. I'm so glad you came to the ranch and are living here with us. I feel that God has great things in store for you. Noah has made it known that he cares for you. I can see it all over his face."

"He told me he was in love with me this morning." Brendy wanted to talk to someone so badly; it might as well be Connie.

"Seriously, he told you that?" Connie whistled. "Guess he didn't bring you here for Brad after all. Well gosh, that's just great."

"It isn't great, Connie. It isn't great at all." How would she make Connie understand?

"Why not? He is a great catch." Connie looked confused.

"That's just it; he is a great catch. He is a very good man who deserves a very good woman."

Connie laughed. "Oh, so now you are going to tell me that you can never be that woman because of some stupid something you did in your past, or because of something you lived through as a child; well, none of that matters. You have to leave yesterday there, and not bring it into today."

"If it were only that simple. Go ahead and rest, and I will talk to you about this later."

"I'll hold you to it." Connie winked and got to her feet. "Come here, woman." Connie pulled Brendy to her feet and gave her a huge hug. "I knew the moment you stepped in our door that God put you here for Noah. Noah isn't like any other man; he is special, and the woman who ends up with him will be blessed the rest of her life."

Brendy didn't say anymore; what could she say? She knew the words Connie spoke were true, but it didn't matter how much everyone tried to sell her on Noah; no one knew the truth, and Brendy wondered how much they would want her with Noah if they knew.

*****

Noah walked back through the front door around seven that evening. Brendy had managed to fix a large bowl of spaghetti and garlic bread; it was one of the few things she knew how to make.

"Smells good, and I thought you said you couldn't cook," he smiled.

"Spaghetti is easy; anyone can fix it. So how is your mother?" Brendy set dishes on the dining room table as she spoke.

"She's coherent but in a great deal of pain, so they are keeping her heavily sedated. She sleeps a lot in and out. She told me to tell you thank you and she loved you."

"Your mother is a sweetheart. I love her, too."

"Maybe you can go see her tomorrow; she would like that. Did you call everyone else for dinner?"

"No need to; we are here," Brad said, coming through the back door of the kitchen with Greg right behind him.

"So where are Rene and Beth?" Brendy asked.

"She's at the house with Beth whipping us up something, I don't think she knew you were cooking. I'm so sorry. I just came to ask Noah how Mom was today. I've been so busy I couldn't get there, and now visiting hours are over. I will get there first thing in the morning."

"She's good; she's asking about everyone, you know Mom. She knew how busy you all are, though, so don't worry, she has been in good hands. I've been there all day," Noah teased.

"Well, I'm going to get out of here then and go home, and Brendy, I truly am sorry about dinner," Greg apologized again.

"Don't worry about it; it probably isn't fit to eat anyway," she chuckled. "Where's Connie. Has she already gone back to the hospital?"

Noah rolled his eyes. "Yes, I'm sorry. I guess it's just me, you, and Brad."

"Oh well, let's eat then, I'm hungry. If you don't like it, I would appreciate it if you would keep it to yourselves."

*****

After dinner, Noah helped Brendy do the dishes. The quietness between them felt awkward. He wasn't sure where her bright smiles and laughter had gone, but they had been gone ever since the day he picked up her cell phone and she became sick. Noah still wasn't sure, but felt certain it had something to do with Jasper Logan, and whatever it was, it was something that Brendy never intended to tell him.

"Dinner really was good, and I'm not just saying that to make you feel good." Noah tried to make conversation; the quietness was driving him crazy.

Brendy handed him another plate to dry. "It wasn't as bad as I thought it would be." She managed to laugh.

"And you made so much, no one will have to cook tomorrow night. We'll just heat up leftovers."

"Well, I thought I was cooking for four others."

"Usually you would have; I think Rene was just trying to be nice because Mom isn't here. I'm sure she had no idea you were cooking."

"Oh that's fine, I'm not upset. I think I will go with you to see Edith tomorrow, though. I hope she wasn't hurt that I didn't come today."

"No way, especially after I told her you were cleaning."

"Oh Noah, that was supposed to be a surprise."

"Sorry, please forgive me. She asked me where you were, so I told her you were cleaning before I thought about what I said."

"It's okay. So how's does everything look?"

"It looks great. I like the way you rearranged the living room, too."

"Do you think she will be upset that I did that?"

"Of course not, she will love it."

"I just hope you're right." Brendy said nervously.

Noah put his arms around her and looked into her eyes when he spoke. "Why do I sense this extreme nervousness with you lately? Are you sure you're all right?"

"Brendy managed to smile. "I am fine, really."

"Really?" he kept holding her, never wanting to let her go.

"Does this bother you?" he asked, referring to his arms wrapped around her waist. He had not felt her tense up like this at the cabin.

"It's hard to explain, actually." When Brendy finished her sentence, Noah dropped his arms immediately.

"I'm sorry; I didn't mean to overstep. I guess that wasn't very respectful."

"Oh Noah, you didn't overstep. I just have so much on my mind that I can't go into right now." Brendy knew that Noah had good intentions and that he wasn't contemplating how to get her into bed, but it brought back so many memories of the night before with Jasper that it had made her shiver.

"Maybe I have pushed too hard and moved too fast. Seems I've been rushing things because I knew I didn't have much time with you before I went back, and I really wanted you to know how I felt before I left."

Brendy smiled. "I know how you feel. I wish you didn't feel that way."

"Well, it's too late," he shrugged. "Now my goal is to be so charming you will feel the same way," he winked.

"Well, you are charming, that's for sure. If you don't mind, I think I will go and lie down; I feel exhausted."

"I can see why; you have been up all day cleaning and cooking. You have earned the right to go to bed early. I'll see you in the morning around nine, and after breakfast we'll ride to the hospital."

"Great. Sounds good. I'll see you in the morning then." Brendy knew Noah wanted to kiss her goodnight, and if she had been a woman of virtue, who had been wholesome and good, she would have granted him that kiss; in fact, she would have initiated it. In Brendy's mind, she wasn't a woman of any worth at all, so she smiled politely and walked out the back door of the kitchen and across the drive to her apartment.

Chapter 19

Noah got up at two a.m. and dragged himself to the kitchen. He had yet to get any sleep. He should have been on his way back to Pittsburgh; at least, that's what he'd planned for today. He had wished so hard over the past week that he didn't have to go back, but he never intended it to be because of his mother's heart.

Noah pushed the button on the coffee maker and sat down to wait for the hot liquid to fall into the pot. What on earth was he doing up at this time of morning drinking coffee? Noah didn't care. As a doctor, he always kept odd hours; why should his trip home be any different?

Noah raked his hands through his hair and sighed. As of the past two days, he was angry. Angry that he hadn't known his mother had a heart condition, angry that he had no idea what was going on with Brendy and why she pushed him away, but more angry with the fact that the woman he had fallen so hard and so fast for seemed to have connections with Jasper Logan. What on earth was it about his friend that always led him to the women he loved?

Apparently Jasper had known her before he came into the picture. It wasn't that he didn't want to believe the things Brendy told him; it was just that her actions spoke volumes. What deep dark secret was she hiding and how did that secret tie in with Jasper?

Noah jumped as Brad walked into the kitchen. "Hey there, big brother, are you finding it hard to sleep, too?" Brad walked over to the cabinet and took out two coffee cups and poured them both full.

"Just sitting here thinking. So why can't you sleep?" Noah took the cup and nodded his thanks.

Brad slid out a chair and sat down. "Well, unless it is about Mom, then we aren't thinking the same thing."

"Then it's partly the same thing," Noah smiled and blew at his steaming cup.

"You know, Noah, after Dad died, it was like a huge part of me died along with him. I never realized how much he did here on the ranch. I guess I took it for granted. Not only did I miss him like crazy, but Greg and I were forced to take over everything. It wasn't easy, but I think we fell into line smoothly enough. But you know, I never once thought that anything would ever happen to Mom, you know?"

"I understand completely; I've been thinking the same thing. Just angry with myself for not knowing anything was wrong."

"How could you? I mean Mom goes for yearly check ups, but when you seem as fit as a fiddle and run around like a crazed woman full of energy, you don't know to look for anything wrong. It's no one's fault, Noah."

"Do you ever resent me, Brad?" That was a question Noah had always pondered; now he finally had the opportunity to ask.

"Resent you for what?"

"That I went away to college? That I wasn't here when Dad died, and took a job so far away there's no way I can help out with the ranch."

Brad grew quiet for a moment thinking about his answer, and used the time to drink a few more sips of coffee. "You know, I was at first. Jealousy would be the right word." Brad shook his head and smiled. "I guess I was jealous because you found a way out. All my life has been spent right here on this ranch. From the earliest age I can remember, Dad had us working, doing chores and sweating. I used to resent it like crazy when I was younger and prayed for the day I could leave and never look back."

Noah looked at his younger brother in astonishment. "Are you serious? Gosh, I had no idea you felt that way."

"I don't anymore. Now when I look back upon my life, all I see is how blessed I was to live in a family that loved me so much. I know now that Dad wasn't being mean to us; he was showing us what was true and good. He taught us that family was everything and that we stuck together, no matter what."

"But I didn't stick. I left and never came back."

"That's right; you didn't."

"How does that make you feel?" It didn't matter to Noah what the answer was; it was something he needed to know. His brother meant the world to him, and he hated that he had waited until now to ask.

"Noah," Brad set down his cup and looked his brother in the eyes. "You were going to school before Dad died, remember? Being a doctor was a dream of yours all your childhood. I remember you used to talk about it all the time. You were the oldest, and Dad was so proud of you. I remember I used to ride with him to town, and everyone he came across he would brag and tell them about you going to school to be a doctor. You gave him such pride."

"I'm sorry, Brad. I can't imagine how that made you feel."

"It got tough at times, until I started doing rodeos. I'm grateful Dad lived long enough to see me do a couple." Brad smiled, remembering. "He was my biggest fan, always sitting right there in the front row cheering me on. It was then that I realized Dad was proud of all of us, just in different ways. He wanted us to be the best we could be in whatever it was we dreamed of doing."

"He was amazing, wasn't he? I don't ever remember him and Mom arguing, not even once."

Brad chuckled, "Neither do I. They weren't only husband and wife; they were best friends."

"They were. That kind of love is rare. But you never really answered my question. Do you resent the fact that I left?"

"No Noah, not anymore. You're a great doctor, Noah, and you're doing what has been in your heart since birth. Not everyone gets to live their dream. I know in order to live that dream you have to go where it is, and you had too good an offer at Magee's to turn it down. Greg and I have talked about this many times."

"You have?" Noah smiled.

"Yes, we have. We are as proud of you as Dad was. This isn't just our land, Noah; it's yours, too. Dad and Mom saw to that long ago when they divided the property out and deeded it to us."

"I know, and trust me when I tell you that there are times I get so homesick, especially now."

Brad looked at Noah and pursed his lips. "You mean now that Brendy is going to be living here with us?"

"That, and knowing Mom's condition. It's something I have really been doing some soul- searching about."

"So this is why I find you up drinking coffee before daylight."

"Yep, this is why. But, what about you? Mom must be on your mind," Noah asked.

"She is. Quite honestly, there has been a lot on my mind lately."

"Then let me have it, little brother, do tell."

"Just life, I guess. What is it I want out of life, you know?"

"And? I mean, do you have any idea? I always thought you were totally happy right here messing with the horses and doing the rodeos."

"I am happy, but lonely."

Noah laughed. "Lonely? Come on, you have at least two different women each weekend. Isn't that what you were telling me?"

"I was bragging, big brother, but yeah, I usually do," he laughed.

"But yet, you are still lonely? It's like that old saying, always lonely but never alone."

"Exactly, so you do know where I'm coming from," Brad agreed.

"You just have no idea how much I know where you are coming from. I'm surrounded by hundreds of people day in and day out, yet at the end of the day when I go home, there is no one there."

"I am beginning to think there is no woman out there for me," Brad got up and placed his cup into the sink.

"Oh, she's out there; you just got to give it some time. I mean, look at me; I'm older than you and I'm still single."

"But not for long. I see the way you and Brendy look at one another."

Noah shook his head and rolled his eyes. "Problem is, little brother, she doesn't see it like I do. I know she feels something, I can tell, yet she constantly pushes me away. For some reason, she doesn't feel that she is good enough for me."

"That *she* is good enough for *you*? Now that's funny," Brad chuckled. "Would you like another cup of coffee?"

"No, I'm fixing to go to bed; morning comes early, but thanks."

"Come on, Brendy will come around and your gloominess will be gone."

"I sure hope so, little brother. You know, there comes a time in a man's life when he gets to be as old as I am that one has to wonder if it is just him, and maybe women aren't as attracted to him as he hopes."

"Surely you don't believe that? That you aren't attractive, that is."

"Well, if she were as smitten with me as I am with her, there wouldn't be a problem, would there?"

"Noah, Greg and I have both said many times that you are the one that got all the good genes. I mean, let's face it, we are a good looking family, but you by far outshine the rest."

Now Noah laughed. "Oh sure, I guess I just got the good stuff 'cause I was the first born and there wasn't any left to trickle down."

"You said it," Brad teased and patted him on the back. "I got to get up in a couple of hours and head to the barn, so I'm going to leave you for now and pray I can get some sleep."

"It was good talking to you, Brad; we don't get that very often."

"No, we don't. And Noah?"

"Yeah?"

"Don't worry about the whole jealousy thing. I have been over that for years now. I am happy for you and so proud to call you my brother. I'm with you no matter what you decide, whether it be to stay in Pittsburgh or to return here to the ranch. I love you and will support you in any decision you make. And I wouldn't worry too much about Brendy; she is young, just give her time."

*****

Brendy knew Jasper had left town, so she had no worries of running into him at the hospital.

She wasn't used to anyone like Noah being so nice to her. He opened her car door and opened the door of the hospital and allowed her to walk in first; he took her hand in the hallway walking towards Edith's room. No matter how she played hard to get, he was not going to let up; that was easy to see. In fact, it made her feel good knowing he cared that much. Even if she knew in her heart she could only enjoy it for a little while. It wouldn't be much longer before she left Summersville, never to return. Still,she had decided to enjoy the day.

"Mom will be happy to see you; I think she likes you." Noah smiled, walking towards the end of the long hallway on the second floor.

Brendy smiled at the comment. "The feeling is mutual."

They walked in quietly to find Edith sleeping and Connie reading the Bible, in a chair beside her. It pained Brendy to see Edith in such condition, so lifeless and pale, with monitors hooked up all around her. There was the steady sound of beeps that told Brendy that even though she looked lifeless, she was still very much alive, thanks to Noah, getting to her on time.

"How is she?" Noah asked Connie,walking over to stand beside his mother's bed.

Connie got to her feet and hugged them both. "She should be waking up soon; she's been out a while. The doctor was here not long ago and he says everything is looking great; they should move her into a private room tomorrow if she is still doing well. She complains a lot about pain, and Noah, you know Mom, she never complains, so it must be terrible. I hate to see her like this." Tears formed in Connie's eyes and she wiped at them. "Just look at me; I'm a mess. I cry all the time now."

"It's okay to cry, so don't worry about it. Besides, you are in the presence of family, and we could care less." Noah hugged her again and allowed her to cry.

"That's right; don't ever feel bad about crying. I've done my share myself throughout my life," Brendy commented.

"Go on home, little sister, and get some rest. Brendy and I are going to stay most of the day and Rene is coming to stay tonight, so you won't have to."

"I need to be here Noah, just in case…." Connie ended her words as if she couldn't bear to finish the sentence. To speak what was in her heart was too painful.

"Mom is going to be just fine, Connie. She has a great bunch of doctors here, and as you said, so far everything is great. If God wanted to take her home, then He would have the other night. He didn't. He chose to let her stay, and as long as she is still breathing, then she still has a purpose in this world."

"I have thought about that, too." Connie tried to control her tears and took a deep breath. "She does have a purpose, and I pray that she doesn't fulfill it for years to come."

"So get out of here; we'll let you know if anything comes up." Noah handed her a purse sitting beside the bed, and pushed her towards the door.

"I was hoping to be here when she awoke." Connie looked back towards Edith, hating to leave.

"Go, she knows you love her, Connie. I will tell her you stayed with her all night. You need some sleep; you look exhausted." Noah urged.

"I am, and I have a couple of riding lessons late this afternoon, so thank you. I will take you up on it and go home, but you call me immediately if anything comes up, or if she wakes up and asks for me, okay?"

"Okay," Noah smiled. "I promise; now go."

*****

The room was quiet after Connie left. Only the sound of the constant beeps reminded them that Edith was still okay, just sleeping.

Noah went to Edith's doctor and left Brendy alone, staring at the older woman she had grown to love. Brendy wondered how her life might have turned out had Edith been her mother. She would never have run to New York, nor would she ever have worked for Caroline Reese. She might possibly still be a virgin, waiting on the man of her dreams to come along and show her what true love really was.

Brendy reached out and gently touched Edith's hand with the tip of her finger. She slept peacefully, with no movement, and Brendy wondered if she was perhaps dreaming of days long ago. Back when her husband was still a very big part of her life, and her four children were running around the ranch playing in the creek or spending time on the mountain in the cabin they had built with love. The very same cabin she was so fond of.

If she had been raised in this family, Brendy knew it would have been easy to believe in God. Why wouldn't she? There would be no reason not to believe that a loving God would bestow His blessings down upon you, because she would have felt as though she had been blessed all of her life.

Instead, there had only been darkness in her life. A life filled with hurt and pain, and the loneliness that creeps upon you when you feel there is nowhere to turn. She'd wanted to run all of her life; it's all she knew how to do. To leave and go somewhere where she could start over from scratch and leave the pain of the past behind. But had she left it behind? A tear fell down Brendy's cheek as she thought of all the times she'd tried to start over, and how that pain had followed her, every step she ever took.

"God," Brendy whispered quietly. "If you are real, then reach down and touch this wonderful woman. Heal her body, and give her strength to keep going. So many people need her, God. I need her, too, even if it's just a little while."

Brendy saw movement and realized that Edith was trying to wake up. Had she heard the words she just spoken on her behalf?

"Brendy?" Edith opened her eyes slowly and smiled at her. Brendy smiled in return, and wiped the tears from her eyes.

Brendy stood up and leaned down so Edith could see her better. "Yes, it's me. How do you feel?"

Edith licked at her dry lips and tried to smile. "Like I have been run over by a truck."

Brendy reached over and got the water bottle that sat on her bedside table, and placed the straw inside her dry mouth. "Here, try to drink a little of this."

Edith sucked at the straw, and relief filled her face as her thirst was satisfied. "Thank you, that was wonderful. I never thought water would taste so good." Edith spoke slowly and stumbled over her words.

"Let me know when you want more, okay?" Brendy set the water bottle back down and smiled at Edith. Silently she thanked God before she even realized what she was doing. Perhaps she did believe in Him, after all.

Edith reached over and took Brendy's hand in hers. Brendy could feel her trembling.

"Are you okay, do you want me to go tell a nurse you're awake? Perhaps you need more pain meds?"

"No, no thank you, not right now; I need to talk to you. Please sit down and listen before I drift off again. I can't seem to hold my eyes open."

Brendy slid the chair as close to the bed as it would go and looked at Edith, waiting for her to speak.

"I dreamt of you."

"Of me? What did you dream?" Brendy could only imagine.

Edith smiled and closed her eyes a moment before she opened them again and looked straight at Brendy. "I think I died and went to Heaven. It was strange. For the longest time

I stayed, but then I knew I had to come back. I came back for you, Brendy."

Brendy immediately felt the knot in her throat and the tears. Nothing she could have done would have stopped them. "For me?" she choked out.

Edith swallowed and slowly spoke again. "Yes, just for you. I saw my Tom in Heaven; he is happy. I saw my parents and all the people that passed before me. It is so beautiful there, Brendy, so much peace."

Brendy sniffled and wiped at her tears. She believed her, and the joy that radiated through her body was indescribable. "But why for me?"

Edith managed to smile weakly. "Because Jesus sent me with a message. He told me to come back and tell you that He is real, Brendy. That He's been with you throughout your entire life. He has seen every tear you ever cried, and felt all the pain you have felt. He has had you in the palm of his hands all of your life and He loves you." Edith licked at her lips again, and Brendy got up to give her more water. Edith sucked at the straw a few more times and continued to speak slowly. Edith was not about to go back to sleep before she had given the message she had to give.

"He says to stop running. You have run all of your life. He says until you stop and face it, it will never get any easier. He wants you to give it all to Him, Brendy. He knows everything about you, and yet he still loves you and still wants you to release it to Him and accept the blessings He has waiting on you."

Brendy laid her head on the edge of the bed and wept. Edith placed her hand on her head and prayed out loud.

"Dear Heavenly Father, please show this beautiful girl that the words I speak are real and are true, and were given to me by You so that she may believe with all her heart that she was never alone, and that she is still here today because she has so much of life still to live, so many blessings still to receive. We ask in Your name, sweet Jesus. Amen"

Brendy looked up with a tear-stained face, and realized that Noah was standing behind her. How long had he been there? How much had he heard? When she looked at him she realized that he, too, was crying. He came to her and got down on his knees right there beside the bed and took her hands in his.

"I heard what Mom told you," he cried. "He wants you to believe in Him, Brendy. He wants you to want Him, too."

"I want Him, Noah, I do." Brendy cried. "I need Him like I need air to breathe. I do believe her. I do believe He loves me now. I am so sorry; I have let Him down all of my life." Brendy's shoulders jerked back and forth as she sobbed.

"Are you ready now? I can pray with you," Noah offered.

"Yes, yes, I am so ready." Brendy bowed her head and closed her eyes, and allowed Noah to lead her in prayer.

"Just repeat after me, Brendy. It is so simple to accept Christ into your life. Now that you believe, all you have to do is ask Him to come inside you and be your Lord and Savior. So I ask again, are you ready?"

Brendy managed a small giggle as she cried at the same time. "I am ready."

"Dear Father…" Noah spoke out loud, and Brendy spoke the same words behind him. "I come to You today as a sinner…….I know I am not perfect, but I know You love me….. I know You came to this earth in the flesh and You bled and died for me……. I know You rose again after three days, and You are now waiting on me to be with You……..Please come into my heart, Jesus, and save my soul from darkness…..For where I am, there You may be also…… Amen."

Noah stood and pulled Brendy up out of the chair and hugged her tightly. Her body still shook from sobs. He held onto her for the longest and allowed her to cry. This time he knew she cried from joy and the peace that had entered her. How amazing was it that God allowed Edith to come back to deliver that beautiful message to a woman who might not otherwise have believed, had it not come straight from Heaven.

Noah looked at his mother, and realized she had fallen back to sleep. She'd managed to stay awake long enough to do what God wanted, and Noah secretly prayed that because his mother had done as she was asked, maybe He would grant her the opportunity to live on this earth a while longer.

Chapter 20

Edith was moved to a private room the next day. The doctors said she had made remarkable progress. Edith didn't tell the rest of the family why God sent her back. Only Brendy and Noah knew. Edith would live the rest of her life anticipating going back to Heaven to be with her Tom. What a gift she had received to be able to visit with him, if only for a moment.

Unexplainable peace entered into Brendy that she had never felt before. She was no longer afraid of Jasper; she knew that she would never again allow him to place his hands upon her.

She also knew that even though God had forgiven her, her past was still her past, and for that reason, she would never be able to have a future with Noah. After all, it would not be fair to love him and not tell him the wickedness of her past sins. It would only be right to tell him how many men she had been with, and because Jasper was one of them, she knew in her heart it would crush him deeply. She prayed Jasper did not return anytime soon, but decided that she would be sitting on ready when he did.

This time, Brendy knew it wouldn't exactly be running; it would be getting away from Jasper, so he couldn't hold anything over her head and would no longer be able to blackmail her. When she got to where she was going she would send Noah a letter asking him never to tell Jasper of her whereabouts. She would tell him the whole story; she owed him that much. If he chose to forgive her, he would know where to find her. If he chose to let her go forever, then she trusted that he would never allow Jasper to know of her whereabouts. It wasn't something she wanted to do; it was something she had to do.

It was the most incredible feeling to be at peace with life, and to know that Jesus forgave her of her past. To know that if she left this world today, she would be in His presence, no matter what she had done. Everything had been wiped clean and she had been given a second chance. If only it were that simple with Noah.

She smiled as she thought of Doris Brubaker, and knew the old woman would continue to pray for her all the days of her life; she could feel her prayers. Maybe some people were just put on this earth to pray for others. Maybe it was their gift or their calling.

Brendy thought of all the people who were bedridden, and couldn't do anything more with their bodies. As long as they had breath, they could pray; they were useful. Maybe that was the most powerful gift of all.

"You seem quite happy today," Connie said, coming in the front door to find Brendy dusting. "What song was that you were just humming?"

"Faithfully, by Journey. They were the most popular before my time, but I still love them."

"I agree; Journey is awesome. You know, there is a stereo in your apartment, and I have some CDs if you would like to borrow some. I would be lost without music."

"I love it as well. The next trip into town I'd like to look at a few. By the way, speaking of that, I really do need to get a few groceries of my own for the apartment. Could you let me know the next time you go so I can tag along?"

"Well, you better get ready, sweet sister, because I am fixing to leave. I have to run into town to pick up a few things myself. Rene spent the night with Mom last night so I got plenty of rest, and Mom insisted I leave an hour after I got there this morning, saying I had things to do and she was fine. I love seeing that woman feisty, lets me know she is going to be okay."

"Yes, sounds like it. Let me run and grab my purse, and I'll be right back." It was nice to know that Jasper was back in New York, and she didn't have to be afraid that she would run into him in town. What a great feeling to be alive and to be at peace with your life.

*****

Since Connie's riding lessons weren't until that evening, Brendy and Connie spent the day in town. Connie showed Brendy around a few places that she liked to shop, like Down Home Candles and Crafts so she could buy a few candles for her apartment, and to the Dollar Tree to buy cleaning supplies. They shopped at Soundwaves Music to buy a Journey CD and a few other oldies that Brendy liked.

They ate lunch at the Dairy Queen, and then went to Wal-Mart to buy groceries. Brendy enjoyed being around Connie, and wished she could tell her new friend the terrible truth about herself, to get her opinion on what she should do about Jasper, but it was easy to see that Connie looked at her with respect, and she couldn't bear to ruin that image. She would know soon enough.

"I don't know why I never moved up here myself. You have this place so cute." Connie helped Brendy carry in her groceries. "You do realize Mom never intended for you to eat here; she loves cooking for everyone."

"I know, but I kind of want to cook for myself. I will eat with her more than she realizes. Her cooking is so good."

"It is, isn't it? I should pay more attention or, one day, when and if I ever get married, I will have no idea what to do first."

"Do you have a boyfriend?" Brendy loved feeling that she had an actual friend; she enjoyed the easy conversation.

"I wish. I don't have time for a boyfriend."

"Why not, doesn't Brad date?"

Connie laughed. "Brad has had women since he has been able to speak. Brad makes time, that's for sure. I guess after a long day of doing what I have to do, I'm just too pooped to do what I'd like to do; besides, there isn't anyone interested."

"Why not? You're pretty and extremely nice."

"Men don't want pretty, Brendy; they want hot, like you." Connie laughed, thinking she had complimented her new friend, but Brendy grew quiet and continued to put away the groceries.

"Did I say something wrong?" Connie asked, after Brendy had been noticeably quiet for too long.

"No, I thank you for thinking that; it's just that me being hot has gotten me into a lot of trouble. Men can be such creeps. I sometimes wish I wasn't pretty at all."

Connie whistled and took a seat at the bar. "Wow, now that must be some story. Is that why you push Noah away?"

"It is." Brendy was not sure how much she should tell, but it was killing her not to tell someone at least part of the story.

"I didn't mean to offend you, Brendy, but gosh, you really are beautiful. I have always longed for that kind of beauty."

Brendy finished putting away the groceries and sat down beside Connie to talk. "No, you don't, not really. I mean, look at yourself, Connie, you *are* beautiful."

"On the inside, right, where it counts." Connie laughed.

"No, not just the inside. You are very pretty, and your smile lights up your whole face. You are a person everyone longs to be around."

"But I'm not drop-dead gorgeous like you. I'm not someone that would make a man want to take a second glance."

"Of course you are, and plus, when a man does take a second glance, you know he likes you for you. I have been told I was hot, gorgeous, drop-dead beautiful, sizzling, tasty-looking, and spell bindingly beautiful. I tell you, it's a curse."

Connie giggled. "Who wouldn't want to be like that, though?"

"Me. I hate men pawing me and looking at me as if they want to rip off my clothes and see what's underneath."

Connie looked dreamingly and sighed, "Yeah, I could see why that would be a problem." Brendy laughed and slapped at her arm.

"Trust me; it gets old."

"That may be true, but what I wouldn't give if, just once, a man looked at me like he would like to take me to bed."

Brendy couldn't stop laughing; she thought Connie was hilarious. "You're a hoot."

"I'd rather be hot," she giggled. "So tell me why you think men are such creeps?"

"I've experienced a few creeps in my time."

"Really? You are so young; I am surprised you've had more than a couple of relationships, or are those the ones you are talking about?"

"Oh, I've had more than a couple."

"Did you have sex with them?" Connie was now glued to Brendy's face, wide-eyed, ready to absorb any details Brendy might be willing to give up.

"I did."

Connie whistled again and smiled. "Oh, do tell. I never get to hear any action; we are all such a boring family here."

"Oh Connie, your family isn't boring at all. In fact, they are wonderful. Edith and Tom taught you all so well, to have integrity and morals. To wait on marriage before you sleep with someone. I think that is just beautiful."

"I guess. But here I sit, a twenty-four year old virgin. I mean, you don't see a lot of those these days."

"Trust me; you aren't missing anything. It's better to wait on the man that loves you than to be taken advantage of."

"Why didn't you just say no if you knew they didn't love you?" Connie asked curiously.

"Because I had no choice."

"Oh my god! Were you raped?" Connie's face filled with terror.

"I might as well have been, but no, I gave consent when I took the job." Brendy knew there was no turning back now. She would just beg her to never tell Noah.

Connie looked at her a while, confused. "You were a prostitute?"

"I was a high-paid escort, but it's the same thing, just a better word." Brendy expected Connie to act disgusted, but she just sat there staring at her.

"Wow, what ever made you do that?"

"I ran away from home when I was sixteen. I didn't have the wonderful life you had. I never knew my father, and my mother beat me daily. When I left, I went to New York and met a woman named Caroline Reese. She ran an escort service, and somehow I got sucked in to it. I was only sixteen."

Connie wrapped her arms around Brendy, and held her for a moment without letting go. Brendy had not expected this reaction.

"You poor girl. How long did you work for that lady?"

"Six torturous years."

"Oh my god, six years? Why didn't you quit?"

Brendy shook her head. "I couldn't. I wanted to, but once you start, you lose your self- worth and just become a robot. Besides, Caroline let me know daily that I belonged to her."

"Shucks, you don't belong to anyone except God; that wasn't right. I wish we had known you then; we would have come and got you out of that mess." Connie sounded angry.

"That would have been nice. One morning I just woke up and decided I'd had enough and I left. I went to the airport, and took a plane to Pittsburgh. That's when I met Noah, and he brought me here."

"Are you telling me that you just met Noah the day you met us?"

"That's right. Your mom knows, but we didn't tell anyone else."

Connie put her hands over her face a second and rubbed at her temples. "So that's why you and Noah aren't that close yet; heck, you hardly know each other."

"That's right, and Noah does not know what I just told you. All he knows is that I ran away from my mother's house and worked in a diner."

Connie half-smiled. "So I am the only one that knows?"

"That's right, and I would appreciate it if you would let me tell Noah in my own time. Now is *not* the right time."

"I certainly understand. Your secret is safe with me."

Brendy placed her hand on top of Connie's and smiled. "Thank you. I've never had a friend before."

Connie hugged Brendy again. "Well, you have one now. You know what, Brendy? I know Noah as well as anyone, and when you do get around to telling him, it isn't going to matter. He loves you, and I don't think that it will make a difference to him whatsoever."

"I don't know," Brendy shook her head. "He's only been with one woman and she broke his heart. He has saved himself, and promised God the next time he will be with his wife, the woman he's been praying for. I'm sure he hopes his wife is as pure as he is."

Connie sighed. "I see why you think that. Noah does believe that you should stay pure, but just as God forgives us, we have to forgive also. I know Noah believes in forgiveness, and it wasn't like you did it against him like Jessie did; what you did was before you met him."

Brendy tried to smile, but her heart wasn't in it. The last night with Jasper was right under Noah's nose, and he'd had no idea it was taking place. "So, now you understand why I keep pushing Noah away. I feel that he deserves better."

Connie looked sad when she spoke. "I do understand your reasoning, but Brendy, if you think you could have a life with my brother, then don't let that keep you from trying. Tell him, as you have told me, and then see what he says. Give him a chance to decide; don't make that decision for him."

If only it were that simple, Brendy thought. She knew that if she could turn back the hands of time, she would backtrack to the day she and Noah met, and she would tell him the entire story from beginning to end, and see what he chose on that day. She wondered, if he had known the truth, would he still have brought her back to the ranch to meet his family, or would he have set her out in town as she had planned?

If she had told him the truth and he still chose to bring her to the ranch, then it wouldn't have been so bad with Jasper because Noah would have already known about her past, and Jasper would not have been able to blackmail her. The worst he could have done was told Caroline, and Brendy felt certain Noah would have protected her.

At least now Connie knew the truth, and Brendy felt better knowing some of the heavy load she carried had slipped off. It was just a matter of time before the rest would come off, as well; she only wished she knew the outcome of the day the avalanche would surely happen.

Chapter 21

Rene cooked tacos for the family. Brendy declined, saying she was going to try a new recipe she'd bought the items for that day. She was excited to cook in her new kitchen and hoping to kick back and watch a good movie, something she never did in New York.

Brendy was serving herself a plate of beef stroganoff when Noah stuck his head in. "You mean to tell me I was forced to eat tacos when you have that?" Noah referred to the aroma in the room.

Brendy laughed. "I would have invited you, but didn't want to upset Rene. Besides, you were still at the hospital."

"I'll forgive you this time. By the way, Mom said to tell you hello and make sure I gave you the message personally."

Brendy smiled and set the plate at the barstool, motioning for Noah to sit down. "She is filled with messages these days for me, isn't she? Here, sit down and try this; I know you have some room in there."

Noah licked at his lips and did as she requested. "Sounds great; I am not much of a taco man. I did manage to eat two, though."

"What would you like to drink? I have soda and sweet tea."

"Sweet tea sounds wonderful, thank you."

Brendy poured two glasses of sweet tea, filled another plate of food, and took a seat beside him. "I'm glad you stopped by. So, how is Edith doing? Connie said they moved her to a private room this morning, and she was doing great."

"They did and she is; thanks for asking. She is being her spunky self. Of course, she is still in pain, but the pain pills help her with that. You know Mom; she is bound and determined to get back on her feet. You may have to put a weight on her head as soon as she gets back, to keep her from doing too much. Mom has never known her limits."

"She's probably never had any limits until now."

"Yes, I guess you're right. I can tell she doesn't have as much energy as she used to, but of course, that has never stopped her from doing anything. I am surprised that she is letting you help her in the house."

"You know, Noah, I believe that she only did that to give me something to do here on the ranch as well. She likes all her little chickadees close to the nest."

Noah smiled and took another bite of food. "That's right, and now you are one of her chickadees, don't forget that; she claims you as her own. In fact, she came back from Heaven just for you."

"Every time I think about that, I have to smile. Just think, Noah, if I had believed, God might have kept her."

"Don't think I haven't thought about that, that's for sure. By the way, this is great. You really can cook, can't you?"

Brendy laughed. "Hardly,I bought a cookbook in town today, and I was trying out a recipe. I still have a lot to learn. Thank God for books."

"Well, it's very good. You need to show this to Mom; she loves learning something new when it comes to cooking."

Brendy laughed out, "Yeah right, I'm sure there is a lot she doesn't know."

"She knows a lot but not stroganoff." Noah took another bite and moaned, making Brendy laugh. She knew he was just trying to make her feel good, but she enjoyed the compliment just the same.

"So, when do they think your mom will be able to come home?"

"Unfortunately, a day or two after I leave on Sunday. I really wish I could be here to help her home, but I know she will be in good hands. Connie hardly leaves her side. You will probably have to push Connie away and make her go to work."

"Connie and I have become quite close; I enjoy her company."

"Really? That's good to know. At first I felt bad about leaving you with a bunch of strangers, but in actuality, you met them all the same day you met me, and everyone seems to have taken to you as much as I have."

"You have a wonderful family. I was blessed the day God sent me here; I realize that."

Noah put down his spoon and smiled at her for the longest time.

"What was that look for?" Brendy grinned.

"I never thought I would hear you say that, you acknowledging God."

"I do believe I said it yesterday, if I remember correctly."

"That you did, one of the best days of my life so far."

"Oh really, I thought the day at the cabin with me was the best so far?" Brendy teased.

"It was until yesterday; now that one has to be the best."

"It was great, that's for sure. When your mother told me Jesus sent her back from Heaven to give me that message, it made me realize how much He loved me and had always loved me."

"So you do believe her? I mean, *really* believe her?"

"Of course I do; your mother wouldn't lie."

"No, she wouldn't. That made my day. I told her today when I got her alone what happened; you do know, she fell asleep before you gave your heart to Jesus."

Brendy laughed. "Poor thing, she was so exhausted; it took her a while to tell me all that. It was all she could do to stay awake as long as she did."

"She stayed awake as long as she needed to; the rest is where I came in. It's weird but I was waiting to talk to Mom's doctor, and the nurse told me he would be there within five minutes, but I had this overwhelming feeling that I had to get back to Mom's room then; it couldn't wait. When I entered, you were transfixed on what Mom was telling you, so I stood still and listened. I prayed you believed her, and I thanked God for sparing Mom's life on your behalf. I know now why I had to get back. God knew you were ready, and He needed me to lead you in prayer."

"Isn't He great? I have been so stupid, Noah. It's a wonder He loves me at all."

"You weren't stupid, just uninformed. You never had the chance to really get to know Him. You weren't brought up in church, so it wasn't your fault. You've had a hard road, but those days are over."

"Thanks to you and your family."

"Brendy, you can give God all the credit and the glory; He is the one who placed you on that bench that day. He knew what He was doing when I came along."

"You know, a woman named Doris Brubaker prayed for me on the plane on the way to Pittsburgh. She prayed that God would put me with the right people and, amazingly, He did."

"There's nothing amazing about it. He always has our best interest at heart."

"I guess He does. Now I just have to get used to thanking Him for everything. I'm not used to that."

"It will get easier in time. Just keep reading your Bible."

"I've already read the four gospels, and instead of going on, I am going back and reading them again. I like those because it is the words Jesus spoke."

"There's a lot to learn in those four books. If you have any questions, let me know, or better yet, ask Mom after she gets home; she will eat that up."

"I bet. Are you still going to text me off and on?"

"You bet, that's why I got you the phone, so I can keep up with you, remember?" Noah smiled. "So what's on your agenda for this evening? Are you going to bed early?"

"I thought I would pop some popcorn and watch a movie. I borrowed The Color Purple from Connie; she said it was one of her favorites."

"It is a great movie, very inspirational. I saw it a long time ago."

"Would you like to watch it again? I would like the company."

He was hoping she would ask. "I would like that very much."

*****

It was after midnight before the three-hour movie went off. It touched Noah's heart the way Brendy cried at least three times during the film. He got a little teary-eyed himself. He'd met Brendy fifteen days ago, yet it seemed he'd known her all of his life.

Noah had gotten used to having a cup of coffee after midnight and decided he was too happy to sleep, so he started the coffee maker and sat down to wait.

It excited him more now about the future because he'd witnessed Brendy's transformation. He'd heard with his own ears and seen with his own eyes the way she came to God broken, and yet God healed her.

He still saw a beautiful woman who appeared to be the same woman he met at the airport two weeks prior, yet everything about her had changed since the day before. She had a glow about her and smiled more. She had been so carefree during the movie and seemed to have let go of whatever it was that had been bothering her so badly before. Noah only wished she would forgive her mother; of course,that would come with time.

Sooner or later Noah knew he would make his way back to Summersville to live the rest of his life. He wasn't sure if he would buy a house in town close to his office or build something, as Greg and Rene had, right on the property. It was certainly big enough and already deeded to him. They could always live in the apartment until the house was finished.

Noah laughed to himself at his thoughts. Here he was, sitting again at the kitchen table after midnight, and all he could think about was marrying a woman he'd only met two weeks before. There was no doubt he loved her and wanted to spend his life with her. The rest was just waiting for it to happen.

Never had he found a woman that he could feel so free around, to be himself, and he was sure that tonight she was being more herself, too; she'd even reached across and held his hand during the movie. It shocked him that she'd made the first move.

He smiled when he thought about the kiss she allowed him when the movie was over, and he was saying goodnight. He couldn't wait until the day he would ask her the most important question of his life. True, he already asked it once in his lifetime, but this time would be the last time.

Noah got up from the table and poured himself a cup of coffee, thankful that his mom kept the cabinet stocked with Folgers. How many nights at the hospital had Folgers kept him awake, patient after patient, as one baby after another made its way into the world? The full moon seemed to be the worst time for it, too.

Noah knew that Brendy was on her way to take a bath and had not yet gone to sleep, so he got out his cell phone and sent her a text.

Thanks for dinner and a movie: best date I've had EVER!

He smiled as he pressed the send button.

*****

Brendy was towel drying off when she heard her phone tell her she'd received a text. She smiled, knowing it was Noah. Quickly she picked up the phone to check her message. He was thanking her for dinner and a movie.

Brendy tied on her robe and sat down on top of her bed. He'd told her tonight was his best date. How could she tell him it was one of her first, as she didn't think the other men actually qualified as a date?

She pressed reply and wished she could be there to see his expression when he received it.

I agree...also the best kiss EVER! Goodnight, sweet man, and sweet dreams.

Brendy waited just a few seconds before she got his reply.

If they are about you, they will be.

Brendy smiled and snuggled under the soft comforter. If only she could have a future with this man, she knew he was a man she could always trust, someone who would never let her down and would take care of her the rest of her life. The only thing now that stood in their way was the same man who had stood in his way with his first love, a man named Jasper Logan.

*****

"Noah told me you accepted Jesus as your Savior," Edith smiled at Brendy, who had come with Noah to see her.

"I did, thanks to your message from God." Brendy reached over and took Edith's hand. She had fallen in love with the older woman and knew, because of her, her life would forever be changed.

"I'm glad Noah isn't here; I need to talk to you again," Edith said. Noah had walked down the hall to talk to Edith's doctor.

"Oh. Do you have another message?"

"Not from the Big Man this time," Edith smiled. "This message is strictly from me."

"Sounds important."

"It could be. I had a premonition, or rather a dream. Not sure, anymore, with me going in and out all the time."

"And it's about me?" Brendy was almost afraid to hear what Edith told her. It was clear she had connections with God.

"I saw you and Noah. Together, I mean. You were married and you were happy. You lived there on the ranch and you had two children, a girl and a boy. It was so real, Brendy; I swear it was."

Brendy smiled, visualizing what Edith told her. How nice that would be if it could ever be true. But that would have meant Noah had forgiven her for the sins she'd committed with Jasper.

"Maybe that was just wishful thinking on your part?" Brendy suggested.

Edith shook her head and looked up, as if she were thinking of something way ahead in the future. "I don't think so. Before Greg and Rene were married, back when I hired her one summer to work on the ranch, they were just friends. They'd been friends since grade school and that was it, just friends. I guess, because they grew up together and she and Connie were friends, no one thought of them being anything more than that. Then, one day, I was sitting on the front porch in the swing, and all of a sudden, everything left me. It was like I was seeing a movie in my head. I know God was giving me a vision. He likes to do that, you know?" she smiled.

Brendy smiled back and rubbed the top of Edith's hand with her thumb.

"Anyway, I saw them in a cabin, the very one that is there today. Of course, back then there was no cabin. I saw them with a daughter, which they now have. It puzzled me at first because I had no idea Rene liked Greg anymore than she did Noah or Brad, but after that I started paying attention; I mean *really* paying attention, and when I told Noah what happened,he smiled and said he knew it all the time. He was just waiting on them to realize it."

"So you think Noah and I will one day get married?"

"I don't think; I know." Edith shook her head up and down in confidence.

"Well, we will have to see, I guess. You know he leaves in five days?"

"I know. He would have already been gone if it weren't for me. I'm sorry I gave everyone such a scare, but what happened to me caused a great chain reaction."

"How do you figure that?" Brendy asked.

"Well, by me dying, I was able to bring a message back from God, and Noah was able to stay another week he hadn't planned. Besides this terrible pain, I would say it was well worth it."

"What was worth it?" Noah asked, coming into the room.

"Me dying, that's what."

"Nothing is worth that," he frowned, "but I will say Brendy accepting Christ was wonderful."

Brendy reached up and took Noah's hand and smiled at him. Edith lay there smiling big at the two, as if she were saying I told you so.

"So tell me," Edith asked, "what's been going on with my baby?"

"Rene has been taking her over to her mom's house each morning. Of course, Beth asks about you all the time," Brendy answered.

"I don't like sharing that girl," Edith laughed, "she is my pride."

"You have her spoiled rotten Mom, that's for sure."

Edith giggled," I do, don't I? Just wait till I have more to spoil." Edith looked at Brendy and winked.

Noah had no idea what was going on between his mother and Brendy, but it was obviously an inside joke he knew nothing about.

"Mom, since you seem to be doing so well, and Brad will be here in just a few minutes, would it bother you if I left early today? I would like to take Brendy down to the Summersville Muddelty Trail and go for a walk."

"I wouldn't mind at all; in fact, go now and take your time. I am capable of being alone a little while."

"Are you sure, Noah?" Brendy stood and looked at him. She had no idea he'd planned this for today.

"Of course, he is sure; now scoot on out of here." Edith made a motion with her hand telling them to go.

Noah laughed. "You heard the woman. I love you, Mom. I'll see you again in the morning. And don't be too hard on these doctors."

"Fiddlesticks, it's not me that's hard on them; it's the other way around."

Chapter 22

"So, just what is the Summersville Muddelty Walking Trail?" Brendy asked, on their way out of the hospital parking lot.

"It's not just a walking trail; it's also for riding bikes. Used to go there as a kid; it was awesome. It's almost three miles of trails under a canopy of trees. Muddelty Creek runs alongside the trail and there are bridges that cross over the creek; it's quite beautiful this time of year."

"I bet. I had no idea there was so much to do here."

"There's so much more than I will have time to show you, so make sure Connie shows you all the fun stuff when I'm gone."

"I think I am going to miss you very badly, Noah."

Noah smiled and quickly glanced in her direction and then back to the road. "I'm glad you feel that way. I know I am going to miss you. I am really dreading that ride back to Pittsburgh alone."

"Do you think your family would mind if I went back up on the mountain to the cabin after you left, for a couple of days?"

"You want to go back by yourself?" Noah sounded concerned.

"Yes, I really would like to."

"Would you not be afraid by yourself, with no power?"

Brendy laughed, "Noah, look who you are talking to. You have no idea what I have been through. There isn't much that scares me." Unless it's Jasper Logan, she thought.

"I'm sure they won't mind, but can I ask why you want to do that?"

Brendy shrugged her shoulders, "I don't know, really, I just love it up there. It's the most beautiful place on earth to me."

"You really think so?"

"I know so. I want to see if I can connect with God the way you did after Jessie hurt you so badly. Maybe God is up on that mountain, and I would like to ask Him a thing or two."

Noah chuckled. "He is, but He is also there in your apartment as well."

"True, but I would really love to go back. What do you think?"

"I think that could be arranged, and I will agree to this, on one condition."

"Oh, what's that?"

"That you allow Brad to go with you just long enough to see you there, carry you in some wood, get your fire started, and allow him to come back in a couple of days to help you back down. You are new at riding still, and I will feel more comfortable if you allow him to do that."

"That's an awful lot to ask of him; he is so busy."

"He's never too busy to escort a pretty lady up the mountain. I will just have to give him strict orders to not be intruding on my girl," Noah laughed.

Brendy laughed as well. "Okay, then, if you don't think he would mind. Of course, I will wait until Edith is home and doing things on her own again; until then, I will be there to help."

"Mom is going to have all the help she can get, trust me, but thanks. I know she loves you, and I know you two are going to become closer than ever."

*****

Brendy thought the trail was as amazing as Noah described. Quite a few people walked hand in hand, and there were also many on bikes. It was a beautiful day to spend walking under the huge trees.

"Thanks for bringing me here; it's beautiful."

"I hate that Mom had the heart attack, but I thank God daily for giving me another week with you. Two weeks just weren't enough."

"And three is?" Brendy asked, smiling.

Noah reached over and took her hand in his as they walked. "Three isn't either, but it's a lot better than two. I'm not sure if a lifetime is even enough. How do you feel about me asking you to be exclusive to me only?"

"Are you asking me to go with you, like they do in high school?"

"I'm asking that you give me a chance. I realize it won't be easy, with me living so far away, but I know it won't be forever; I'm working on a surprise."

"A surprise?"

"Yeah, but before I put this surprise in motion I need to know you feel the same about me as I feel about you."

Brendy stopped on the side of the trail and looked at Noah. "Ever since you have started pursuing me I have steadily pushed you away. There are still things you don't know about me."

"And I don't have to know......." Brendy put her finger over Noah's lips to stop him.

"I wasn't finished," she smiled. "As I was saying, there are things you don't know about me, but I am sure you will know it all sooner or later. There is no one else I want to date, Noah. So don't worry about me finding someone else. As I have said before, I am not interested in being with anyone at the moment. I don't mean to hurt you, but I still don't think I'm right for you. Look how educated you are. Noah, I quit school when I was sixteen and ran away from home. I don't even have a high school education, much less college."

Noah wrapped her in his arms, not caring who might be watching. "Do you think I give a hoot what kind of education you have?"

"Look how much younger I am than you."

"That bothers you, doesn't it?" he asked.

"No, but does it bother you? You are a doctor, for crying out loud. I'm a waitress, and now a housekeeper."

Noah shook his head and rolled his eyes, "There you go again, cutting yourself short."

"It might not bother you now, but in the future it might."

"Brendy, let's take one day at a time, okay? Let's see where that leads us. As I was saying, I promise you that I will leave all the nurses alone, and not take anyone else to dinner or to the movies or where-the-heck-ever," he laughed, "if you promise to be my girl and give me a chance. I know we are far apart, but I plan to come back more than once a year, and we can stay in touch by phone and text daily. What do you say?"

Brendy looked into his eyes. There was so much love there; never had she felt that a man actually loved her the way Noah did. She lifted her arms around his neck and kissed him more passionately than before. Caught up in the moment, she forgot they were standing out in public in the broad daylight, and Noah didn't seem to mind, either.

"Wow," he blinked. "I take that as a yes?"

"Yes Noah, but let me warn you now, as you find out more and more about me and my past, just remember this day and how good it is right at this moment, and try not to hold it against me."

"I promise you, no matter what, I will love you as much today as I did yesterday and more tomorrow."

Noah and Brendy took their time walking the Muddelty Trail. They were in no hurry to get back to the ranch, back to the life they knew would come to an end within the next five days when Noah went back to Pittsburgh. No matter how much they were allowed on the phone or how many texts they received a day, it would never amount to the time they'd spent together in the heat of the summer in Summersville, West Virginia.

*****

So much had happened to Brendy in a little over two weeks, but more so in the past few days. As she looked into the mirror the next morning, she pinched herself to see if she were dreaming. Did she really tell Noah she would be his girl, just the day before?

Why did she do that? How could she lead him on this way?

"Ugh!" she screamed out to herself. "What have you done?"

The day before was so wonderful Brendy wanted to live for the moment and not worry about what was to come in the days and weeks ahead, but now that she had slept on it, she realized that Noah was going to be leaving in four days thinking she belonged to him. He would go back to the hospital and make a lot of nurses unhappy because he would be off-limits. What if she ruined his chance of finding the woman God wanted him to spend his life with? Was that fair to him?

Brendy walked to the kitchen and got out the box of pancake mix. It was nice, cooking in her own kitchen, with the sun streaming in from the outside, nothing like Spanish Harlem. She dreaded the day Jasper would show up and she would have to leave, but for now, she would enjoy the time she had. Hopefully it would be several months before he returned.

She wasn't looking forward to hurting Noah. She prayed that when he read the letter she sent him and had a few weeks to ponder it, he would have enough love in his heart to forgive her.

It seemed so strange to her, that out of all the men in the world, only one man was Noah's enemy. The same man who grew up with him was the same man who tore him apart from his first love, and could very well be the one who caused him to never look at her the same again.

Brendy heard Noah's car leave for the hospital to visit Edith. She'd told him the night before that she was going to stay home today and mess around the house some. The main house couldn't get any cleaner than it already was, and her apartment sparkled as well.

After she ate breakfast and finished the dishes, she packed a few things in a shoulder bag, including a Karen Kingsbury book that Connie let her borrow, and set off to the back yard to the trail that would lead her to the stream and the hammock under the trees.

Everything was beautiful by the stream, just the way it had been the last time she'd made her way here. Brendy lay back in the hammock and opened the book to read. It felt great to have time to enjoy life. Since she'd given her heart to Jesus, everything seemed so much brighter; she wasn't afraid of Caroline Reese anymore. If, by some slim chance, Caroline ever found out about her whereabouts, she would go to the law and get a restraining order; no one was going to tell her what to do, or treat her as if they owned her.

The only person she had to answer to was God, and for the rest of her life she never intended to let Him down as she had before. She knew from time to time she would stumble, but she would never again fall so far she couldn't claw her way out.

*****

"I'm proud of your progress, Mom, you're doing great." Noah sat beside Edith in the hospital room. "Your doctor seems to think you will be able to go home Monday, but you are going to have to take it easy for a few weeks, is that understood?"

Edith smiled at her son. "Since when did you become my boss?" she teased.

"Since you had a heart attack."

"I guess, because you are a doctor, you think you know everything?" Edith giggled. She loved it when Noah tried to take care of her. He was so much like his father.

"If I were a heart doctor I would say yes, but in this case, I am not. Now, if you were having female problems or having a baby, I would be your man."

Edith reached over and patted Noah's hand. "Out of all the different kinds of doctors, why did you pick an OB/GYN?"

"The female anatomy has always interested me." Noah rolled his eyes and made Edith laugh and then moan out from the pain.

"Oh son, don't make me laugh; it hurts when I laugh."

"Sorry, Mom. The truth is, I absolutely love bringing babies into this world. There's something about following a woman's progress almost from conception to birth. To be able to witness the joy the father and mother share when they see what they created together out of love. Unfortunately, so many nowadays having babies, the father is nowhere to be found, and the mother is just a baby herself."

"Have you had anymore time to think about what you intend to do?"

"You mean about staying in Pittsburgh or coming back to Summersville?"

"Yep, that's what I mean."

"I'm still weighing my options. As it is, I have obligations to my patients in Pittsburgh for the next several months. I know it isn't necessary that I see them through to the end; there are many good doctors there; it's just the way I am."

"I understand. Have you made yourself clear to Brendy that you love her?"

"I have. I asked her yesterday as we were walking to be exclusive to me."

Edith smiled. "And what did she say?"

"She says she isn't interested in being exclusive to anyone just yet,but that I didn't have to worry; she wouldn't be dating anyone else. I'm counting on the phone and texting to be enough for a while."

"I guess this means we will see you more than once a year now?"

"Yes, there is no way I would wait a year to come back. I will be back at Christmas for sure, but don't tell Brendy; I want to surprise her. In fact, don't tell anyone."

"Oh, I just love it when I am the only one that knows a secret."

"You have known quite a few in your time," Noah laughed.

"Yep, I sure have. You used to come up to me and say, Mommy, if I tell you something bad I did, do you promise not to tell Daddy?"

Noah chuckled, remembering. "I have no idea why I didn't want you to tell Dad; he was such a pushover."

"He was at that. I sure wish he could have lived long enough to see his grandbabies. Beth sure is special."

"She is, looks just like her mother and acts just like her father."

"You got that right. Anyway, you know, you do not have to come and see me every single day; I'm perfectly fine. What is Brendy doing today?"

"I'm not sure. She said she wanted to mess around the house."

"Then why don't you go mess around with her?"

Noah rolled his eyes, "And what do you mean by that?"

Edith slapped at him, "Not what you're thinking, young man. You have spent much of your life with me, and you talk to me daily. You have just met your future wife, so go and find her; see what she is doing and have a good time."

"Future wife? You sound so sure of yourself."

"It has been confirmed; now go, before I do something drastic."

"Drastic? Like what?"

"I am not sure, but if you give me time, I will think of something."

*****

Brendy had read twelve Chapters by the time she started back. Evening had approached, and she was already anticipating what she would fix for dinner. Sloppy Joes and French fries sounded easy enough, and, if she could catch Noah in time, she could invite him as well.

"You must have been down at the creek," Greg said, as Brendy rounded the corner of the barn.

"I have. I've been down there reading; it's so peaceful there."

"It is. There are a lot of peaceful places on this ranch. How did you like the cabin?"

"Oh, I loved it; it's my favorite place in the world."

"Me too. We have a lot of memories up there."

"That's what Noah told me. You have a great family; I thank you all for making me feel so welcome."

"Well, you are quite welcome. You know, Mom and Dad deeded each of us kids part of this ranch, and that mountain with the cabin belongs to Noah."

"Is that so? Too bad he never gets use of it."

"I have a strange feeling that he won't be in Pittsburgh forever, not now that you're here in Summersville."

Brendy laughed. "So it might take me to make him return to his roots?"

"It might. Of course, if it does, we will welcome him back with open arms; it has never seemed right here without him."

"I can imagine. You have a wonderful brother."

"Yes, he's the best."

"Well, I guess I better head up the hill. It was nice talking to you."

"You too," Greg smiled, and returned back inside the barn.

Brendy could see Noah's car sitting in the driveway and wondered what he was up to. She wanted so badly to go into the house and invite him to come and eat with her, but knew that might upset Connie, who was supposed to be cooking for the family tonight. Maybe she would just go to her apartment and hope he showed up like he had a couple of nights before.

As she entered the bottom door and started up the stairs, her heart dropped; she heard a noise and realized someone was inside her apartment. Her first thought was that Jasper Logan was back. But why would he have come back this soon and in broad daylight? Surely, he wasn't that bold.

Brendy opened the door to her apartment slowly to peek inside. She smiled when she saw Noah sitting at her bar working on a laptop. He had no idea she was watching him. He was so handsome sitting there, and she wondered what he was up to.

"Do you always enter into people's homes when they aren't there?"

Noah jumped with fright and laughed. "You scared me."

"Not before you scared me." She walked in and closed the door. "What are you up to?"

"I was hoping to find you here, to show you your new toy I bought for you, but you weren't here so I couldn't wait. I hope you aren't upset that I let myself in."

"Not at all, I was only joking, but what do you mean, my new toy?" Brendy walked over and looked at the pink laptop that now lay open in front of him.

"I am trying to get this thing working so you will have the Internet. Have you ever used a computer before?"

"I know this is going to sound crazy, but no."

Noah laughed, "I thought as much, but there is really nothing to it. I have also made you an email account in case you want to write more than just a few texts; it makes it easier."

"I see." Brendy kept looking at the laptop, as if it were a foreign object.

Noah leaned way back and watched her, wondering what was in her mind. "Are you upset with me that I bought this? Maybe I am overstepping here; I'm just trying to think of ways you and I can stay connected, after I'm gone."

"No, I'm not upset at all. In fact, if I don't seem excited, it's because I don't know what to say. That is such an expensive gift."

"I figure, if I were here, I would spoil you rotten and take you out as much as possible, and since I'm not, I am really saving tons of money."

Brendy laughed. "Oh, so that beautiful pink laptop is nothing compared to what you would have done if we could actually date?"

"That's right."

"Well, in that case, how can I refuse?"

"Would you like me to show you how to use it?"

"If you don't, I will never use it," she laughed. "But first, let me fix us some dinner, and afterwards, you can have my undivided attention."

"Wonderful, so what's for dinner?"

"Sloppy Joes and French fries; my cooking ability is limited."

"That works for me. Would you like some help with anything?"

"Nope, I think I have it covered." Brendy walked over to the refrigerator and took out the ground beef to start cooking. Everything had worked out the way she wanted. Noah Garrett was eating dinner with her again, and afterwards they would spend time together. It couldn't have worked out better if she'd planned it all herself.

Chapter 23

Noah loved watching Brendy cook, even if it was sloppy Joes and French fries she put on a cookie sheet and placed in the oven. Just watching her make her way around the kitchen made his heart soar.

It was easy for Noah to imagine them, later in life in their own home, with children running under their feet. He had no idea how the dream he held in his heart would come about, but he knew it would, if he spent the rest of his life trying to make it happen.

"Have you ever given any thought to having children some day?" Noah asked.

Brendy turned around and looked at him and laughed. "Now, that was random."

"I guess, as an obstetrician, I wonder about things like that."

"A few days ago, my answer might have been no, but now I think I would like to have children, yes."

"Why now?"

"Because now, God has changed my life. Now maybe I can be a good parent; at least, better than my mother was."

"Do you remember your old address when you were with your mother?"

"I do. It's the old house my grandparents used to live in, why?"

"Do you think she still lives there?"

"My mother? Why would it matter?"

"Brendy, I know you don't want to hear this, but you owe it to yourself to find out about your mother. She cannot hurt you anymore; you are a grown woman. It just seems that you would benefit if you wrote her a letter and poured your heart out to her and told her how you felt."

"I wouldn't know where to start. Forgiving my mother will be the hardest thing for me; I am not sure I can."

"You can. I have faith in you. Brendy, forgiving is the first step in healing. And who knows, maybe your mother has changed too, after all these years, but she didn't know where to find you."

Brendy sighed. "I don't know, Noah; I'll give it some thought."

"Please do. I truly believe that, when you pour out your heart to her, a heavy weight will be lifted, and hopefully, she will answer."

"What if she has moved or died?"

"You won't know until you try."

"Maybe you're right. Maybe the only way to move on will be to leave the past in the past, and the only way to do that is to tell my mother how I feel and forgive her, but I know in my heart that it certainly won't be easy."

After they had eaten dinner and washed the dishes, they spent the next two hours going over everything on Brendy's new computer. Noah even set her up a Facebook account. Brendy figured it would be okay, because no one in New York knew her as Brendy Blake; she was always known as Sasha, and the girls she knew never touched a computer.

"Would you like to search and see if your mother has a Facebook account?" Noah asked.

"I'm sure she doesn't; she's probably still drinking up every penny she has and doesn't have the money for a computer or the Internet."

"Let's at least try; if she does, she will never know you looked, unless you friend-request her. What's her name?"

"Louise Blake." Brendy watched as Noah put the name into the search engine. "There are six Louise Blakes. Where does she live?"

Brendy felt a chill go through her; surely one of these six weren't her. "She lived in Magnolia, Delaware."

Noah typed in more letters and then moved back for Brendy to take a close look. "Is that her?"

Brendy got close to the screen and took a good look at the woman that stared back at her. A woman that looked every bit as old as fifty-five, yet Brendy knew she was only thirty-eight. "Oh my god, that's my mother!" Brendy placed her trembling hands over her mouth.

Noah got off the bar stool and wrapped his arms around her. "It's okay, baby; she can't hurt you anymore. It says she is married. Was she married when you left?"

"No, she had never been married, not even to my father."

Noah turned back toward the screen. "Let me show you something. All you have to do is click here where it says message, and it will send a message straight to her. You can wait to see what her reply is, or even if she sends a reply, before you actually friend-request her. That is, if you want to. That will be up to you."

"Noah, I thought I would be writing her a letter; this is so soon."

"No one is rushing you. Take your time. This way, even if she has moved from that certain address, you know she will get your message. At least she still lives in Delaware."

"I just can't believe she has a Facebook, which means she has a computer. And she is married, too. My gosh." Brendy looked as though she was in shock.

"Brendy, a lot can happen to a person in six years."

"Almost seven now, I am almost twenty-three," Brendy smiled.

"Oh, really? When's your birthday?"

"August the fifteenth."

"I'll have to remember that," he winked. "So, as I was saying, a lot can happen in seven years. Maybe she got help, who knows? She doesn't look that bad in the picture; she actually looks happy."

Brendy was trying not to look at the picture; the less she saw of her mother, the better off she would be. "Give me time, Noah, I promise I will message her. I just really need to think about what I'm going to say and how I'm going to say it."

"I understand. I'll not rush you, and you are right. You need to think about the way you say things. When you are done, go back and reread it to make sure it is how you want it before you click send; once you click that, there is no changing anything or no turning back. I'm going to be praying, Brendy. I'm going to pray that God heals your heart, and that if your mother isn't already close to God that He draws her near."

Noah took her in his arms and kissed her goodnight before he left. It made him feel great to see the response he got from her each time their lips met. He hated leaving Summersville after such a short time, but at least he was leaving feeling confident that she was going to give him the chance he asked for.

*****

Brendy tossed and turned all night. Each time she dozed off to sleep she dreamed of her mother yelling at her and calling her names. Names a child should never have been called. So many times she woke up during the night, covered in a cold sweat, thinking of her mother. What would she say; how would she even begin?

Brendy got out of bed and dragged her tired body to the pink laptop that still sat on the bar, turned on. With one touch of her finger, it came alive, and her mother stared her in the face. Noah left it to this page for a reason, she thought. But of course he did. Her writing her mother meant a lot to him. He truly believed that everything would be okay once she poured out her heart,yet Brendy didn't feel so sure.

"What happened to you,Louise?" Brendy whispered.

Brendy got up to start the coffee; she wanted to be alert to think about what she needed to say. It might as well be sooner than later; it would drive her crazy knowing she had promised she would write to her mother, and then constantly putting it off. She might as well get it over with.

After she poured herself a cup of coffee and got comfortable on the barstool, she clicked on message as Noah had shown her. Brendy had never typed on a keyboard before.

She knew she would be slow, but she had all day and figured it just might take that long.

Louise,

I honestly don't know where to begin and I have no idea why I sit here now writing to you except for the fact a very dear man I know seems to think it will bring me closure, and that is something I desperately need in my life.

I was quite shocked to see you have a Facebook, which means you must have a computer and the Internet, does that mean you actually have a job and are not drinking up your income?

Seven years have passed since I left that stormy night. I'll never forget it. After I planned on leaving I had to wait for weeks until a storm hit. I wanted to make sure you didn't hear me; I couldn't bear to be beat anymore than I had been since your parents died.

I'd been stealing money out of your purse for months. It took me a while to save up even a hundred dollars because you never had more than a few at a time. You were drinking badly that Friday night. Fridays were always the worst, perhaps because it was payday for you? You would spend most of it on booze then feel guilty and come home and take it out on me.

I walked two miles in the pouring rain to the bus stop. No one questioned my age, I looked eighteen instead of sixteen, always have looked older than I was. I took a bus to New York, I figured it would be easy to get a job there in the big city, but I was wrong.

I lived off the streets for weeks, digging food out of garbage cans and living in a back alley under a deck in a cardboard box. You don't know what it's like to eat other people's leftovers; you'd be amazed at what people waste.

Thankfully a man that ran the diner there noticed me and allowed me to come inside and wash up in his bathroom. He fed me and gave me a job. He even allowed me to sleep in his stock room; I was grateful.

Here I was, sixteen years old and I had nothing. But at least I wasn't on the streets anymore and I wasn't getting beaten each day when I had done nothing to deserve it.

I have lay awake at night and often wondered why you used me as a punching bag? What did I ever do to you that made you hate me so?

You never hit me until your parents died. After that I lived in pure hell. I hated you Louise, I hated you with everything I had in me. I hated God too, and after a while I stopped believing in Him altogether. Why would I believe, He'd never done anything for me, right? All those nights I lay under my bed shivering and praying to Him asking Him to help me, He never came, yet the abuse continued day after awful day.

As much as I want to tell you that I still hate you, I can't. I can't because I read in the Bible that God won't forgive me if I can't forgive you; crazy, isn't it?

Yes. I do believe in God now. I finally accepted Him as my Savior and for the first time in my life things are looking up. I no longer blame Him for what happened to me. He never caused you to hit me; that was a choice you made.

I have no idea what life is like for you now. It saddens me to think that you and I never really knew each other. There were no mother-daughter hugs or bedtime stories; all there were was fear and darkness.

I see that you are married now. I hope that you love this man and are not just using him for his money, for I can't imagine, for the life of me, you even knowing what love is.

I went to church the other day the first time in my life. I pray that if you have never been that, one day, you get the courage too.

I hope you know that forgiving you is one of the hardest things I have ever done, and Louise, I have done more than most. I no longer wish to have flashbacks and nightmares and wake up screaming in the night, remembering the pain I endured from your anger. No child should have to live through that. No child deserves that.

Instead I am now giving it all to God. I forgive you, Louise, even though you never asked and probably never will. It doesn't matter, it's over...finished.

I guess I will end this letter here. I can't imagine the anger you may feel towards me when you get it, but I hope you realize I never once deserved your punishments, and running away was the only thing I had left that I could do.

I pray that God touches your life the way He has mine.
Brendy

Brendy read and reread the letter many times during the course of the day, correcting mistakes and changing little things here and there; it had to be just right. Finally, around noon, Brendy took a deep breath and clicked the send button. There it was, gone to Magnolia, Delaware just by the click of a button. Wasn't the Internet amazing?

Brendy wondered how long it would be before her mother replied, or if she would reply at all. Perhaps she would read it and say a few choice words and then delete it, never thinking about it again. Oh well, what did it matter? She had spoken her piece and told her mother the truth about how she felt and what happened on the night she ran away. The only thing she had not spoken of was Caroline Reese, and Brendy wasn't sure she ever wanted to speak of that again. Besides, it wasn't her mother's business anyway.

*****

"Something smells wonderful. What are you cooking?" Brendy sniffed, coming into the kitchen of the main house.

"It's homemade vegetable soup; I'm sure it isn't as good as Edith's, but maybe it's edible." Rene smiled, stirring the soup and sampling just a tiny taste.

"What are you doing, Aunt Brendy?" Beth asked, from the table, where she was coloring a picture of Joseph and the coat of many colors.

Brendy looked in Rene's direction, and Rene smiled. "I hope you don't mind. I told her she could call you Aunt Brendy; we are all family here."

"I was just coming in to see if anything needs to be done in the house today. What are you doing? That's a very pretty picture you have there."

"It's Joseph, and see his coat here? It's got all the colors of a rainbow. Joseph's daddy gave him this coat because he was his favorite. His brothers hated Joseph, though,' cause they was jealous of him."

"Is that so? I guess I have a lot still to learn about the Bible." Brendy rubbed Beth's head and walked over to the stove beside Rene.

"So, are you going to be eating in here tonight or at your place?" Rene asked.

"Does it bother you when I eat there?"

"Of course not. Besides, you have been keeping Noah company, and I have never seen him so happy." She grinned.

"Well, this smells so good; I think I will eat in here tonight, if you don't mind. Looks like you have plenty."

"We do, and that would be fine. All I have left to do is make some cornbread, and we're all set."

"Have you heard from Edith today?"

"Yes, Beth and I went to see her this morning. I got permission from the doctor to let Beth in. They are not fond of little ones going in, but they said it was okay. Taking away Grammy from Beth is like taking away nuts from a squirrel."

"I know Edith has missed her; every time I have gone to see her, she always asks about her."

"Edith is doing okay this morning. Beth and I stayed until Noah got there. I don't think Noah has missed one day so far."

"He hasn't, but then that's why he extended his vacation another week."

Rene chuckled, "That's not the only reason, and you know it. Edith just gave him an excuse to do what he wanted to do all along."

"Maybe that's true," Brendy agreed. "But it was still awful that Edith had a heart attack."

"Oh, I agree. And it's going to be very hard for her to take it easy for a few weeks when she gets back. I am still contemplating on whether I should keep sending Beth to my mom's each day or let her stay here with Edith."

"You know, Rene, Beth might just keep Edith company. Why don't you wait and play it by ear? I will be here to do things in the house, and Beth could keep her from getting bored to death."

"We can color pictures together, Mommy," Beth said, eavesdropping into the conversation.

"We'll see what Grammy wants to do first, okay?"

"Okay, Mommy, but you know what she will say; she loves me a whole lot."

Rene laughed, "You're right, sweet pea, you are so right."

*****

Dinner went well and everyone took a fit over Rene's soup, telling her it was just as good as Edith's, but Rene knew better.

Brendy loved seeing Rene and Greg together and wondered if they ever argued. Surely, no couple got along as well as they seemed to without some sort of conflict every now and again.

She wondered how much Greg and Noah were alike. All three boys resembled each other, yet each had their own uniqueness and personality.

Noah loved watching Brendy converse with his family; it was like she'd always been here, always been as much a part of the Garretts as he was. What would have happened to her if he'd not given her a ride that day? Where would she be today?

If fate was as real as Noah thought it was, he felt that even if they had not met that day they would have met sooner or later. Somehow, God would have found a way to place them in each other's path.

He loved watching her with Beth, and Beth seemed to have fallen in love with her as much as he had. Brendy was great with kids, and he knew she would make a wonderful mother someday. His plans he secretly carried now were going to be great, what a surprise for Brendy. He only hoped she was as excited about them as he was.

Chapter 24

Brendy paced back and forth wanting to turn on the computer the next morning. It was driving her crazy, wondering if her mother had responded to her message, yet she couldn't bear to find out.

Even though she'd sat for a couple of hours the night before with Noah, on the front porch swing, she had not told him she'd actually written to her mother. She decided to wait and see if she wrote back, and then show him both at once.

It didn't bother her to show her letter to Noah; in fact, she wanted to. Perhaps if she showed him, he might understand her a little better. He wanted a glimpse inside and she'd only allowed him a tiny window. As for now, she couldn't imagine ever allowing him more, but she knew in her heart that a day would come when he would know everything; that would be the only way to keep Jasper from blackmailing her: to tell Noah the truth, every last ugly detail of it.

The sun was raging high in the sky before Brendy mustered the courage to turn on the computer. To her surprise, a number one showed up in the top left hand corner indicating a message. She felt her heart start thumping harder in her chest. Her mother had written her back? Perhaps she was taking this opportunity to scream and cuss at her like always, telling her what a terrible child she'd been, especially for leaving at sixteen when she was finally old enough to get a job and help with the bills.

Slowly she clicked the number one, and the same screen she'd written her mother on popped up. It was Lousie Blake's message board, and there it was, a letter her mother had actually taken the time to write. Brendy quickly scanned the time it was written. Her mother had written her around midnight the night before. The same time Brendy was having trouble falling asleep, her mother was in Delaware answering her letter.

Brendy,

I am sure when you read this letter you are probably not going to believe a word of it, but here goes...first of all I have to say I cried when I received your message, so many years have passed and I thought I would never hear from you again.

You have every right to feel the way you do about me. I imagine I was quite terrible to you. Honestly I only remember bits and pieces of my life back then because I stayed intoxicated most of that time.

Brendy, it could have been weeks before I realized you were gone. I guess I thought you were hiding from me like you always did. But then I guess if I had been in your shoes I would have hid too. I never told the police you were missing; I had no idea what to tell them, you left because I was abusive.

I have no excuse for doing to you what I did. You never knew the real Louise. My parents knew the real me when I was younger, back before they died and I started drinking so bad. I guess I chose the bottle instead of dealing with all the pain I felt faced with. The pain of losing my parents and the man I loved, your father; and I resented being left alone.

I know now that I was never alone, I had you and I should have cherished you but I resented you instead. I felt that you were a burden to me; a responsibility that I couldn't handle nor wanted to handle.

Brendy, I need to tell you something that I never thought I would be able to tell another soul for so long. I didn't work in the diner like you thought; I was a prostitute for years, selling my body for the rent and a bottle of booze. Then I got on drugs and there was no turning back. It's a terrible life to live, and now I realize you were better off without me. I was neither a good mother nor role model and I am glad you didn't witness the worst of me.

About a year after you left I was arrested for dealing drugs and sent to prison for two years, after that I had to do a year of rehab. Rehab changed my life...sure, I had not done alcohol or drugs in the two years I was in prison but rehab kept me off of them after I got out of prison.

I met my husband in Rehab; he was and still is a counselor there. He is a reformed alcoholic himself and now he spends his life helping others. He was a Godsend to me. Not only did he help me through out that year with my addictions, but he also taught me about God and I too accepted Him as my Savior a couple of years ago.

I fell in love with Michael from the beginning, I like to think he fell in love with me that quickly too, but in actuality it took him a bit longer. We have been married now a little over a year and things are good between us. It's amazing what kind of life you can have when you put God first. I only wish I had done this years ago and maybe then I could have saved us.

I used to sit in prison and think about you, wondering where you went and what your life was like. I'm sorry you have struggled so. After I found God in Rehab I started praying for you daily, that wherever you were God would take care of you and protect you.

I don't know what to say except to tell you how very sorry I am that I did that to you. You never deserved it as you said and you are right. No child deserves that, it was never your fault, it was all mine. I know you said that you forgave me, but I hope by me asking it myself you not only find it in your heart to forgive but maybe you can give me another chance?

I know I don't deserve a second chance, and I can never go back and make up for all those years you had to hide from me, but I pray that we can stay in touch here on face book and finally get to know one another, like we never have.

I would love to hear about your life now...are you still working in the diner in New York? If you never answer me again I will understand, but I promise to answer you each time you write to me. Who knows maybe someday we can actually see each other, I know with God anything is possible, and I am so glad you have God in your life.

Louise

Brendy realized her face was covered in tears, and she used the palms of her hands to wipe them away. She read the letter four times thinking perhaps she'd overlooked something, but she hadn't; it was all there. Her mother had also been a prostitute. Like mother like daughter. The apple doesn't fall far from the tree.

The letter was nothing like Brendy thought it would be. Instead of bad language and ridicule it was warmth and compassion. Her mother actually told her she was sorry. She was still living in Delaware and married to a drug abuse counselor, and more than anything else, what shocked her was the fact that she was no longer addicted to anything, and was living a happy life as a Christian. That was living proof people could change if they wanted to,if they allowed God to move in and take control.

Brendy poured herself a glass of water and looked out the window to the barn below. She could see Brad riding towards the barn on a black horse. Life on the ranch was peaceful. It was a life she never thought she would or could ever have.

There was so much she wanted to ask her mother, but it would all come in due time. If there was one thing she'd learned in the last few days, it was to take life one day at a time, treasure every moment, and never look back.

*****

Noah hadn't seen Brendy all day when he sat at the dinner table, with the rest of the family, eating hamburgers and fries Connie had made. With only one more full day to go before he left, he had spent the day with his mother and told her he was going to spend the last with Brendy. He made plans to stop by the hospital the day after, on his way home to Pittsburgh.

"Has anyone seen Brendy today?" he asked.

"I saw her this afternoon looking out her kitchen window," Brad answered, but I haven't seen her come out all day. She usually takes walks down to the creek."

"Come to think of it, I haven't seen her in the house all day, either," Connie added, but then the house is spotless; there wasn't anything left for her to do."

Rene reached to give Beth more fries and smiled at Noah, "I bet you are really going to miss her, aren't you?"

"That's putting it mildly. Did anyone invite her to come to dinner?" Noah was having a hard time enjoying his food now, feeling guilty for not asking her to come and eat.

"Go on, big brother," Greg laughed, putting in his two cents worth. "Why don't you run and ask her to come eat?"

"She likes to be independent. I'm sure if she wanted to eat, she would have come out; she knows she is always welcome." Noah took another bite of his burger, acting as if it didn't bother him as much as it did.

Connie laughed. "Man, oh man, my big brother is finally in love again, and this time it's for real. It's written all over your face."

Noah chuckled. "Gets worse everyday."

Laughter was heard around the table. The only thing that was missing was Edith. Noah loved his family and wished he'd never left, but then he would never have met Brendy, and maybe that was God's plan all along. Now that he'd met her and she was here, perhaps God was now calling him home, back to Summersville, West Virginia, where life was simpler than in the big city of Pittsburgh.

*****

After dinner, Noah made his way outside and up the stairs to Brendy's apartment. He couldn't bear to let a day pass and not look at her face, especially with only one day left.

"Brendy, are you okay?" Noah yelled out, knocking on her door.

"Come in; it's unlocked," she called back.

Noah opened the door to find her sitting with her legs underneath her on the couch, still wearing her pajamas. "Are you okay?" He had never seen her looking so distant and far away.

Brendy jumped off the couch and ran to him, crying. He wrapped his arms around her and held her close. "What's wrong, baby, why are you shaking?"

"Oh Noah, I haven't left all day; I think I am still in shock. I just keep thinking about the past and how terrible my mother was, and what God has done in her life."

"I'm confused. Have you heard from her already? Did you write to her?"

"Come and look." Brendy pulled him toward the bar and showed him the computer, still on the same place it had been all day.

Noah sat down and started to read, first her letter to her mother, and then her mother's to her. He smiled with tears in his own eyes.

"Brendy, this is wonderful, but how do you feel about this?"

Brendy went around the bar and started the coffee. "I'm not sure, exactly. I mean I am so happy that my mother found Jesus, too, you know? It's just that there is so much to forgive."

"Are you upset that she was a prostitute?"

Brendy looked at Noah, wondering what it was he thought about that fact as well.

"No, not at all. I've made my own share of mistakes, Noah; how could I hold that against her?"

"That's good to know. So, what you are saying is that there is so much to forgive as far as the abuse?"

"Yes. And I know I do forgive her. I mean, I wrote it all in the letter, you know, but in here," Brendy touched her heart and started to cry again, "in here, it still hurts. I thought I could write her a letter and forgive her and everything would be better, yet I have sat here all day and kept thinking why couldn't she have found Jesus sooner, Noah? Why couldn't this have happened before I ran away, so I wouldn't have..." Brendy cut her words short, not knowing how to speak the ugly truth.

Noah got off the stool and took her hand in his, walking with her back to the couch. There he sat with her and held her against him, letting her cry on his shoulder.

"I'm sorry, baby. I'm sorry that your life has been filled with struggles. I don't have the answers, except to say that I believe things happen the way they do for a reason, and that our struggles make us stronger individuals and stronger Christians."

"I haven't felt very strong today, Noah. In fact, I have felt very weak. I have questioned God all day and been very bitter with Him."

"That's okay; God wants us to talk to Him. He expects us to be angry from time to time, because talking to Him means you acknowledge Him, and He loves that. It sounds to me as if you and your mother both are walking, talking testimonies for Christ."

"My mother was a prostitute, Noah; how does that make you feel?" Brendy looked Noah in the eyes, knowing that what he said would determine whether they had a future or not.

"As you said, Brendy, how can I condemn her when I have made mistakes, too? Besides, God has forgiven her, and what God has set free is free indeed."

"It just blows my mind, though, that this man would marry her knowing all the men she'd slept with."

"He must really love her, Brendy. When you love like that, it doesn't matter about the past. I'm glad your mother has found happiness. It sounds like she is doing well for herself. Are you going to write to her again, try to see if you can build a relationship?"

"I've been thinking about that all day. If I continue to write to her, at some point she is going to want to see me, and I am not sure how I will handle that. When I see her face, will I run to her with open arms, or will I resent her for all those years I lived in fear?"

"Brendy, that depends on how close you two become before that meeting. Sure, if you met her today, it wouldn't be easy, but as the days roll on and you two become closer, all that pain is going to slowly, but surely, fade away, and that meeting will get easier to handle."

Brendy hugged Noah tight. "I love you, Noah; thank you for bringing me and my mother together."

Noah smiled at her for the longest. He wasn't sure if Brendy even realized what she'd said to him. "I love you, too, Brendy, more than I ever dreamed I could ever love anyone again. I'm going to miss you something terrible when I leave here, day after tomorrow."

Brendy had not realized she'd said those words until they were already out, and she couldn't take them back. But she did love Noah, right? She loved him with every fiber of her being and wanted to spend the rest of her life with this man, the first man to ever treat her with respect and kindness. She dreaded the days and weeks ahead, and that dreaded day when he would finally learn the awful truth about her, that she, too, had been a prostitute. She wondered then if he would still feel the same, especially when he learned that the man she'd spent the most time with had been his best friend.

"I'm going to miss you too, Noah. More than I thought possible."

Noah pulled Brendy close and kissed her. Each time she was in his arms he wanted to melt there with her. It took all the strength he had, not to carry her to bed and make love to her. Noah promised God long ago that he would never go that route again; that, if given another chance, he would do things God's way, not his way.

Noah pulled away and chuckled. "I'm sorry. You would think awful of me at times, if you only knew what went through my head."

Brendy smiled. "Oh Noah, you are only human, and I think quite the opposite. I love you so for treating me with respect; no one has ever done that before."

"That's because you were with creeps," he joked.

"You can say that again. So, how was your mother? I'm sorry I haven't asked before now."

"She was great. In fact, I don't see any reason they won't allow her to come home Monday. I wish I could stay longer, but I can't."

"I am sure she understands. You have practically stayed all day everyday since she has been in the hospital."

"I stayed longer today because I don't plan to go tomorrow."

"Oh, why is that?" Brendy asked curiously.

"Because tomorrow is my last full day, and I am taking you whitewater rafting at the Gauley River."

"I thought you said I wasn't ready for that yet."

"Oh, you're ready," he laughed. "We are going to have the time of our lives. I have already called ahead and gotten us tickets with a group. It's better to have a guide, and safer. The Gauley is ranked seventh in the world's raftable rivers. We like to call it The Beast of the East."

"The Beast of the East, and you are taking me there?" Brendy looked terrified.

Noah laughed. "You will be fine; you will have on a life jacket and be okay. I will be right beside you."

"If you say so." She loved the way Noah planned out their days; she had never been disappointed.

"So, are you okay now, I mean about your mother?"

"I'll be okay. Just had a lot on my mind. I will wait until you leave before I write her back, but I will write her back, I promise."

"You don't owe me anything, Brendy. You do what's in your heart, but I think you two have already taken a huge step; it would be a shame not to see where it could lead you."

"I know; you are right. I am curious, myself. Thank you for what you did for me."

"I didn't do anything. You are the one who wrote her."

"But you got me a computer, got me on the Internet, and showed me Facebook. Without that, I never would have made contact with her."

"Yes, you would have, just in a different way. God already had this planned. He works all things to His good, even something like this."

Brendy smiled and kissed him lightly on the lips. "He does, doesn't He? So what time are we leaving in the morning?"

"At eight o'clock. Our tour starts at nine."

"Why am I nervous?"

"Because you don't know what to expect, but trust me; you are going to have so much fun."

"If you say so, Noah. I can hardly wait."

Chapter 25

"We are a team here, folks," the instructor called out, as Brendy and Noah stood with seven other rafters listening to him go over everything that would be required for safety. He showed them how to put their life jackets and helmets on properly and gave them the rundown of what to expect, and what to do in case they should fall off.

It wasn't long before everyone was making their way down to where they would all get into the water. Noah assured Brendy that this was the section that everyone started with to polish their paddling skills before they tried it on the lower section. Still, Brendy was nervous. The water looked like it was moving way too fast and dangerous, and there were knots in her stomach that she'd never felt before.

"Noah, I am not sure about this," Brendy said, trembling, as she stepped into the raft.

"Are you going to be okay? We don't have to do this, you know."

Brendy looked around at the others taking their seats, excited with anticipation of what lay ahead. She took her seat and looked across at Noah.

"I'll be fine; we are a team, remember? It's just that I've never done this before."

A blonde in front of her, who introduced herself as Tina, heard her comment and looked back and smiled at her. "Trust me, you are going to have a ball; just don't get nervous. Ron is a great guide; I have been with him many times."

"Okay people, are you all ready to do some rafting?" Ron yelled out.

"Let's do it!" everyone yelled. Brendy looked over at Noah, and Noah could see that concerned look on her face, and for a moment he felt badly about asking her to do this. She looked so cute in her life jacket and helmet, and he knew that once they took off, there would be no turning back until they reached the end.

Noah smiled at her and mouthed the words, I love you.

Within a few seconds, they were off and moving down the Gauley. Ron called back and forth telling them which way to paddle. Over and over they went through areas where there were huge dips that took Brendy's breath and left them soaked from the water splashing up and over the raft.

After about ten minutes, Brendy was finally getting the hang of it and let out the breath she had been holding. Noah was right; white water rafting was incredible. There was so much she hadn't done in her life, so much she would probably never have done if it hadn't been for Noah.

At the end of the day, when the ride was finally over and they were getting out of the raft, Brendy felt breathless with sheer euphoria. How afraid she had been when it had first started, and now she couldn't wait for the day she could go again.

"So, how did you like it? You seemed to be having fun." Noah asked, on their way back to the car.

"I think that was one of the most incredible things I have ever done. It was amazing, and the scenery was awesome. Promise me that when you are here next summer we will go again."

Noah smiled, knowing she was already planning next summer. He had planned even after that.

"I promise we can go every summer, if you like it that much. I had a feeling you were going to enjoy it. So tell me, how you like Chinese?"

Brendy laughed, "What does Chinese have to do with whitewater rafting?"

"Nothing, but since it's dinner time I thought I would take you out."

"In that case, I love it. And for the record, I am starving."

"Good, I'm taking you to the Peking Chinese Restaurant. First, we are going to stop by the house and change clothes; I don't know about you, but I am soaked."

*****

The restaurant was crowded, since it was Saturday night. Noah found a private table in the corner with the lights down low. He loved watching Brendy eat, enjoying her food and talking like she'd known him all of her life.

"This is really good; thank you for bringing me here."

"I'm glad you like it. I wanted to take you somewhere nice tonight."

"Noah, you have done so much for me over the past three weeks. I want you to know that I enjoy just being with you. You never have to do anything to entertain me, honest."

"If I could be with you all the time, I would take you somewhere nice or somewhere entertaining all the time; not because I think I have to, but because I want to."

"This is a personal question, but I have to ask before you leave here tomorrow." Brendy took a bite of her sesame chicken, and chewed slowly, trying to think of a way to ask.

"Okay, so let me have it; I can't wait to hear the question."

Brendy smiled. "You asked me to be yours, exclusively. I was just wondering how many nurse's or doctor's hearts you are going to break when you get back to Pittsburgh, and you let everyone know that you are taken."

Noah chuckled and drank a sip of his iced tea. "Several, why?"

"So, out of that several, there was not one single person you wanted to be exclusive with?"

"No, absolutely not. I'm not looking for a good time; I'm looking for a lifetime. I think I have found that in you."

"You think I'm someone you really want to spend your life with?"

"I know you are."

"No matter what my past holds, right?"

"That's right. I just have to convince you that you want the same thing."

Brendy smiled at his comment, knowing that he might not feel the same if he had any idea what the truth really was.

"So, can you tell me what her name is?" Brendy loved teasing around with Noah.

"Excuse me?"

"Her name, the one whose heart you are going to break. Surely,there is one above the rest who has her heart set on you."

"Her name is Candace Wright. She is a doctor at Magee's."

Brendy laid down her fork and stared him in the eyes. "Are you serious, or did you just make up a random name?"

Noah had to laugh at her comment. "You asked me, and I told you the truth. Her name is Dr. Wright. I have dated her a few times, but it never went any further than just friendship. I'm sure she would like it to go further, but I knew that it never could."

"Why is that?" Brendy was eager to know everything about Candace Wright,not because she was jealous, but because she didn't want to make the same mistakes.

"Because she is stuck on herself and her title. She is very beautiful, but she is also very self-centered. That is not attractive to me."

"So, why do you date her?"

"Because she is a friend and colleague. I am not dating her exclusively. I date others as well."

"And how many others is that?" Brendy asked curiously.

"Are you jealous?" Noah loved this conversation and the fact that he had nothing to hide.

"No, I just find it very interesting that you have all these wonderful females, yet you still asked me to be exclusive. You do know that I will never know what you do in Pittsburgh. How will I know if you date anyone else?"

"First of all, all these females are *not* wonderful or I would already be in love with one of them. Second of all, you are right; you might not know what I am doing in Pittsburgh, but you better believe that I won't be dating another woman. If there is one thing about me that you will find out, it's that I am a man of my word."

Brendy shook her head and sighed. "Poor Candace Wright, I can't imagine how you will break the news to her."

"I'm sure she won't take it easy," he teased, knowing he spoke the truth more than he cared to think about. If there was one thing he dreaded almost as much as he knew he would miss Brendy, it was telling Candace that he was now off-limits to her.

*****

Noah placed his suitcases in his car before daylight and looked up at the apartment above the garage. The lights were off, and his heart had never felt so heavy. He wanted so badly to tell her goodbye before he left but didn't want to wake her.

He'd told her goodbye the night before and kissed her one last time. If he closed his eyes, he could still taste her lips upon his. How sweet was her kiss; it made him hungry for more.

He stood at his car before opening his door and looked back at the huge house he'd grown up in. Not only would he miss Brendy, he would really miss his family and the ranch this time, maybe more now than ever. Never had he had such a strong pull to be back and spend the rest of his days here on this land where he'd left his heart years ago, to be with the woman he wanted to grow old with.

Noah opened the door and climbed inside. In just a few minutes, the sky would start to grow brighter, and daylight would be upon them. He would stop by the hospital for a quick goodbye and be headed back to Pittsburgh.

He'd cranked his car and started to back out when he saw Brendy running towards him, wearing a light pink housecoat. Noah stopped the car and got out, meeting her halfway. Brendy threw her arms around him and hugged him tightly.

"You were trying to sneak off without saying goodbye to me?" She breathed heavily from the jog across the driveway.

"I didn't want to wake you."

"Noah, don't you ever do that again, do you hear me?"

Noah laughed at her. "Yes, ma'am, I promise that I will never do that again. Now give me one more kiss before I start on my journey."

Brendy pressed her lips gently to his; she wanted her last kiss to last longer than any she'd ever shared with him. She hoped he felt the love she had for him just by touching her lips to his. She prayed that when he left her, he would only have to close his eyes and remember her embrace, and that would be enough to carry him through the weeks and months ahead. She also prayed that it would be enough when the day came that he would learn the truth about her, and that love would win over hurt and pain.

"I love you, Brendy Blake," Noah whispered.

"And I love you, Noah Garrett. Please drive safely and stay in touch with me."

"Are you serious? I am going to drive you nuts." Noah kissed her once more on top of her forehead, and then wiped the tears out of her eyes. "I will be back as soon as I can; in the meantime, enjoy your new life here and your new relationship with Christ. Make everyday a fresh new beginning."

After one last hug, Brendy stood in the driveway and watched Noah until the lights of his car were out of sight and headed out of town.

Three weeks ago, she had no intention of falling in love with Noah Garrett. Three weeks ago, she never would have dreamed that a man actually existed that would be so God-centered and treat her with such respect. Nor could she have imagined that his same God would also forgive her and give her a new life, a new beginning. And as she stood for the longest time, now looking out at the long empty driveway, she realized she had been given her first chance at love and her second chance to do things right this time.

As she felt the loneliness set in, without Noah, she smiled through teary eyes because no longer would she ever be alone, for now she had God, and as she had been told often the past three weeks, with Him she could face anything.

*****

"It's so great to be home," Edith said as she made her way slowly into the house, with Connie right behind her.

Brendy hugged Edith and helped guide her to the couch. "It's good to have you home."

Edith looked around the house and whistled. "Goodness Brendy, this place looks amazing! You have made it look better than I do."

"Thank you, but that's not true. Your house always looks wonderful; it was hard to tell I had done anything."

Connie laughed, "Don't listen to her, Mom; wait till you see your bedroom. And speaking of your bedroom, why don't you come on and lay down?"

Edith clucked her tongue and shook her head at her daughter. "Now, since when did you become my boss, young lady?" she teased.

"Since you parked yourself on the couch and not in the bed. Come on, you know the doctor said he was only letting you go home now, instead of a week from now, because you promised you would spend this week in bed and not do anything."

"Did I promise that?" Edith loved playing around with her daughter.

"You did, and I was sitting there when you did, so come on."

"But I want to see everyone when they get here this evening," Edith pouted.

"And you will; I think each of them know where your bedroom is." Connie walked over to Edith, ignoring her protests, and helped her off the couch and down the hallway to her bedroom. Brendy loved watching the mother-daughter love between the two and prayed that maybe someday she could be half as close to her own mother; at least they had gotten started in the right direction.

"Oh my god," Edith yelled out. Brendy took off down the hall to see what had happened.

"What's wrong?" Brendy asked, coming into the bedroom.

"My room looks absolutely gorgeous! I was dreading so badly spending an entire week in this bed,having to look around at the mess everywhere. Wherever did you put it all?"

Brendy smiled. "I'm glad you like it. It wasn't that difficult; I just organized everything."

"Well, you have a knack for organizing." Edith looked over at Connie, who placed a pitcher of ice water on her bedside table with a glass. "Could you leave Brendy and me alone for a moment?"

"Alone? Oh, we have secrets, do we?" Connie teased.

"We will have if you will leave the room."

"Okay mom, you don't have to hit me over the head with a brick. Besides, I have a riding lesson to give; I will see you later. Brendy, don't allow this woman to lift a hand, please."

"You got it," Brendy nodded.

When Connie left the room, Edith patted the bed beside her, indicating for Brendy to sit down. "I thought she would never leave. That girl has been on me like white on rice ever since the sun came up this morning. I am surprised she will even let me pick my nose."

Brendy laughed. "She just loves you; she's a good daughter."

"She is; they just don't come any better. So tell me, what all went on here when I was gone?"

Brendy giggled. "Is that all? Gosh, I thought you had some great secret to tell me."

"That will come in a bit; right now, I need to hear the gossip."

"There is really nothing to tell. Everything went great."

Edith looked puzzled. "So, all this time they have been telling me the family would completely fall apart without me, but everything was fine, no problems whatsoever?" Brendy could see the disappointment on Edith's face.

Brendy took Edith's hand and smiled at her. "It's true; everything was fine, but the house was not the same. It seemed like everyone walked around like a zombie, not knowing what to do or how to act."

"Really?" Edith half smiled. "Who did all the cooking?"

"Rene, Connie, and I took turns. It was nothing grand, like we are used to getting from you, but it was edible."

"Is that so? Well, I like to think I am good for something."

"Oh, Edith," Brendy reached over and hugged her tightly. "It just isn't the same around here without you. Thank you for letting me stay here and for coming back from Heaven for me."

"Oh baby, it was so beautiful. I will never regret dying, and I certainly won't regret coming back." Edith winked at her, and Brendy saw Edith flinch.

"Are you okay? Are you in pain?"

"Just a little. Could you give me my purse? I have some pain pills in there. I am trying hard not to take too many, but there are times I need one just to knock off the edge."

"That's understandable; there's no harm in that." Brendy helped Edith get her pills and poured her a glass of water.

"I'm going to start dinner and leave you alone to rest."

"Don't you want to hear the secret first?" Edith pursed her lips and raised her eyes, making Brendy laugh.

"Only if it's a good one."

"Noah came to see me super-early yesterday morning, and his eyes were all swollen and red from crying."

"Crying? Why was he crying?"

"I don't know. I thought perhaps you might tell me?"

"I'm not sure. I told him goodbye before the sun even came up, right before he..." Brendy stopped in mid-sentence. "Do you think he was crying because he hated to leave?"

"I am almost positive. But I think it was because he hated to leave you."

"I cried, too." Brendy chuckled. "Dang, we have it bad, huh?"

"I'd say. I am not sure what that boy is cooking up; he won't tell me, but I am sure it has something to do with being around you full-time."

"Edith, there are still things about me Noah doesn't know. I don't have the nerve to tell him. I don't want to lose him."

"Is it something you think he needs to know?"

"It is something he *has* to know. I just don't know how to tell him."

"Just tell him the truth. Perhaps it would be better to tell him over the phone or write him a letter than to look him in the eyes; it might be easier."

"I think you're right, and I will in due time. As for now, I am going to take care of you. Noah gave me orders to take care of you, and I don't want to be yelled at, so if you would cooperate with me you would make my job much easier."

"Okay, I will cooperate. But this staying in bed is for the birds." Edith fluffed up her pillow and let out a breath of air.

"Just this week, then we will retire you to the couch, I promise."

Chapter 26

After three weeks on the ranch wearing jeans and boots, Noah felt strange wearing his blue scrubs and tennis shoes. He would like to say he was glad to be back walking the hallways of Magee's, but his heart just wasn't in it.

He'd only been back three days and had already delivered seven babies and performed three hysterectomies. His life was never dull.

Noah told the hospital no more double shifts; there were other doctors besides him. He was tired of trying to be Superman. Besides, he wanted the time to spend talking to Brendy on the phone. He loved hearing her voice and longed for the next call each time they said their goodbyes.

Brendy was doing a great job taking care of his mom, and he could tell that their relationship was getting closer by the day. He was proud that his mother could be that for Brendy, a mother that she'd never had.

Brendy told him she'd written her mother another letter, and her mother had responded. He prayed that God would draw them near as a family, the way they should have been from the very beginning.

"It's good to have you back, Dr. Garrett," a tall blonde nurse said, walking into the nurses' station where Noah was going over charts.

"Wish I could say the same," he chuckled.

"Were your three weeks not long enough?"

"Three years would not have been long enough, I'm afraid." Noah put down the chart and looked at Amy, a young nurse, who had worked at Magee's for almost as long as he had.

Amy looked him in the eyes and smiled. "Do tell; I detect a new love interest."

"Then, you are good," Noah agreed.

"Does Dr. Wright know about this love interest?" she giggled.

"Not yet, she has been gone since I got back, but she should be in later today."

"I would sure love to be a fly on the wall to hear how this all goes down." Amy took a sip of her ice water and shuffled through a few files. "She is going to be none too happy."

"Dr. Wright is only my friend; we have never been anything more than that."

"Humph, then go tell her that. To hear her talk, you two are an item and have been for a very long time. Just ask anyone in this hospital."

"I don't care what she thinks. I have dated several women here, not just her."

Amy laughed. "I know, and she gets highly upset each time you do."

"Really? I had no idea."

"Come on, Dr. Garrett, surely you know she has the hots for you."

"But then, who doesn't, right?" Noah loved kidding around with Amy; she was one of the few who never came on to him. He enjoyed working with her.

"That's for sure. You just better be glad I am married and very in love with my husband, or I would have had my hooks in you, too."

Noah got up and spun her around, making her laugh. "You always know just what to say. It was good talking to you; I have to run and check on a patient, and hide out from the frightening Dr. Wright." Noah made a scary face and claw hands, making Amy laugh.

*****

Noah jumped, as arms wrapped around him. He hadn't heard anyone else come into the doctors' lounge; he was in a hurry to get home and make his nightly call to Brendy before she went to bed.

"Are you hiding out from me?" Candace pouted. Noah had known he would run into her sometime before he went home. Five more minutes, and he would have been out the door.

"Of course not." Noah turned around to face her and smiled down at the doctor most men would have given their eyeteeth to have. Candace was a head shorter than he, with short auburn hair and brown eyes. She was a walking billboard for beauty, but her self-centeredness had always turned Noah off.

"That's good to know. How is your mother? I heard you had to take another week because she was in the hospital."

"I did, and she's great, thanks for asking." Noah continued to take off his shoes and place them in his locker, getting out the ones he normally wore home.

Candace laughed. "Noah Garrett, since when are you in a hurry to go home?"

Candace was right. In the past, he would have sat around and talked and been in no hurry at all; after all, there had been nothing to go home to.

"I need to make a call."

"I haven't seen you in over three weeks, and your call is more important than me?" Candace hung her head to the side and poked out her lips, trying to be as seductive as possible.

"It is important." Noah grabbed his keys out of his locker and stuck them in his pocket. "In fact, at the moment, besides God, it is the most important thing in my life."

Candace smiled and walked in front of the door, blocking his exit. "Then, do tell, please. What on earth has changed you so, since you went to that one-horse town?"

Noah sighed; there was no way out of it, and why should he care? He'd never once let her believe they were anymore than friends. "I met someone, and I am going home to call her, since she lives too far away to stop in and say hello."

Candace looked mortified. "You what?"

"I met someone. It's been great talking to you, but I need to run." Noah tried to brush by her, but she wasn't budging an inch.

"You did what? Just when did you plan on telling me this?" Candace raised her voice a level and was clearly not happy with the situation.

"Since when do I have to clear my personal life with you?" Noah was becoming frustrated. He'd had a feeling she would not take the news lightly.

"Since everyone in this hospital thinks you and I are an item!"

"Candace, you are the only one in this hospital that thinks you and I are an item; everyone else just thinks you are trying to make us become an item."

Candace opened her mouth to speak and stopped, staring blankly at Noah. "What about all those dinners and the times you kissed me goodnight? I thought you cared about me."

"I do care about you, Candace, but I have dated a lot of women here at Magee's. I have never gone exclusively with anyone since I have been working here, and you know that. I am sorry if I hurt you. You know, as well as I do, that you could have anyone you wanted here, and several doctors would give anything for a date."

"Except you, right? I can't have *you,* Noah."

"I'm sorry, Candace, but no. In fact, I am not sure how much longer I will be working here."

Tears formed in her eyes as she stepped away from the door. "Go then, enjoy your phone call, but don't think you can come crawling back to me when this woman doesn't work out for you." Candace turned her back on him and crossed to the other side of the room to pour herself a cup of coffee.

Noah stood for a moment, watching her, not knowing if he should leave or try to explain. "Candace, I never meant to..." Noah was cut short by Candace's comment.

"Go Noah, just go."

Noah left the lounge and headed for the front doors of the hospital,to the parking deck. He'd known it wouldn't go down well, but he'd had no idea she would be that upset. What had he done that gave her the impression they were an item? Even their few goodnight kisses had not been anything passionate. Maybe,as a guy, he'd failed to see the signs. On a few occasions she'd invited him in, yet he'd always declined, knowing that wasn't a good idea.

He'd known from the very beginning that Candace was not someone he wanted to spend his life with. He regretted that he'd known this, yet continued to date her off and on. He should have made it clear to her that he only wanted a friendship and not a relationship, and now he felt foolish for not seeing it sooner.

As Noah drove out of the parking deck, he thought about several nurses he'd also dated. Even though he'd never done anything more than take them to a movie or to dinner, he wondered how many thought he might like them for more than just friendship? Up until now, he'd never really thought about it. The last thing he wanted to do was hurt someone; he knew all too well what that felt like.

*****

Brendy managed to keep Edith in bed as much as possible throughout the first few days. They were becoming closer, and Brendy loved the time spent with this wonderful woman of God. Each day, for several hours, they would open their Bibles and read aloud. Brendy wanted to learn as much as she could, and Edith enjoyed teaching her all she knew. Brendy was like a sponge, absorbing every word that Edith spoke.

Each night, when the sun set and the dishes were washed and dried and put away, Brendy went back to her apartment and, after a hot shower,she would crawl into bed and wait for Noah to call her.

She could imagine what his townhouse looked like. She imagined the color of his towels he used to dry off after a hot shower, and even what sort of books he liked to read. She loved it when her cell phone rang and she could hear his voice, like magic, no matter how many miles were between them; thanks to technology, he was only a phone call away.

"Hi there, pretty lady, what's going on?" Noah asked, getting comfortable on his sofa.

"Not much at the moment, just laying here in bed waiting for the phone to ring." Noah could hear the smile in her voice and knew she was as happy to be talking to him as he was to her.

"How's Mom today; she giving you fits about staying in bed?"

"I'd say; she is not one to rest, but she has done pretty well. She will lie for hours, though, when we are reading and studying the Bible."

"She does love that. She always said she loved eager young minds, so quick to learn."

"Well then, she must really love me; I hang on every word."

"That's good to hear; you will learn a lot from Mom. If there is one thing she is good at, that's knowing that Bible."

"She is at that; I have learned so much. So what about you, have you been busy today?"

"That's putting it mildly. It's always busier during a full moon. Thankfully, though, all the babies I have delivered since I've been back have all been healthy."

"That's great news. It must be devastating when something goes wrong."

"It isn't fun, that's for sure. How's the rest of the family?"

"They seem to be good. Everyone stays so busy with their jobs I hardly see anyone until suppertime."

"Your being there has made it easier on everyone, I'm sure." Noah loved talking to Brendy every evening and hearing her voice. It was almost like they were right there beside each other.

"I hope so. So tell me, I have been dying to ask all week. Have you run in to Candace Wright yet?"

Noah chuckled. "You are great at remembering names."

"Only my competition."

"I ran into her tonight, as a matter of fact."

Brendy snuggled deeper in the bed and smiled. "Oh really, do tell all."

"Well, it seems she thought we were more of an item than I thought, and she isn't too happy at the moment."

"Is Candace pretty?"

"She is beautiful, but only on the outside. I think we have gone over this before."

"Noah, if this woman cares about you, maybe you should think twice before you let her go."

Noah was quiet for a moment before he spoke again. "Where did that come from?"

"I know you always get upset when I do this, but seriously, she would make a great catch."

"I don't think so. I think you make a great catch."

"That's only because you think you know me. You have made me out to be something in your mind that I'm not."

"I may not know a lot of things about you, but I know I am in love with you. I know you are the woman I want to spend my life with."

"And so, we will have a life of phone conversations," Brendy laughed. "That should be interesting."

"It's safe," Noah teased her.

"I'd say, very safe." They both laughed. Noah loved kidding around with Brendy. She acted so much older than her age, wise beyond her years.

"So what are you going to do about Candace?" Brendy knew that Candace would make a better match than she would but couldn't bear the thought of it.

"Nothing, there is nothing to do. She will be all right. Every doctor here would love to go with her; she will find someone."

"But you aren't interested, right?" Brendy loved hearing him say it. She felt like a teenager having her first boyfriend, something she had not yet experienced.

"That's right; I'm not interested at all. But I'm very interested in a pretty young girl I met at the airport a few weeks ago."

"Oh really," Brendy giggled. "Do you think this girl is interested in you, too?"

"Oh yes, I'm almost positive she is. In fact, when I talk to her each night, I can hear that she misses me in her voice."

"Oh really, you can hear that in a voice?"

"I can. What does my voice tell you?"

"That you are a crazy man for being interesting in some young girl you just met recently when you really don't know that much about her."

"Then you aren't as good as reading voices as I am, because you are dead wrong."

"Oh well," she laughed. "I guess we can't be good at everything."

"That's true. Well, baby, it's late and morning comes early for both of us."

"Don't remind me. If I am not up by six, I'm afraid your mother will try to fix breakfast."

Noah laughed. "You are probably right about that. So what's for breakfast?"

"A glass of OJ and a bowl of cereal; I am not that great with breakfast foods."

"Well, it's better than nothing," he chuckled. "Goodnight baby, I love you and sweet dreams."

"Sweet dreams to you, too, and don't be too hard on Candace Wright."

After Brendy closed her cell phone and placed it on her bedside table, she lay back and sighed. How many more nights like this would she have before Noah learned the truth about her? How much longer could she keep up with this charade? She'd never in her life loved anyone, until Noah, and she was certain, that when it was finally all over, she would have a pain in her heart that would go with her the rest of her life.

Chapter 27

"What are you doing out of bed?" Brendy asked, as Edith came into the kitchen.

"It's been five days since I have been home and I can't take it any longer; you just have to let me do something before I go crazy."

"Noah and the rest of the family will be upset with me if they knew you were out of bed." Brendy was peeling potatoes to make potato salad for dinner, to go with the shake-and-bake fried chicken and macaroni and cheese.

"They won't be upset with you; it will be with me, and I don't care what Noah and the rest of the family think. I am fine, really. Now tell me what I can do before I pull my hair out."

Brendy laughed and got off the stool and handed Edith the potato peeler. "You can peel these potatoes and then shell the eggs; I am terrible at the eggs. I always peel the egg away with the shell."

"Watch them until they come to a boil, and time them for exactly five minutes; then take them off and place them in cold water." Edith took the peeler and grabbed a potato, happy to be able to do something.

"Is that the secret? I have been boiling them too long."

"That would do it. Have they started boiling yet?"

Brendy walked over and looked at the pot. "Not yet, but any minute now."

"Then watch them closely and the shells will fall right off, but no more than five minutes."

"I want to thank you for all you have done for me." Brendy stood at the stove and watched, knowing that a watched pot never boils.

"You have already thanked me so many times. It is I who should be thanking you; you have helped me so much with the house and waited on me hand and foot the last few days."

"It was my pleasure; I have enjoyed it."

"By the way, I have been meaning to ask you how you like the apartment, now that you have had time to stay there a while."

"Oh, I love it; it is so cute and comfortable. I am surprised no one has lived there before me."

"Nope, no one at all. I thought Connie might have moved up there after she graduated high school just to give her that sense of privacy, but she never did."

Brendy looked at the clock to time the now boiling pot. She'd learned so much from helping Edith in the kitchen, and for the past five days, she'd gone back and forth from her bedroom to the kitchen to ask questions about something she was preparing for dinner. She knew she would never be as good as Edith when it came to cooking but felt certain she would be able to cook well enough to get by.

"Well, it's a beautiful apartment and I love it. Have you heard from Noah today? He usually texts me a few times before now, but I haven't heard a word from him." Brendy was beginning to get worried. She often wondered if Jasper would skip her altogether and go straight to Noah with the truth, but why would he do that? He would miss out on torturing her a little more, making her pay for something that he was just as guilty of.

"No, come to think of it, I haven't. He usually calls me on his lunch break for a few minutes just to say hello. He knows I don't know anything about texting."

"I didn't either until he showed me. I hope nothing is wrong. I would call him but he might be in surgery, so I let him call me."

"Yeah, I'm the same way, never want to bother him so I let him call first. He stays so busy there at Magee's. I may be a little prejudiced, but I know he's one of the best doctors there. They are lucky to have him."

"He does seem like he would be a very kind and compassionate doctor." Brendy turned off the burner and removed the eggs.

"He is. In fact, it really hits him hard when something goes wrong with one of his patients or a baby is stillborn or born with complications. He treats everyone the same as if they are his own family. Other doctors have told him not to take things too personally or get too attached, but that's just Noah. It wouldn't be him if he was otherwise."

"You raised him well. He is such a wonderful man, but then, all your children are wonderful."

"Thank you, they are, aren't they? I am proud of each and every one of them. I think Brad was a bit jealous at first, of Noah, going off to school and becoming a doctor. But, of course, we would have sent Brad, too. He just chose the ranch and the horses. Did you know he is one of the best in the rodeo for this state? He is really good at what he does. Makes me crazy watching him, though; he chose such a dangerous sport."

"Noah told me he was into that, but I had no idea he was so good. I can imagine it must be very frustrating to watch."

"And Greg's heart and soul is right here on the ranch. Of course, I think each of them feels that way, but Greg has never desired to do anything other than work with horses. He is great at breaking them in. Brad tried to get him to do rodeo, too, but Greg won't hear of it; he doesn't want to take the chance that something might happen to him with his family. He and Rene are great together. They have been married seven years now. I told them they could live here in the house with me; it's not like there isn't plenty of room, but they wanted a place of their own. That's why Greg built the cabin."

"It's a nice cabin," Brendy commented. "I love the way it faces the mountains. It must be so beautiful in the fall, out on that back deck."

"Oh it is; Rene spends a lot of time there. Did you know she is an artist, too? That girl can paint like you wouldn't believe."

"I didn't know that; she never mentioned it."

"Oh she wouldn't. She doesn't like to brag, but she deserves all bragging rights; she is that good. She painted the picture behind the couch in the living room."

"She is good. I love that picture, but when I look at it, it looks so familiar."

Edith laughed. "That's because it's a picture of the mountain behind us; only it's in the fall of the year when the trees come alive with color. She gave it to me about five Christmases ago, and I treasure it."

"I can see why. Has she ever thought of selling any of her work?"

"She has from time to time. Unfortunately, she doesn't get that much time to paint. She is so busy doing trail rides and tending to Beth it keeps her hands full."

"What about Connie? What are her hobbies?" Brendy enjoyed this conversation, getting to know the family a little better through the eyes of their mother.

Edith chuckled. "I have never been too sure about her. As far as I know, her only hobby is riding horses. She's been a cowgirl since the day she was born. I would love for her to fall in love and get married and have children. I am afraid that if her Mr. Right doesn't walk right up here on the farm and face her eye-to-eye, she will never find him. She is too busy to go looking for him herself, and she hardly has any friends to hang out with; not that she would, I'm afraid. I am glad you are here. You both are so close to the same age, and I pray that you become someone she can open up to. She is very private when it comes to her feelings."

"I do like Connie, and we have become quite close." Brendy knew Connie was the only one, so far, that she had opened up to. Connie had proven that she could be trusted with a secret.

"That's good to know; she needs that. So, would you like for me to mix this potato salad together?" Edith asked.

Brendy giggled. "It might be a good idea, if you want to enjoy dinner a little better."

*****

"Don't take it so personally, Noah. You know that, in our profession, things like this happen from time to time; there is no escaping it." Candace tried to console him.

Noah looked at her with a blank stare. "I am not in the mood to hear this right now, Candace."

"To hear what, the truth?"

"Candace, a man just lost his wife and his child this morning; I am sure he isn't thinking right now that these things just happen and that this is all a part of life. If you don't mind, I would like to be left alone to grieve with him." Noah had gone to lie down in the doctors' lounge to be left alone. The morning had gone all wrong from the very beginning.

Candace shook her head. "Maybe you need to change professions,Noah; you aren't cut out for this."

Noah got up, feeling quite tired of this conversation. "Maybe I do. As for now, I think I will go home early and call it a day."

"So, instead of facing things, you are running from them," she said, matter-of-factly.

Noah did not comment on her accusation. He'd had enough trauma for one day. All he wanted was to go home and think about what had gone wrong. What could he have done differently that might have saved their lives?

Noah wasn't aware of his surroundings as he drove out of the parking deck of the hospital. He didn't see a couple of the nurses throw up their hands to wave. He didn't hear the parking assistant tell him to have a great day.

Noah's mind was only on Brendy and her smile. All he could think about was what if they'd been married and had just gone through nine months of pregnancy, so excited with anticipation, just waiting for the day their son would be born. How would he be feeling now, if he'd lost them both in one day, within a few minutes apart?

He was numb as he drove through the city on his way to Heavenly Heights, where he had lived the past few years. All he could think about was the ranch and getting back to the woman he'd fallen so in love with. He wanted to hold her in his arms and protect her, for the rest of her life.

Noah shook his head, realizing that all the protection in the world would not have stopped her or the baby from dying, if things had gone as they had this morning.

The Andrews had done everything right during their pregnancy. They had a beautiful home and successful careers. She had eaten right and taken care of herself. She never missed an appointment, and had taken her prenatal vitamins. How could everything have gone so wrong?

Noah opened his garage door and drove his car inside. All he wanted to do was take a hot shower and lie down a bit. He couldn't wait to call Brendy, just to hear her voice. It was still early yet, and he figured she would be finishing up dinner. He would wait until he knew she was back in her apartment, so he could have her undivided attention.

For now, Noah knew he needed to cry; he had felt it building all day. He made his way to his bathroom and started the shower. He needed a good cleansing to wash all the tears away.

*****

Brendy raced to the phone from her kitchen later that evening. She'd left her phone on the bed and didn't want to miss Noah's call; she'd waited on him all day and still no word. She was beside herself with worry.

"Hello?" she said, out of breath.

"God, it's so good to hear your voice. Is everything okay?"

"Everything is great, except for the fact that I have been worried about you. Usually, by now, you would have sent me a dozen text messages. Are you okay?"

Noah hesitated, and Brendy thought for a moment that they had lost their connection.

"Noah, are you there?"

"I'm here." Noah sniffled, and Brendy could tell he was crying. What on earth was wrong with this strong man to make him cry?

"Something's wrong. Tell me, Noah, what happened? Are you okay?"

Noah took a moment to contain himself. It was just so overwhelming, hearing her voice, and he thanked God for this wonderful woman, knowing that everything was going to be okay. Then, in a flash, he thought of Roger Andrews, and what he must be going through at this very moment, knowing that come tomorrow he would be making plans to bury his wife and his son. The pain hit him so hard it doubled him over.

"I'm okay physically. Give me just a moment." Noah made his way to his couch to sit down before he fell. He had only lost one other patient in his career and four other infants, but it was never easy, and this time seemed to be the hardest, because not only had he became close to Roger and Ava Andrews, but he'd lost both Ava and their son on the same day.

Brendy could tell something was terribly wrong and her heart hurt for him. She wished she were beside him, so she could hold him and let him cry on her shoulder the way he'd allowed her to.

She waited for him to respond. She could tell he was moving about the house to find somewhere to sit. She could tell, by the way he was breathing and by hearing his sniffles, that he was heartbroken over something. Oh God, had Jasper told him about her? Was this what was making Noah so upset? Her heart sank, dreading to hear what he would say to her.

"I lost a patient and her son today. It's just been a very rough day."

"Oh Noah, I am so sorry. I can't imagine what you're going through. Was she married?"

"Yes, she was. He isn't taking it so well, but then who would?"

Brendy took a deep breath when she realized Jasper had not said anything. She was still safe a little while longer, yet her heart went out to Noah for all the pain he was feeling.

"What happened? Do you want to talk about it?"

Noah breathed in deeply and let it out slowly before he spoke. "I have been going over this in my mind ever since this morning. I swear I didn't foresee one single problem. In fact, there were no problems until the delivery. The baby turned at the last moment and was coming out breech. I saw there was a problem, and we were rushing her into the operating room from her private room where she had been going to deliver. The cord was wrapped around the baby's neck, and it cut off his oxygen for way too long."

"Oh, Noah."

"It all happened so quickly. Ava started hemorrhaging very badly. I did everything in my power to stop it, everything I was taught to do. I even prayed for God to help me, but nothing I did seemed to work; I lost them both anyway."

"Was her husband there when she died? Was he in the room?"

"He was, until we started rushing her down the hallway; then it all happened so fast we left him outside when we rushed her into the operating room. So no, he did not see his wife die. I had to go out and give him the news. God, I hate that."

"Noah, I don't know what to say. I feel heartbroken for him and for you. I wish I could help you. I wish I was there with you so we could cry together."

Noah realized that Brendy was nothing like Candace Wright. She didn't even know Roger or Ava Andrews, yet she wanted to cry with him. She had compassion for strangers and their grief. Noah knew, for the rest of his life, when trauma happened in the hospital he would always have her to come home to, just to lie beside and have her kiss away his tears. She understood him like no other woman ever had.

"I keep thinking that maybe it was good he didn't see her die," Noah said. "Yet, would it have been better for her if he'd been there for her, to be beside her as she took her last breath?" Noah couldn't help himself as he visualized that morning's events over again in his mind, and once again, the tears started to fall.

"Oh, sweetheart, I am so very sorry." Brendy's heart was breaking for him and for the loss of this family. Before she could stop herself she, too, started crying. How could she help him when he was so far away?

"I keep thinking, what if I had done things differently? What if I could have foreseen this and given her a C-section? None of this might have happened. But everything was going so well. There were no complications, so, as doctors, we always try to have a natural delivery when at all possible. In fact, Ava didn't want anything for pain. She asked me to allow her to have her son natural."

"I know you, Noah, and I know you did all you could. Does this make you angry with God?" Brendy had to ask; it was something she wondered.

"It makes me question God, but not get angry. I know Ava was a Christian woman, and she and her son are in Heaven now. I just wish God had allowed them more time on earth. I know God has a plan for Roger. He doesn't leave you hanging like that. They already have a daughter who is three years old. Melinda looks just like her mother, so at least he will have his wife's memory living on inside of her."

"That's good to know, but it hurts to think about. That poor man's life has just been turned upside down. I hope this doesn't make him turn against God."

"I have really been praying for him; I always worry about the same thing. It's enough to drive anyone away, I guess. You know, I will probably be sued for this."

"Why? You did all you could; how can they blame you?"

"I should have foreseen it. Even though I did all I could, the truth is, if I had given her a C-section this probably would not have happened."

"But having it natural was what she wanted."

"True, but I am the doctor, and that's how the courts will see it."

"Do you think he will sue you?"

"I'm not sure. I know Roger personally from my church here in Pittsburgh, but people aren't themselves when something like this happens. Most tend to be influenced by others."

"Will you lose your job?"

"Losing my job would be a small price to pay for him losing his wife, but no, I won't lose my job, but I could lose a lot of patients. As a doctor, I have to have a lot of insurance to cover such things. As of now, I have no idea what he will do. I plan to go to the funeral and set up an appointment with him afterwards to talk."

"I wish I was there. I would go with you and stand beside you. I'm sorry there is nothing I can do."

"There is something you can do. You can pray for Roger and for Melinda. They have just lost a very important part of their life, and I am partly to blame."

"Oh Noah, my heart is heavy. I will pray, I promise."

"Well, I am going to get off this phone and do some praying myself. Please tell Mom that I am sorry if I worried her by not calling her today; you can explain for me. Tell her I will call her tomorrow during lunch like always. I love you, sweet lady, more than I have ever loved any woman in my life."

Brendy smiled. "And I love you, Noah. Try to get some rest. I will be praying for you as well."

Chapter 28

Noah wasn't afraid of being sued. That was the last thing he was worried about. No matter how much Candace and other doctors warned him not to get too involved with his patients, he couldn't help himself.

He could remember the very first ultrasound that Roger and Ava had had. They had been so excited to find out they were having a son. He would have been Roger Junior. Now all that Roger Sr. had left were memories, and it haunted Noah. If he could have foreseen all the heartaches that came with being a doctor, he might have chosen another profession altogether.

Noah knelt down beside his bed and prayed. He'd never been a man to kneel, but on this occasion he felt it was appropriate.

"Dear Heavenly Father...I come before You today to ask that You wrap Your loving arms around Roger Andrews. Please give him the comfort and peace he will need to get him through these next few days and even the next few years.

Father, You tell us that You know the plans You have for us. You teach us that You are always with us and that You have our best interest at heart. But Father, when things like this happen, it is so confusing.

I know I am not one to question You. You tell me to lean not on my own understanding, and I realize You were with me today even though I couldn't feel You. I tried everything I knew to do to save her, but nothing worked, and Father, if there is something that I didn't do and should have, please forgive me.

Help me, Father, to be a better doctor and to be able to handle this. Help me to understand that all things happen to the good of You, it's just that right now that is hard to see.

Please be with me tomorrow as I help other patients, for they do not know what happened today, and help me be able to smile and carry on for them. My patients have entrusted

*me with their most precious gift, so help me be there for them,
and give me the knowledge I need when things go wrong.*

*But most of all Lord, please be with Roger Andrews on
this night and help him to find rest and peace that I know can
only come from You.*

In Jesus' Name...Amen.

*****

"Are you ready to go?" Brad smiled at Brendy as she
walked into the barn with her backpack over her shoulder.

"I am so ready; you just wouldn't believe how ready," she
laughed.

"You deserve a little time away after the way you have
been taking care of Mom. I know she appreciates it. But are
you sure you want to go back up on that mountain alone?"

"I'm not alone; you're taking me. And I must say that I really hate the fact that you and Noah feel that you have to take
me. I will be all right going by myself." A week and a half
had passed since Edith came home, and now that she was
back on her feet doing little odds and ends, Brendy knew this
would be a good time to go. Ever since Noah had taken her
to the cabin on the mountain, she'd longed to go back.

"It's perfectly okay, gives me a break from the everyday
chores and gives me a change of scenery. Besides, I haven't
been up there for a while, so I will enjoy it. But are you sure
you want to stay up there by yourself for a couple of days?
It gets quite dark there at night," Brad grinned that cowboy
grin she thought was so cute. It amazed her that Brad didn't
have a special someone in his life.

"I will be just fine; I'm not afraid of the dark. Besides,
I am hoping I can get reception up there. That way, if I get
spooked, I can call you."

"Well, if you do, don't expect me to get there quickly, but
I will come as fast as I can."

Brendy laughed, "I appreciate that, but I am sure I will be
just fine. Edith has packed enough food for me to stay a week."

"That's Mom for you. Well, follow me, little lady. I have Beauty all ready for you. Looks like we're just going to have to say Beauty is yours; she seems to like you."

Brendy climbed up on the quarter horse and patted her. "Hey there, Beauty, ready to take another ride to the top of the mountain?"

"She's been ready and waiting." Brad clicked his tongue and started off, with Brendy right behind him.

It was almost like following Noah up the small steep trail;he and Brad looked so much alike from behind, and it made Brendy miss him terribly. She hoped that his meeting with Roger Andrews would go well today. He'd told her that they were meeting at noon to go over everything. She had been praying for him all morning and asking God to be with him and to guide his words.

It was amazing when she thought about all the ways she had changed since she left New York. Praying would have been the last thing she would ever have thought of doing in a crisis; she had not felt that God was with her for so long she would have no reason to pray, but now she knew, beyond a shadow of a doubt, that He was with her. In fact, He'd sent Edith back to tell her that very thing.

*****

"Come on in," Noah smiled, shaking the hand of Roger Andrews. He'd known Roger ever since he moved to Pittsburgh. Roger played a very big part in the church they attended, as one of the youth pastors. Today was the first time Noah and Roger had spoken since briefly exchanging a few words at the funeral.

Roger took a seat in Noah's office and looked around for a moment without saying anything. Noah could feel there was tension there, but he had expected that.

"I have relived that day over and over, Noah, and still I can't figure out exactly what went wrong." Roger looked Noah in the eyes, through tears.

Noah looked across at his friend and could see the pain that was still so fresh. "What happened to Ava just doesn't happen everyday, but unfortunately, it does happen. I didn't foresee anything because everything had gone so well, at first. Ava hadn't had any complications when I delivered Melinda, and I thought it would be smooth sailing as before. When your son turned at the last minute, not only was he breech, but the cord wrapped around his neck so tightly. He was already trying to push his way out, and this is why we were rushing to the operating room. I'm so sorry, Andrew, there just wasn't enough time."

"Because of this, it caused Ava to hemorrhage. We tried everything in our power to stop the bleeding, but were not able to; it all happened so quickly. The huge amounts of blood Ava lost, plus the trauma of the delivery, caused her to go into cardiac arrest. Several doctors assisted me with her; we worked for some time doing all that we were taught to do. I'm so sorry,Roger; I know that there are just no words to excuse what happened. Please know, if I had known your son was going to come out feet first and every-thing happen as it did, I would have planned a C-section from the beginning."

Roger leaned back in his seat and folded his hands to-gether. "Noah, I have known you several years now. You have become a very dear friend. Ava thought the world of you. She would never have chosen another doctor over you to de-liver our son. You did a wonderful job with Melinda, always making us feel like family. You don't find many doctors like you, Noah. You are one of a kind."

Noah intended to stay strong, as a professional doctor would have, shedding no tears, but it seemed that lately he wasn't like most doctors, and he couldn't help it when he, too, got teary-eyed.

"But I wasn't able to save them, Roger. I just don't have the right words to tell you how truly sorry I am."

Roger sat up straighter in his chair and smiled for the first time since the day Noah had seen him smile at Ava, just before everything erupted. "No, you weren't able to save her, and I feel with all my heart no other doctor would have been able to, either. I know you, Noah, and I know you truly did all you could. I feel that you have hurt and suffered right along with me, and I want to thank you for coming to Ava's funeral. I'm sorry I wasn't able to talk to you more then; it went by in a blur to me. I don't remember half the people there."

"That's understandable. I just hate so bad that things didn't turn out the way we wanted them to, and I'd give anything if I could go back and do things differently."

"Yeah, you and me both. As a man of God, I've decided that He had a reason for this. That reason may never, in my lifetime, be revealed to me, and I must tell you that I am very angry and bitter with God right now, but I don't hate Him. How could I? I know when we are born we are never promised tomorrow; this is what I teach the youth all the time, to always be ready. When we leave this earth, it is a part of life. We are born to get back to our maker; unfortunately, some of us don't have as long as others."

Noah reached over his desk and patted Roger's hand. Is there anything at all I can do for you and Melinda? Just name it."

"Just pray for us." Roger tried to smile again. "I know you have been; I can feel it. Pray that she will understand. At three, she doesn't understand where her Mommy is, and she still asks me when I am bringing her baby brother home. She had been so excited about that. We had taken her to her grandma's to wait for us to come back with Little Roger, but I was the only one to pick her up, with red swollen eyes, and I had no words to say. I still don't."

Noah shook his head. "I will continue to pray for you daily, and remember, if you need me to explain more about what actually went wrong, I can do that, too."

"I guess at this point it doesn't really matter; I know you did all you could. There was no way you could have foreseen what happened, and all the explaining in the world just won't bring Ava back to us." Roger got up from his seat and reached across to shake Noah's hand once more.

"Thank you, for doing all you could. Thank you for trying. I hope this doesn't ever cause you to stop what you are doing. You are a very great doctor who has compassion for your patients. I will always consider you my friend."

Noah choked back tears as Roger spoke kind words to him. He certainly had not expected this meeting to go as it had.

When Roger got to the door he turned back once more. "You know, everyone advised me to sue you." Roger chuckled. "They told me I could stand to make a fortune, but from what? I don't think I could spend a single penny of money, knowing I only had it because Ava was no longer here. Besides, knowing in my heart you did all you could, and knowing the man of God that you are, I would be the one in the wrong."

"I appreciate that, Roger. And I thank you for your kind words."

Roger smiled once more and left Noah's office. Noah stood for a moment staring at the closed door, still numb from the meeting. How he wished he could rewind a few days and give Roger his wife back and Melinda her mommy back, and have her little brother cooing up at them, but that just wasn't possible. For some reason, God called Ava and her son home way too soon.

*****

"Are you sure you don't want me to carry in any wood and start a fire for you before I go?" Brad asked.

"In this heat, I don't think so. Besides, I am going to live off sandwiches and finger foods the next couple of days; I will be fine."

"It does give you a lot of light when it gets dark, though." Brad couldn't imagine a city girl up on this mountain alone.

"I have oil lamps. There must be at least a dozen or more here."

"That's true, do you have matches?"

Brendy smiled and reached into her pocket. "I sure do; that's the last thing your mom handed me."

"Good old Mom, you got to love her. Well then, I guess I will head back down the mountain. Check and make sure your phone works up here."

Brendy opened her cell phone and smiled. "Looks like it. I will be fine. I have been looking forward to this ever since Noah brought me up here the last time. Go back down and get to work; I know you have things to do."

"You got that right. Okay, I'm leaving you, then. I will be back the day after tomorrow early afternoon to see you back down. I am leaving Beauty with you. She has already been taken care of. Just give her a little more feed tomorrow, and make sure her water stays full. I don't want you not to have a way back, if you should need it."

Brendy shook her head. "You are so much like your brother; you both worry way more than you should."

"It's not our fault, believe me. We have our mother's genes, so we come by it naturally."

Brendy watched as Brad got back up on his horse and headed out of sight. She still had the day ahead of her and a full day tomorrow.

She felt safe here on this mountain, with nothing around her but wildlife. Even Jasper Logan didn't know were she was. She'd planned out her time wisely and brought paper and pen. She'd even brought her Bible, and planned to spend much of the time reading and learning. She would take notes of everything she didn't understand, and make it a point to go back later and ask Edith to explain. Edith seemed to love to pore over the Bible and teach Brendy all she knew. She had learned so much from her.

One of the main things Brendy intended to do was write the letter to Noah that would explain her connection to

Jasper. She hoped that coming to the mountain would clear her mind enough to write the truth of her past.

As much as she wished she never had to speak of her ugliness again, she knew it must come out. Just yesterday, Edith had read a part in the Bible where Jesus was talking to the Jews who believed him and he told them in John 8:32

Then you will know the truth, and the truth shall set you free.

That one verse stuck in Brendy's mind like a phantom. She had not been able to shake those thirteen words. Even though Jesus had been talking to the Jews about believing in Him, she felt in her heart that there was also hidden meaning there. That maybe Jesus was trying to say that by always telling the truth you would be free. By telling the truth, there would be no lies to hide or cover up.

Brendy hoped to use the weekend to pray and ask God for guidance on how to tell him. She knew it would be the hardest thing she ever done and she wished she could look him in the eyes, but she couldn't bear to see the hurt she would cause.

*****

Noah walked into the nurses' station after a hard day. He tried to smile and make eye contact with everyone, but his heart hadn't been in it. He hoped he hadn't allowed it to show through to his patients. The last thing Noah wanted was for his patients to see the turmoil he seemed to be going through each day since he'd lost Ava and her son.

Now, each time he went to deliver a baby, he second-guessed himself. Maybe this is the way he should be, more concerned, paying more attention to every detail. Only it was driving him nuts. He never wanted to experience what happened to Ava and her son again, and he surely never wanted to tell another husband that he done everything humanly possible, but his wife and child had passed away despite the fact.

"Tough break the other day, Doc," a female nurse said, looking up at him from the computer.

"Excuse me?" There was something in the tone of her voice that rubbed Noah the wrong way.

"The Andrews woman and her baby, it's the talk of the hospital. We all know you did all you could; you're one of the best doctors here. That's just life, though, full of tough breaks."

"What in the world is wrong with this place? Am I the only one here who has any compassion at all?"

Marge looked shocked by his comment; never had she heard Dr. Garrett raise his voice to anyone. "I just meant I was sorry for what happened."

"Yeah, I hear you, tough break." Noah shook his head and picked up the patient's file he had come after. He was tired of everyone's remarks and wished they wouldn't treat people as if they were just a number.

Noah started to leave the nurses' station, with Marge still looking at him. He stopped and turned towards her again. "Sorry, Marge, I still haven't quite gotten over it; I shouldn't have taken it out on you."

Marge tried to smile. "It's okay. I guess I should have said it a little differently. It never gets easy seeing things go wrong. I guess I have just gotten used to it and don't take it as personal as I used to. Working in a hospital has a way of making you cold."

Noah thought about what she'd said to him, as he drove home that evening. If he continued to work at Magee's, would life do the same to him as it had to her? As he drove into his garage and shut the door behind him, leaving the world outside, he sat in his car a while and thought about life in Pittsburgh.

Pittsburgh had never made him happy. It was just a place that he laid his head and worked. His townhouse was beautiful, and Noah was sure he could get a good price for it. He had a job that didn't just exist in Pittsburgh. He had a job that he could do from anywhere in the world. Why had he ever thought that working in a busy hospital would make him happy?

Maybe he'd watched too many doctor shows all his life and thought that a big well-known hospital would give him the satisfaction that he always craved. But life isn't like sit-coms. Life is very real and very painful.

Noah leaned his head back on the headrest of his car after turning off the engine. There were women in Summersville. Those women needed doctors, too. They had babies just like the women in Pittsburgh. There had to be places for lease where he could open a practice and work out of Summers-ville Memorial Hospital.

Not only were there women in Summersville who needed doctors, but the woman he had planned to spend his life with was there, also. He had planned when he left Summersville that he would work another year and put in his notice, but why was he waiting? In a year he would only be another year older, and in all that time he would be away from Brendy.

Noah closed the door of his car and opened the door lead-ing into his kitchen with a smile on his face; never had any-thing been so clear to him. Tomorrow he would call an agent in Summersville, and have them start looking for an office building to lease to open an OB/GYN practice. He decided he would wait about telling Brendy or the rest of the family until everything was set in stone. Then, he would go home and surprise them.

Chapter 29

Brendy tore up the letter she had written and threw it in the trash. It was her second attempt, and nothing was coming out right. How could she possibly tell him she had been a prostitute for the past six years and slept with Jasper right under his nose? There just weren't any words to let him down gently. No matter how she said it, she knew it would crush him.

Brendy got up from the table and walked to the window to look out. It was so peaceful here on this mountain. She felt almost like Moses in the Bible, when he had gone to the mountain and spoken directly to God through the burning bush. Edith had told her that story, and how God had sent him to go back and lead the Hebrew people out of bondage.

She wished God would speak to her and help her write the letter. If she could just say the right words...

Dear Jesus....I know I am new at this, I am no expert in praying and still feel very unworthy of your blessings, yet I know You blessed me that day in the airport when I met Noah and then his family. I know You blessed me when I sat by Doris. You had me in Your hand even then, even when I did not believe, and You led me to the place You knew I would find You.

I have nothing to hide from You, for You were with me through all of it. You have been with me since the day I was born.

I do love Noah. I love him so much and I know that I will never find another man that loves me the way he does. I don't have to tell You what I am struggling with; You already know every detail of my life.

Please help me find the words to tell him. I don't want to hurt him, but I see no other way around it. Even though I know You are here, there are times I don't feel You around me at all. This is one of those times, Lord; please help me feel Your presence. I need You now more than ever....Amen.

Daughter...I will never leave you nor forsake you......

Brendy jumped and looked around. Where had that come from? It was like He had spoken directly to her spirit, not out loud, but she heard it just the same.

Brendy walked back to the table and lit another lamp. Darkness was starting to close in around the cabin, and she knew she must light all the lamps before it finally set in completely.

Sitting down at the table, she picked up her pen again and began to write, knowing it didn't really matter how she told Noah the truth, as long as she poured out her heart the best way she knew how.

Dearest Noah,

As I sit here alone in the most beautiful place in the world, my hand is shaking from trying to write to you. It's so peaceful here in the cabin, and as darkness closes in all around me, I know I am not alone; nor have I ever been alone, for God has been with me since the beginning of time.

There is so much I haven't told you, Noah, so much I wanted to tell you from the very beginning, but never had the courage or the words to speak them out loud. I do hope you forgive me for doing it this way.

If you have received this letter, then it means I am no longer on the ranch. And as I write this I cannot even tell you where I am going because right now I don't know where that will be. But thanks to you, I have a phone and if you choose to forgive me please call and I will tell you where I am. If you decide that you cannot live with the truth, then please just send me a text saying goodbye, that way I will know and move on.

First of all let me say that when you met me in that airport I had just come from New York that morning, it was the first time in my life I had ever been in Pittsburgh. I only chose that city because it was the next flight out with a vacant seat. I like to think it was fate.

Fate because I met a woman on that plane that talked to me about God and even took my hand and prayed for me. She prayed that God would lead me to the right people and the right place, and I realize now that God knew what He was doing all the time. As you said, I did not believe in Him but He believed in me, and He did everything He could to lead me to Him so that I would believe and gave me every opportunity in the world to love Him.

I thank you, Noah, for believing in me even when I didn't believe in myself. Thank you for seeing the good in me even when I knew there was really no good to see. When you look at me you see a pretty woman that has a past of abuse. You know all about my mother and why I left home, and it was you that even brought me close to my mother and gave me a relationship with her that I never thought possible. Because of you my mother and I now email each other daily and I have been able to find forgiveness for her in my heart. You taught me that, Noah, you and Edith; how precious she is. She came back just for me....how great is that?

You know so much about my life when I was growing up but what you don't know is what I did during the six years I lived in New York. That was a part of my life I have never told you about. All you know is that I worked as a waitress, which is the truth, yet I failed to tell you that I only worked there a few months before I left and went to Spanish Harlem.

I met a woman named Caroline Reese. She ran a very high class escort service and she offered me a job. I was so young and naïve when I was sixteen. I had no idea what an escort service really was and all I could see was dollar signs in my young eyes and the promise of my own place filled with nice things.

I am not proud of what I did Noah, selling my body to men for a few trinkets and nice clothes. I knew right away I wanted out. I even tried to leave many times, but Caroline had a hold on all us girls and we were intimidated by her. I am not sure now why I was so afraid, but I was. Until the day I met you I was like a robot doing whatever she told me and only making myself more miserable.

Noah, you told me you have only been with one woman. I can and never will be able to tell you the countless men that have took advantage of me and I willingly let them. I have done things that would make me blush if you were looking at me now face to face. You see, I know when I accepted Christ that day in the hospital He wiped all that away and gave me the second chance I had desired. That's also the day I knew that no man would ever treat me that way again. The day I decided to tell you the entire ugly truth about myself. Even if it meant losing you forever, you had the right to know.

I can only imagine what you are thinking at this very moment, and maybe you have already decided in your heart to forgive me because I know you believe in forgiveness, you have told me so. But what I tell you now might cause you to change your mind about wanting a life with me. If so, then I understand, I can't say as I blame you, but I hope we can still be friends through texting, at least for a little while. I honestly have no one in the world I could call my friend except you and your family, and after you hear the rest you probably won't want to ever look at me face to face again, that is why I left....hang with me, you will understand when you read the rest of this letter.

When I was in New York there were several men who would pay me to escort them once a month, sometimes more. There were certain men I saw more than once. I had no control over which men I was with. Caroline made the appointments and I went wherever I was told. There was a man that she sent me to on the second night I worked for her. I was still frightened at the time because the night before had been terrible, the night I lost my virginity to two different men who could care less if they were gentle or not, so by the second night I was just as terrified, maybe more so.

Anyway, on this night I met a man on a yacht. He was a good-looking man who was kind to me. This is the same man that I spent one night a month with for the next six years. I never allowed myself to get attached to him or anyone for that matter. I had no idea this man was married or a doctor or anything about his personal life. Caroline always told us to never ask questions because they weren't any of our business, our job was just to please and leave. I know this sounds disgusting, but that's the way it was.

Noah please believe me when I tell you that I love you with all my heart and I have fallen so deeply for you, yet I know when I tell you this next part your feelings for me might change, but just know they will never change my feelings for you. You are the only man that ever treated me with respect. I have never given my love to anyone before, only my body. I have spent the past six years as a robot doing a job that left me feeling dirty and ashamed. Those days are over and I know God has set me free, yet as I sit here tonight at this table in a cabin high up on a mountain I have tears in my eyes and a knot in my throat as I know I am about to lose the only thing besides God that ever mattered to me.

Noah, that man that I am speaking of is the same man you grew up with. It is the same man that took Jessie away from you and married her. That man is Jasper Logan.

When I saw him in Summersville Memorial that night after your mother's surgery I thought I would die. I thought I had him out of my life forever.

Noah, I am sick in the pit of my stomach but that isn't all. You didn't realize when you talked to Jasper what you were doing but you told him I was staying in the apartment above the garage. He came to the apartment the night after your mother's surgery when you were in the house sleeping. He parked his car at the end of the drive so no one would see him and walked up. I thought it was you when I opened the door. I was devastated. He blackmailed me, Noah. He told me that he would tell you and the family, and as much as I hated for him to do that, that part didn't scare me as bad as when he said he would tell Caroline Reese where I was. I was so afraid one of her men would come after me and take me back.

Oh God, Noah, please believe me when I tell you I didn't want to do what I did next. I slept with Jasper that night, right across the drive from you. I felt sick about it. I didn't want to do it but I was so afraid, and I didn't want you to hate me, you had said the most wonderful things to me and treated me like I was special. No one has ever made me feel like that, like I mattered.

When I got saved in that hospital I made up my mind that Jasper Logan would never touch me again. I would wait for him to return and when he did I would tell him to leave and never give into him again. After he leaves, then I too would leave and go somewhere where he would never find me again and never be able to send anyone after me. So if you now have this letter that is what has happened. I didn't give into Jasper and I never will again. I am so sorry, Noah, I never loved Jasper. I have never loved any man but you.

I know that this letter leaves you angry, confused and maybe even disgusted, and I am so sorry for that.

As I said, I have left the ranch and it breaks my heart. Please tell your mother and everyone else that I am okay. It is up to you if you want to tell them the truth. It will be okay with me, after all, the truth shall set me free.

I love you Noah, I pray that you forgive me for the terrible things I have done.

Love you always.....Brendy

Brendy laid her head down on the table and cried. It was done, finished. The letter she hoped he never had the chance to read because maybe Jasper would stay away and not come back. Maybe she wouldn't have to leave the ranch and the people she loved, but then that would mean one day she would have to tell him face to face, and that wouldn't be easy at all. Either way, she would break his heart, the very man who loved her like she always dreamed to be loved.

Brendy made sure the door was locked, turned out the oil lamps and crawled into bed. The darkness around her should have left her afraid, but Brendy knew she wasn't alone. For the first time in her life, she felt more at peace than ever before. Even though she knew Noah didn't yet know the whole story, just by writing it all down she felt that she could now breathe. One way or another it would all be over soon. Brendy only wished she could see into the future, and know if she would spend her life in another town or spend it with Noah. If there was one thing for sure, only time would tell.

Chapter 30

Noah put in his notice two days after he found an office to lease in Summersville. He had never done anything this spontaneous in his life, and he wasn't sure if he was excited or frightened, or maybe a little of both.

He had been saving all he could for the past couple of years, so money wouldn't be a problem for a little while until he opened his practice and was able to take on a few patients. There was so much he had to do and he knew he needed to be in Summersville to do them. He still had not told anyone in the family. He wanted to go back and see the office first, himself, before taking Brendy over. The pictures on the Internet looked great, and it had even been a doctor's office before and still had much of the same equipment there. It was as if God had everything already worked out.

All he had to do was run an ad in the paper telling the town he was now open for business and hire a couple of nurses and a receptionist. He would start off small at first and build up, maybe even allow another doctor to share a space with him. It was always easier when there were two involved; that way he wouldn't have to be on call twenty-four seven.

He'd gone to the hospital administrator and put in his notice that morning, giving them thirty days. That would give him enough time to wrap up things with his patients and turn them over to other doctors. Surely they would be happy for him. He hated turning a few over to others, but there was no way around it.

He called an agent in Pittsburgh and placed his townhouse up for sale. He prayed it sold within thirty days, but if it didn't, so be it; perhaps it wouldn't take much longer.

Noah decided to live in the main house instead of renting an apartment in town. He wanted to be as close to Brendy as he could. He never wanted to leave her again, and hoped that someday she would agree to be his wife. Noah didn't intend to take too long about asking her.

He would go through the rest of his life regretting that he couldn't do more for Ava Andrews and her infant son, but, because of that, it gave him the courage to move on and start fresh. He looked forward to the years ahead when he could go back to his hometown church at New Life Assembly. Nothing had been the same since he left Summersville and he longed to get back to a life that seemed slower-paced and normal, a life that he would find in the town of his birth with the woman that he loved.

*****

"Man, oh man, you did a lot of studying in the word up on that mountain, didn't you, girl?" Edith laughed, reading over all of Brendy's notes. "It does a woman good to see a baby of the Lord take this much interest in the word."

"Oh Edith, I can't begin to tell you what happened to me up there. I have never felt anything so strong in all my life. I felt like Moses walking on holy ground."

Edith smiled. "I remember when the kids were all little and we stayed our first night there in that cabin. We all anointed that cabin and prayed over it asking God to bless it. We had so many good times there; it is certainly a special place."

"Noah told me he went there and closed himself in for three days after he and Jessie called off the wedding."

"He did. That was a terrible time in his life. I'll never forget the day he walked in and told me and Connie they called off the wedding and asked if we would call everyone and tell them. Two days later he packed a bag and rode up the mountain. I knew where he was going, and even though I worried about him and wanted to ride up after him or send someone to go check, I knew he was a strong man of God, and I knew he needed that time with God alone for however long it took, and just like Moses, when he rode down off that mountain there was a light in his eyes again. He has never been the same since. I don't know what happened to him up there, but God met him there, that's for sure."

"Yep, that's a special place. So, do you think you will be able to help me with a few things on that list?" Brendy smiled, knowing she'd given Edith four pages of notes.

"I think I might can. Where do you want to start?"

"Let's just start from the beginning and go from there," Brendy teased.

"The beginning sounds good." For the next several hours, Edith went over all the notes that Brendy had written down and tried as best she could to explain it to Brendy. In fact, by the time everyone came inside for dinner,neither Edith nor Brendy had started it and they laughed at having lost track of time. Edith made it a fend-for-yourself night with sandwiches and cans of condensed soup.

Brendy was eager to get home and wait for Noah's call. He'd texted her several times that day with short messages, but she always looked forward to hearing his voice and finding out about his day. She had no idea when things would be over and she enjoyed each day one at a time and was grateful for every one God allowed her with this wonderful family.

*****

After Brendy hung up the phone with Noah, she put on her pajamas and took a seat at her bar in front of the computer. For the past week, her mother had been sending her an email and she managed to send one back before going to bed. All the walls were being torn down around her heart for her mother, and she was starting to like the woman who'd given birth to her.

Dear Brendy,

Receiving your emails has become the bright spot in my day. I so look forward to hearing from you each day and the things you are up to. The trip to the mountain top on horseback seems fascinating. I bet Summersville, West Virginia is beautiful, you are lucky or maybe I should say blessed to be there. God is looking out for you.

Edith sounds wonderful. I am glad you met her and only wished I could have been that great of a mother to you. At least now we are talking and finally getting to know one another. Did you know my favorite color is lime green? I know that was random, I just wanted you to know that. What's your favorite color? As a mother I guess I should know that, but sadly I don't.

It has been raining off and on here all day but we needed the rain so I won't complain. It helps cool things off a bit. It's so hot now.

I know you will have a birthday in a few days, I know you may not believe this but I have always thought about you on August fifteenth. I just wish I could go back to the night you were born and do things right this time.

Anyway, just wanted to say hello and tell you I love you and I am proud of you.

Sweet dreams...... Louise

Brendy got off the stool and poured herself a glass of ice water before going back. She loved this routine with her mother; it had become a nightly ritual. Sometimes they only left short letters, but the fact that they each were thinking about the other made the notes special. Maybe it was time she started calling Louise Mother; that way, her mother would know she'd been forgiven.

Dear Mother,

I had no idea your favorite color was lime green. Mine is pink. I remember when I was little Grammy buying me this pretty pink dress. I wore that thing everywhere and was so proud of it. I think that's what made me fall in love with the color pink. Don't laugh but my cell phone is pink and my computer is pink and I even have a pink Bible. Noah bought them for me.

This is embarrassing for me but I have no idea when your birthday is. I remember it was in December but I cannot remember what day.

Edith and I have spent hours today going over the notes I made from the Bible. There is just so much I don't understand, but I am learning more everyday. Edith says I am a baby in Christ because I just now came to accept Him. We studied so much that we lost track of time and forgot to cook dinner; Edith said that was a first for her.

It was cloudy here today but no rain. We could use the rain though so if you want to send some down our way we will appreciate it. Ha!

Anyway, it is late and six comes early. I love you too, and take care.

Love always...... Brendy

Brendy looked at the clock above the counter. It was almost midnight. She wondered if Noah was already sleeping in Pittsburgh.

Brendy shut down the computer, turned off the lights, and headed for bed. It would be nice if she and Noah were married, and he was already sleeping in her bed. She would crawl in the bed beside him and wrap her arms around him. She could almost feel the warmth of his body and hear him breathing softly beside her.

Brendy pulled the covers up around her shoulders and turned to her side, pulling the other pillow close to her. For now this would have to do.

*****

Brendy hurried to the front door when she heard the doorbell ring. Edith was out back talking to Rene about Beth, who had just gone to her first day of kindergarten, and Rene was still crying and heartbroken because she felt she was losing her baby.

Brendy opened the door to a large bouquet of red roses in her face. "Can I help you?"

The man looked around the roses and smiled. "I'm looking for Brendy Blake."

"That's me. Are these for me?"

"That's what it looks like." He handed the flowers to
Brendy with a clipboard and pen. She placed the vase filled
with flowers on the floor for a moment and signed his paper.

"Thank you very much."

"No problem, have a nice day." Brendy closed the door
behind him and picked up the roses. Never in her life had she
received roses from anyone, and she raced to the table to set
them down again and to look at the card.

*I hope you enjoy these roses and think of me. Happy Birth-
day, my love....Noah*

Brendy stuck her nose into the petals and breathed in
deeply.

"My, oh my, what is this?" Edith clapped her hands, coming into the dining room with Rene.

"Noah sent me roses. Wasn't that nice of him?"

"What's the occasion?" Rene asked.

"It's my birthday. I'm surprised he remembered."

"Your birthday? Why didn't you tell me?" Edith handed
the vase to Brendy and made a motion with her hands for
her to go."

"What are you doing?" Brendy giggled.

"She's trying to tell you to go home and take the day off,"
Rene answered.

"That's right, now go. No one is supposed to work on their
birthday; it just wouldn't be right. Go home, take a load off,
read a book, whatever, but go."

"That's not necessary," Brendy said.

Rene went to the front door and opened it. "You better
do as you're told; you really don't want to see this woman
angry."

Brendy laughed and headed for the door. Maybe a day
off would be nice. "Okay, you win. I will see you all in the
morning, then."

"No, you will see us tonight. Make sure you come back
at seven." Edith gave her a tiny kiss on the cheek and went
back to the kitchen. Brendy could tell there was no use

arguing with this woman; she would never win over her anyway.

*****

Brendy set the vase filled with roses on her bar and stood back to admire them. They were beautiful and smelled wonderful. Brendy got her cell phone and went to Noah's name. She never texted him first but couldn't wait to thank him for the flowers.

You remembered...thank you so much...I love you.

Within five minutes, her cell phone was ringing with his name on her caller I.D.

"Hi there, I can't believe you remembered!" Noah could hear the excitement in her voice.

"It hasn't been that long ago since you told me. If I remember next year, I will be doing something great," he laughed.

"They are beautiful, Noah. I have never received flowers before."

"Are you serious? I thought you had dated a few men."

"Yes, but never gotten flowers."

"Then you dated a few losers."

Brendy laughed, "You got that right. So are you not at the hospital?"

"I am. I'm between patients. I was hoping you would text me as soon as they came, and I hope it was you that answered the door."

"It was; your mom was trying to console Rene. She's been crying this morning because she left Beth at her first day of kindergarten."

"That's right, she did start this year, didn't she? I bet Mom will miss her, too."

"Oh yes, I am not sure who is really consoling who here. How's everything going there?"

Brendy loved hearing about Noah's time in the hospital; it fascinated her, almost like hearing bits and pieces of a soap opera.

"Everything is great so far this morning. I just delivered my first baby, and both are healthy."

"That's great. I pray for you each day. I think God is getting used to hearing from me now."

Noah chuckled. "Yeah, just like a woman, never shuts up."

"Hey now, that isn't funny," Brendy laughed.

"I'm only kidding. baby, I hate to cut you short, but I need to run; I have other patients to check on. I hope you have a great birthday, and I will talk to you later tonight at our usual time."

"Okay, have a great day at work, talk to you soon." Brendy closed her cell phone and fell back on her couch and giggled. Finally,after twenty-three years, she'd found her happiness. She'd met the love of her life and made peace with God and her mother; now if only it could continue on and never end. At least she would be able to keep two out of three, and two out of three wasn't bad.

Brendy sighed and made her way to the kitchen window. She loved looking out at the pasture filled with horses and the mountain she had grown to love so.

The huge barn was as beautiful as the house, maybe even bigger. She could stand all day and watch the activities going on around it, with Brad, Greg, Rene, and Connie going in and out on different horses. At times, there would be people she didn't know, getting ready for trail rides or having riding lessons. So much went on each day, that just watching, one would never get bored.

Brendy smiled to herself, knowing what she would do. It was her birthday, after all, and Edith wanted her to spend it the way she desired. She would spend the day down by the creek, in the hammock, reading her book. God had certainly given her a beautiful day for it.

*****

Each time Brendy found herself at the creek, she noticed something she hadn't noticed before. There were always beautiful flowers blooming, and the jasmine she had been watching was growing even thicker around the arbors you went underneath before you crossed the bridge.

Brendy got comfortable and was on the fourth chapter when she saw Connie approaching her.

"Well, hello, I saw you giving a riding lesson; how did you get away?" Brendy asked.

"It was almost over. I thought I saw you head down this way with a book in your hands. I was supposed to give you something this morning after your flowers arrived, but I was busy and didn't realize you had them yet."

"So, you knew I was going to get flowers? Your Mom and Rene seemed surprised."

"I was the only one that knew. Noah told me yesterday and also told me to go to Dodrill Jewelers and pick up what he ordered for you." Connie handed Brendy a gift-wrapped box that was long and skinny.

Brendy took the box. "But he sent me the most beautiful roses; why did he do this?"

Connie let out what appeared to be a chuckle. "You just don't know my brother. If you hang with him, the best is yet to come."

"But I talked to him not long ago, and he didn't say anything about a gift."

"Yeah, when you didn't mention anything to him but the roses, he called me and asked me if I had given you the gift yet. So here I am, doing my duty for my big brother. Go on and open it; I can't wait to see your reaction."

Brendy peeled off the pink wrapping paper slowly and gasped at the beautiful diamond tennis bracelet that lay inside. "Oh my god!"

Connie laughed. "Now that was a great reaction! I knew you would like it. I told Noah, if you didn't like it, he could always give it to me as an early Christmas present."

"It's so beautiful. There must be fifty diamonds on this thing!"

"There is actually one hundred,to be exact, but who's counting?" Connie loved seeing Brendy so excited. "Here, let me put it on for you." Connie took the bracelet and clasped it around Brendy's arm. "Now, that's beautiful."

"I have never been treated so well. He is spoiling me."

"That's Noah for you. I have often wondered if Jessie regretted doing what she did and losing Noah. And now she is with that creep, Jasper. Serves her right."

Brendy looked at Connie and wasn't sure how to react to her statement. Connie had no idea she even knew Jasper Logan.

"Why do you think Jasper is a creep?"

"I just know these things. I never liked him as a kid either, when he was hanging around the house all the time. He used to do things to me I never told anyone about."

"Oh my god, Connie, what do you mean?"

Connie shook her head. "That was a long time ago. He never went too far, but he would touch me in places I knew was wrong and try to kiss me when no one was around. I bet if the truth be known he probably cheats on Jessie. That man can't be trusted."

Brendy wanted so badly to tell Connie the rest of the story but didn't think this was the right time. She was too excited over the beautiful bracelet on her arm.

"I'm sorry, Connie. I wish you had told someone."

"Well, like I said, he never carried it too far, but it made me resent him, and when everything went down between him and Noah and Jessie, it didn't surprise me at all. Jasper likes going after things he can't have just to prove that he can. He is a real snake in the grass. But anyway, I don't want to spoil your day. I need to get back to my next lesson and let you get back to reading."

"Well, thank you for bringing this down for me; it's beautiful."

"You're welcome and happy birthday."

Brendy watched Connie walk back up the trail and disappear through the trees. A part of her wished she had told

Connie the truth about Jasper. After all, she knew about her being a prostitute; she just wasn't sure if Connie would be so loyal to that particular secret, knowing how much she loved her brother.

Brendy found it hard to concentrate on her book after that. Her mind was clogged with pictures of Jasper Logan and everything she'd gone through with him, and now learning that poor Connie had gone through things as well, as a child. He was certainly a man who could never be trusted.

Brendy held her arm up to the sunlight and watched the diamonds sparkle. It was the first piece of jewelry she'd ever owned that was given to her out of love, not something she'd bought with devil's money.

Brendy laid down her book and closed her eyes. The breeze felt wonderful on her face. She never wanted to forget this day, but to treasure it always, a birthday that would probably turn out to be her favorite in her memories for the rest of her life. A birthday filled with love.

Chapter 31

"Surprise!" Everyone yelled at the same time, as Brendy entered the main house that evening for dinner.

"Oh my goodness, what's all this?" Brendy looked wide-eyed. A beautiful birthday cake sat on the kitchen table with the candles lit, and several gifts sat beside it. She'd never expected anything like this.

"We went right to work after you left this morning. Of course, we took turns doing a little shopping, and I made you the vegetable soup you love so much for dinner, but first you are going to blow out your candles and make a wish." Edith motioned for her to come closer.

Brendy's heart filled with love. Everyone in the family, except, of course, Noah, stood around the table in a circle and sang Happy Birthday to her. Tears fell down her cheeks. Brendy knew that none of them realized this was the very first birthday party or cake she had ever had. Never had she been allowed the privilege of blowing out candles or making a wish. Little things, that so many took for granted, Brendy treasured.

Brendy looked down at the candles and closed her eyes. Her wish was easy. She wished that when Noah finally learned the truth, he would be able to forgive her and still want to share his life with her.

She blew hard and all twenty-three candles went out. "I did it! I didn't know I had it in me," she laughed.

"That means your wish will come true, Aunt Brendy." Beth jumped up and down and clapped her hands. "Can I have a piece of cake now?"

"Not yet, young lady," Greg said, picking her up in his arms. "First of all, we are going to eat a bowl of soup."

"But what if I don't want any soup, Daddy?"

"Then you won't get any cake, either," Rene answered.

"Aw, that's not fair." Beth stuck out her lip and pouted, making Brendy laugh.

Brendy ruffled her hair and poked out her lip, mocking her. "So, how was the first day of school, big girl?"

"It was so much fun; I got to color and everything!"

"That's great; I'm glad you liked it. So what did you learn?"

Beth thought for a moment and then smiled real big. "I learned to do this when I need to go potty." Beth raised her hand high in the air, and everyone laughed.

The soup was delicious and the cake, too. Beth ate two pieces, even though Rene was afraid that, with all the sugar, she might not go to sleep so easily. Of course Edith had insisted it was a special occasion and birthdays didn't come everyday, so Rene gave in.

Greg and Rene got Brendy a beautiful candleholder to set on her coffee table and the candle colors matched the colors of her apartment.

Beth drew a picture of her, sitting on top of Beauty, wearing a cowboy hat and boots. Brendy laughed at the likeness. "The only problem is, I don't own a hat or boots," she teased.

"You do now." Connie handed her the next gift from her. Brendy screamed out when she opened the box to find a cowboy hat and a beautiful pair of boots.

"Thank you, but how did you know my size?"

"Okay, so I have a confession," Connie said. "I did some snooping in your closet while you were down at the creek."

Brendy laughed. "Well, I love it, but I am afraid I will have to borrow one of your horses to make this picture real."

"You don't have to borrow anything." Brad handed her a piece of paper that told her she was now the owner of Beauty, the quarter horse she had been riding.

Brendy looked at Brad for a moment, in shock. "But Beauty is your horse."

"Not anymore, I think she likes you better. Don't get all happy just yet; there is a lot that comes with owning a horse. So, if you accept the gift, you will have to learn to take care of her, so you can build a bond."

"Oh yes, I will accept. Thank you so much, Brad. She is beautiful."

"And last, but not least," Edith handed Brendy the last gift. Brendy opened the box to find several different Bible study books that made the Bible easier to understand, and also a beautiful journal filled with blank pages.

"Oh Edith, thank you so much; these will really come in handy. And the journal is beautiful. I have never had one."

"It is filled with blank pages because your story hasn't been written yet, Brendy; with God, it can be whatever you want it to be, so make it a good one."

Brendy thought about her comment for a minute, and realized that as badly as she wanted her story to be filled with Noah and his wonderful family, it wasn't really up to her, but to Noah after he learned the truth.

"Thank you all for making this day so special for me. I will never forget it as long as I live." Brendy stood and went around the room, giving each family member a hug. It was too bad America wasn't filled with families like the Garretts; what a wonderful country it would be. Then again, maybe it was. She had spent her life not really realizing how wonderful life could be, in the situation she grew up in, but one thing was for certain; she would never again take her life for granted, and would be appreciative for everything God gave her.

*****

Brendy stared at the phone that night, willing it to ring. She wanted so badly to call Noah and thank him for the beautiful bracelet but didn't want to disturb him. She jumped when the phone finally rang as she was holding it in her hand, and laughed.

"Finally, what took you so long!" she screamed.

Noah laughed. "I take it you received all of your gifts."

"I did. Oh Noah, the bracelet is beautiful, but it is way too expensive. The flowers were plenty."

"The flowers weren't the gift. They were just to say happy birthday, and that I loved you. The bracelet was the gift. And as soon as I am able to get back there, I will take you out to eat somewhere nice, so you can wear it in style."

Brendy giggled. "I will never get tired of you."

"I certainly hope not. So, what did the rest of the family do? If I know my family, they didn't let your birthday go unnoticed."

"You aren't kidding. Edith made the prettiest cake and that homemade soup that I love. She gave me Bible study books and a journal. Rene and Greg got me candles,and Connie gave me a cowboy hat and boots."

Noah chuckled, visualizing Brendy opening her gifts. "So now you are a certified country girl, are you?"

"I am; in fact, this country girl now owns her own horse."

"So Brad gave you Beauty, did he?"

"You knew about that?"

"No, but I thought he might. You and that horse were made for each other. But did he tell you there is a responsibility that comes with owning a horse?"

"He did. In fact, he is giving me a lesson in horse care tomorrow. By the time you get back, I should be a pro."

Noah smiled to himself, knowing he would be back sooner than she thought. He couldn't wait to come through the door and surprise her. In fact, he wouldn't only surprise Brendy but the whole family.

"Yep, it won't take you long at all. When you learn how to saddle that horse and do things by yourself, you will prob-ably go to the cabin quite often, I'm sure."

"That would be nice. It's just so peaceful there, Noah. I think I could live there with no trouble at all."

"Really? You would live up on that mountain with nothing around but wildlife?"

"I could; it would be wonderful."

Noah had never thought of living in the cabin, his cabin. All sorts of thoughts went through his mind and he knew that was something he needed to look into.

"I'm glad you had a great birthday; I'm just sorry I couldn't be there."

"That's okay; I know you were here in spirit, and that's what counts."

"I was there in spirit, all right; I thought about you all day long. I was wondering something, though."

"Oh, what's that?" Brendy asked.

"I have a feeling today was your very first party ever, am I right?"

"Yes, you are right. It was also my very first cake."

"Seriously? You've never had a birthday cake before?"

"Never. Your family has made everyday special and I will never forget any of you."

"You will never forget us because you are going to spend the rest of your life with us." He laughed.

Brendy grew quiet for a moment and prayed that what he said was true. "That would be nice; I can't imagine anywhere else on earth I'd rather be."

*****

Noah put down his cell phone and headed for his kitchen. His stomach had been rumbling since five and now, at nine, he still had not made time to eat dinner. He made a mental note, after opening his refrigerator, that he needed to stop by the market on his way home tomorrow and pick up a few things. He'd been so busy he hardly had anything to eat at all.

Noah shut the refrigerator door and grabbed an apple out of the wooden bowl on the table; at least it would be food in his stomach.

As he was headed back upstairs to take a shower, his doorbell rang. That was weird. It was after nine o'clock; who would come to visit at this hour? He headed back down to see who was there, knowing he was not in the mood for company. He had hoped to take a hot shower and go to bed.

Candace Wright stood in front of his door wearing a provocative black dress and smiling as if something were up her sleeve. "Good evening, Noah. I was in your neighborhood and thought I would drop by."

"Candace, it's late and I'm really tired."

Candace pushed her way in beside him and walked towards his living room area. Noah rolled his eyes, shut the door, and followed after her. "I guess you didn't hear what I said."

"Oh, I heard you, Noah. If this night ends the way I hope, you will go to bed sooner than you think." Candace pushed her body up against his and tried to kiss him. Noah took a step backwards and pushed her away.

"Have you been drinking? I can smell alcohol on your breath."

"A little, but not enough to not know what I am doing. In fact, I am very aware that you put in your notice at the hospital without even telling me, and I am here to find out why."

"Candace, as I have told you before, my life is my life. I do not have to share my plans with anyone, including you."

Candace looked at him with sad eyes and closed the distance between them. "We were so good together, Noah. When we kissed, I felt passion. Take me upstairs, Noah, and let me show you how good we can be."

"Candace, you are drunk. I am going to take you upstairs and put you in my guest room and let you sleep this off."

"I am not drunk!" she screamed. "I know what I am doing, Noah. I have wanted you from the first time we met. What is wrong with me? Why don't you want me, Noah?"

"Nothing is wrong with you. You are a very beautiful woman, but I am not in love with you. I am in love with someone else."

"But, how do you know you can't fall in love with me? Give us a chance; take me upstairs and make love to me."

Noah took hold of her arms gently and pushed her off of him again. "Candace, love isn't just about making love. Love comes from within. There is no way I can make love to a woman I don't love; it doesn't work that way with me. I have to honor God."

"I'm so sick of hearing about your God. Everyone is sick to death of it! You're not even a man, Noah. No *real* man would refuse me!"

"Well, this man has. Come on and let me put you in the guest room; I don't want you driving like this."

Candace broke away from his hold and screamed out loud. "I'm not drunk; can't you see that I am throwing myself at your mercy? Can't you see that I love you, Noah, that I have loved you ever since we met? We can be so good together, Noah; please don't send me away. Just give me one night to prove to you that we can be good together."

"So what if we had awesome sex, what then? What happens when we wake up in the morning and we find that, other than being doctors, we have absolutely nothing else in common?"

Candace shut her eyes and took a deep breath. "Do you really feel that way? Do you really feel that we have nothing in common?"

"I do. You are a beautiful woman, and there are many men who would give their eyeteeth for just one night with you, but I am not that man. I would not do anything in this world to hurt Brendy, or to dishonor God."

Candace looked at him with sorrow in her eyes and smiled. "This Brendy is a very lucky woman. I hope she realizes what she has and treasures it always." And with that said, Candace Wright walked out the door and left Noah standing alone.

Candace was not the first woman to throw herself at Noah since he moved to Pittsburgh. If he desired, he could have a different woman each week, but ever since those three days on the top of the mountain when he cried out to God and promised to do things right this time, he had kept his promise and knew now that because he'd stayed true to his word, God was blessing him with the woman he'd prayed for all of his life.

Noah wanted love. He desired passion just like any other man, yet he wanted it with the woman he loved. Making love wasn't just a statement; it was a feeling. A beautiful union between a man and a woman after they had made a commitment to love one another all the days of their life, and he wanted that more than anything but could never see himself with any woman other than Brendy Blake.

*****

Brendy felt sick when she turned on her computer expecting to find a message from her mother and instead found a message that Jasper Logan had privately sent her on her Facebook page. She had not thought about Jasper knowing her real name.

Her heart beat faster as she feared what it said. Her life here on the ranch may be over sooner than she'd hoped. Brendy clicked on the message, wanting to get it over with, and took a seat on the barstool.

Brendy,
How interesting to know you have a Facebook page. You, of all people. I guess it's a good thing that Caroline doesn't know your real name...or does she?
I find this arrangement better for me because now I won't have to waste any more money. The only problem is I can't get there each month as I did in New York. Don't worry though, my princess...I will be there soon enough. I know how much you miss me. We are so good together, don't you think?
I was thinking that if things don't work out between you and Noah I would consider having you come and live close to me....that way I can see you as often as I like. I guess if Noah knew the truth you would have no other option but to turn to me.
As much as I would love to have him know the truth about your dirty little secret, I am in no way eager for him to find out I was one of your clients....makes me look trashy, and for that reason your secret is safe with me for now.

Of course, I can't promise you the same when it comes to Caroline.....in fact, I ran into her just the other day and she asked me if I had seen you. She seemed very concerned. Of course, I told her I hadn't.

You will get a kick out of this, but she has no idea you left town. She actually thinks you are lying dead somewhere and no one has found you yet, isn't that amazing? Seems I am the only one who really knows the truth.

Until we meet again........Jasper

Brendy was disgusted with Jasper's letter. She quickly deleted it and blocked him altogether from her Facebook page. Noah had taken a picture of her the night he made her a page, and now she wished she had never allowed it.

Did Jasper actually think she would ever turn to him, as if he was the only other man on earth besides Noah? It made her sick to think about.

Brendy put the name Caroline Reese in the Facebook search engine, and nothing came up. Thank God she didn't have a Facebook page. Caroline knew her first name but had no idea what her last name was, so maybe she was safe.

Brendy was angry with herself for allowing Jasper to have such a hold over her. She wished she could go ahead and send Noah the letter and leave; that way it would be over with sooner rather than later, but how could she do this now, today, after everyone had been so nice to her and given her gifts? They would never understand and would be so hurt.

How could she have let things get so out of hand? She should either have told Noah the truth from the very beginning or moved on and never allowed herself to get attached. It was too late now; the damage was done.

Chapter 32

The next three weeks went by more quickly than Noah thought they would. With only one more week to go before he headed back to Summersville, West Virginia, he was dancing on air with anticipation.

"Looks like someone is happy for a change," Marge said as he entered the nurses' station. "Don't tell me this hospital has made you grow cold already." She laughed, remembering a few weeks before when he had become angry with her.

"Nope, I'm as compassionate as always. Just excited this is my last week."

"Yeah, I heard that. We are sure going to miss you around here. Magee's won't be the same without you."

"I appreciate that. I'll miss you too, Marge. If you were living in Summersville, I would hire you as my receptionist."

"Ooh wee, don't tempt me, I'm liable to pack up and go with you," she winked.

"I truly am sorry about the other day; I shouldn't have talked to you like that."

Marge just smiled and rolled her eyes. "Don't worry about it, Doctor, you had a rough few days; it's understandable."

"And still do have rough days every time I think about it. I'm not sure I will ever get over it, you know?"

"I understand. It takes time, like anything. How is Mr. Andrews doing? Is he any better?"

"He is dealing with it. I saw him at church Sunday and we spoke for a few minutes. He has finally gone back to work. He and his daughter are going through counseling; it is helping her understand and deal with the fact that her mother isn't coming back. But they are good. I just pray God sends him another woman to love. I know no one could take the place of Ava in his heart, but maybe she would help fill the void and be a mother to Melinda."

"That's so sad, Doctor. I will keep them in my prayers and you, too, for that matter, leaving here in a few days and starting a new adventure in your life. You must be beside yourself with excitement."

"I am. Not only am I excited about starting a new practice and moving back to my roots, I also plan to ask the most incredible woman for her hand in marriage."

"Is that so? And just when did you meet this incredible woman?"

"A couple of months ago," he laughed.

Marge whistled. "Just two months ago, and already you know for certain that she's the one?"

"I do. I have never been more certain of anything in my life."

"I suppose this woman lives in Summersville?"

"She does. How did you know that?" Noah and Marge laughed at his comment. Noah would miss Magee's and all the friends he'd made here, but he knew there would be others that God would send into his life. His time here was over, and it was time to move on.

*****

"If you baby that horse anymore than you have the last few days, you are going to spoil her," Brad said, walking up behind Brendy in the barn.

"Does spoiling a horse hurt them?" Brendy brushed her back. She'd followed the same routine ever since the day after her birthday. She loved the way the horse smelled, and the way Beauty always seemed excited to see her.

"No, I can't say as it does. I'm glad I gave you that horse; now that's one less that I have to take care of. By the way, you are doing a great job with her."

"Thank you. I have fallen in love with this horse," she smiled.

"I think the feelings are mutual. Do you feel comfortable enough about putting a saddle on yet?"

"Yes, I have pretty much gotten the hang of it, and Connie has given me a few lessons. In no time at all, I should be able to ride back up on the mountain without you having to lead me."

"You really like it up there, don't you?"

"I do. Too bad you can't get there by car." Brendy patted Beauty's neck and talked to her softly.

"Yeah, now that's an idea you will have to talk to Noah about. By the way, how is he doing? I know he talks to you and Mom, but I haven't spoken to him since he went back to Pittsburgh."

"He is good, staying busy in the hospital. I had no idea a doctor's life could be so time- consuming."

"Yep, about like the life of living on a ranch."

Brendy laughed at Brad's comment. "Yes, you are so right. I watch you out my kitchen window, and you never stop, all day long."

"That's my life, but I do enjoy it."

"Do you, really? I mean, this is none of my business, but do you do it because you really love it or because you feel obligated?"

Brad grew quiet for a moment, and Brendy knew she'd overstepped her boundaries. "I'm sorry, Brad; that was none of my business. It was just something I wondered about."

"It's okay. I do feel obligated. I guess when Dad died and Noah was already in college, that left me and Greg to carry on. I do sometimes wish I had more free time, but I love this life, working with the horses and doing rodeos when I can."

"I pray that one day you meet a wonderful woman."

Brad chuckled. "Don't pray too hard; I don't have time for a woman unless, of course, she is a horse."

"I can see you have plenty of those around here screaming for your attention."

"Yep, and now it's one less. Are you sure you don't need two horses? I can always give you another one."

"Oh no, I think one is plenty, thank you."

*****

After dinner had been eaten and the dishes were washed and put away, Brendy was on her way home when she found Edith sitting on the front porch swing.

"I wondered where you'd wandered off to," Brendy said, sitting down beside her.

"You and Connie were doing such a fine job with the dishes and having that wonderful conversation; I thought I would leave you two alone, and another reason was that I just felt like being lazy."

Brendy patted Edith on her leg and smiled. "You deserve it. You were supposed to take it easy for six weeks."

"And it has been right at six weeks."

"No, not quite." Brendy reminded her.

"Well, who's counting? Anyway, with all you have been doing with the house, all I really have to do is cook, and I enjoy that."

"And you are so good at it. Can I ask you a question?"

"Sure." Edith turned her body to face Brendy.

"Are you okay? I mean, are you really feeling all right? You haven't been quite yourself the past few days."

"I feel fine physically; it's hard to explain."

"I would love to be the one you can talk to; you have certainly been there enough for me."

"There's really no way of explaining how I feel. Unless I say that I'm homesick. I'll be okay, really."

"Homesick? I'm afraid I don't understand."

"When I died on that kitchen floor and Noah fought hard to bring me back, I didn't just lie there. Well, my body did, but our soul never dies. I crossed over, Brendy. I saw the other side. I saw my Tom and my parents. As much as I am glad to be back here with all of you, I'm still homesick for all of them. Do you understand that?"

Brendy took Edith's hand and rocked on the swing beside her for the longest without saying a word. This was a time that there were no words that needed to be said. She did understand. If she had gotten to see Noah after so many years of being away from him, she wouldn't have wanted to come back, either.

After a while of sitting in silence, Brendy spoke. "Thank you, Edith. For coming back for me, I mean."

"Don't thank me, child, I really don't think I had a choice, but if I had a choice I would have definitely come back for you."

"I know you would have. I'm so sorry you couldn't stay, but I'm so glad you came back. Not only did I find Jesus through that,I have gained something I never thought I would have. All my life I have hungered for a mother's love, and even though my mother and I have gotten closer, I have never known what that was like until you."

Edith put her arm around her and pulled her close. "Oh child, you are so easy to love, and I have enjoyed spending time studying the Bible with you. You are a delight to spend time with."

"Is that all that has been bothering you? I have really been worried."

Edith chuckled. "I think you are the only one to notice that my mind has been elsewhere lately."

"That's only because everyone else stays so busy, and I'm around you all day."

"That's right, you are. I don't know; it's just this feeling I get. I've always had this sixth sense when it comes to things. I just feel that something mighty is brewing in the air, and it isn't good."

Brendy fidgeted on the swing. Was it her Edith had sensed? Could she actually *feel* what was about to go down? "What do you think it is?" Brendy asked.

"I have no idea; that's why I have spent the last couple of days praying. Whatever it is, I have asked God to have His hand on it and work it out for His glory. I guess only time will tell."

"Yes, I guess you're right; only time will tell."

*****

After getting off the phone with Noah that evening, Brendy could tell he was acting as strangely as Edith. She was on a low and he was on a high. He was so upbeat compared to a few weeks ago. It was good to hear him laugh again and seem more like himself.

Brendy turned on the computer, as she did every night, to read the letter her mother had sent her and send one back in return. She thought of going to visit her mother if things didn't work out with Noah, but she hoped it didn't come to that. Brendy did want someday to see her mother again, but she hoped, when that time came, Noah was by her side.

Brendy wondered if Jasper was angry that she'd blocked him off her Facebook. Maybe she should have kept him unblocked. At least, that way he might have told her when he was coming; now she would never know, and she lived each day wondering when the night would come that he would knock on her door.

She played it out in her mind a hundred times how it would all go down and what she would say to him. In her mind, she could be a strong woman of God and not be afraid of Jasper Logan or what he could do to her.

In her mind she knew all the right words, for she rehearsed them over and over. She even went so far as to watch herself in the mirror, and how she would look when she said them.

Anybody on the outside looking in would have thought she was crazy, but Brendy knew that Jasper was dangerous and she wasn't about to allow him to get the upper hand, even if she died defending herself. She would go out fighting and standing up for what she believed in.

Not only had Brendy gone over what she would say to Jasper, but also what she would say to Noah if her original plan didn't work and she had to face him instead of giving him the letter she still had in her bedside table.

She knew talking to Jasper would be easy compared with talking to Noah. She didn't care about Jasper or what he thought of her. She could care less how angry or bitter he became with her or what he threatened. She would never go back and cow down to anyone again. Being with the Garretts had given her the courage she needed to stand up and fight.

Noah, on the other hand, would not be so easy. If it came down to having to look him in the eyes, how would she say what was on her heart? Brendy had never been good with words or expressing herself face to face, and, up until now, she had always run from everything and had become a coward when it really counted.

In her heart, she knew the storm that was brewing, and Edith felt it, too. Edith was feeling what was about to happen between her and Jasper and Noah. Almost the same thing that had happened with Noah years before, and she wondered if he would,once again, ride to the mountaintop and close himself in. Her heart ached for him and what he was about to go through. She wished she could spare him the pain he would have to endure, but there was no getting around it; sooner or later Jasper Logan would be there, and everything she had would be gone in a moment. Only Noah could bring it all back.

And even if he did choose to forgive her, would it ever really be the same? Would they be able to start over, with him knowing she'd slept with Jasper? Would he ever be able to hold her in his arms again or kiss her lips? How could he erase the picture he would have in his head of her and his friend. He would go the rest of his life wondering what the two of them had done. Would he go so far as to ask her questions?

Brendy closed her eyes and lay back on her bed. It was after midnight, and she knew sleep would not come easy.

After fifteen minutes of hearing the clock tick beside her, she got out of bed and down on her knees. Where else could she go? Who could she turn to, besides God?

Dear Heavenly Father,
Even though I am saved I still feel lost. My heart is heavy
with sadness. I know You forgave me of my past but that same

past is haunting me now. I realize that the truth will set me free, but it is that same truth that will hurt Noah.

Father, I feel the truth of my life closing in on me. I feel that I am suffocating and can't breathe. I can't take this much longer. Even though I wish I could go on as things are now, I know that when Noah finds out, everything will change, and I pray when that time comes You show me what to do and where to go. Starting over won't be easy, but with You, I know I can make it.

In Jesus' name….Amen.

Brendy went to bed and tried again to find sleep. It seemed that each time she prayed she always found peace, but not this time.

Edith told her that on nights she couldn't sleep, she always felt that God was trying to show her something, so she would get up and open her Bible and pray, asking God to reveal the words He wanted her to read. After praying, she would let her Bible fall open and place her finger on a verse. Edith laughed and said many might find her crazy, but that was always a fun game she and the Lord played.

"Are you trying to tell me something, Father?" Brendy felt no stirring in her spirit and felt crazy. She was new at being a Christian and wasn't sure how she went about listening to that still, small voice. So far, she had only heard it once before.

Brendy sat up in bed and turned on the lamp on her bedside table. She took out her pink Bible and silently asked God to reveal the words He wanted her to read. She let her Bible fall open and placed her finger between the verses of Luke 6:27–28

Love your enemies. Do good to those who hate you. Pray for the happiness of those who curse you. Pray for those who hurt you.

Brendy read the verses over several times. Was God trying to show her she needed to pray for Jasper and Caroline? What would she pray? She was so worried about herself she'd never thought about praying for them. Surely God loved them just as much; after all, they were His children, too.

Brendy placed the Bible on the bedside table and, once again, hit the floor on her knees. Praying was not something she was used to, and never had she prayed for her enemies, for people who cursed her or hated her or hurt her. She remembered Edith teaching her about loving your enemies, but it seemed that saying you loved someone and actually praying well over them were two different things.

Dear Father,
Forgive me when I forget to pray for others. It isn't easy praying for those who hurt me. You have proved to me that You still loved me even when I was living in sin. You loved me enough to lead me here. You never once gave up on me, and I realize that you love Caroline and Jasper the same.

Lord, I pray that you draw them near, lead them also to the right place with the right people. Help Jasper to see that he is living in sin. Show Him that You love him the way You showed me.

Send someone into Caroline's life that helps her to see what she is doing is wrong. Show her, too, that You love her and draw her near You.

And Lord, please help all those girls that are afraid of her. Help them have the courage that You gave me to get away and start a new life. I know You love each of them, no matter what they have done.

And last but not least, be with my mother. Bless her abundantly, Lord, for being faithful to You. Help her to help others by sharing her testimony, and thank You for bringing us back together through Noah.
In Jesus' Name...Amen

Brendy smiled as she crawled into bed; suddenly, she felt sleepy. There was much to learn about praying.

Chapter 33

"Are you serious? I never dreamed it would sell so quickly." Noah paced back and forth in the doctors' lounge as he spoke to the real estate agent on his cell phone.

"I'm scheduled to leave on Monday. Is there anyway I can sign those papers by Friday of this week?" Noah waited for Gail's response as he observed Candace walk into the lounge and take a seat. He nodded his hello and turned his back to her.

"Okay, that would be great. I'll come by Friday morning and sign off on my part. Everything sounds wonderful, and thanks for doing such a great job."

Noah slid his cell back into his pocket and turned to face Candace. "So, what's up?" He tried to be polite, even though their last meeting didn't go that well. It was the first time he had spoken to her since she'd showed up late on his doorstep.

"Looks like things are finally going your way?" she smiled.

"Yeah, I just sold my townhouse, looks like they are paying cash for it. I'll be signing papers on Friday and pulling out of Pittsburgh on Monday."

Candace shook her head and looked off for a moment. "We will miss you here, Noah, especially me."

"Magee's has other doctors; this hospital can survive without me."

"I need to talk to you, do you have a minute?" Candace patted the seat beside her.

"I don't have long; I have two patients in labor that I need to check soon."

"It won't take long. I really don't know how to start. I am so embarrassed about the other night. Never in my life have I pushed myself on anyone." Candace chuckled. "Gosh, I've never had to. You are the first man who ever turned me down."

"Candace, it's nothing against you." Candace put her hand up, stopping him from speaking anymore.

"I'm not finished." She took a deep breath and continued. "I'm sorry about what I said about your God. The truth is, Noah, your God is my God. I was brought up in church. I was taught the ways of the Lord, and even saved as a teenager. I guess working as a doctor and seeing so much death all around; it starts to take a toll."

Noah shook his head; he understood more than anyone.

"I understand what you mean about honoring God. You caused me to think a lot about my own life since that night, and the fact that I haven't been honoring God myself. I've done a lot of praying since then. I think the Lord might have been shocked to hear from me at first; it's been a while."

"I shouldn't have let you drive that night."

"Oh Noah, I wasn't drunk. Sure, I'd had a drink, but I knew what I was doing. I would like to tell you I was out of my head, but the truth was I have been after you ever since I laid eyes on you. All my life I have been spoiled; my parents never hurt for money, and now I don't, either. The one thing I really wanted that I couldn't have is you."

"I'm sorry, Candace. I pray that you find that special someone that will make you happy. Keep praying and honoring God, and He will bless you as He did me."

Candace smiled and turned toward him more. "She must be awfully special."

"She is. I know God put her in my path for a reason. I didn't understand at first what it was, but now I do."

"She's a very lucky woman."

"I'm the lucky one, Candace; Brendy is special."

Candace got off the couch and took Noah's hand, pulling him to his feet. "Can I at least have a hug?"

Noah put his arms around the woman he'd spent the last several years with. The same woman he'd taken to dinner numerous times and kissed goodnight at her front door. The woman he could never love.

When Noah pulled away, Candace had tears in her eyes. "I truly am sorry for the other night. I don't want that to be the last memory you have of me."

"It won't be," Noah smiled. "We did have some good times and a lot of laughs."

"Yeah, we did." Candace walked towards the door and stopped. "Take care of yourself, Noah. I wish you the best."

Noah watched her leave, feeling that it would be the last time they would speak. If he saw her again in the next couple of days, it would only be in passing. A part of Noah hurt for her. As beautiful as Dr. Candace Wright was, she was not nor would she ever be the woman God had chosen for him; he knew that now more than ever.

*****

"Why are you leaving again so soon?" Jessie walked into the bedroom and found Jasper packing.

"Why do you care? I'm sure you won't miss me." Jasper continued to pack, not stopping to look at Jessie.

"What is that supposed to mean?"

"Take it anyway you want to. You never acknowledge that I'm here anyway, so why do you care when I go?"

Jessie walked close to Jasper so she would be in his view when she spoke. "We both lead busy lives, Jasper; as doctors, neither one of us is home much. And you know as well as I do that I acknowledge you every bit as much as you acknowledge me."

Jasper shut his suitcase and zipped it up. "I have a business trip to go to. I should be back in a few days."

"You and your business trips, why don't you just tell me the truth, Jasper? What's her name?"

Jasper looked at Jessie for a moment before he spoke. "She's no one you know. Is that what you want to hear?"

"So, there is another woman? I mean, I know you have had rendezvous with nurses at the hospital, but these business trips you have been taking have nothing to do with nurses, do they?"

"Jessie, you and I have not been man and wife for years now. There is no use trying to pretend that either of us is happy. Frankly, I am tired of the effort."

Jessie laughed out. "The effort? Do you really think you have been giving our marriage any effort?"

"As much as you have. Don't think I don't know about your rendezvous."

Jessie took a deep breath and let it out. "So what does this mean? Do you want a divorce?"

"I've wanted one for a long time."

"Then why haven't you asked?"

"I was waiting on you to ask. I know you haven't loved me for a long time, if ever."

"You're right; I haven't. I suspect the same from you?"

Jasper shook his head and agreed. "You can keep the house. I will move into an apartment. As a matter of fact, you can keep it all. I'll come back in a couple of days and move my clothes."

"So, that's it?" Jessie said. "Just like that, it's over?"

"Jessie, as we have agreed, it's been over a long time; there's no use dragging it out any longer than it has to be."

"You know, we both made mistakes, but our biggest one was hurting Noah."

"You say that with sadness," Jasper smiled.

"We both hurt him, Jasper, you and I both; he didn't deserve that."

"If you care so much, he is still single; you know where to find him."

Jessie shook her head, "No, he may not be married, but he is very much in love. I saw it in his eyes the last time we were in Summersville and I ran into him and his girlfriend."

"Well, he isn't married yet, so he is still up for grabs."

"You will never change, will you, Jasper? It's a pity I didn't stick with Noah. I've often wondered how my life might have turned out differently."

Jasper picked up his suitcase and started for the door. "I will tell you how it would have turned out. You two would not have been married as long as you and I, because Noah would never have put up with your infidelity the way I have."

"Just as I have put up with yours. I don't know who this woman is, Jasper, but I hope she truly knows the kind of man you are."

Jasper laughed as he walked out the door. "Goodbye, Jessie. I'll let you draw up the papers anyway you want. Take care of yourself."

Jessie sat on the edge of the bed and listened for his car to start and pull out of the garage. She felt numb, absolutely emotionless. Her husband of five years was leaving, and she couldn't even bring herself to tears. Her life was such a mess, and had been ever since she'd allowed Jasper Logan to own her, body and soul.

Jessie lay back on the bed and stared up at the ceiling. How long had it been since she had prayed? How long had it been since she had gone to church or felt good about life? She had everything she'd ever wanted, but, in the process, had lost the only things in life that really mattered to her: God and Noah Garrett.

*****

Jasper drove out of town and headed south. He would stop at a hotel after a hundred miles or so and finish the rest of the trip tomorrow. He planned to be in Summersville way after dark, so he wouldn't be noticed.

Everything was starting to fall into place. Since he didn't have to worry about going back to Jessie, he would persuade Brendy to leave with him. He knew for certain she would put up a fight, but she would give in, just as she always did. His hold was Caroline Reese, and if he promised he would keep Caroline from knowing her whereabouts, she would come.

He wasn't worried about Noah; Noah had been a pushover for way too long. Even as a child growing up, Noah had been a coward, always trying to work things out instead of standing up and fighting like a man. No wonder he had lost Jessie, and now, because of his God, he would lose Brendy, too.

Noah's God had kept him from living, and Jasper was sick of hearing about it. All his life, growing up, Noah had put God first, but look where it got him. Noah was now a thirty-two year old man who was still unmarried.

Jasper laughed to himself when he thought of Noah's beliefs. What did it matter, anyway? If Noah's God was really as loving as Noah said, then He would forgive him, right? It was better to live for the day and not think about the consequences.

Jasper smiled when he thought of how it would all go down with Brendy. He'd had a lot of women in his life, but none he ever really wanted to keep until Brendy. He wasn't sure what it was about her, but it gave him such power to think about finally owning her, once and for all.

It had been easy when he could pay for her time. Like clockwork, she was always there, always eager to please, but now, even though no money exchanged hands, he had to bribe her and threaten to expose her.

He hated the word blackmail, and would much rather think of this as him saving her from sure heartache later on. Sooner or later, Noah was bound to find out the horrid truth, and what then?

Did Brendy actually think Noah would forgive that? If so, then she didn't know Noah the way he did. Noah had turned against Jessie for being with one other man. What would he do when he found out she'd been with hundreds?

No, he would be devastated and disgusted with her, and she would be left out in the cold, all alone, with no one to turn to except him.

He wasn't doing anything wrong, and she would thank him for it later. He was sure that if he could ever get her alone for any length of time, she would realize that it was him she'd always loved. Not a man like Noah Garrett, but a real man. A man who wasn't afraid to go after what he desired, and right now he desired her.

*****

"Don't you just hate this storm?" Brendy asked Edith, coming into the kitchen not long after sunup.

"Actually, I like a good storm if tornado warnings aren't involved. It gets the family in the house and gives us some one-on-one time together."

"So where is everyone at, then?" Brendy walked to the coffee pot and poured herself a cup of coffee.

"They will be in soon. There will be no trail rides or riding lessons on a day like today. Of course, the boys will still be busy in the barn, but us women can sit around and gossip," Edith laughed.

"So, what are we gossiping about?" Connie asked, coming into the kitchen.

"Anything and everything," Edith answered. "I am hoping Rene comes here before going home, after she drops Beth off at school; us four girls could have us a powwow."

"So call her and ask her to stop by here first. Never mind," Connie said, getting out her phone. "I'll do it. You just better make sure we have plenty of something to munch on."

Brendy laughed and looked at Edith after Connie's comment. Edith winked at her and took a strawberry cheesecake out of the refrigerator.

"Ooh, that looks delicious." Brendy licked her lips.

"It will be, but this will come after breakfast. I am fixing the works."

Brendy walked over to Edith and put her arm around her. "You always fix the works. Eating with you is better than any restaurant."

"Thank you." Edith put the cheesecake back into the refrigerator and turned to Connie. "So, what did she say?"

"She said she would be here in a few. What's for breakfast? I'm starved."

"Gravy and biscuits, hash browns, and bacon."

"If you keep cooking like this, you will never get rid of us kids," Connie joked.

"Why do you think I do it? I don't want to lose any of you." Edith brought the biscuits out of the oven and placed them on the counter; at the same time, a crack of thunder rolled right above them, making Brendy jump.

"Goodness," Edith laughed. "I have felt a storm brewing for days, but I had no idea it would be so bad.

Brendy smiled at Edith, knowing in her heart that this was not the storm she'd felt brewing, and it frightened her to think about the one that would hit when Jasper Logan drove back into town.

*****

Chapter 34

Noah looked around his townhouse and smiled. The movers had already left and were headed to Summersville to place his items in a mini storage there. He would leave his belongings there and live in the main house until he figured out what his plans would be for the future.

He thought about what he wanted to do but wasn't sure Brendy would like the idea. If his idea worked, then the cabin on the mountain wouldn't be a place she could ride off to to be alone; it would be a place she would live each day. There were so many details that he would have to take care of before that could actually become a reality.

Taking one last walk through his townhouse, he knew this should be a moment that most became saddened, realizing that they would never walk this way again, but Noah was filled with nothing but happiness.

He met the Franklins Friday morning and was glad that his house would be filled with love and children. Robert Franklin was moving to Pittsburgh because of his job, and Elizabeth was a stay at home mom with two girls. He imagined the beautiful townhome filled once again with furniture, and the kitchen filled with the smell of bacon, as children sat at the table coloring.

Noah wanted to get an early start, but last minute details at the hospital kept him most of the day. He thought about waiting until Tuesday morning and getting to Pittsburgh about noon, but he couldn't contain his excitement. He could imagine how excited Brendy would be when he got there,after dark, not long after he hung up the phone with her. She would be sitting at the bar in front of her computer, writing her mother before bedtime when he knocked on the door.

Noah had so much he wanted to say to her. He wanted to hold her in his arms and promise her that he would never again leave her.

He would sneak in the main house with his key without anyone knowing and surprise the family in the morning for breakfast. Then he would drive Brendy to see his new OB/ GYN office in town and meet with the agent to sign the papers. His life had never been so blessed and so well planned out.

Noah started the engine of his car and backed out of the driveway. He paused at the end and took one last look. As he drove away, he silently thanked God for the blessings he'd been given and promised to live the rest of his days allowing God to work through him to fulfill His purpose.

*****

Even though the rain and storms had kept the ranch from its usual busy day, Brendy had a blast with all the women who where forced to stay inside. They laughed and talked and even played board games.

As much as Brendy loved everyone in the Garrett family, the last thing she wanted to do was hurt them. What would they think when she left with no warning? Would Noah tell them the truth?

Brendy turned on the lights in her apartment and looked at the clock. Noah would be calling within fifteen minutes, so she quickly jumped in the shower. Her every-night ritual had become something she loved.

"So, how has your day been?" Noah asked with excitement. He couldn't wait to surprise her within the hour.

"It's been great. Rained here all day, and all of us girls did nothing but laugh and play board games; it was fantastic."

Noah laughed at her. "That sounds like something women would do."

"And what would men do?"

"Sit around and watch football and talk about women," he teased.

"Yeah, that sounds about right. So how was your day?"

Noah paused. "If I told you, you wouldn't believe me. But it was great; probably one of the best days I've had since I moved to Pittsburgh."

"Really? So how many babies did you help bring into the world today?"

"None, actually."

"None? You must have had the day off."

"You could say that. Of course, it doesn't sound like I've had as great a day as you women, playing all those board games."

"Yet, it was your best so far? Now that sounds interesting. Can you tell me about it?"

Noah chuckled. He knew her well enough to know she wouldn't give up easily. "Not just yet, maybe later."

"Later as in before we get off the phone, or later as in another day?"

"Just later. So, have you written your mother today?" Noah changed the subject.

"No. You know I always write her after you and I talk; you're just trying to change the subject, Noah Garrett. I was not born yesterday."

"No, you sure weren't. That would make you way too young for me."

Brendy laughed at his comment. "You're funny. Okay then, I won't pry, but in the future, if you can't finish telling me what you started, don't start it at all, drives me nuts."

"Does it? That's only because you are a woman."

"Come on now, that's not very nice," she giggled. "You are definitely up to something."

"You know me so well. I have a feeling, after this, you are going to know me so much better."

"That would be nice; I can hardly wait. Don't laugh, but do you know that today was the first time I've ever played Monopoly in my life?"

"Seriously? How did you like it?" Noah looked forward to firsts with Brendy. There was so much she'd missed out on so far.

"I loved it, once I got the hang of it. Of course, your mother won; she wiped us all clean."

"Yep, that sounds like her; she takes pride in that, too."

"You've got that right. She will probably rub it in for days to come."

"But, of course she will," he laughed. "My mother is just an overgrown child."

"That's why she is so much fun. I was thinking that it would be great if, one day, your mother and my mother could get together. Now that my mother seems so normal, it would do her good to have a friend like Edith."

"Mom would like that; she can't get enough friends. Maybe one day we can arrange a meeting and invite her and her husband to the ranch."

"I never thought I would say this, but I would really like to do that. I feel I have missed out on so much with my mother, and I have a lot of making up to do."

"It makes me feel great, Brendy, knowing that you two are talking and that you have forgiven her."

"So you think I forgive her?" Brendy wasn't so sure herself.

"You have. I can hear it in your voice. You used to sound very down when you talked about her, but now you are always upbeat and making plans for the future; that's great."

"That's scary. I can't believe how much I've changed since I met you in Pittsburgh. Sometimes I can't even believe it's me."

"It's always been you, Brendy. It's just that you no longer have such a low self-esteem. And speaking of that, I would like to talk to you about getting your GED and perhaps going to college."

"Me going to college? Now that would be a trip."

"Do you realize you can go to college right there in your own home on your computer? Almost every subject imaginable is offered online now. What have you always wanted to be?"

"I haven't really thought about it. I think you've asked me this question before," she laughed.

"Well, I want you to think about it. Search your heart and go for it. I'd love to help you get started with anything you can dream of."

"Well, that does sound interesting. I will definitely think about it."

"Well Brendy, it's getting late, and I know you have to write your mother." Noah smiled with excitement, so eager to pull into the driveway.

"Yeah, and you have all those babies to deliver tomorrow. You know what, Noah?"

"What's that?"

"I really miss you."

"That's good to know. I hope you know the feelings are mutual. I wish I'd never had to leave."

"Me, too. Well, goodnight, Noah. I will talk to you tomorrow."

"Okay baby, I love you, goodnight."

"Love you, too." Brendy hung up the phone and stared at her computer screen. It was so easy to tell Noah she loved him, but then she *did* love him. She only wished she'd met him six years before, when she could have considered herself someone worthy of him.

*****

Jasper parked at the end of the driveway and turned off the engine. The house looked dark and deserted. He'd timed it just right; everyone had gone to bed.

He was glad Noah was back in Pittsburgh; that was one less person he had to worry about, and, knowing Greg and Brad went to bed with the chickens, he didn't have to worry about them, either.

He looked up at the window above the garage and smiled. Brendy's light was still on. She was a night owl. He guessed her new schedule was driving her crazy. After tonight, she would no longer have to worry about it.

Jasper climbed the stairs slowly that led to her front door, and listened carefully, making sure no one was there besides her. He had no idea what he would say should he run into someone other than Brendy.

Several weeks had passed since he was last here, and he couldn't wait to have her for his own again. He listened closely at the door and only heard the distant sound of someone typing on a keyboard. Obviously, she was alone.

He turned the doorknob slowly, and the door started to open. Crazy woman had forgotten to lock her door, but then, this was Summersville, not New York.

*****

Brendy finished the letter to her mother and was shutting down the computer, when something to her right caught her eye. Her doorknob was turning slowly to the left. Oh my god, had she not locked the door?

Brendy wasn't sure if she should run towards the door and slam it shut and lock it, or run to her bedroom and lock the door there. So much ran through her mind in a split second. Brendy knew it was Jasper. Her heart had been warning her for days; even Edith had felt it.

Before the door opened all the way, Brendy rushed to it and pressed her body against it with all she had, but Jasper was too strong and shoved the door open so hard it sent her flying backwards, and she hit her head on the edge of the coffee table.

Brendy looked up, feeling dazed, as Jasper stood over her. She wanted to scream out with everything inside her, but, for some reason, her body would not cooperate. Brendy tried hard to open her mouth to speak, to tell him to go away, that she was no longer his toy to do with as he wished, but all that came out was a faint moan, before her world went black.

Jasper checked to make sure she was still among the living and realized that the hard hit had only knocked her unconscious. Within a few minutes, she would regain consciousness and be able to talk to him. He would help her pack her clothes, and they would be on their way within the hour.

She was so beautiful lying there, and Jasper couldn't wait until she was finally his, anytime he so desired. No more paying for her time, or having to get days off and sneak around hoping not to get caught. Now there would be just the two of them, and she would be his forever. She might put up a fight at first, but she would soon realize where her place was, and that was with him.

Jasper slowly caressed her arm, touching the softness of it. She was the most beautiful woman he'd ever seen. She was like an addiction to him, and each time he left her, it drove him crazy until he was with her again. No wonder Noah was in love with her. At least his friend was smarter than he gave him credit for.

"You are mine now, my love. Wake up and look at me." Jasper rubbed Brendy's face gently, trying to get her attention.

Brendy moaned out again and slowly opened her eyes. Terror filled her face when she realized Jasper Logan was kneeling beside her.

"Looks like you hit your head pretty hard, glad to see you back in the land of the living."

Jasper smiled, and ran his hand down her leg.

Brendy jerked away and tried to sit up. Dizziness overcame her, and she fell back. Why wouldn't her body cooperate? How could she tell him no if she was paralyzed?

"Good girl, you don't have to move. Just lie still." Jasper started to unbutton her blouse as he whispered to her. "You are so beautiful, Sasha. I'm sorry it took me so long to get back. I have wanted you so badly."

Brendy tried to shake her head from side to side, but, each time she moved, the room spun around her. "No Jasper, please no."

"Shhh, don't try to talk now. Just lie real still. After I'm done, we will get you packed. I have some good news for you, Sasha. I'm getting a divorce. You will be able to come and live with me."

"No Jasper, stop!" In Brendy's mind, she screamed out, but Jasper only heard a faint whisper. She was too weak to fight him, and now he would win again. How would she ever tell Noah that she'd allowed this twice since she met him?

Would he ever believe that she never wanted for it to happen again?

Jasper leaned down and tried to kiss her lips, but Brendy turned her head to the side. "I said no, you will never touch me again. You are a pig, and you disgust me!" Brendy wasn't sure if she was saying the words out loud or inside her head, and she prayed that he heard her.

"You are mine, Sasha. You have always been mine, since that first night on the yacht six years ago, and now you will be mine forever." Jasper started to unsnap her pants, and Brendy jerked to the side.

"I said no!" she screamed out, as loud as she could. "Get off me!"

No one heard Noah enter. No one knew how long he'd been listening or watching. No one knew that, at first, he thought his world was crashing in like the last time he'd found Jasper with the woman he loved.

It had not taken Noah long to realize that Brendy was hurt and Jasper was taking advantage of the situation. This was the woman he loved, and no one was going to hurt her ever again.

Rage filled him as he flew across the room and pulled Jasper back by his collar. Jasper turned quickly, thinking Greg or Brad had walked in, and realized it was Noah.

"Not this time, my friend," Noah said with rage, as he balled up his fist and knocked Jasper across the room, knocking him unconscious.

Noah knelt down beside Brendy, who was still lying on the floor, confused about what was taking place. She was so dizzy and could have sworn she saw Noah walk in and pull Jasper off of her. But how could that be? Noah was in Pittsburgh; she had talked to him no more than an hour ago.

"Baby, are you okay?" Noah lifted her gently off the floor and cradled her in his arms. There was a pool of blood on the floor where her head had been. "You're bleeding; did Jasper do this to you?"

"Noah, you're here?" Brendy was confused.

"I'm here, baby, and I am never leaving you again. I'm taking you to the hospital. Just hang on to me." Noah lifted Brendy off the floor and carried her down the steps to his car. As much as he wanted to go back in and hash it out with Jasper when he woke up, he knew he had to get Brendy to the hospital quickly.

Noah drove at record speed to Summersville Memorial Hospital. So much was racing through his mind. For the life of him, he couldn't figure out what Jasper was doing there, and how they knew each other.

Ever since the night in the hospital after his mother's surgery, he'd had a sick feeling there was more than he knew, and he was hoping Brendy would tell him in time.

Brendy rolled her head back and forth and moaned again. Why was she in Noah's car? What time was it? She tried to focus but she kept going in and out of consciousness.

"Where are we?" she whispered.

"Don't talk, baby, we are going to the hospital. I think you have a concussion, and you definitely need stitches. I want to check and make sure you're okay."

"What happened?"

"You must have hit your head, but we will talk later. Just rest, we will be there shortly."

As much as Noah wanted to ask a hundred questions as to why, he knew now was not the time. When Brendy was up to answering questions, he wanted her alert and able to focus. To Noah, it didn't matter what the answers were, as long as she was okay.

*****

"What happened?" Dr. Phillips asked Noah, after giving Brendy a CAT scan.

"I'm not sure. She was lying on the floor when I walked in. I think she fell and hit her head on the edge of the coffee table."

"She's lucky; it could have been worse. She does have a concussion, and I will have to stitch her up. But the CAT scan shows no sign of internal bleeding."

"Thank God for that. She has been in and out of consciousness, and I haven't really been able to ask her what happened."

"And she will be pretty out of it the rest of the night. We have her pretty sedated. I'd like to keep her tonight just to observe her. If everything goes as I think it will, I will send her home tomorrow."

Noah shook Dr. Phillips hand. "Thank you, sir, I appreciate you taking care of her."

"Just call me David, and it's good to have you here. I heard through the grapevine that Dr. Noah Garrett was about to start working out of our hospital."

"That's right. I'm opening my practice here in town."

"Well, from the rumors, you are one of the best. Glad to have you join us."

Noah smiled. "Thank you, David, and thanks again for everything."

Chapter 35

Noah looked down at Brendy, sleeping peacefully in the hospital bed. Even though her head was bandaged, she was still beautiful. What were the secrets she was withholding, and why did she think she couldn't trust him with them?

What sort of hold did Jasper have on her, and how did they know each other? So many things were now starting to make sense.

Noah hated the fact that Brendy felt she couldn't confide in him. Something terrible had happened between her and Jasper; he only wished he knew what it was. The day in the cell phone store when she suddenly became ill, and the day in the hospital when terror was written all over her face, told him she was afraid of Jasper Logan.

Jasper had known her by another name, but they'd covered it up. Why could he not have read between the lines? Had he always been so blind to the obvious? Jasper had asked him so many questions about her afterwards, and he had led him right to her.

Brendy stirred a little, and Noah reached down and took her hand, squeezing it gently. "How do you feel, baby?"

Brendy struggled to open her eyes. "Noah......"

"Everything is okay. They are keeping you tonight for observation. Just try to get some rest, and we will talk in the morning."

"But what are you doing here?" she said slowly.

"It's a long story. Get some rest. I'm going back to the ranch and grab an outfit for you to wear home tomorrow; you have quite a bit of blood on what you were wearing."

"I'm so confused." Brendy knew Jasper had been there and Noah had walked in. What had happened? What was he thinking?

Noah leaned down and kissed her softly. "We'll talk later; now get some sleep. I'll be back as soon as I can."

Brendy closed her eyes and within minutes was sleeping. Noah left the hospital, telling the nurse at the nurses' station he was leaving and would be back shortly, to please keep an eye on her. It didn't matter that he was not a doctor yet at Summersville Memorial; he still found himself acting like he belonged here. Besides, Brendy was the woman he loved.

*****

When Noah pulled into his driveway, he noticed that the car parked at the end was now gone. He hadn't paid much attention to it before, but now he knew it must have been Jasper's.

The main house was still black, with everyone sleeping, oblivious to what had taken place. How would he tell them what had happened, when he didn't know himself?

Noah found the door to Brendy's apartment still open and all the lights still on. He wondered when it was that Jasper left and where he had gone. Surely he was around here somewhere, either at his parents' or at a hotel.

Noah walked into Brendy's bedroom and opened the closet, looking for a pair of pants and shirt that would be comfortable for wearing home. There was no dresser in the room except for a bedside table with a few drawers. Perhaps she put her underclothes there, he thought. Noah opened the top drawer, and something caught his eye. It was a letter in a long envelope with his name on it.

Noah took the letter out of the drawer and sat down on the edge of the bed. The envelope was not sealed. When had she intended to give this to him? Should he open it?

So many questions were in his mind, so many unanswered questions, that he felt whatever was inside the envelope might shed more light on what had happened.

Noah slowly opened the envelope and pulled out a hand-written letter to him from Brendy and began to read.

*****

Noah was filled with so many emotions driving back towards the hospital. He could imagine Brendy sitting all alone on the mountaintop late at night, with just the lamplight. He could visualize her, sitting at the table he'd sat at so many times growing up with his parents, as she cried and poured out her heart to him in a letter she was going to mail if Jasper ever came back.

So many times he could remember her telling him that she wasn't right for him. She had tried to tell him in so many words but could never find the right ones. When he thought about her life, his heart hurt for her. Until now, she'd lived her life doing what others told her and never what she wanted, forced to quit school at sixteen and go to a city filled with strangers at such a young age.

He wondered how many other young girls fell into the same trap, thinking that selling their bodies was their only option, and then not able to get out.

It wasn't Brendy's fault those things had happened to her. It was, first, her mother's, who was young herself and facing fears she didn't know how to handle. Then being controlled by Caroline Reese and made to feel that she didn't have an option or a say-so in what happened to her own body. And now, when things were finally going good for her, she meets the man who has as much hold over her as the others.

Noah gripped his steering wheel hard and gritted his teeth. He silently asked God to forgive him for his thoughts. He was angry at Jasper for taking advantage of the situation and trying to blackmail her into letting him have his way. All Jasper's life he'd thought he could take anything he wanted, but no more.

Noah turned away from the hospital and started down the long road that led to Jasper's parent's house. His parents were usually in Italy this time of year, and maybe he would get lucky and find him alone.

As he approached the front of the house, he saw only one car. It was the same car that was at the end of his drive earlier. Jasper was there, and he was alone.

Noah got out of the car and took a deep breath before walking to the door.

Be with me, Lord, and help me keep my cool even when I will want to lose it.

I'm with you always, Son.....

Noah heard that still, small voice in his spirit and knew that whatever happened between him and Jasper, God would be with him.

Noah knocked on the door and waited for several minutes before knocking loudly. "I know you're in there, Jasper, you might as well open the door before I kick it in!" Noah yelled. He was bound and determined he would not leave until he spoke to Jasper face-to-face. So many years were bottled up, and tonight would be the end of it.

Jasper opened the door with an ice pack held against his eye. "Did you come to finish me off?"

"We need to talk." Noah didn't wait to be invited in; he pushed past Jasper and went towards the living room area.

"Why did you hit me? Couldn't you see I walked up on an accident and was only trying to help her? I'm a doctor, for crying out loud."

Noah walked as close to him as possible and didn't cow down to his friend, who had always made him feel he had the upper hand. Jasper always won at everything growing up, and even stole Jessie right out from under him.

"I know, Jasper. I know everything."

"You know what? What do you know, Noah?"

"I know you were blackmailing Brendy. I know you have run around on your wife for years with prostitutes and young girls who didn't know better. I know you took advantage of Brendy's accident and were about to rape her."

"Rape her?" Jasper laughed. "Is that what she told you? Noah, you, of all people, know that rape is when it is forced; Sasha has been giving it to me freely for years now. Just ask her."

Noah grabbed Jasper by his collar and pushed him up against the wall. "I pity you, Jasper Logan; other than being a great doctor, you are selfish and self-centered. You are a cheat and a liar. You don't care who you hurt, or how you get what you want. You have always thought that life is handed to you on a silver platter, but it's not. There are just some things that money can't buy, and Brendy is one of them." Noah shoved him aside and walked towards the door.

He turned and looked back at Jasper, who was standing with his mouth agape. "If you ever come back on the Garrett property, I will have you arrested and expose you for the man that you are. I am sure Mr. and Mrs. Logan would be very proud of their son if they knew the truth. Goodbye, Jasper."

Jasper watched Noah leave, not believing that he had taken Sasha's side over his. Why would he want to build a life with a prostitute? Noah would never change, always trying to bring out the best in people and be everyone's savior.

Jasper flipped up his cell and pressed his contact list button. Caroline Reese's name stared at him. How easy would it be for him to make one call? What would happen if she knew that Sasha was alive and well and hiding out in another state?

Jasper closed his cell and threw it on the couch. How would he benefit from that? Maybe it was best to let it go. After all, Caroline was hiring new girls every day; he would just find another one the way he found Sasha. He would start home tomorrow and give her a call. By tomorrow night, he would be back on his yacht with someone new and be able to put all this behind him.

*****

Brendy was sleeping when Noah walked into the hospital room, just before daylight, and sat down beside her bed. Knowing Brendy's past, he smiled to himself and looked up towards the heavens. Why would God have sent someone who had lived Brendy's life to someone who'd always had such high standards? Perhaps God knew it was time to lower those standards and to show him that He loved all people, no matter what their past. He died to cover our sins, not to condemn us for them.

He squeezed Brendy's hand gently, and she opened her eyes and smiled at him. "I had the most wonderful dream."

Noah smiled back at her. "So, tell me about it."

"First, I have to talk to you about something. I'm sorry I waited so long, Noah."

"Are you feeling better?" he asked.

"I'm coherent, if that's what you mean, but I have a heck of a headache."

"I thought you might. Would you like me to get you some pain medication?"

"No, Noah, I don't want to go back to sleep. I have something to tell you and I need you to let me talk, okay?"

"In other words, you want me to shut up?"

Brendy tried to laugh, but squinted her eyes, from the pain racing through her head. "Yes, that's what I want, for you to let me talk. I am just not sure where to begin."

"Why not start at the beginning?"

"Yes, that's a good place. Noah, I had a letter written to you, and I wish I had it here because I really thought about the way I wanted to tell you this in that letter. Now my head is all fuzzy, and I'm afraid it won't come out right, but I'm going to do my best."

"Hang on, I think I have it right here, if it will help." Noah reached in his pocket and pulled out the letter and placed it in Brendy's hand.

Brendy looked at the letter and back at Noah. She felt paralyzed with fear. How did he have the letter? She'd never mailed it to him.

"How did you get this?" Brendy's voice trembled.

"I went back to your apartment to get you some clothes, and I went snooping for underclothes, thinking you might appreciate it if I brought you back something to wear home. It just happened to be lying there, and, since it had my name on it, I thought it was for me."

"And you read it?"

"I did. You did want me to, right?"

Brendy closed her eyes and couldn't stop the tears. "Oh Noah, I never meant for this to happen this way."

"No, I think you were going to run off again, right? But you had not decided where you were going. Well, you don't have to run anymore, Brendy. Summersville can stay your home forever, if you want it."

"What are you saying, Noah? I know I have hurt you terribly."

"Nothing you did, Brendy, was done against me. You didn't even know me when you were in New York. I am so sorry you endured all that. No one deserves the life you have been dealt, but that's all over now. No one will hurt you anymore."

"Jasper will come back. You don't really know him, Noah; he is not a good person, and he will never give up."

"Jasper Logan will never bother you again, Brendy, and neither will Caroline. No one owns you. We will call the law if anyone steps foot on our property."

"Noah, I'm confused. How can you get over this so easy? I have been with countless men, some I didn't even know their name."

"Because I was with you in that hospital room the day you asked God to forgive you. Brendy, it is not my place to forgive you; you did none of those things to me. I love you just as I always have. It is your place to forgive yourself."

"You mean you don't care that I'm a prostitute?"

Noah laughed. "You *were,* Brendy, but you're not anymore. You are a wonderful Christian woman that I happen to love with all my heart."

Tears fell down Brendy's face, and Noah reached over and wiped them with his fingers. "Do you love me, Brendy Blake?"

"I do, Noah. I love you so much."

"Do you love me enough to marry me and grow old with me?" Noah reached back into his pocket and pulled out a small box. "I was going to do this tomorrow at my new office, but what the heck." Noah pulled out a beautiful diamond ring and placed it on her finger.

Brendy tried to laugh. "Oh Noah, of course I will marry you. I would love to be your wife and…" Brendy paused. "What do you mean, at your new office?"

"Well, that was another surprise. I sold my townhouse and leased an office space in Summersville. I am opening an OB/GYN practice. I will work out of this hospital instead of Magee's."

"You mean you aren't going back to Pittsburgh?"

"Nope, not ever. Is that okay with you? I mean, I know how much you hate the city."

Brendy looked as if she were in shock. "Does your family know this?"

"Not yet. In fact, they don't know you're in the hospital, or I am in town."

"Oh my goodness, Noah, they will be worried sick about me. We are going to have to tell them what happened. They will think I'm terrible." Brendy closed her eyes again, thinking of the worst.

"Why? Because you are clumsy?"

"Clumsy?" Brendy was confused.

"Yes. Last night, when I got to your apartment to surprise you, I found you lying on the floor unconscious, so I picked you up and brought you to the hospital. Why would that make them think you were terrible?"

Brendy looked at him with such love in her eyes it made his heart melt. "I love you, Noah Garrett, and I can't wait to get out of here so we can start over with no secrets."

"Well, I do have one, or maybe I should say it's a surprise."

"I like surprises, so what is it?"

Noah laughed. "If I told you, it wouldn't be a surprise, would it?"

Brendy rolled her eyes at him and smiled. For the first time in Noah's life, he felt like he finally had a focus. He was back on the land he loved with the woman he'd prayed all his life for God to send him. He had no idea what tomorrow held for them, but he knew who held tomorrow, and with God's help, anything was possible.

It's not over yet. *The Seasons of Change Series* next book is *Fall's Undying Promise.* Join Greg and Rene as they get heartbreaking news that no couple wants to hear. Will their faith in God be enough to carry them through the challenging road that lies ahead?

Look for these upcoming books:

Fall's Undying Promise . . . Greg's Story
Cold Winter's Chill . . . Brad's Story
The Fragrance of Spring . . . Connie's Story

Karen Ayers is the author of *The Secrets of Westingdale* available now at:
http://SBPRA.com/KarenAyers

When Maria Taylor purchases Westingdale, a huge mansion that overlooks the sea, she hopes to turn this beautiful house into an historic bed and breakfast and also hopes that it will bring her and her sixteen-year-old daughter back together following the death of her husband and Janie's father the year before, as they have drifted apart. But the long-vacant home has problems of its own. Little do they know that Westingdale is haunted.

Join with a mother and daughter as they start a new life. You will laugh and cry as their story unfolds and be left with the knowledge that it is okay to love again. What is *The Secrets of Westingdale*? For some, it is as simple as finding forgiveness.

A LETTER FROM KAREN:

I hope you enjoyed *Sweet Summer Rain* as much as I enjoyed writing it. I wanted to show the reader that, no matter what our past is, it can be made clean with God. He died to cover our sins, not condemn them.

I allowed Brendy to start this journey not believing in God because, so many times throughout her life, she felt He was never there for her, as so many do in this life. It saddens my heart when people take God for granted or say they don't believe Jesus Christ was the Son of God.

God sent His only-begotten Son, Jesus Christ, to this earth to die for our sins, and all we have to do is believe in Him to have everlasting life.

For God so loved the world, that He gave His only begotten Son, that whosoever believeth in Him, should not perish but have everlasting life. John 3:16

This has always been my favorite Bible verse because, to me, it says it all. The word whosoever means: anyone, everyone, all of us, if we JUST believe, we can have everlasting life when this life is over. Isn't that great? It doesn't even matter what we have done or where we came from; Jesus loves us all the same. He died for all of us, not just some of us.

If you have never asked Jesus into your heart, and believe that He is the Son of God, born of the virgin Mary to live on this earth and die for our sins, and that He rose again after just three days, then humble yourself and ask Him today:

Dear Lord, I believe that You are the Son of God. I believe that You came to this earth and died for my sins. I am asking You today to fill my heart with Your Holy presence and save my soul. Forgive me, Lord, and cleanse me from past sins. Today, Dear Jesus, wipe the slate clean and allow me to start again, as Your child. Thank you, Lord Jesus, for becoming my Savior. Amen

If you have just prayed the prayer of salvation and asked Jesus to become your Lord and Savior, then the advice I want to give you is this: Make sure, if you don't have a Bible, that you go buy one today. The King James Version or the New Revised Version are both good. If you cannot afford a Bible, then write to me and let me know and I will mail you one, free of charge. I advise you to seek a Bible-believing church and get to know the people there. Learn from them, and grow deeper in your relationship with Jesus.

If *Sweet Summer Rain* touched your heart in anyway, please email me at:

karenyp46@gmail.com I would love to hear your comments.

If you found any mistakes in this book, they are my own, as I choose to be my own editor. I also want to thank Strategic Book Publishing and Rights Co. for being wonderful in every stage of getting this book ready. Everyone there is very prompt and very professional, and I pray God's blessings over each and every one of them.

CPSIA information can be obtained at www.ICGtesting.com
Printed in the USA
LVOW06s1406250713

344637LV00001B/15/P